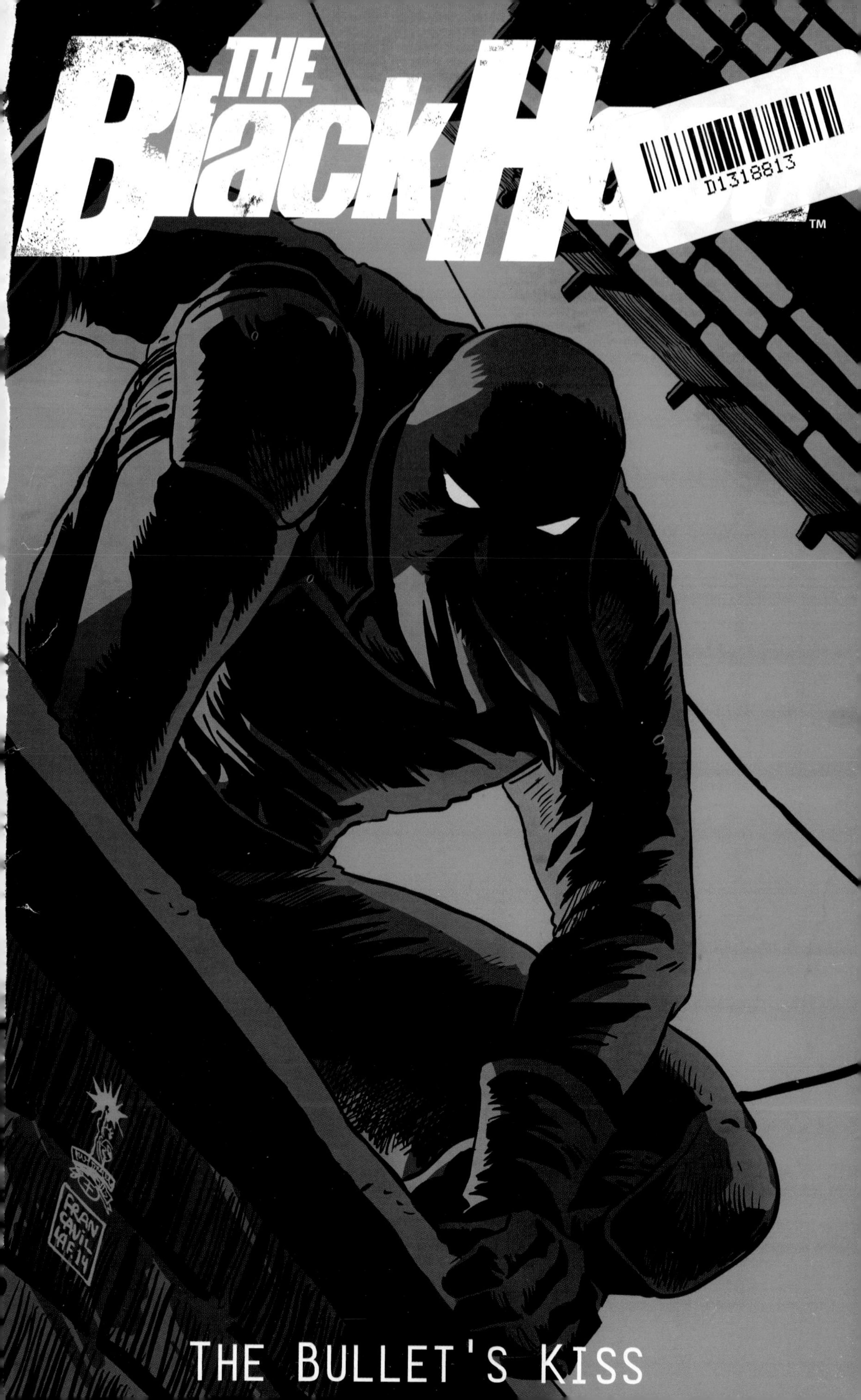
THE
Black
™
FRAN GAVIL
THE BULLET'S KISS

STORY
DUANE SWIERCZYNSKI

ART
MICHAEL GAYDOS
ISSUES 1-5

HOWARD CHAYKIN
ISSUE 6

COLORING
KELLY FITZPATRICK
ISSUES 1-5

JESUS ABURTO
ISSUE 6

LETTERING
RACHEL DEERING

EDITOR
ALEX SEGURA

ASSOCIATE EDITOR/GRAPHIC DESIGN
VINCENT LOVALLO

PUBLISHER
JON GOLDWATER

INTRODUCTION BY LAWRENCE BLOCK

If I remember correctly (and that's an increasingly iffy proposition as the years mount up) I first met Duane Swierczynski four years ago at a panel discussion at the Mysterious Bookshop, Otto Penzler's store in Lower Manhattan. I was the moderator, and my chief challenge for the evening lay in pronouncing Swierczynski. Megan Abbott was also on the panel, along with a strange young man who was exposed a few days later as a compulsive serial plagiarist who lifted whole passages word for word from the novels of Robert Ludlum. (You can't make this shit up—and, evidently, neither could he, poor devil.)

After that auspicious beginning, Duane and I caught up with each other a year later in his hometown of Philadelphia, where he interviewed me onstage at NoirCon, leading me down the primrose path of Memory Lane. (While I can't claim to recall what either of us said, you won't be surprised to learn that it's available online, lurking among the cat videos and the colorful skateboard accidents.)

We read each other's books, kept up with each other via social media, friended each other on Facebook, followed each other on Twitter. And then in July of 2014 I got on a train at Penn Station and got off it at Philadelphia's 30th Street Station and took a cab to Rittenhouse Square, where I'd contrived to rent an apartment for a month.

I had a book to write, and it's been my custom for years to hole up somewhere and isolate myself with the work. I've done this at writers colonies in Illinois and Virginia, in hotel rooms and apartments in Key West and New Orleans and Fire Island and Listowel and Lambertville, on a cruise ship sailing from Phuket to Athens and another on the North Atlantic. (I'd even done so once before in Philly, some 45 years ago, in a hotel that was no great loss when the wrecking ball got around to it. That particular book never got finished, and it was no great loss either.)

Now, back in Philly, I had a few friends in town I could have called, including an actress I'd known in New York and a girl from my graduating class at Buffalo's Bennett High. But I didn't call anybody, or—aside from the waitress at the sushi place and the counterman at the coffee joint—I didn't really talk to anybody.

The writing went well, and the book was done before my month was up. I was eager to get home, but gave myself a day or two to decompress. I was, God knows, tired and wired, and some human contact was in order. A dinner at some place that didn't serve sushi, say, with a familiar face on the other side of the table. Who ya gonna call? The actress? The classmate?

I shook my head and emailed Duane, and the following evening I followed his directions and met him at a restaurant. And I had the kind of calming and comforting post-book dinner conversation one can only have with another writer.

How'd this happen? I'm supposed to be introducing *The Bullet's Kiss*, the outstanding new graphic novel written by Duane and illustrated by Michael Gaydos. (But if you're reading this, you already know all that, because you've got the book in your hand. Never mind.)

Yet all I seem to be doing is nattering on about Duane—and, alas, about myself. Until now, although I've read several of Duane's novels, most recently the superb *Canary*, I've never had a look at his comic books. Novels and comics are two very different horses, and few writers can sit comfortably astride both of them. Duane does so with enviable balance, and you can see the verve and raw strength of the comic book in his novels, even as the literary depth of prose fiction lends gravitas to his comics.

And, in every panel of *The Bullet's Kiss*, you see Philadelphia. It's a powerful presence here, and I can think of no one better positioned to get it on the page, and get it right.

Oh, that book I wrote on Rittenhouse Square? As I write these lines, I've got four hours before it's time to launch it at the place it all began, the Mysterious Bookshop. Nice how it all comes full circle, innit? The title, I'm self-seeking enough to tell you, is *The Girl with the Deep Blue Eyes*, and it takes place in neither New York or Philadelphia, but in hot and steamy Gallatin County, Florida. It is, according to my film agent, like James M. Cain on Viagra.

You know what? It just might make a hell of a graphic novel...

ISSUE ONE

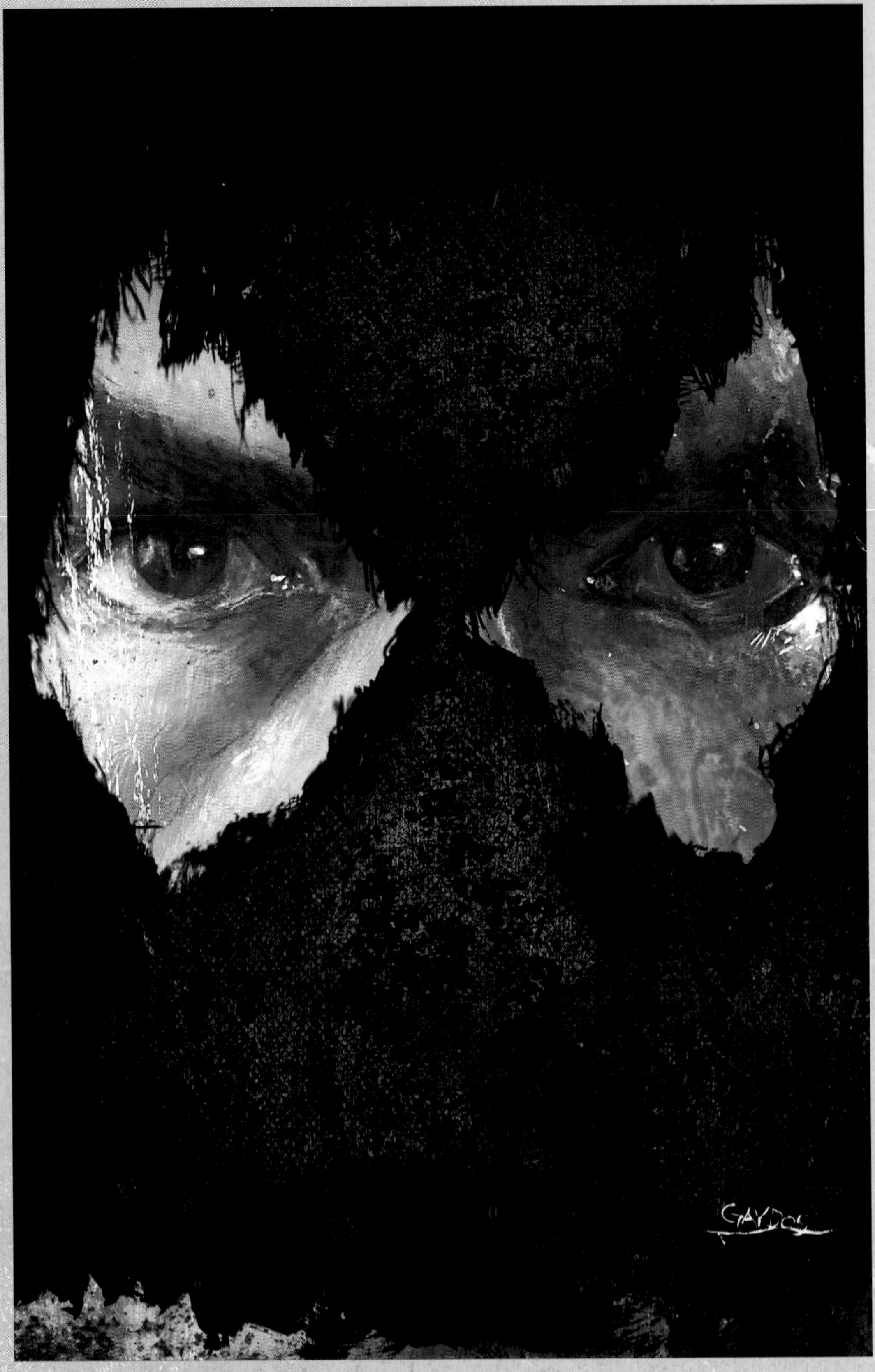
GAYDOS

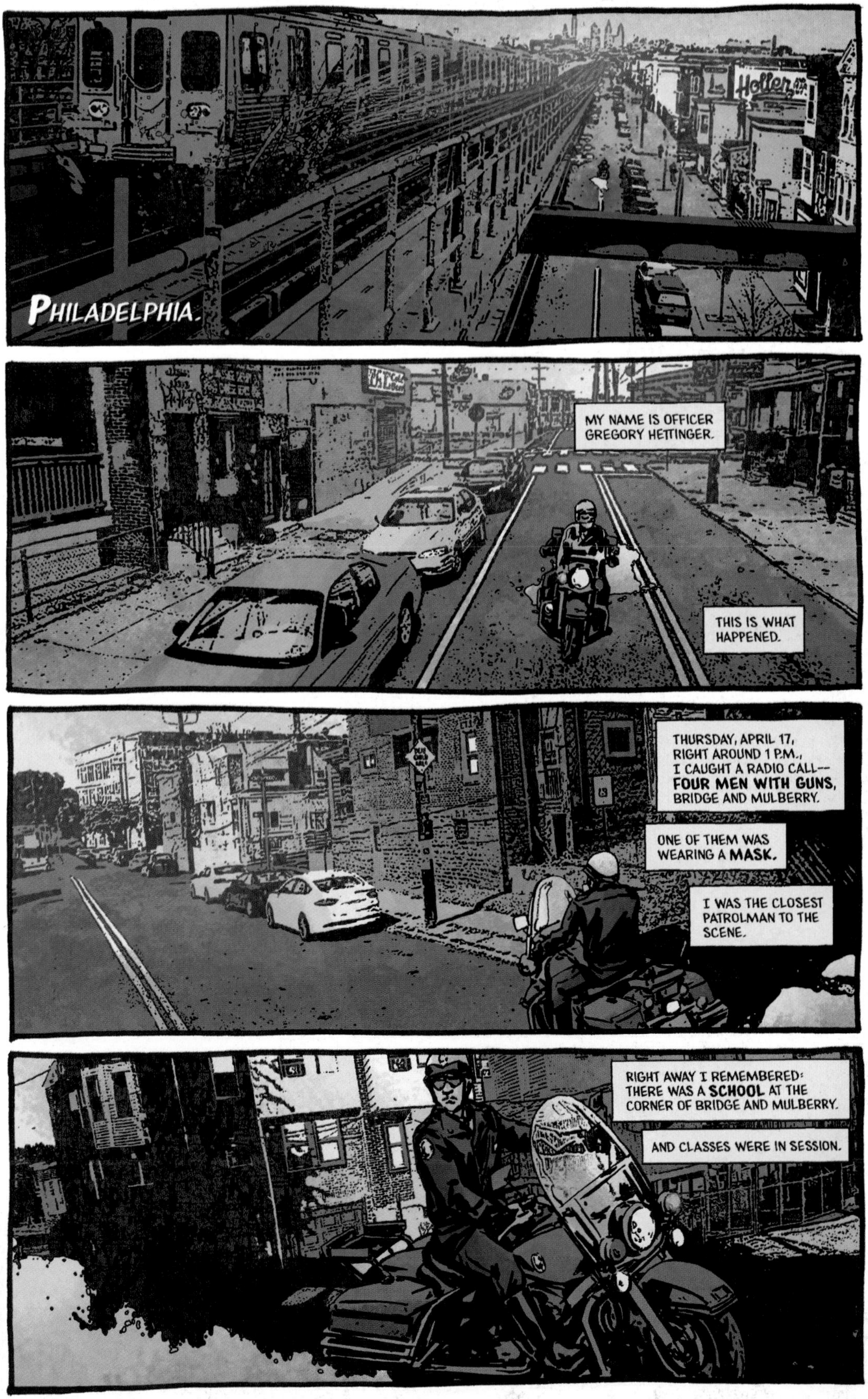
PHILADELPHIA.
MY NAME IS OFFICER GREGORY HETTINGER.
THIS IS WHAT HAPPENED.
THURSDAY, APRIL 17, RIGHT AROUND 1 P.M., I CAUGHT A RADIO CALL-- FOUR MEN WITH GUNS, BRIDGE AND MULBERRY.
ONE OF THEM WAS WEARING A MASK.
I WAS THE CLOSEST PATROLMAN TO THE SCENE.
RIGHT AWAY I REMEMBERED: THERE WAS A SCHOOL AT THE CORNER OF BRIDGE AND MULBERRY.
AND CLASSES WERE IN SESSION.

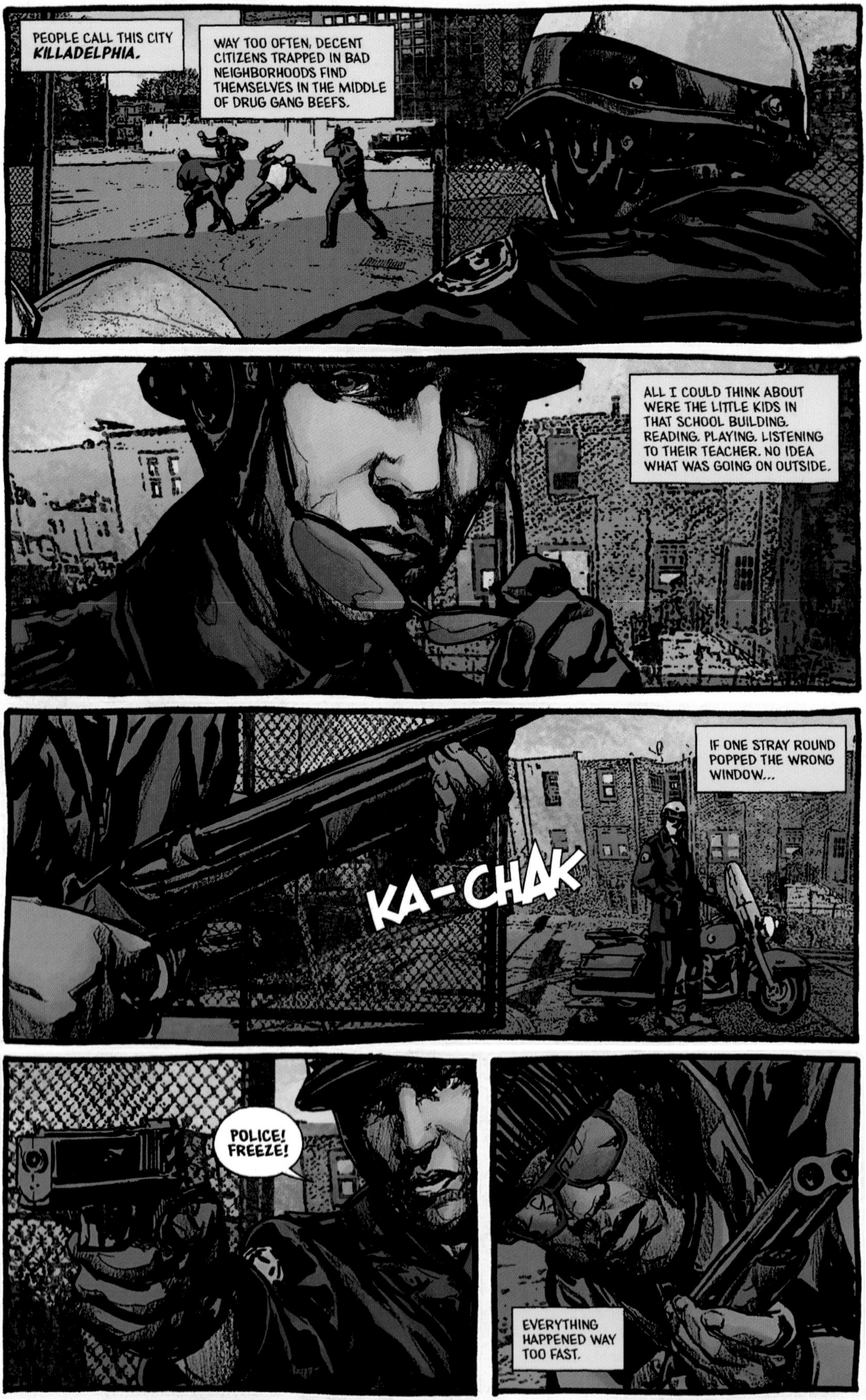
PEOPLE CALL THIS CITY **KILLADELPHIA.**
WAY TOO OFTEN, DECENT CITIZENS TRAPPED IN BAD NEIGHBORHOODS FIND THEMSELVES IN THE MIDDLE OF DRUG GANG BEEFS.
ALL I COULD THINK ABOUT WERE THE LITTLE KIDS IN THAT SCHOOL BUILDING. READING. PLAYING. LISTENING TO THEIR TEACHER. NO IDEA WHAT WAS GOING ON OUTSIDE.
IF ONE STRAY ROUND POPPED THE WRONG WINDOW...
KA-CHAK
POLICE! FREEZE!
EVERYTHING HAPPENED WAY TOO FAST.

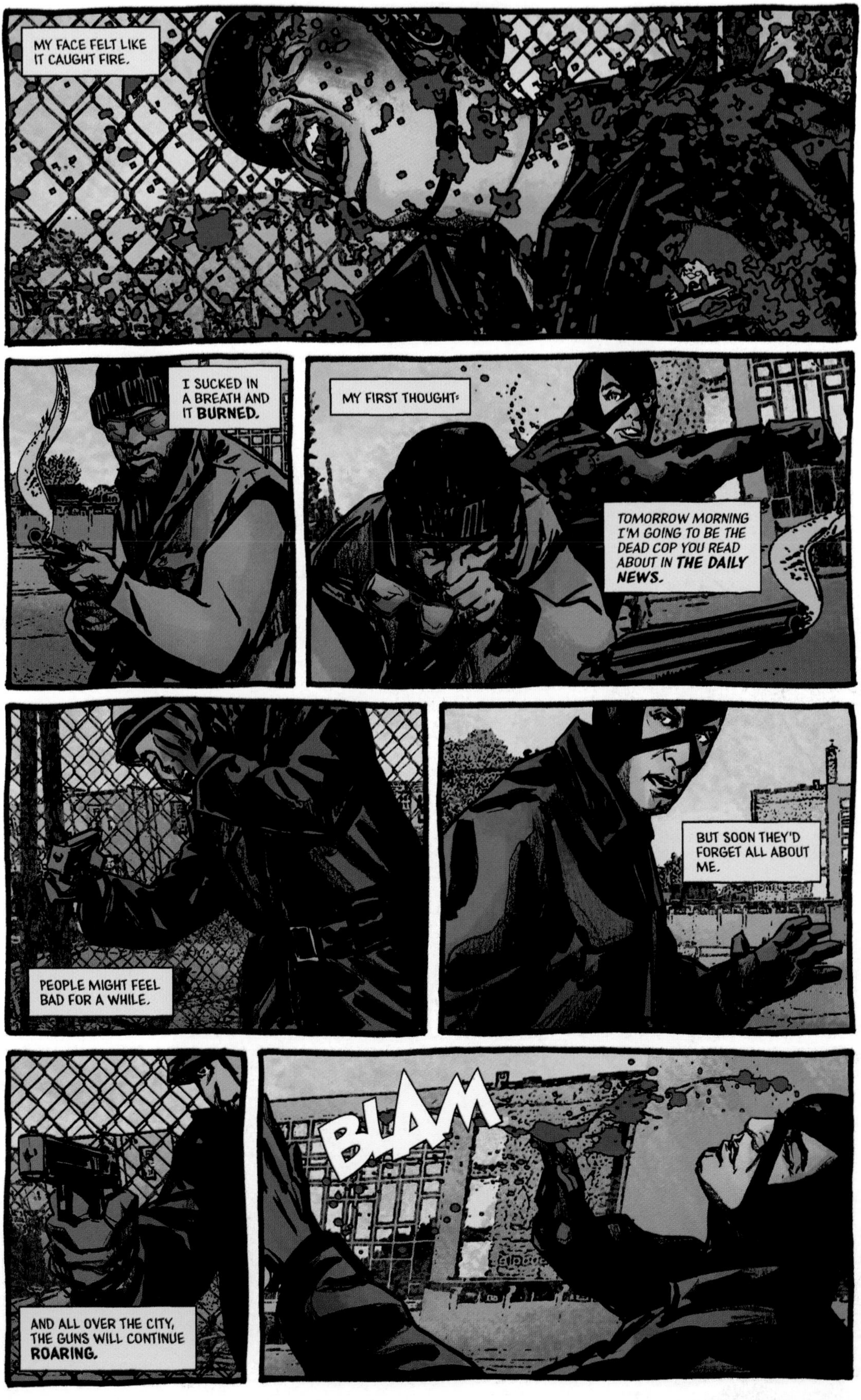
MY FACE FELT LIKE IT CAUGHT FIRE.
I SUCKED IN A BREATH AND IT **BURNED.**
MY FIRST THOUGHT:
*TOMORROW MORNING I'M GOING TO BE THE DEAD COP YOU READ ABOUT IN **THE DAILY NEWS.***
PEOPLE MIGHT FEEL BAD FOR A WHILE.
BUT SOON THEY'D FORGET ALL ABOUT ME.
AND ALL OVER THE CITY, THE GUNS WILL CONTINUE **ROARING.**
BLAM

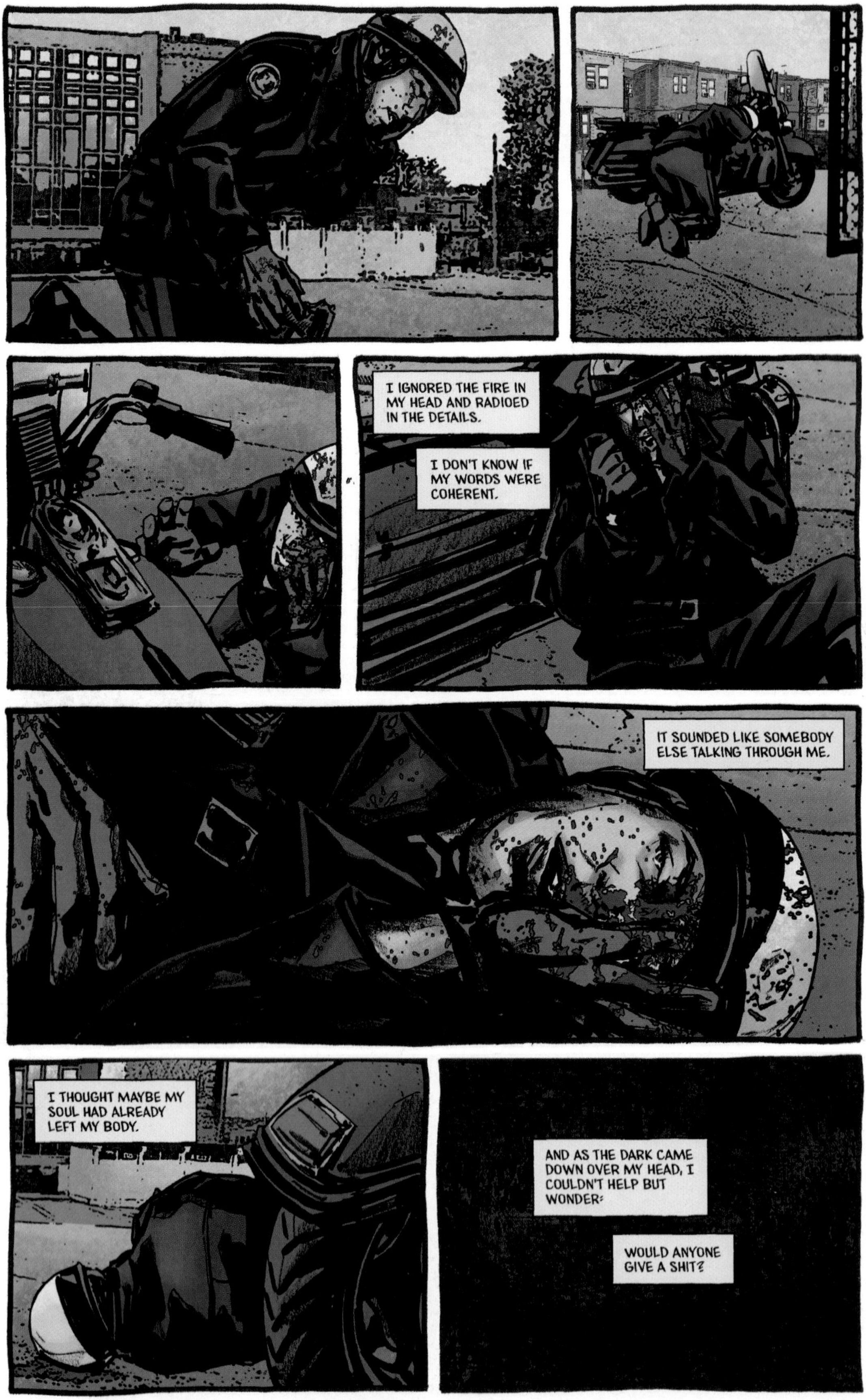
I IGNORED THE FIRE IN MY HEAD AND RADIOED IN THE DETAILS.
I DON'T KNOW IF MY WORDS WERE COHERENT.
IT SOUNDED LIKE SOMEBODY ELSE TALKING THROUGH ME.
I THOUGHT MAYBE MY SOUL HAD ALREADY LEFT MY BODY.
AND AS THE DARK CAME DOWN OVER MY HEAD, I COULDN'T HELP BUT WONDER:
WOULD ANYONE GIVE A SHIT?

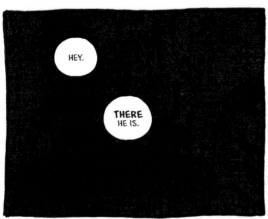

HEY.

THERE HE IS.

THERE'S THE **HERO**.

I TRIED TO ASK MY CAPTAIN WHAT THE FUCK WAS GOING ON -- HERO? -- BUT I COULDN'T RECOGNIZE THE NOISES COMING OUT OF MY MOUTH.

IT WASN'T ENGLISH.

GO EASY. YOU'VE GOT SOME STITCHES AROUND YOUR MOUTH AND YOU DON'T WANT TO POP THEM.

YOU PROBABLY HAVE NO IDEA WHO YOU TOOK DOWN, DO YOU?

"HIS NAME WAS KIP BURLAND. THEY CALLED HIM THE **BLACK HOOD.** A VIGILANTE IN A MASK. REALLY CREEPY BASTARD.

"WE'VE BEEN TRYING TO NAIL HIS ASS FOR YEARS."

WHUH?

DON'T SPEAK-- FOR REAL, SON. YOU'RE NOT SOUNDING LIKE YOURSELF.

I'VE GOT DANNY CHITWOOD FROM CHANNEL 48 OUTSIDE. HE WANTS A QUICK SHOT OF US, OKAY?

IT'S IMPORTANT THAT PEOPLE KNOW YOU'RE OKAY.

ONLY I WASN'T OKAY. I HAD JUST BEEN TOLD THAT I KILLED A MAN.

VIGILANTE OR NOT... I'D TAKEN A LIFE.

ANYTHING YOU'D LIKE TO TELL THE PEOPLE OF PHILADELPHIA, OFFICER HETTINGER?

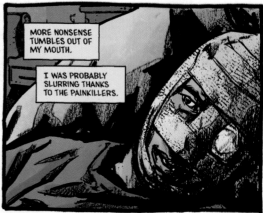

MORE NONSENSE TUMBLES OUT OF MY MOUTH.

I WAS PROBABLY SLURRING THANKS TO THE PAINKILLERS.

EVEN THEN I TOLD MYSELF: DO YOURSELF A FAVOR AND GET OFF THIS SHIT AS SOON AS POSSIBLE.

I KNEW TOO MANY PEOPLE WHO PLAYED AROUND WITH A FEW PERCOCETS AND ENDED UP CHASING A $500-A-DAY HABIT.

I ASKED THE DOC HOW BAD IT WOULD BE, ONCE THE BANDAGES CAME OFF.

I COULDN'T FEEL ANYTHING. I ASSUMED MY HELMET TOOK THE WORST OF IT.

THEN THE DOCTOR **SHOWED ME.**

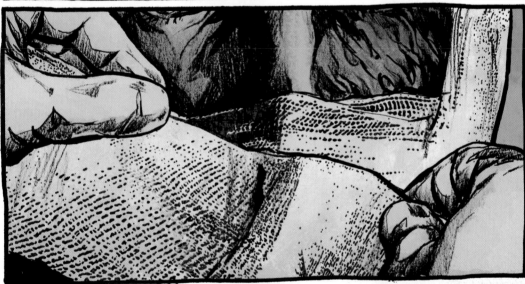

I SHOULDN'T HAVE ASKED.

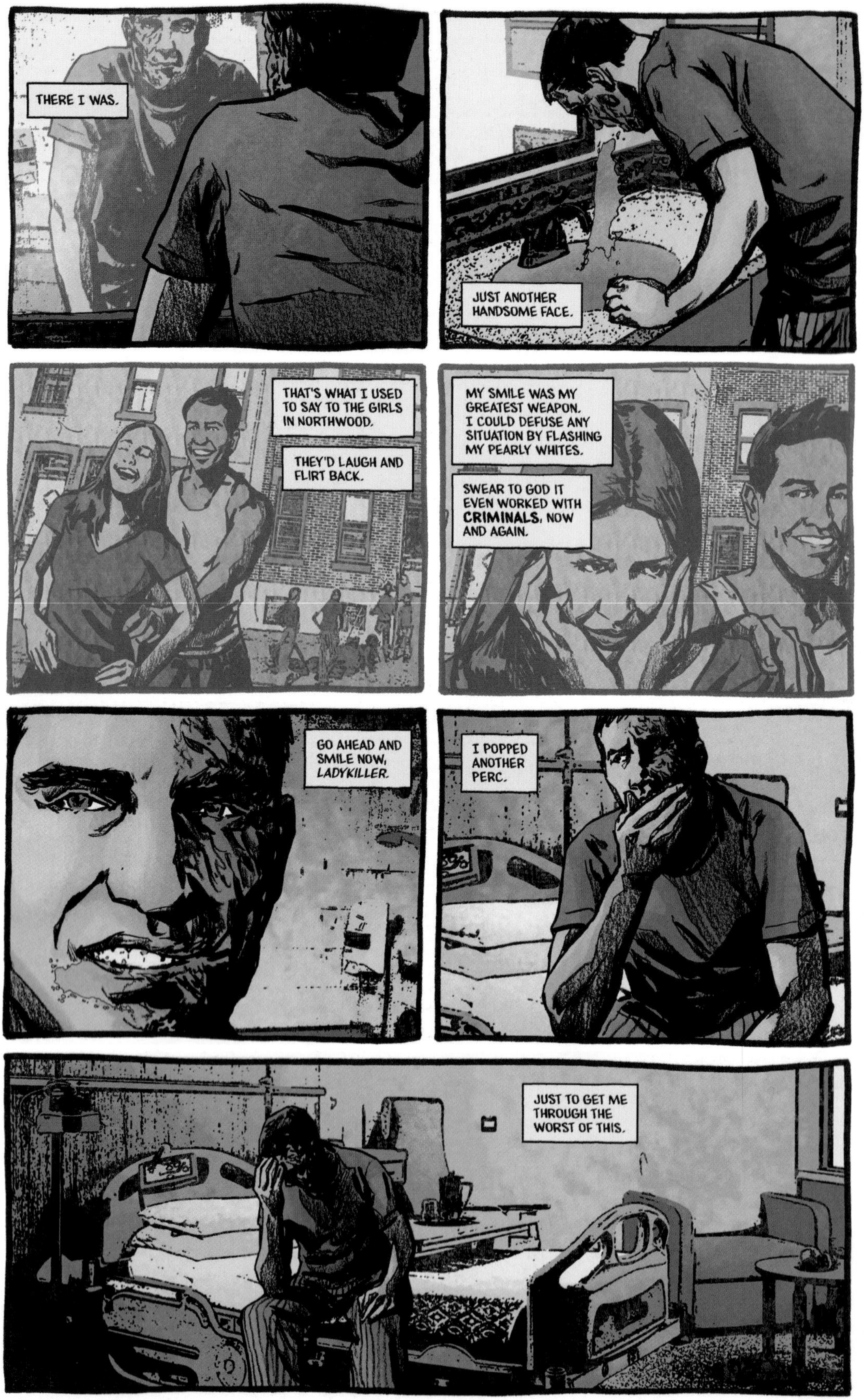
THERE I WAS.
JUST ANOTHER HANDSOME FACE.
THAT'S WHAT I USED TO SAY TO THE GIRLS IN NORTHWOOD.
THEY'D LAUGH AND FLIRT BACK.
MY SMILE WAS MY GREATEST WEAPON. I COULD DEFUSE ANY SITUATION BY FLASHING MY PEARLY WHITES.
SWEAR TO GOD IT EVEN WORKED WITH CRIMINALS, NOW AND AGAIN.
GO AHEAD AND SMILE NOW, LADYKILLER.
I POPPED ANOTHER PERC.
JUST TO GET ME THROUGH THE WORST OF THIS.

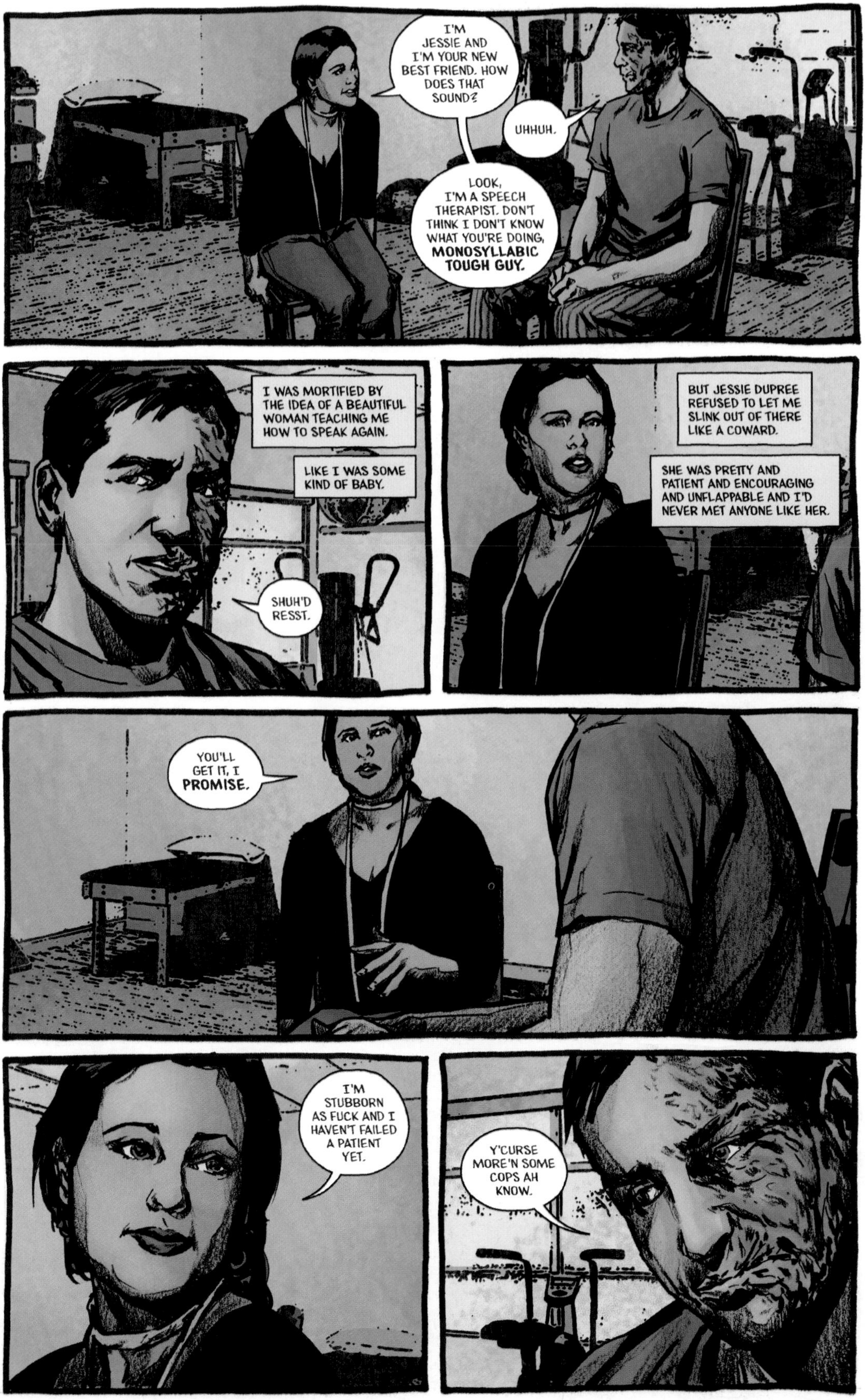

I'M JESSIE AND I'M YOUR NEW BEST FRIEND. HOW DOES THAT SOUND?
UHHUH.
LOOK, I'M A SPEECH THERAPIST. DON'T THINK I DON'T KNOW WHAT YOU'RE DOING, **MONOSYLLABIC TOUGH GUY.**
I WAS MORTIFIED BY THE IDEA OF A BEAUTIFUL WOMAN TEACHING ME HOW TO SPEAK AGAIN.
LIKE I WAS SOME KIND OF BABY.
SHUH'D RESST.
BUT JESSIE DUPREE REFUSED TO LET ME SLINK OUT OF THERE LIKE A COWARD.
SHE WAS PRETTY AND PATIENT AND ENCOURAGING AND UNFLAPPABLE AND I'D NEVER MET ANYONE LIKE HER.
YOU'LL GET IT, I **PROMISE.**
I'M STUBBORN AS FUCK AND I HAVEN'T FAILED A PATIENT YET.
Y'CURSE MORE'N SOME COPS AH KNOW.

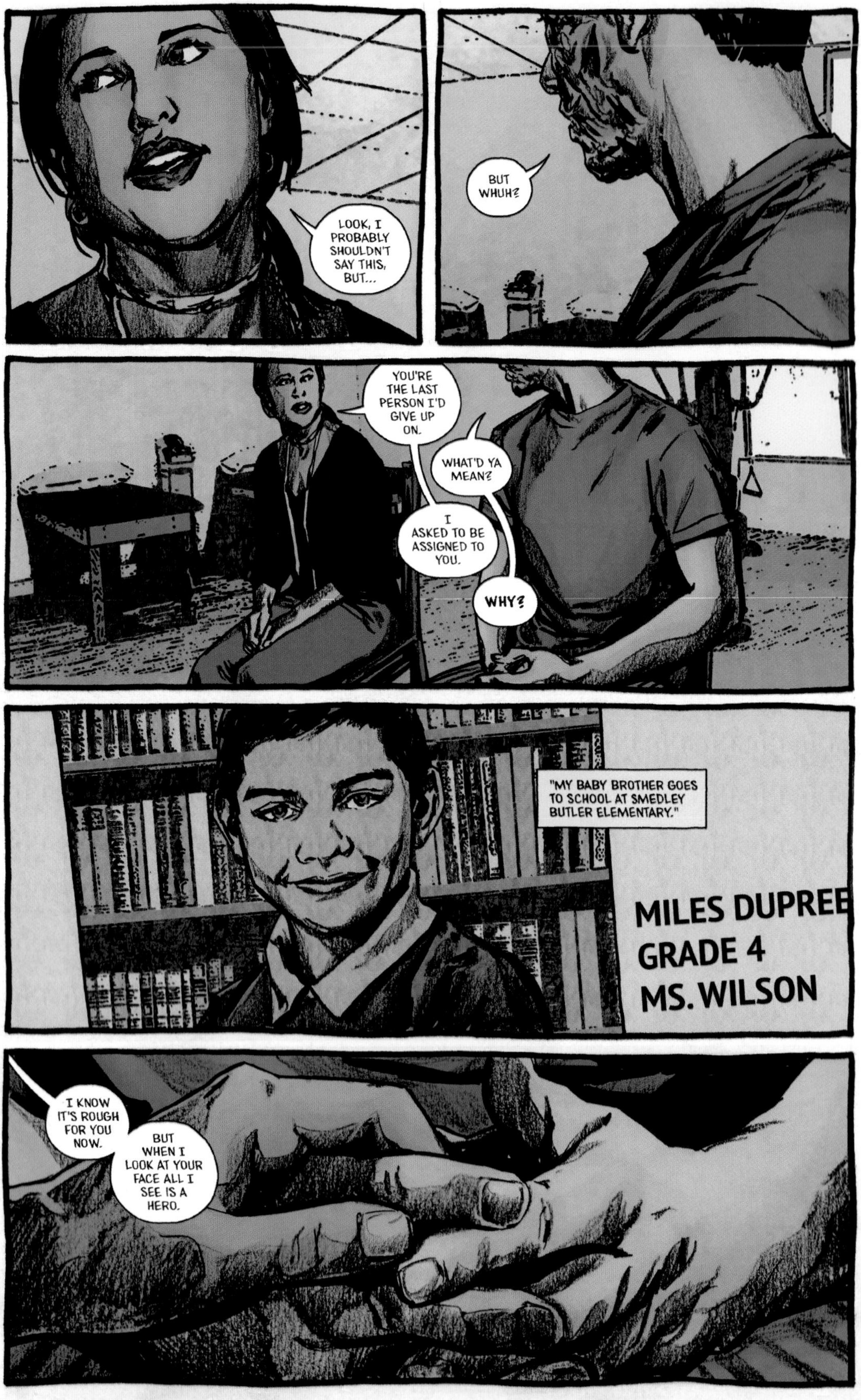
LOOK, I PROBABLY SHOULDN'T SAY THIS, BUT...
BUT WHUH?
YOU'RE THE LAST PERSON I'D GIVE UP ON.
WHAT'D YA MEAN?
I ASKED TO BE ASSIGNED TO YOU.
WHY?
"MY BABY BROTHER GOES TO SCHOOL AT SMEDLEY BUTLER ELEMENTARY."
MILES DUPREE
GRADE 4
MS. WILSON
I KNOW IT'S ROUGH FOR YOU NOW.
BUT WHEN I LOOK AT YOUR FACE ALL I SEE IS A HERO.

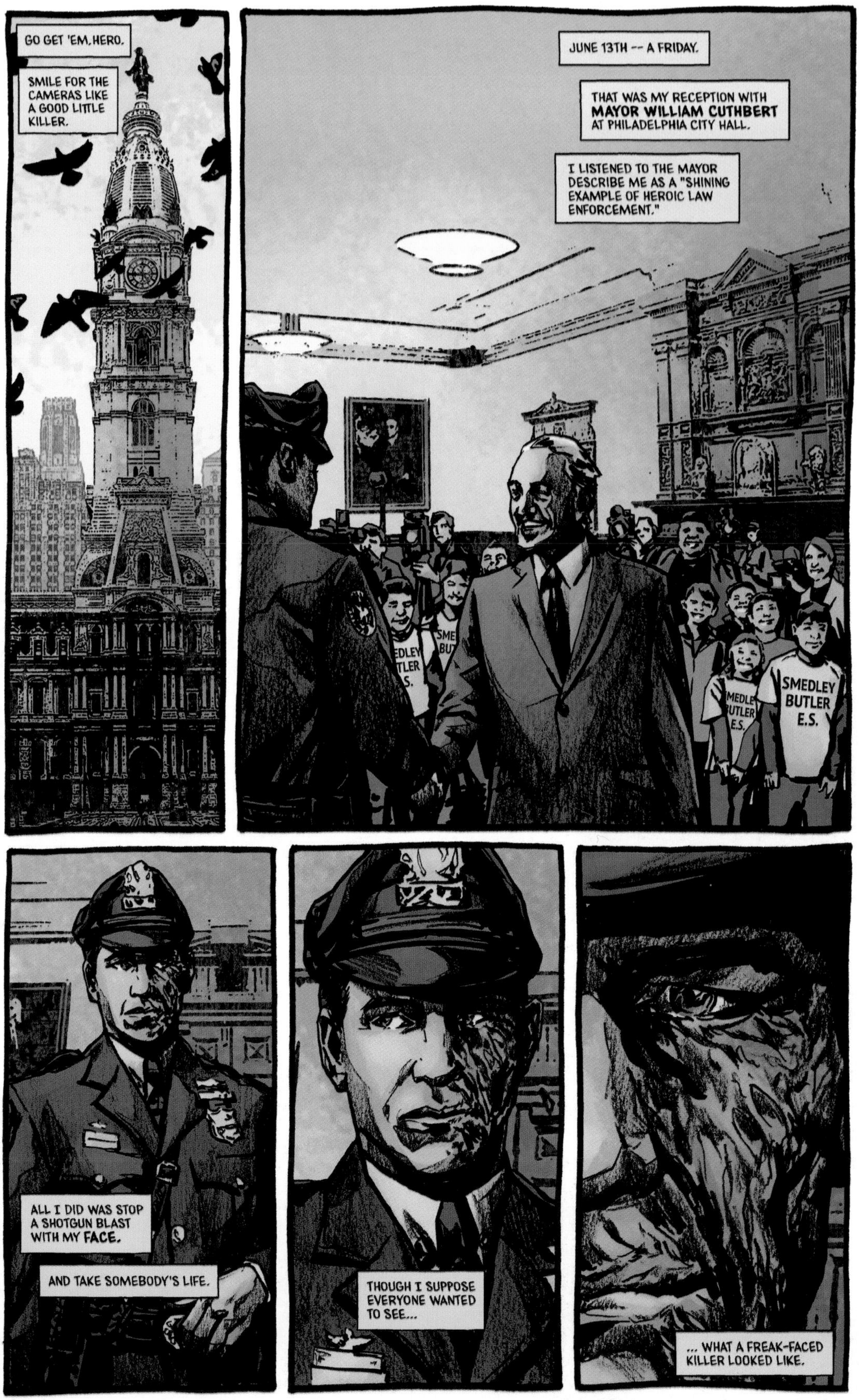
GO GET 'EM, HERO.
SMILE FOR THE CAMERAS LIKE A GOOD LITTLE KILLER.
JUNE 13TH -- A FRIDAY.
THAT WAS MY RECEPTION WITH MAYOR WILLIAM CUTHBERT AT PHILADELPHIA CITY HALL.
I LISTENED TO THE MAYOR DESCRIBE ME AS A "SHINING EXAMPLE OF HEROIC LAW ENFORCEMENT."
SMEDLEY BUTLER E.S.
ALL I DID WAS STOP A SHOTGUN BLAST WITH MY FACE.
AND TAKE SOMEBODY'S LIFE.
THOUGH I SUPPOSE EVERYONE WANTED TO SEE...
... WHAT A FREAK-FACED KILLER LOOKED LIKE.

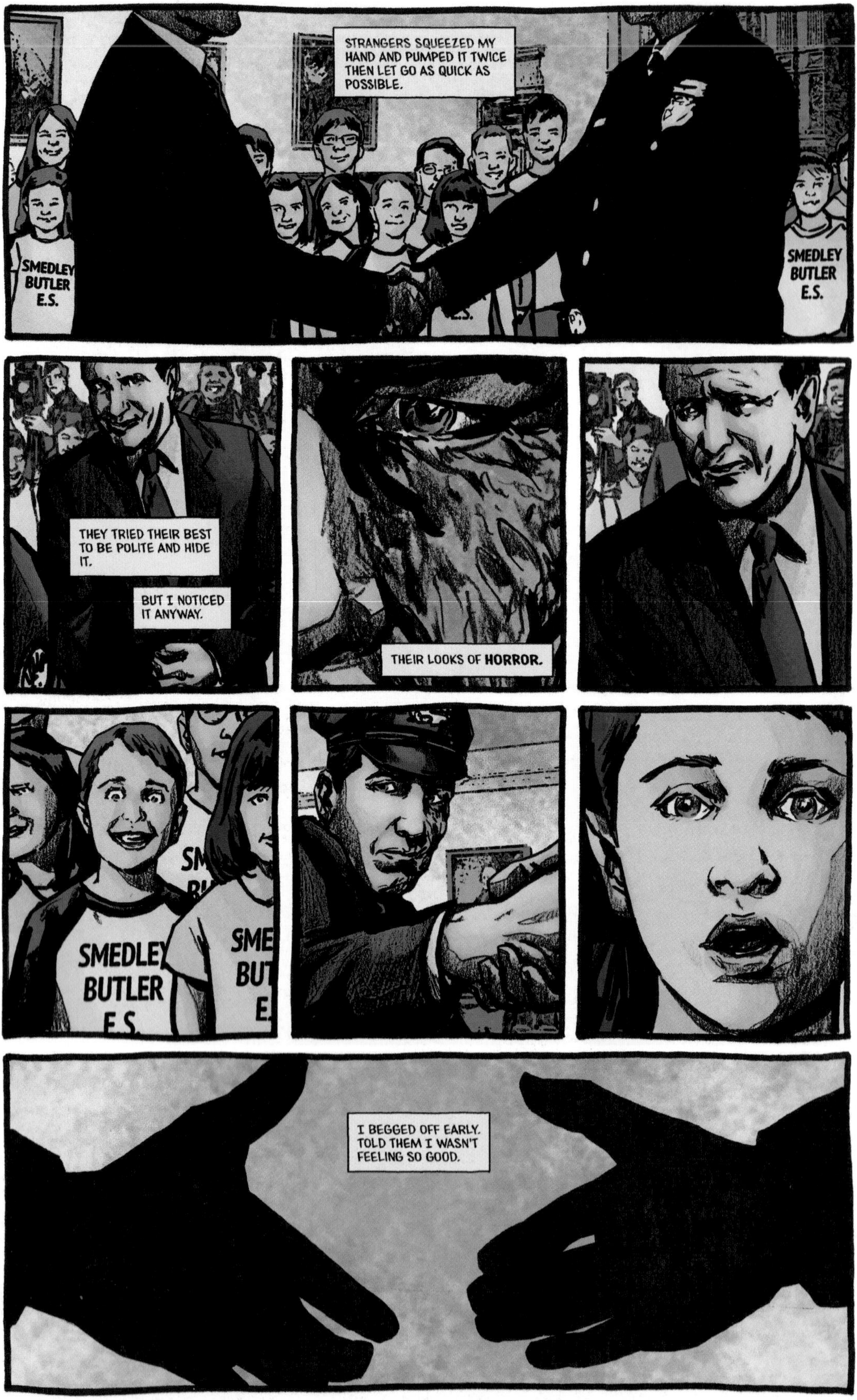
STRANGERS SQUEEZED MY HAND AND PUMPED IT TWICE THEN LET GO AS QUICK AS POSSIBLE.
SMEDLEY BUTLER E.S.
SMEDLEY BUTLER E.S.
THEY TRIED THEIR BEST TO BE POLITE AND HIDE IT.
BUT I NOTICED IT ANYWAY.
THEIR LOOKS OF **HORROR.**
SMEDLEY BUTLER E.S.
I BEGGED OFF EARLY. TOLD THEM I WASN'T FEELING SO GOOD.

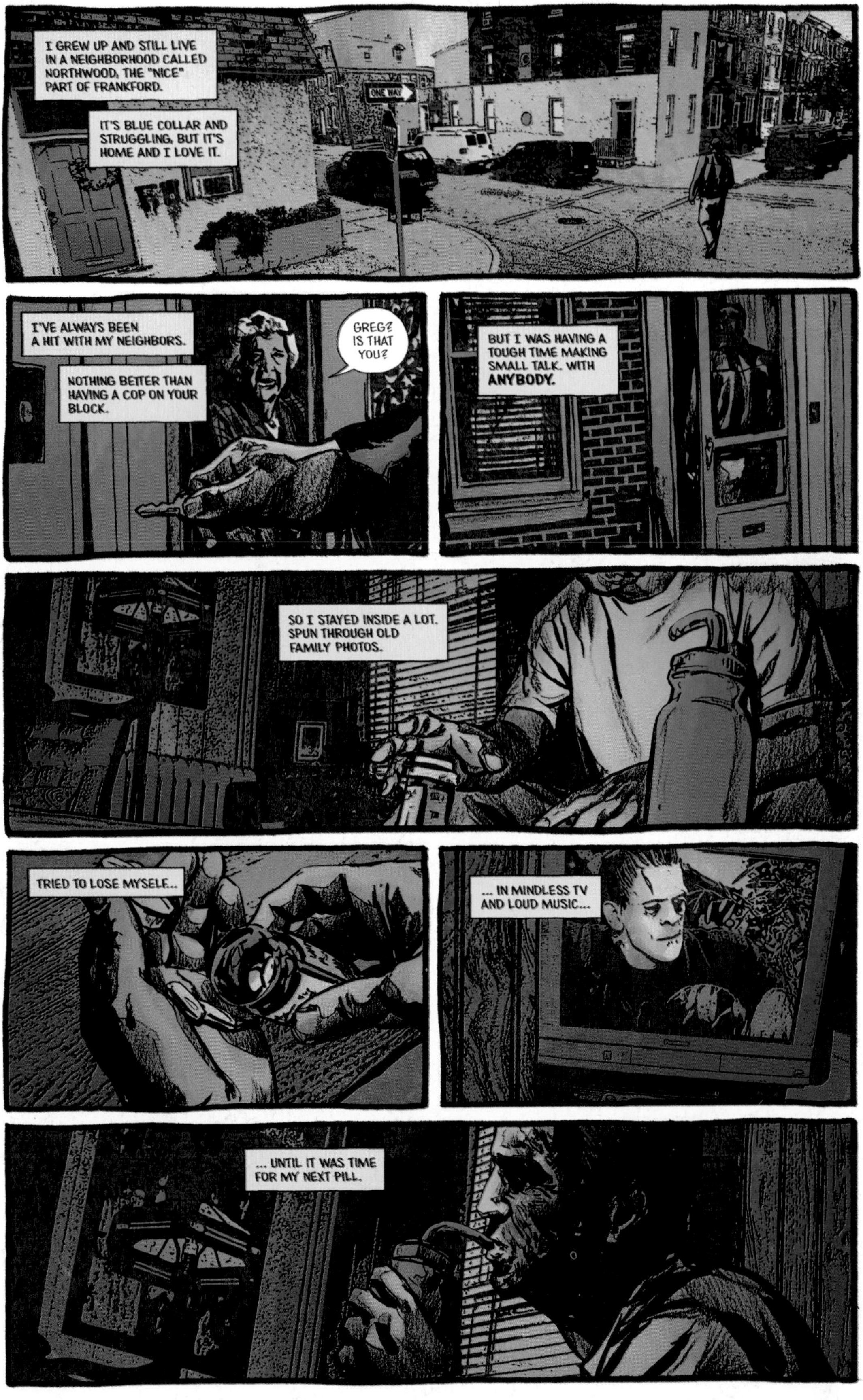
I GREW UP AND STILL LIVE IN A NEIGHBORHOOD CALLED NORTHWOOD, THE "NICE" PART OF FRANKFORD.
IT'S BLUE COLLAR AND STRUGGLING, BUT IT'S HOME AND I LOVE IT.
ONE WAY
I'VE ALWAYS BEEN A HIT WITH MY NEIGHBORS.
NOTHING BETTER THAN HAVING A COP ON YOUR BLOCK.
GREG? IS THAT YOU?
BUT I WAS HAVING A TOUGH TIME MAKING SMALL TALK. WITH ANYBODY.
SO I STAYED INSIDE A LOT. SPUN THROUGH OLD FAMILY PHOTOS.
TRIED TO LOSE MYSELF...
... IN MINDLESS TV AND LOUD MUSIC...
... UNTIL IT WAS TIME FOR MY NEXT PILL.

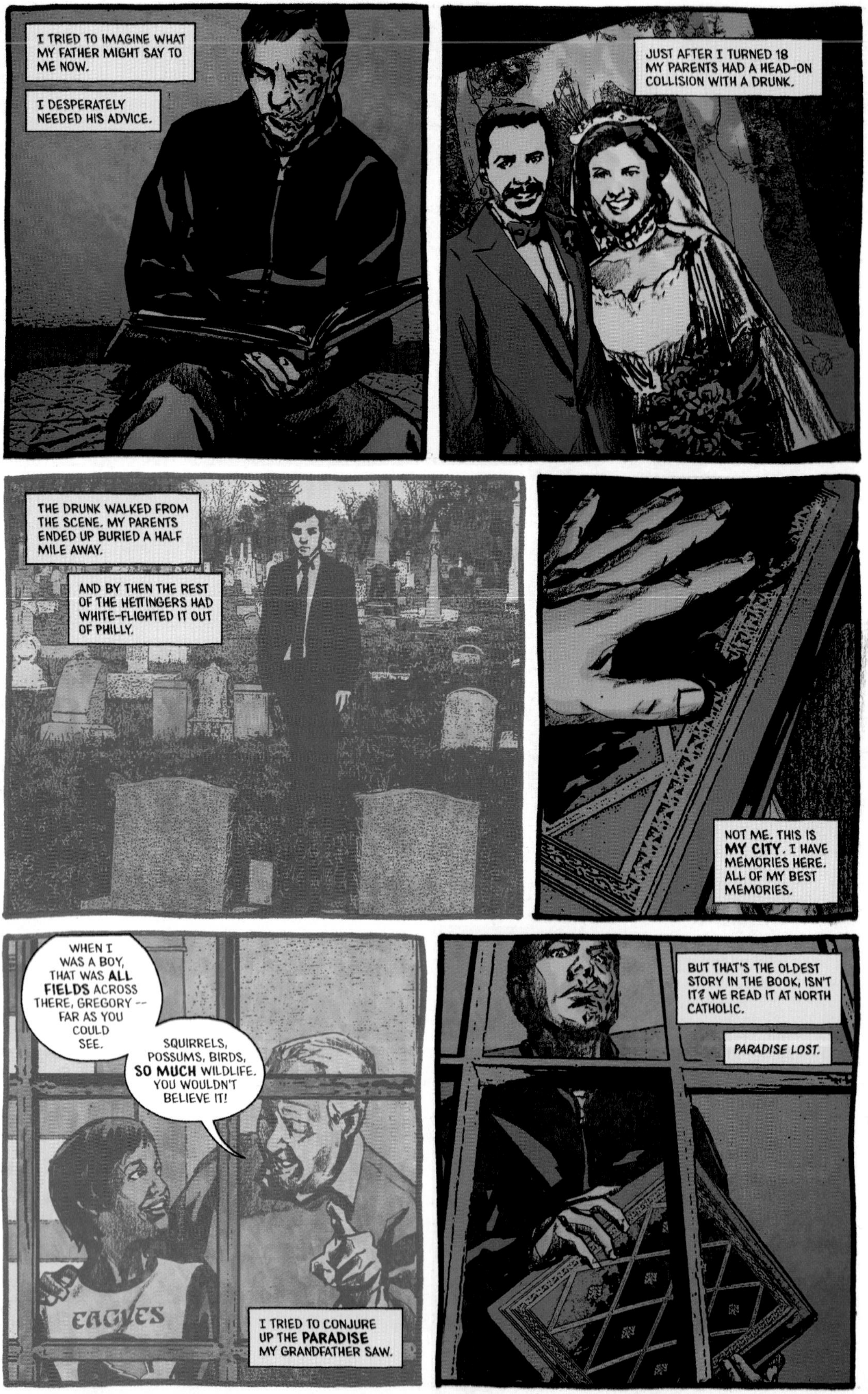
I TRIED TO IMAGINE WHAT MY FATHER MIGHT SAY TO ME NOW.
I DESPERATELY NEEDED HIS ADVICE.
JUST AFTER I TURNED 18 MY PARENTS HAD A HEAD-ON COLLISION WITH A DRUNK.
THE DRUNK WALKED FROM THE SCENE. MY PARENTS ENDED UP BURIED A HALF MILE AWAY.
AND BY THEN THE REST OF THE HETTINGERS HAD WHITE-FLIGHTED IT OUT OF PHILLY.
NOT ME. THIS IS **MY CITY**. I HAVE MEMORIES HERE. ALL OF MY BEST MEMORIES.
WHEN I WAS A BOY, THAT WAS **ALL FIELDS** ACROSS THERE, GREGORY -- FAR AS YOU COULD SEE.
SQUIRRELS, POSSUMS, BIRDS, **SO MUCH** WILDLIFE. YOU WOULDN'T BELIEVE IT!
EAGLES
I TRIED TO CONJURE UP THE **PARADISE** MY GRANDFATHER SAW.
BUT THAT'S THE OLDEST STORY IN THE BOOK, ISN'T IT? WE READ IT AT NORTH CATHOLIC.
PARADISE LOST.

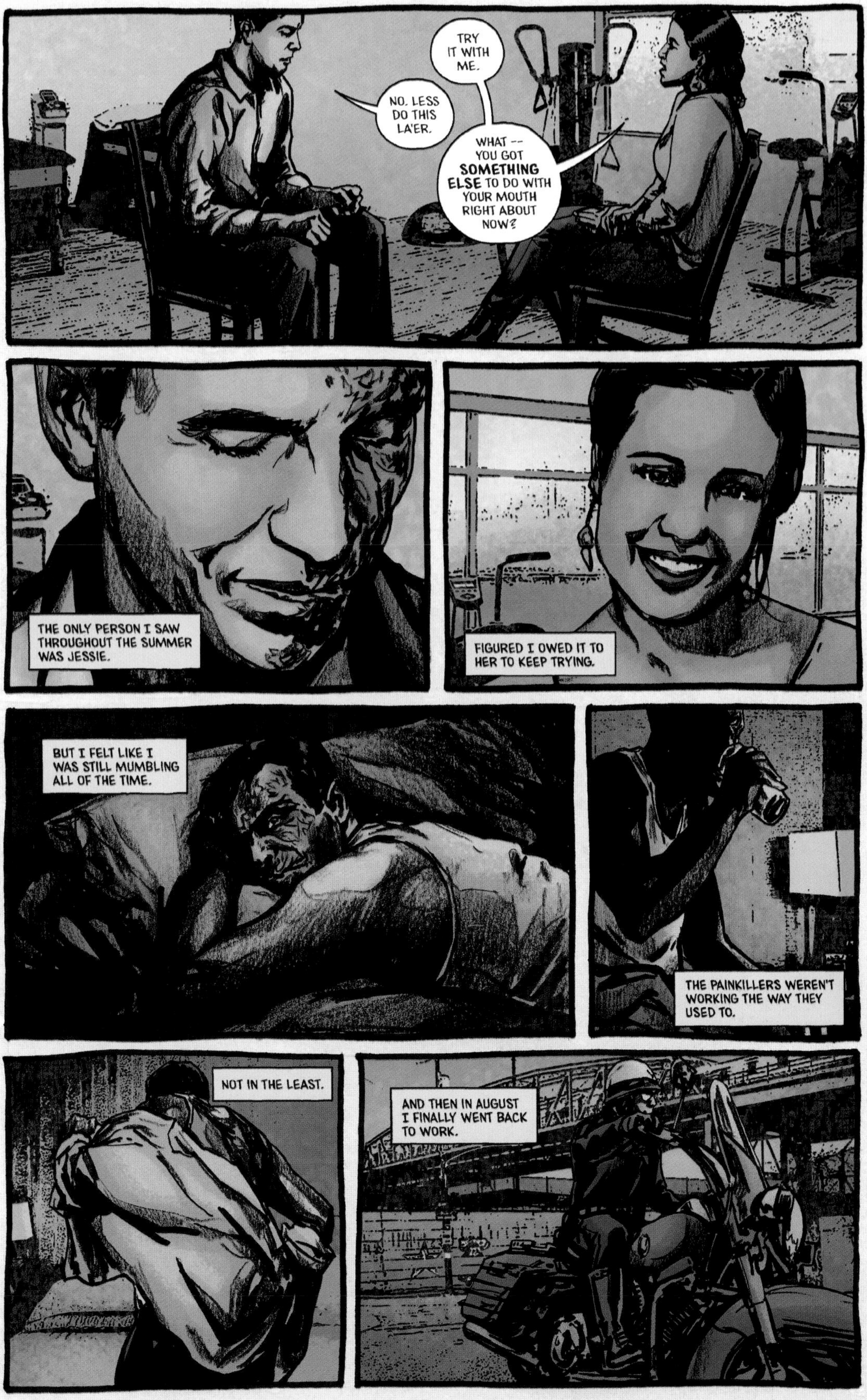
TRY IT WITH ME.
NO. LESS DO THIS LA'ER.
WHAT -- YOU GOT SOMETHING ELSE TO DO WITH YOUR MOUTH RIGHT ABOUT NOW?
THE ONLY PERSON I SAW THROUGHOUT THE SUMMER WAS JESSIE.
FIGURED I OWED IT TO HER TO KEEP TRYING.
BUT I FELT LIKE I WAS STILL MUMBLING ALL OF THE TIME.
THE PAINKILLERS WEREN'T WORKING THE WAY THEY USED TO.
NOT IN THE LEAST.
AND THEN IN AUGUST I FINALLY WENT BACK TO WORK.

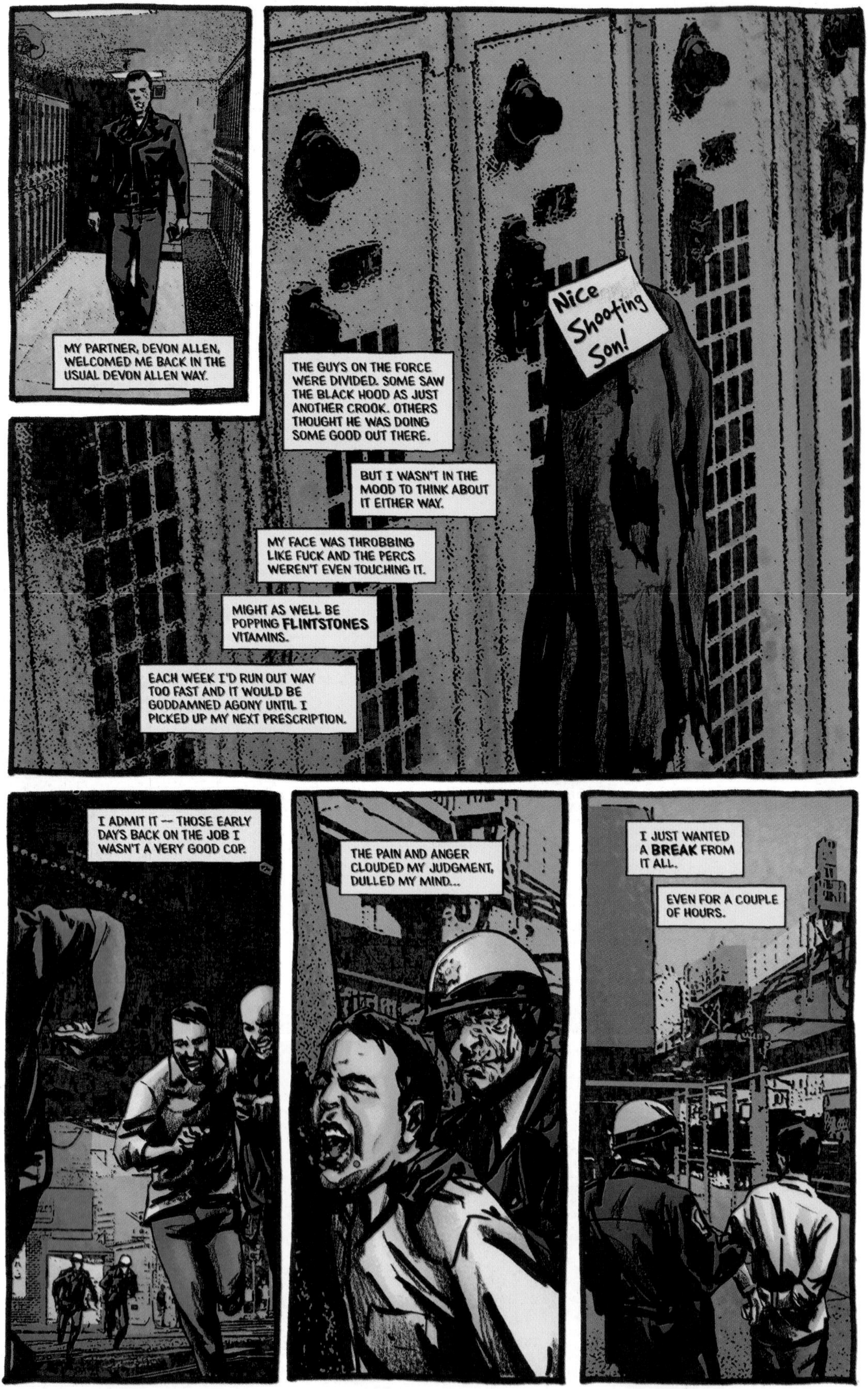
MY PARTNER, DEVON ALLEN, WELCOMED ME BACK IN THE USUAL DEVON ALLEN WAY.
THE GUYS ON THE FORCE WERE DIVIDED. SOME SAW THE BLACK HOOD AS JUST ANOTHER CROOK. OTHERS THOUGHT HE WAS DOING SOME GOOD OUT THERE.
Nice Shooting Son!
BUT I WASN'T IN THE MOOD TO THINK ABOUT IT EITHER WAY.
MY FACE WAS THROBBING LIKE FUCK AND THE PERCS WEREN'T EVEN TOUCHING IT.
MIGHT AS WELL BE POPPING **FLINTSTONES** VITAMINS.
EACH WEEK I'D RUN OUT WAY TOO FAST AND IT WOULD BE GODDAMNED AGONY UNTIL I PICKED UP MY NEXT PRESCRIPTION.
I ADMIT IT -- THOSE EARLY DAYS BACK ON THE JOB I WASN'T A VERY GOOD COP.
THE PAIN AND ANGER CLOUDED MY JUDGMENT, DULLED MY MIND...
I JUST WANTED A **BREAK** FROM IT ALL.
EVEN FOR A COUPLE OF HOURS.

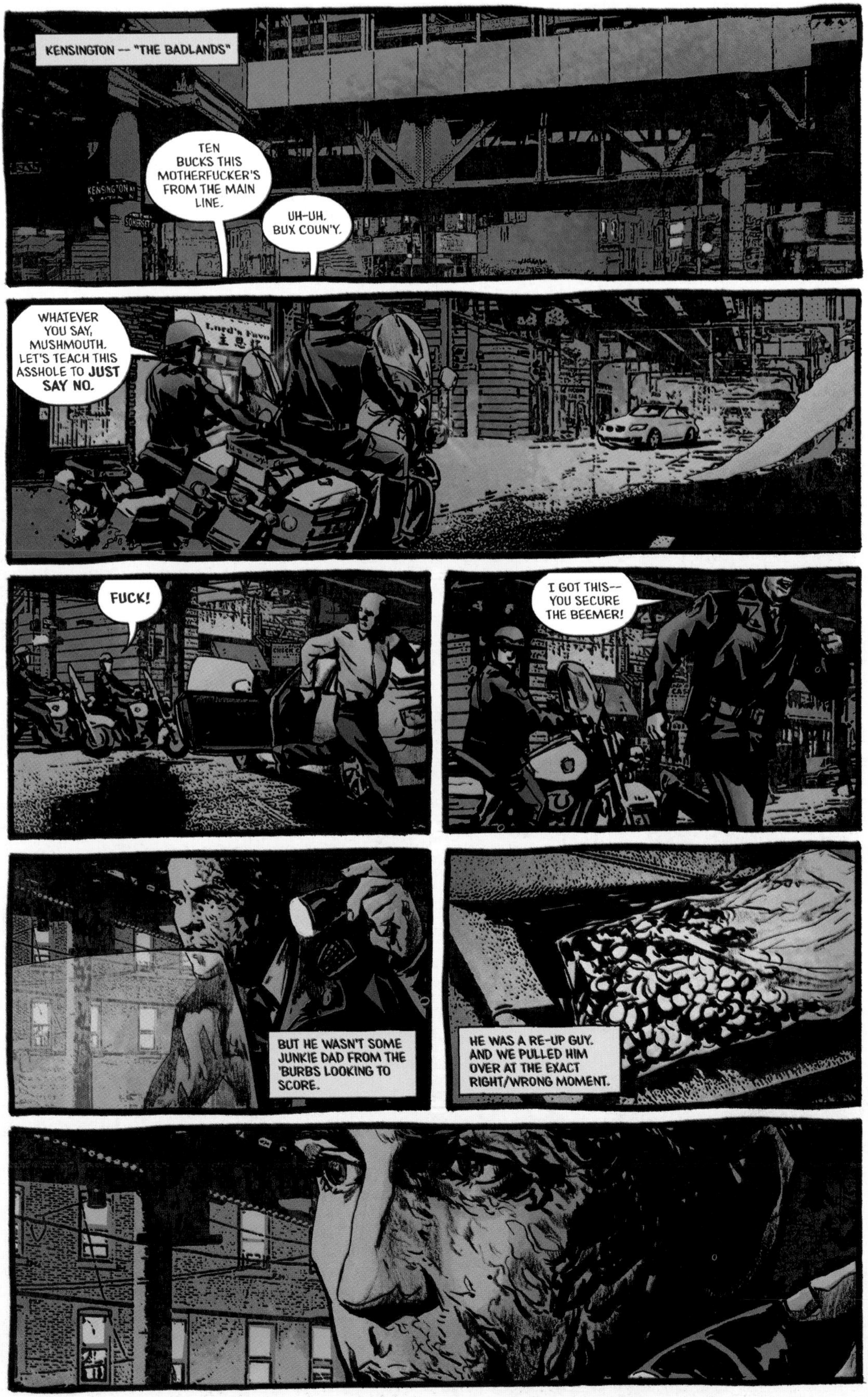
KENSINGTON -- "THE BADLANDS"
TEN BUCKS THIS MOTHERFUCKER'S FROM THE MAIN LINE.
UH-UH. BUX COUN'Y.
WHATEVER YOU SAY, MUSHMOUTH. LET'S TEACH THIS ASSHOLE TO JUST SAY NO.
FUCK!
I GOT THIS-- YOU SECURE THE BEEMER!
BUT HE WASN'T SOME JUNKIE DAD FROM THE 'BURBS LOOKING TO SCORE.
HE WAS A RE-UP GUY. AND WE PULLED HIM OVER AT THE EXACT RIGHT/WRONG MOMENT.

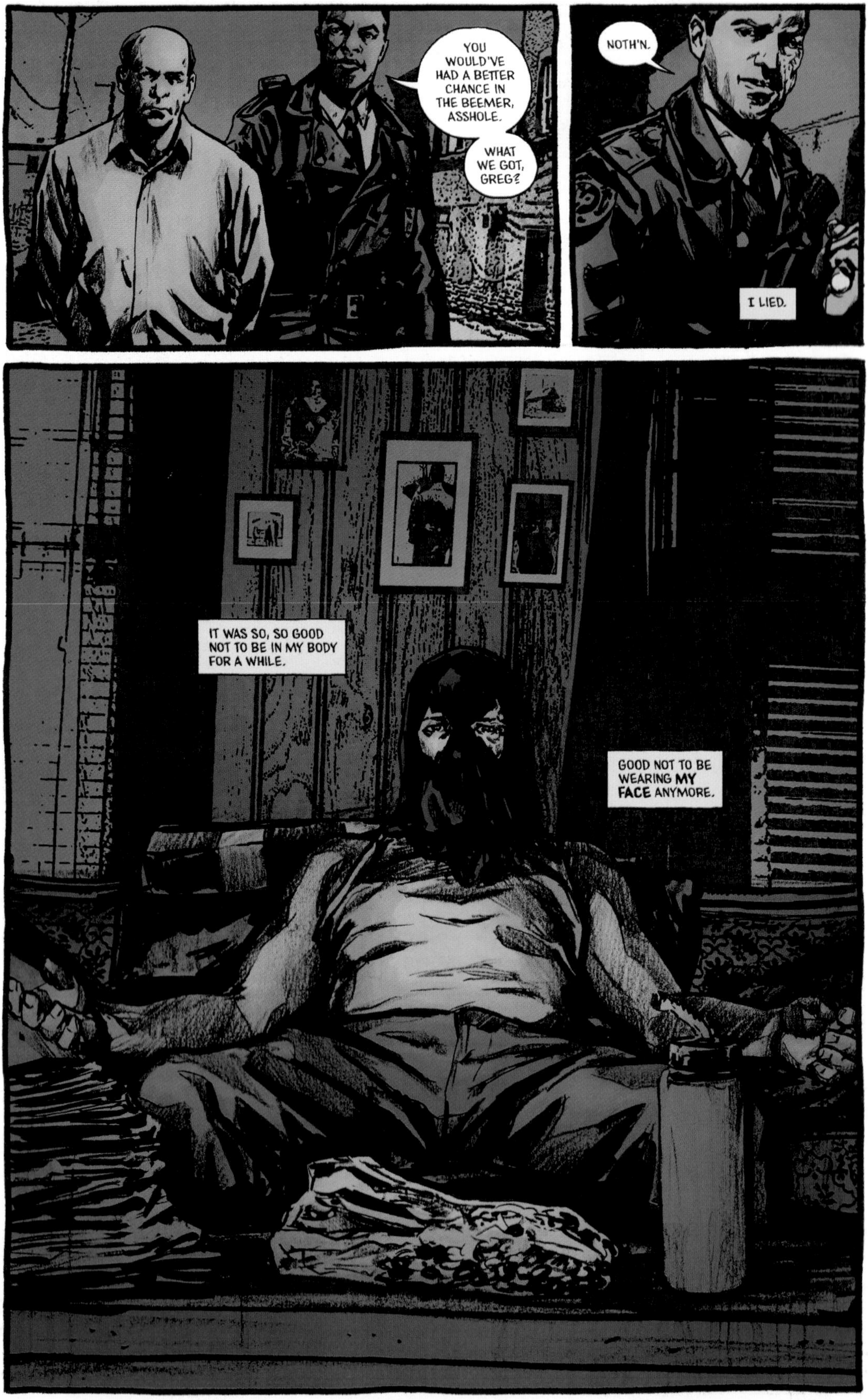
YOU WOULD'VE HAD A BETTER CHANCE IN THE BEEMER, ASSHOLE.
WHAT WE GOT, GREG?
NOTH'N.
I LIED.
IT WAS SO, SO GOOD NOT TO BE IN MY BODY FOR A WHILE.
GOOD NOT TO BE WEARING **MY FACE** ANYMORE.

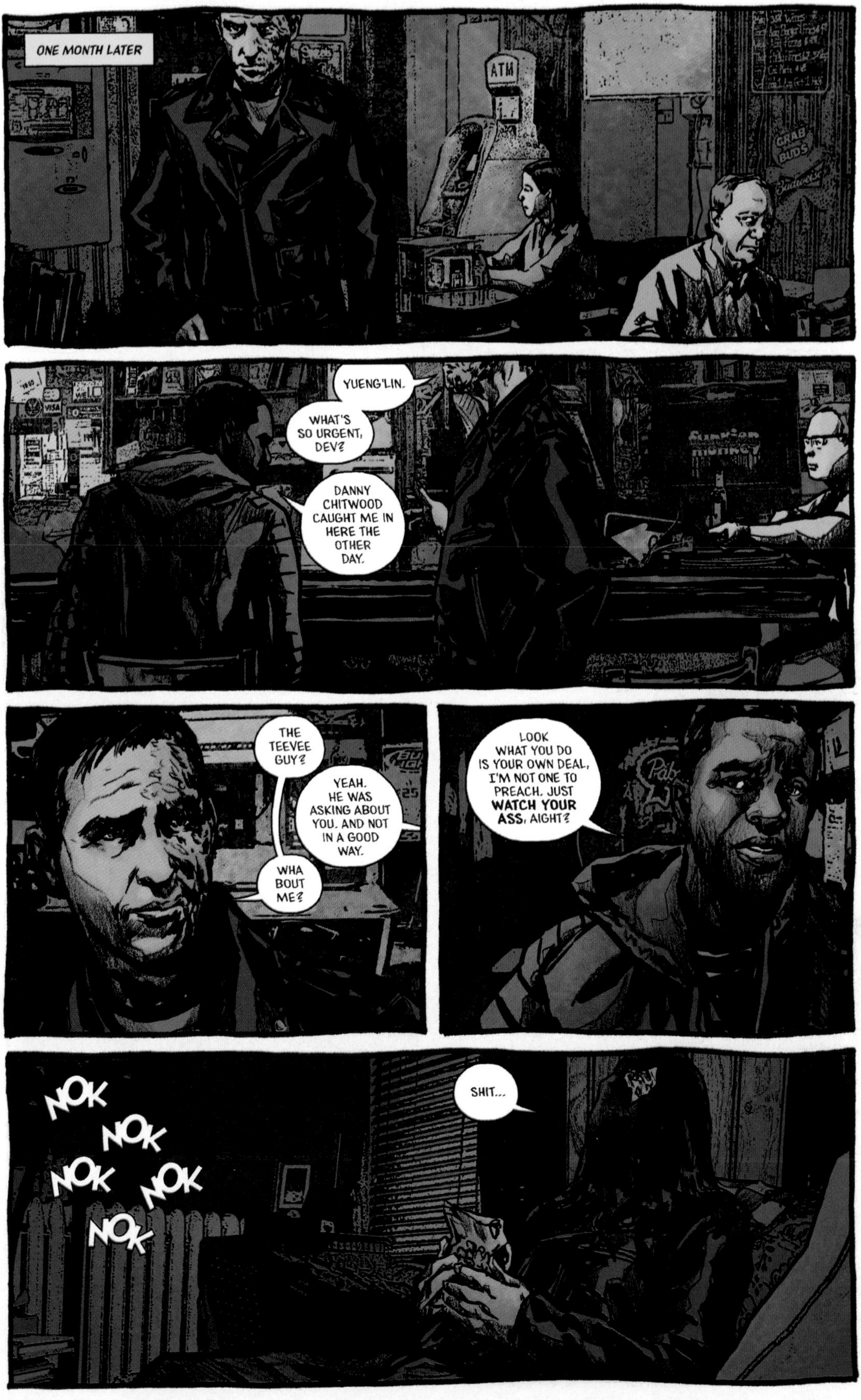
ONE MONTH LATER
YUENG'LIN.
WHAT'S SO URGENT, DEV?
DANNY CHITWOOD CAUGHT ME IN HERE THE OTHER DAY.
THE TEEVEE GUY?
YEAH. HE WAS ASKING ABOUT YOU. AND NOT IN A GOOD WAY.
WHA BOUT ME?
LOOK WHAT YOU DO IS YOUR OWN DEAL, I'M NOT ONE TO PREACH. JUST WATCH YOUR ASS, AIGHT?
NOK NOK NOK NOK NOK
SHIT...

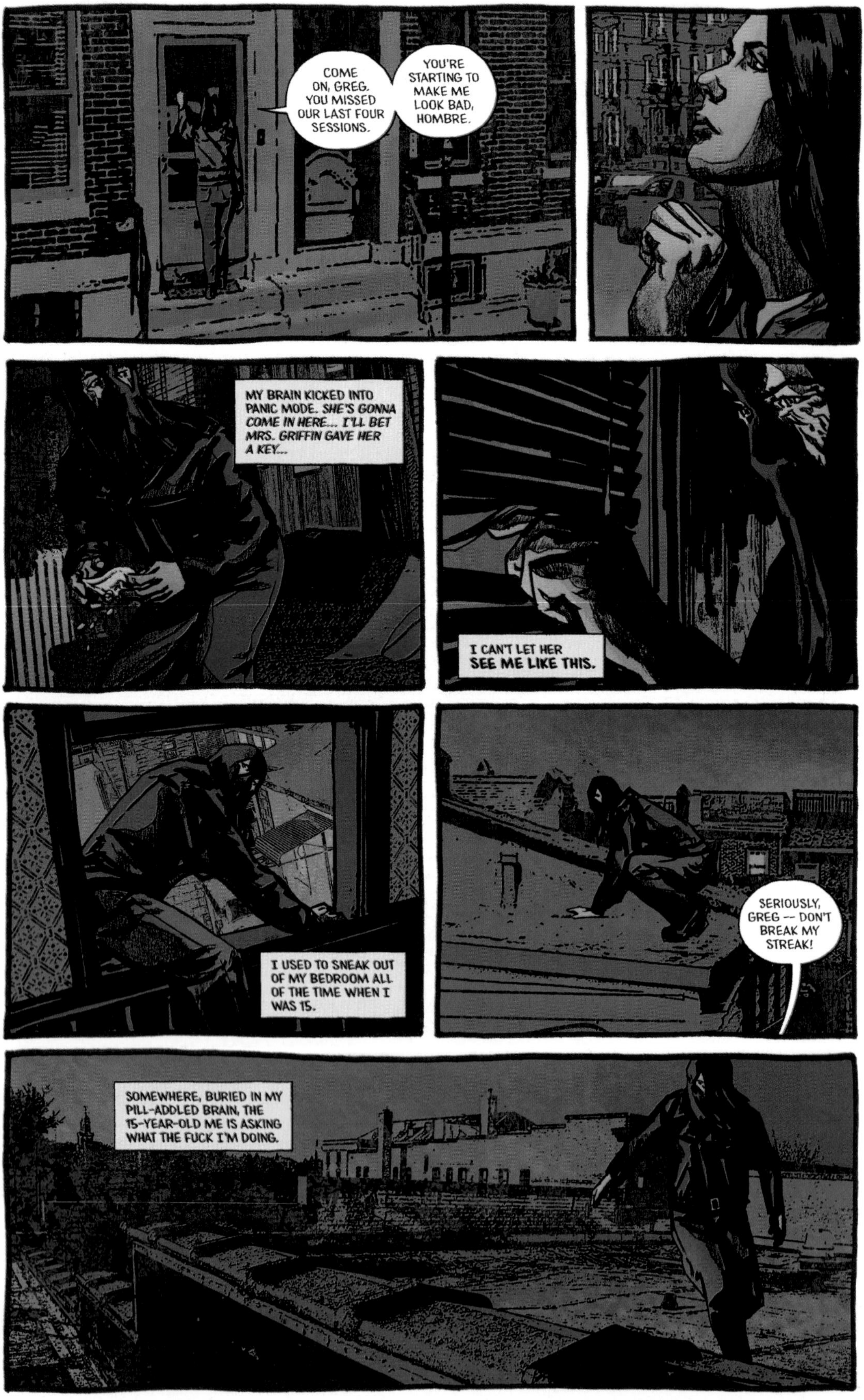
COME ON, GREG. YOU MISSED OUR LAST FOUR SESSIONS.
YOU'RE STARTING TO MAKE ME LOOK BAD, HOMBRE.
MY BRAIN KICKED INTO PANIC MODE. *SHE'S GONNA COME IN HERE... I'LL BET MRS. GRIFFIN GAVE HER A KEY...*
I CAN'T LET HER **SEE ME LIKE THIS.**
I USED TO SNEAK OUT OF MY BEDROOM ALL OF THE TIME WHEN I WAS 15.
SERIOUSLY, GREG -- DON'T BREAK MY STREAK!
SOMEWHERE, BURIED IN MY PILL-ADDLED BRAIN, THE 15-YEAR-OLD ME IS ASKING WHAT THE FUCK I'M DOING.

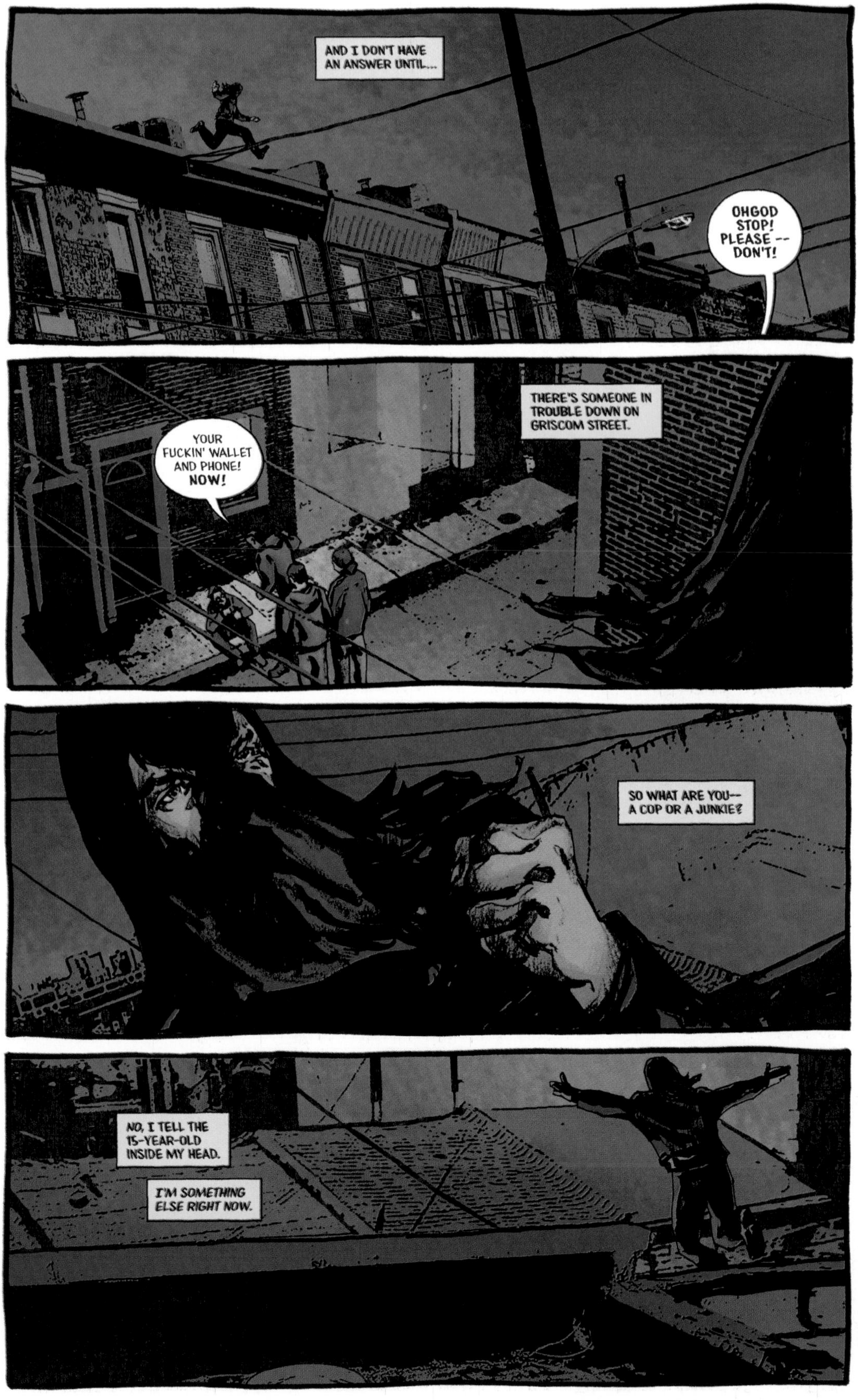
AND I DON'T HAVE AN ANSWER UNTIL...
OHGOD STOP! PLEASE -- DON'T!
THERE'S SOMEONE IN TROUBLE DOWN ON GRISCOM STREET.
YOUR FUCKIN' WALLET AND PHONE! NOW!
SO WHAT ARE YOU-- A COP OR A JUNKIE?
NO, I TELL THE 15-YEAR-OLD INSIDE MY HEAD.
I'M SOMETHING ELSE RIGHT NOW.

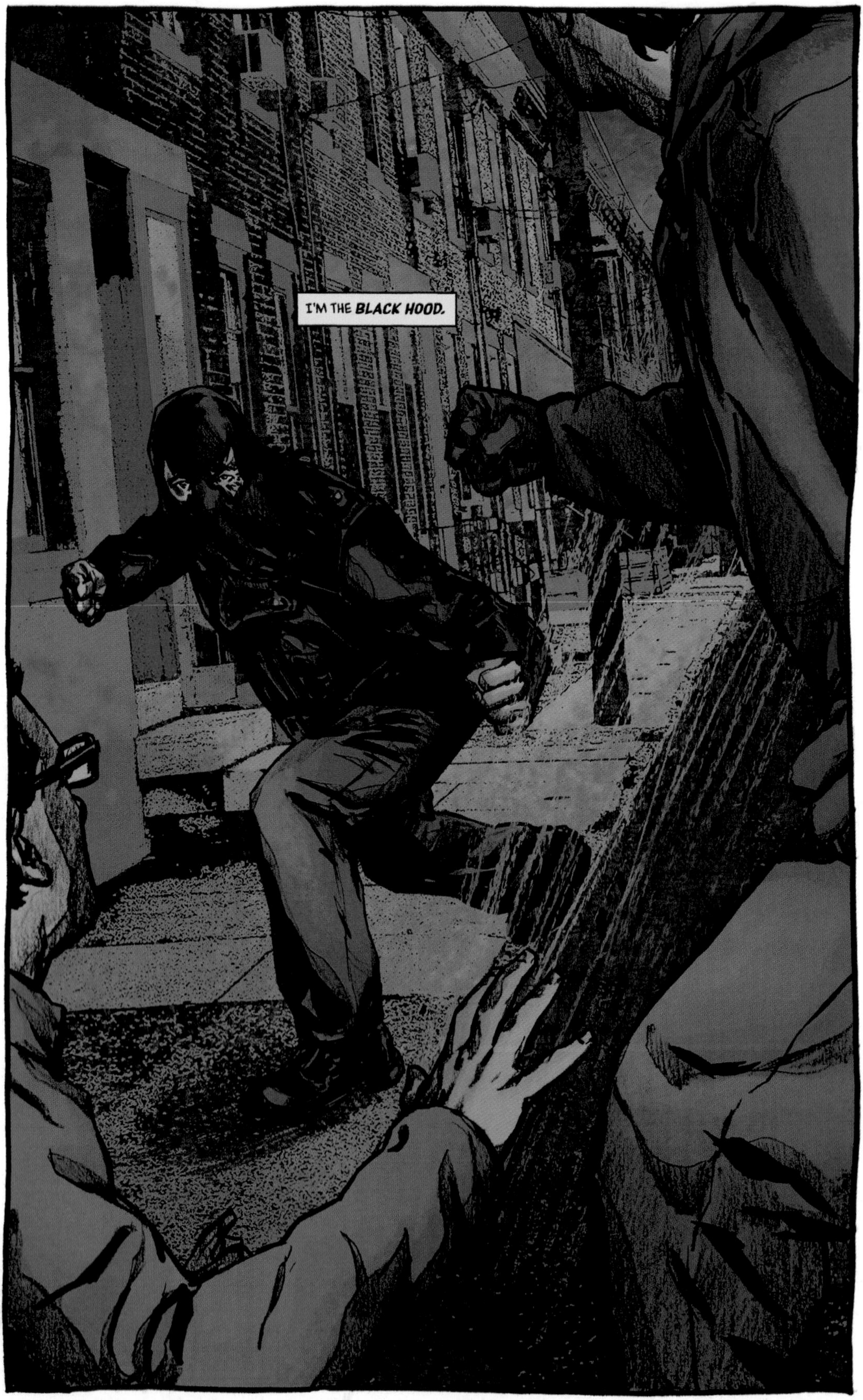
I'M THE BLACK HOOD.

ISSUE TWO

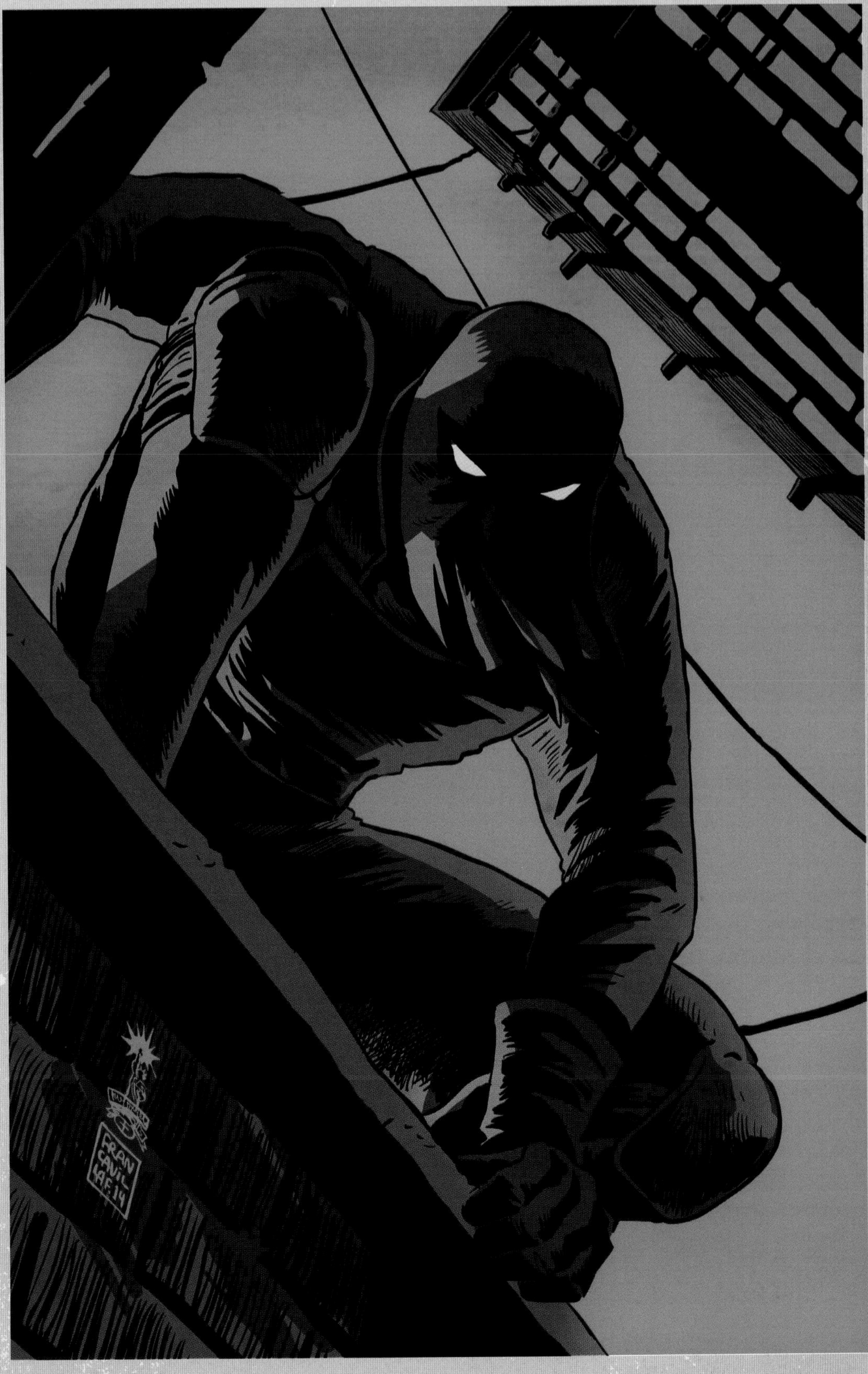

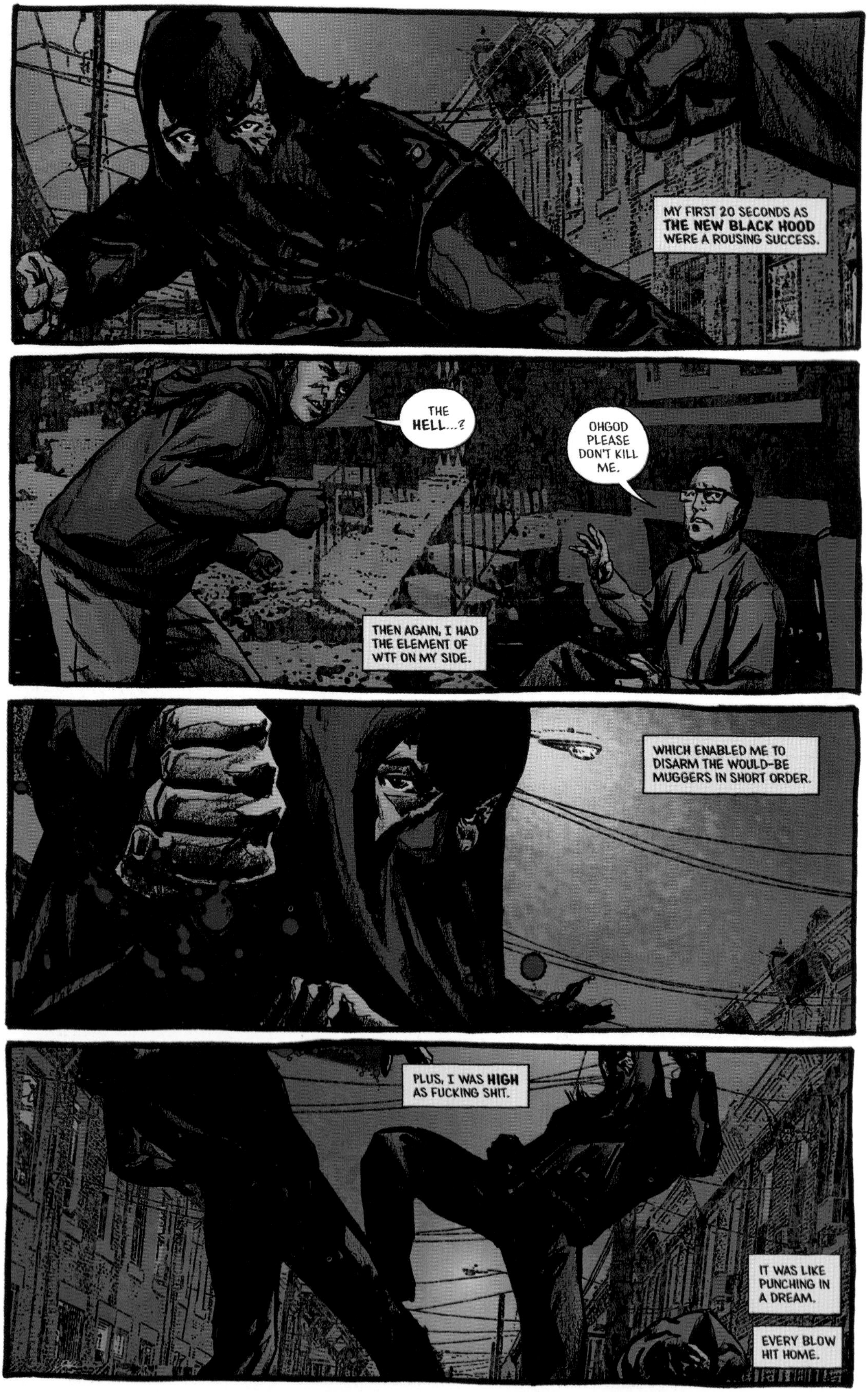
MY FIRST 20 SECONDS AS THE NEW BLACK HOOD WERE A ROUSING SUCCESS.
THE HELL...?
OHGOD PLEASE DON'T KILL ME.
THEN AGAIN, I HAD THE ELEMENT OF WTF ON MY SIDE.
WHICH ENABLED ME TO DISARM THE WOULD-BE MUGGERS IN SHORT ORDER.
PLUS, I WAS HIGH AS FUCKING SHIT.
IT WAS LIKE PUNCHING IN A DREAM.
EVERY BLOW HIT HOME.

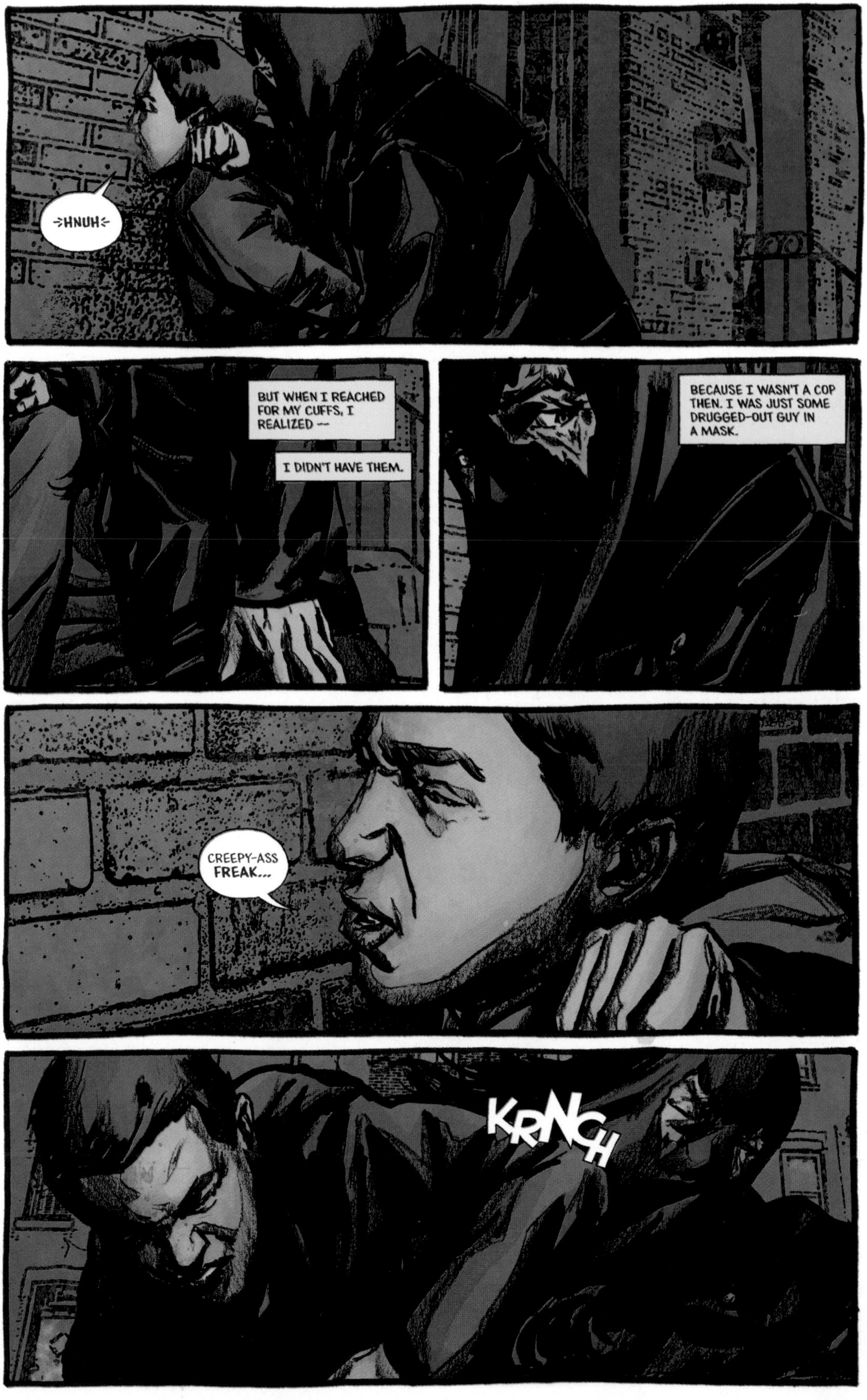
HNUH
BUT WHEN I REACHED FOR MY CUFFS, I REALIZED --
I DIDN'T HAVE THEM.
BECAUSE I WASN'T A COP THEN. I WAS JUST SOME DRUGGED-OUT GUY IN A MASK.
CREEPY-ASS FREAK...
KRNCH

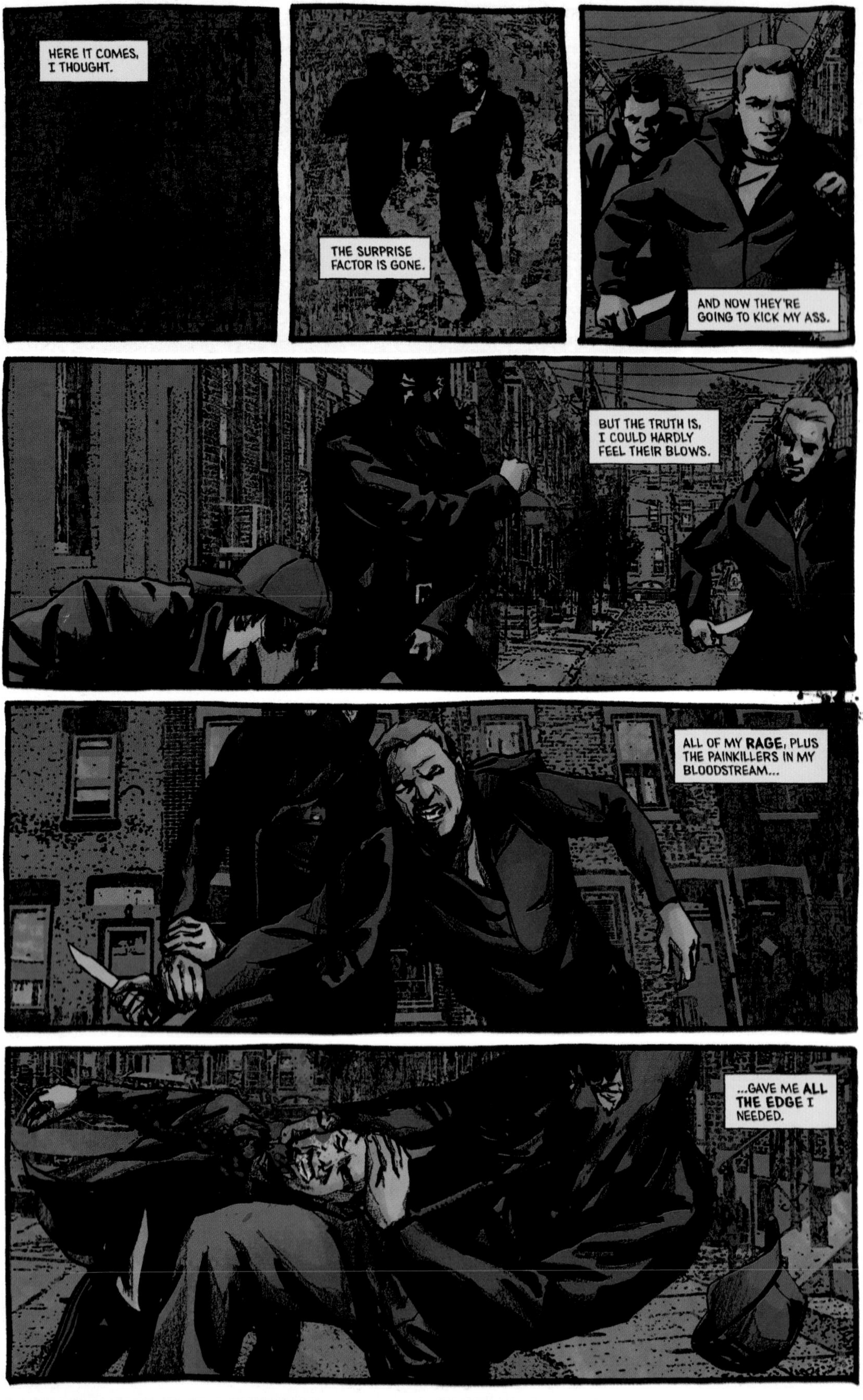
HERE IT COMES, I THOUGHT.
THE SURPRISE FACTOR IS GONE.
AND NOW THEY'RE GOING TO KICK MY ASS.
BUT THE TRUTH IS, I COULD HARDLY FEEL THEIR BLOWS.
ALL OF MY RAGE, PLUS THE PAINKILLERS IN MY BLOODSTREAM...
...GAVE ME ALL THE EDGE I NEEDED.

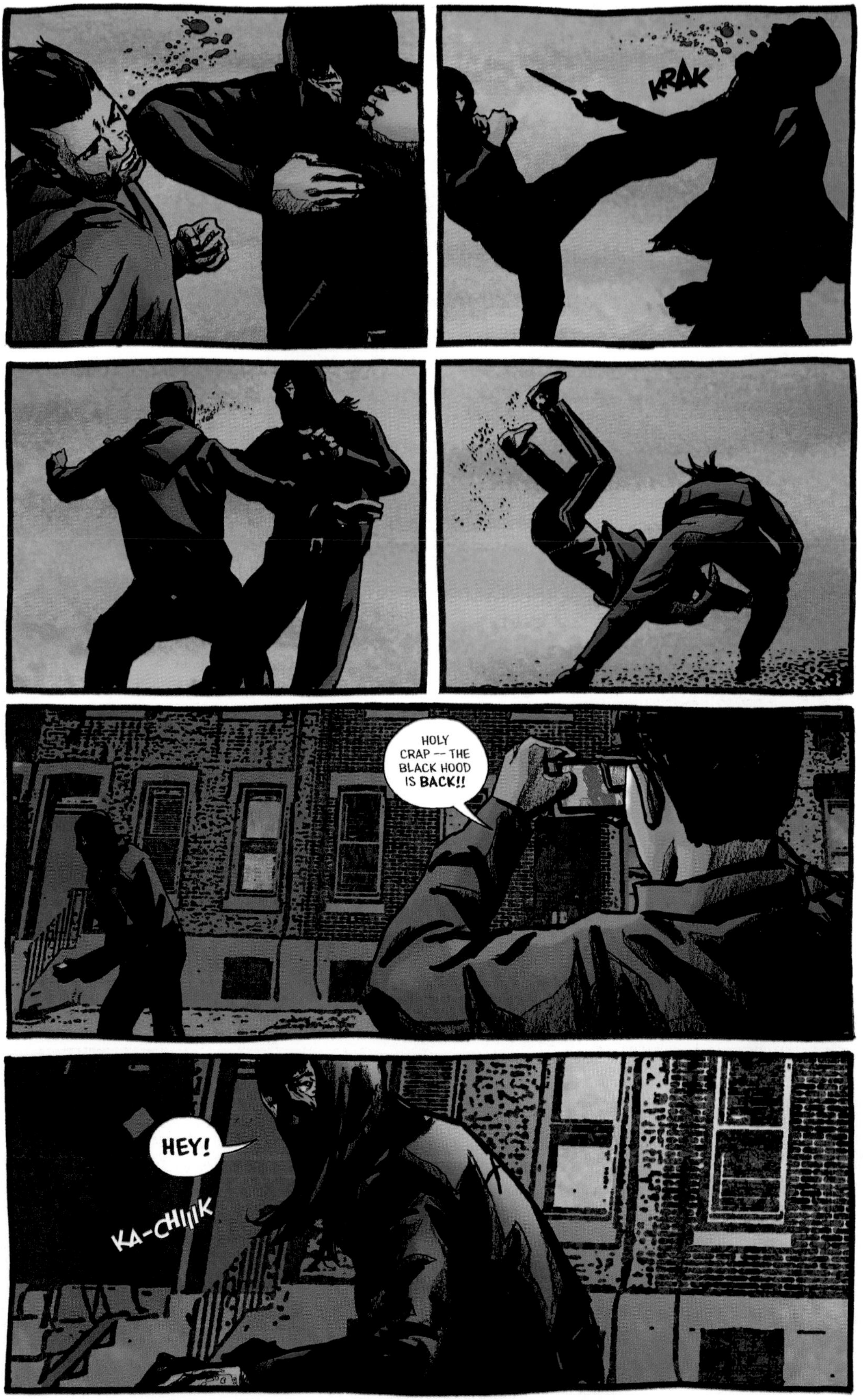
KRAK
HOLY CRAP -- THE BLACK HOOD IS BACK!!
HEY!
KA-CHIIIK

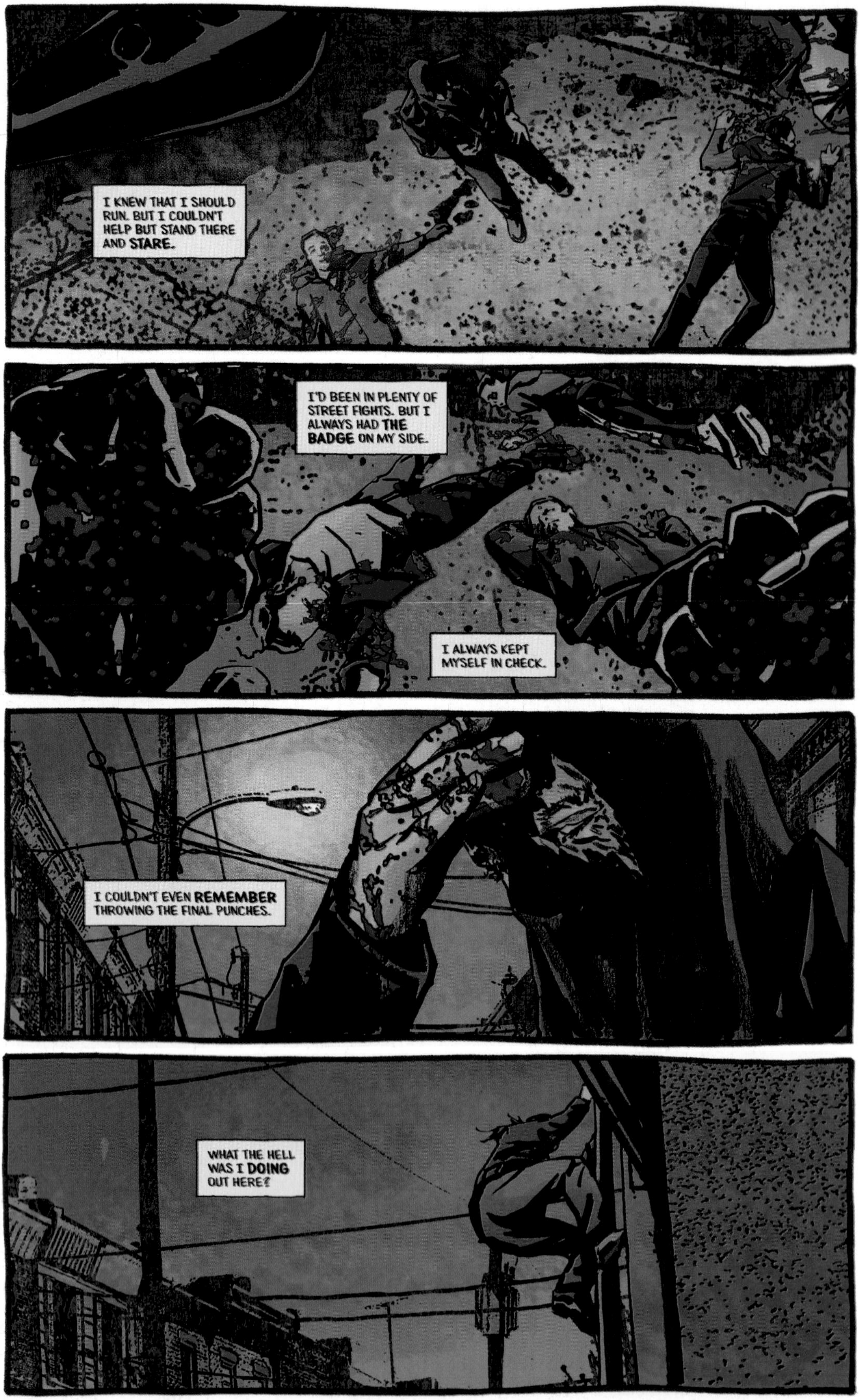
I KNEW THAT I SHOULD RUN. BUT I COULDN'T HELP BUT STAND THERE AND STARE.
I'D BEEN IN PLENTY OF STREET FIGHTS. BUT I ALWAYS HAD THE BADGE ON MY SIDE.
I ALWAYS KEPT MYSELF IN CHECK.
I COULDN'T EVEN REMEMBER THROWING THE FINAL PUNCHES.
WHAT THE HELL WAS I DOING OUT HERE?

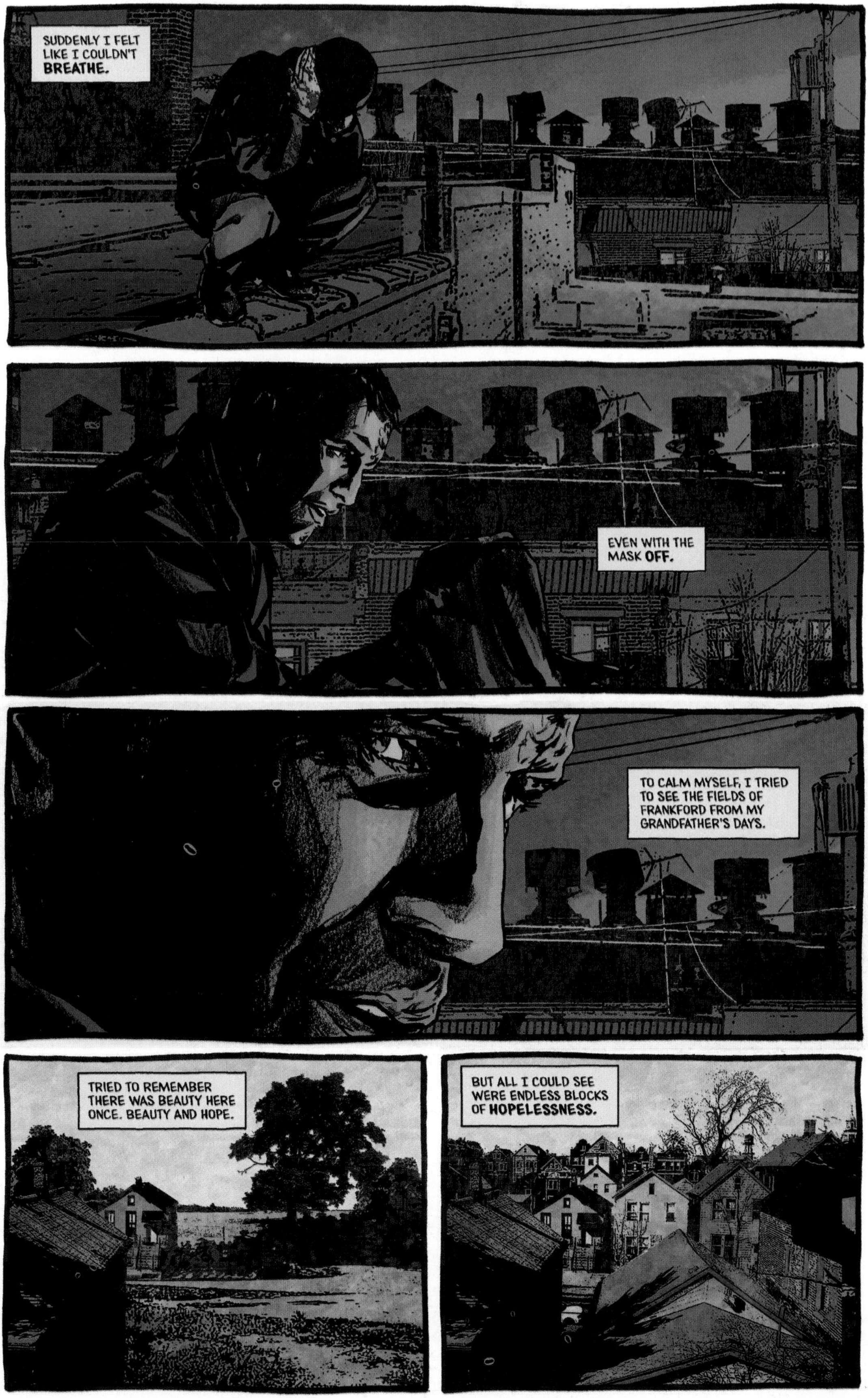
SUDDENLY I FELT LIKE I COULDN'T BREATHE.
EVEN WITH THE MASK OFF.
TO CALM MYSELF, I TRIED TO SEE THE FIELDS OF FRANKFORD FROM MY GRANDFATHER'S DAYS.
TRIED TO REMEMBER THERE WAS BEAUTY HERE ONCE. BEAUTY AND HOPE.
BUT ALL I COULD SEE WERE ENDLESS BLOCKS OF HOPELESSNESS.

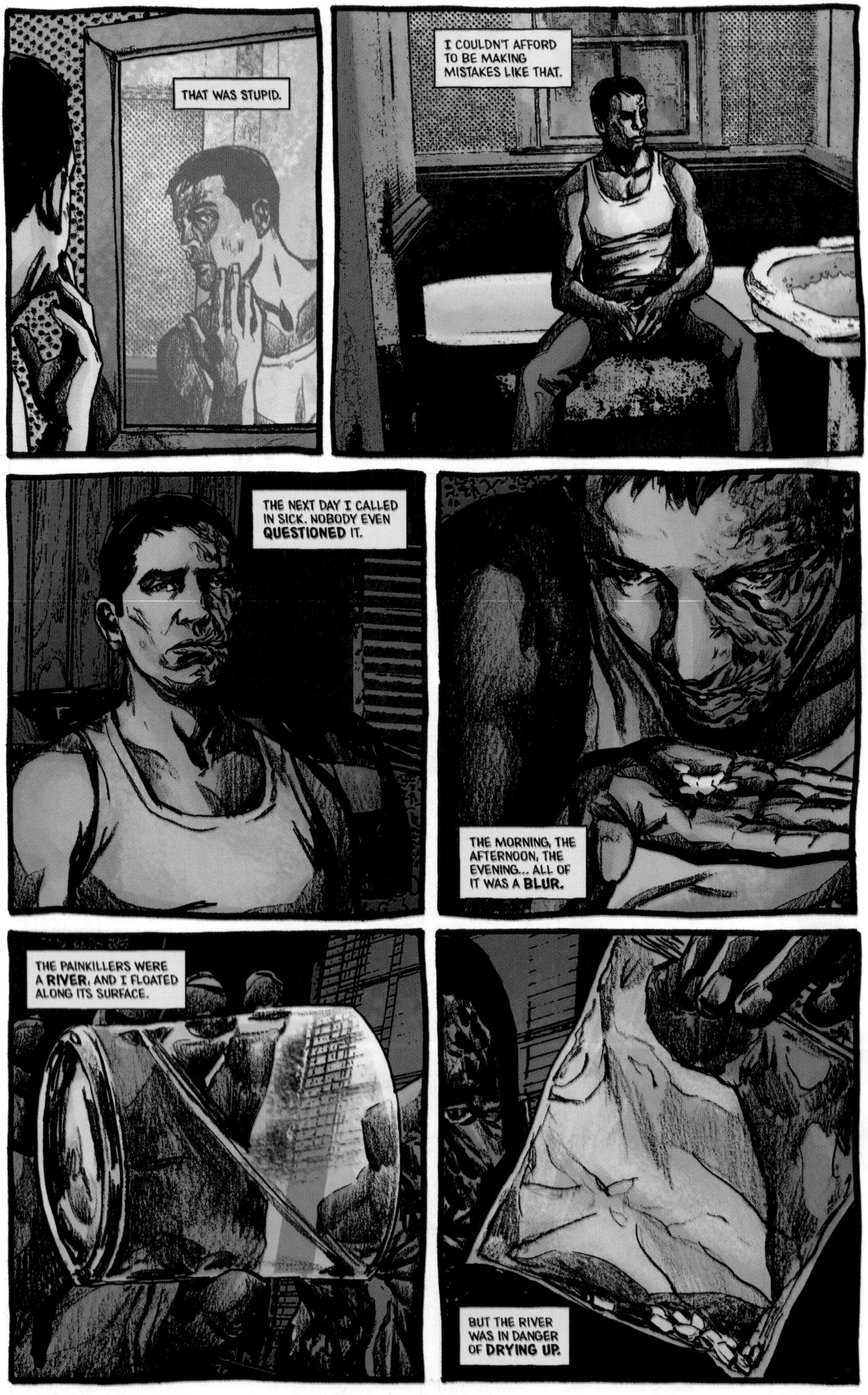
THAT WAS STUPID.
I COULDN'T AFFORD TO BE MAKING MISTAKES LIKE THAT.
THE NEXT DAY I CALLED IN SICK. NOBODY EVEN QUESTIONED IT.
THE MORNING, THE AFTERNOON, THE EVENING... ALL OF IT WAS A BLUR.
THE PAINKILLERS WERE A RIVER, AND I FLOATED ALONG ITS SURFACE.
BUT THE RIVER WAS IN DANGER OF DRYING UP.

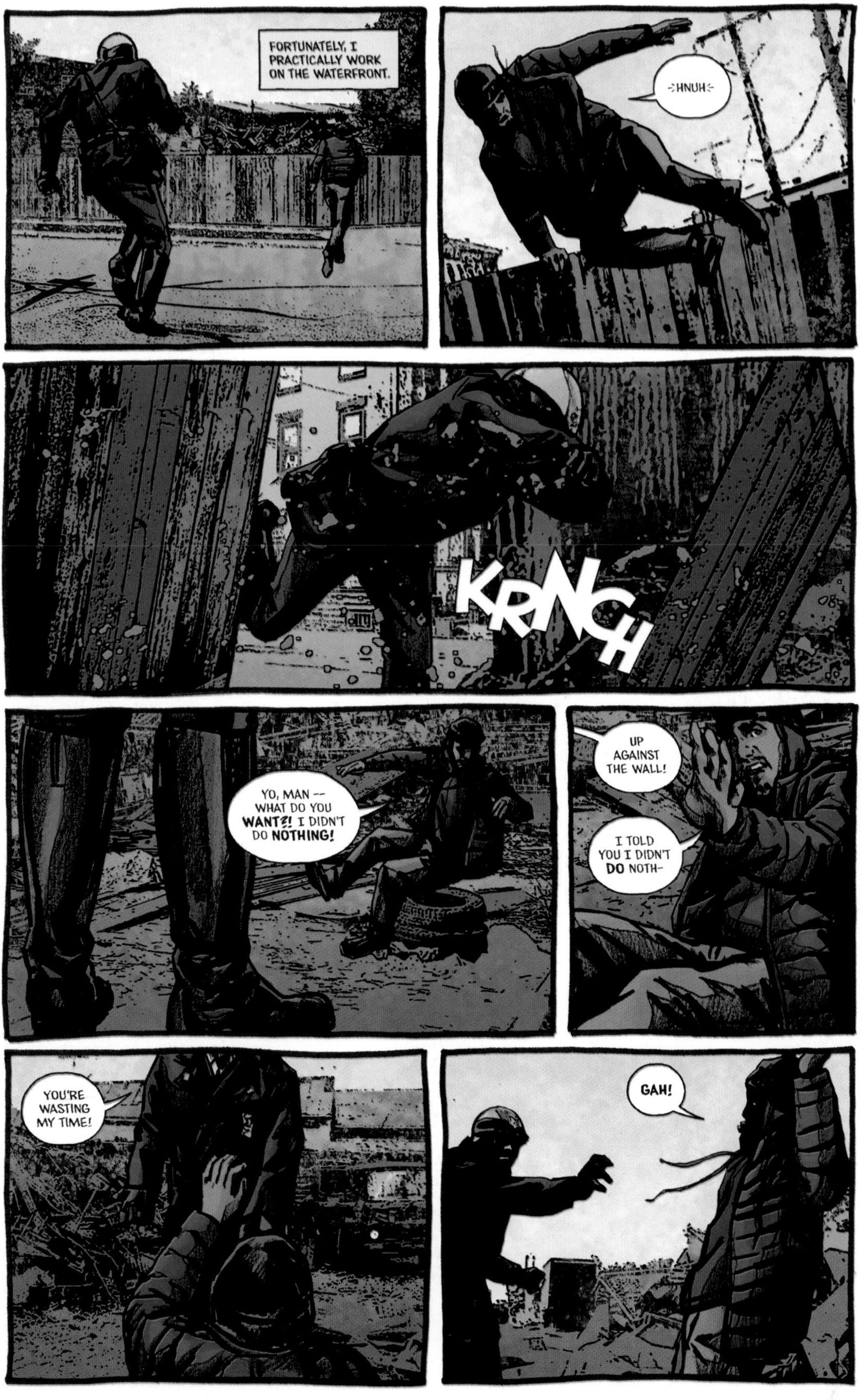
FORTUNATELY, I PRACTICALLY WORK ON THE WATERFRONT.
HNUH
KRNCH
YO, MAN -- WHAT DO YOU WANT?! I DIDN'T DO NOTHING!
UP AGAINST THE WALL!
I TOLD YOU I DIDN'T DO NOTH-
YOU'RE WASTING MY TIME!
GAH!

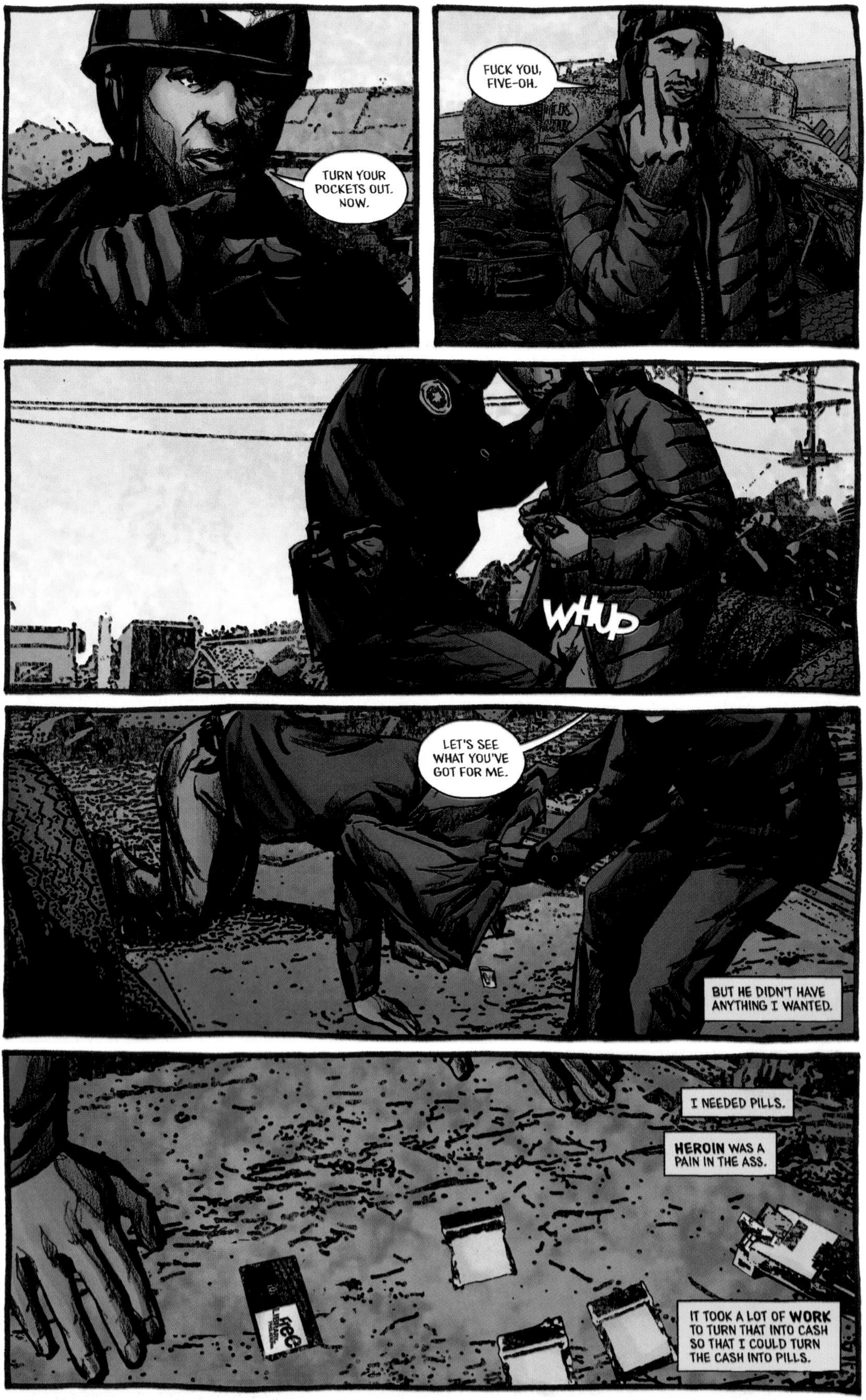
TURN YOUR POCKETS OUT. NOW.
FUCK YOU, FIVE-OH.
WHUP
LET'S SEE WHAT YOU'VE GOT FOR ME.
BUT HE DIDN'T HAVE ANYTHING I WANTED.
I NEEDED PILLS.
HEROIN WAS A PAIN IN THE ASS.
IT TOOK A LOT OF WORK TO TURN THAT INTO CASH SO THAT I COULD TURN THE CASH INTO PILLS.

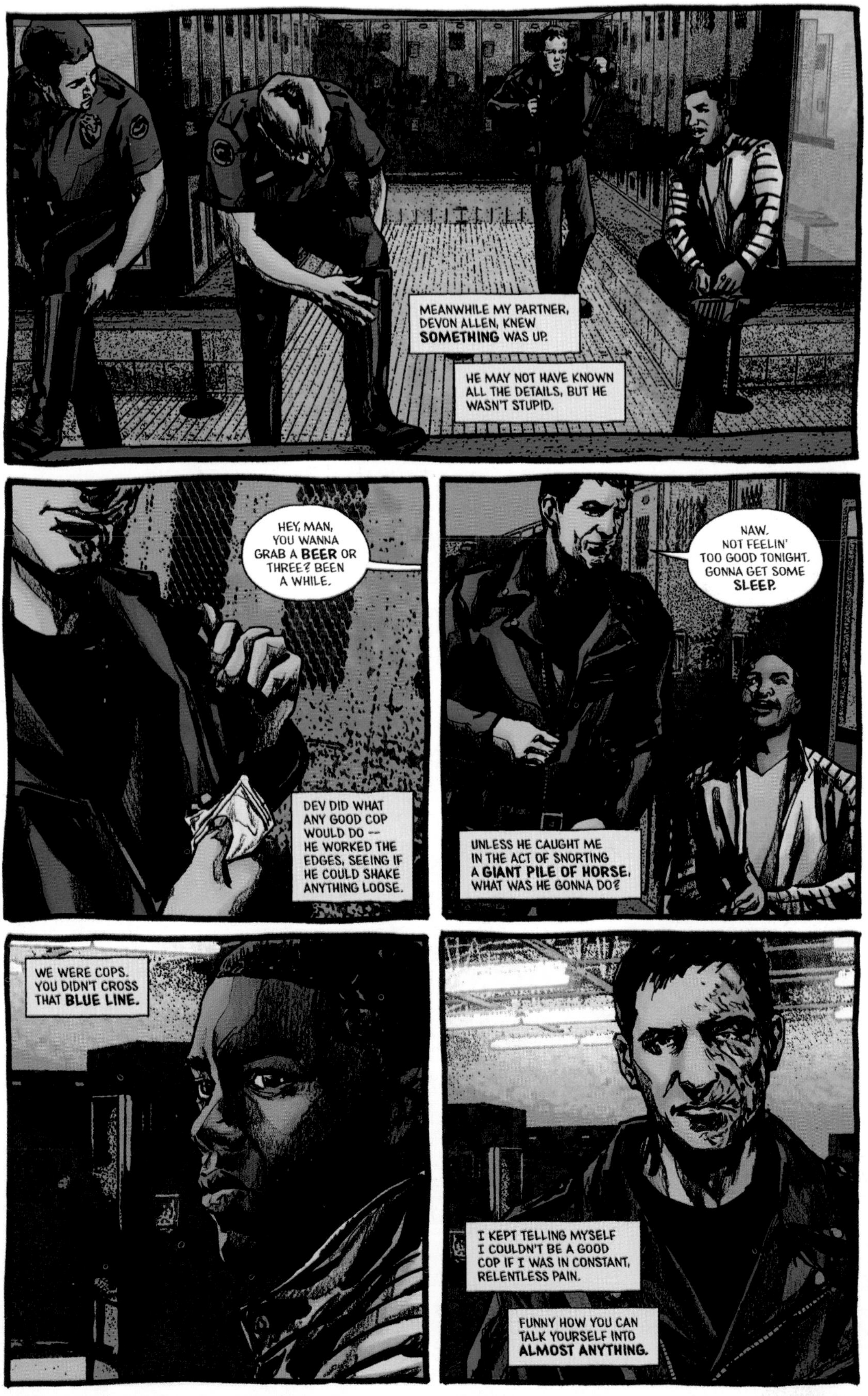
MEANWHILE MY PARTNER, DEVON ALLEN, KNEW SOMETHING WAS UP.
HE MAY NOT HAVE KNOWN ALL THE DETAILS, BUT HE WASN'T STUPID.
HEY, MAN, YOU WANNA GRAB A BEER OR THREE? BEEN A WHILE.
DEV DID WHAT ANY GOOD COP WOULD DO -- HE WORKED THE EDGES, SEEING IF HE COULD SHAKE ANYTHING LOOSE.
NAW. NOT FEELIN' TOO GOOD TONIGHT. GONNA GET SOME SLEEP.
UNLESS HE CAUGHT ME IN THE ACT OF SNORTING A GIANT PILE OF HORSE, WHAT WAS HE GONNA DO?
WE WERE COPS. YOU DIDN'T CROSS THAT BLUE LINE.
I KEPT TELLING MYSELF I COULDN'T BE A GOOD COP IF I WAS IN CONSTANT, RELENTLESS PAIN.
FUNNY HOW YOU CAN TALK YOURSELF INTO ALMOST ANYTHING.

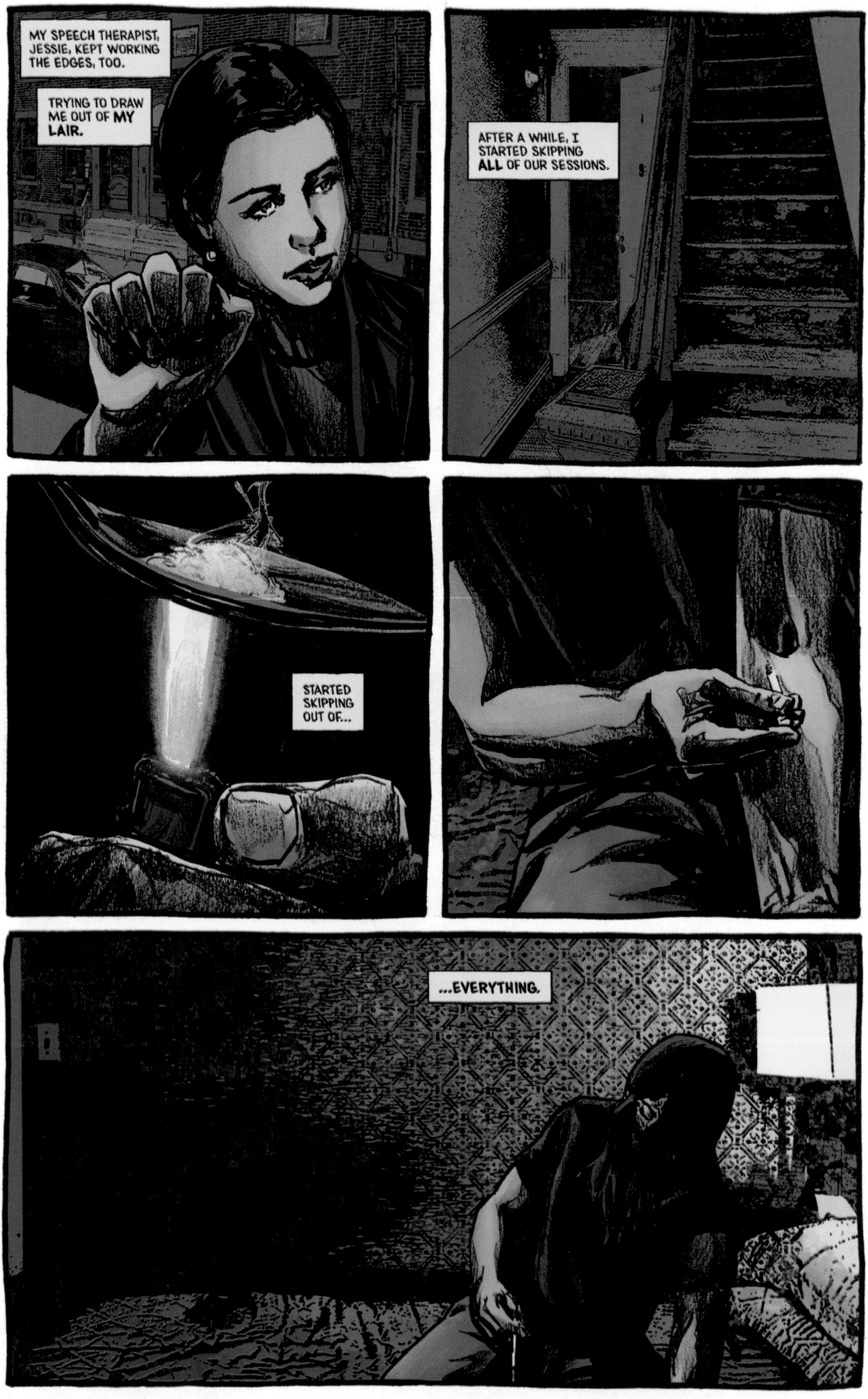
MY SPEECH THERAPIST, JESSIE, KEPT WORKING THE EDGES, TOO.
TRYING TO DRAW ME OUT OF MY LAIR.
AFTER A WHILE, I STARTED SKIPPING ALL OF OUR SESSIONS.
STARTED SKIPPING OUT OF...
...EVERYTHING.

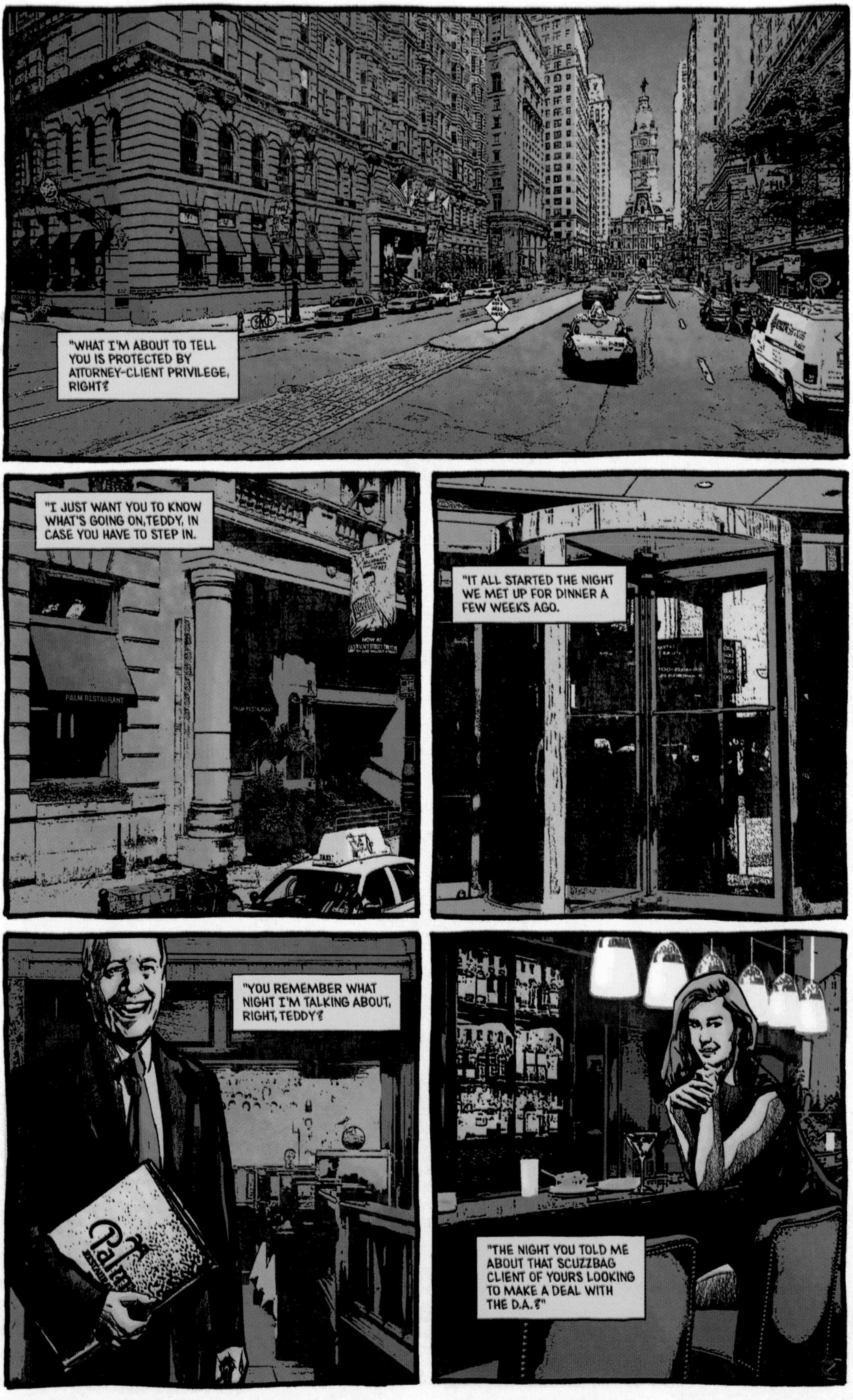
"WHAT I'M ABOUT TO TELL YOU IS PROTECTED BY ATTORNEY-CLIENT PRIVILEGE, RIGHT?
"I JUST WANT YOU TO KNOW WHAT'S GOING ON, TEDDY, IN CASE YOU HAVE TO STEP IN.
PALM RESTAURANT
"IT ALL STARTED THE NIGHT WE MET UP FOR DINNER A FEW WEEKS AGO.
"YOU REMEMBER WHAT NIGHT I'M TALKING ABOUT, RIGHT, TEDDY?
"THE NIGHT YOU TOLD ME ABOUT THAT SCUZZBAG CLIENT OF YOURS LOOKING TO MAKE A DEAL WITH THE D.A.?"

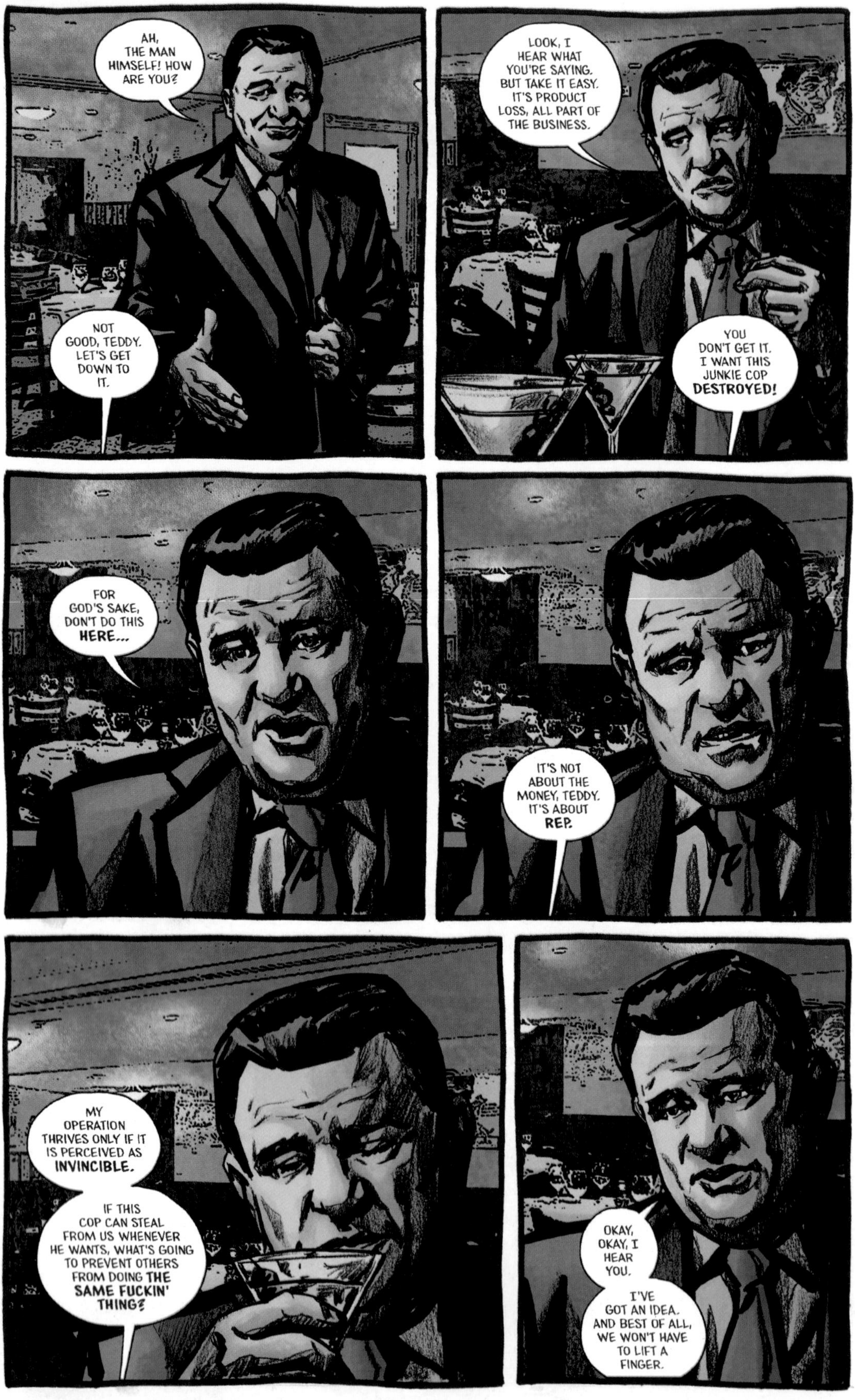
AH, THE MAN HIMSELF! HOW ARE YOU?
NOT GOOD, TEDDY. LET'S GET DOWN TO IT.
LOOK, I HEAR WHAT YOU'RE SAYING. BUT TAKE IT EASY. IT'S PRODUCT LOSS, ALL PART OF THE BUSINESS.
YOU DON'T GET IT. I WANT THIS JUNKIE COP DESTROYED!
FOR GOD'S SAKE, DON'T DO THIS HERE...
IT'S NOT ABOUT THE MONEY, TEDDY. IT'S ABOUT REP.
MY OPERATION THRIVES ONLY IF IT IS PERCEIVED AS INVINCIBLE.
IF THIS COP CAN STEAL FROM US WHENEVER HE WANTS, WHAT'S GOING TO PREVENT OTHERS FROM DOING THE SAME FUCKIN' THING?
OKAY, OKAY, I HEAR YOU.
I'VE GOT AN IDEA. AND BEST OF ALL, WE WON'T HAVE TO LIFT A FINGER.

ONE DAY LATER.

I APPRECIATE THE TIP, I REALLY DO.

I HEAR A **BUT** IN THERE.

BUT... I'M HAVING A HARD TIME COMING UP WITH **ANY** EVIDENCE THAT HETTINGER IS CROOKED.

NOBODY'S TALKING.

WHAT ABOUT THAT **CORNER PUNK** WHO MADE A DEAL?

SILENCE WAS PART OF THE DEAL.

LOOK, YOU'VE GOTTA BE CAREFUL GOING UP AGAINST THE BOYS IN BLUE.

IF I GO AFTER ONE WITHOUT A VERY GOOD REASON, I LOSE AT LEAST A **DOZEN** SOURCES.

LET ME HAVE MY MEN DO A LITTLE DIGGING, DANNY. I KNOW I'M RIGHT ABOUT THIS.

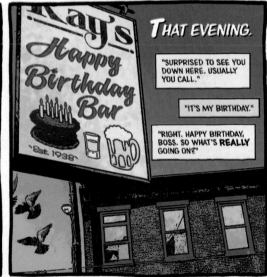

Kay's Happy Birthday Bar

"Est. 1938"

THAT EVENING.

"SURPRISED TO SEE YOU DOWN HERE. USUALLY YOU CALL."

"IT'S MY BIRTHDAY."

"RIGHT. HAPPY BIRTHDAY, BOSS. SO WHAT'S **REALLY** GOING ON?"

I NEED SOME DEGREE OF **PRECISION** WITH THIS ASSIGNMENT, MR. GRAHAM. AND NO POSSIBLE CONNECTION TO MY BUSINESS INTERESTS.

WE'RE ALL ABOUT PRECISION AND DISCRETION. AM I RIGHT, MR. SAVITZ?

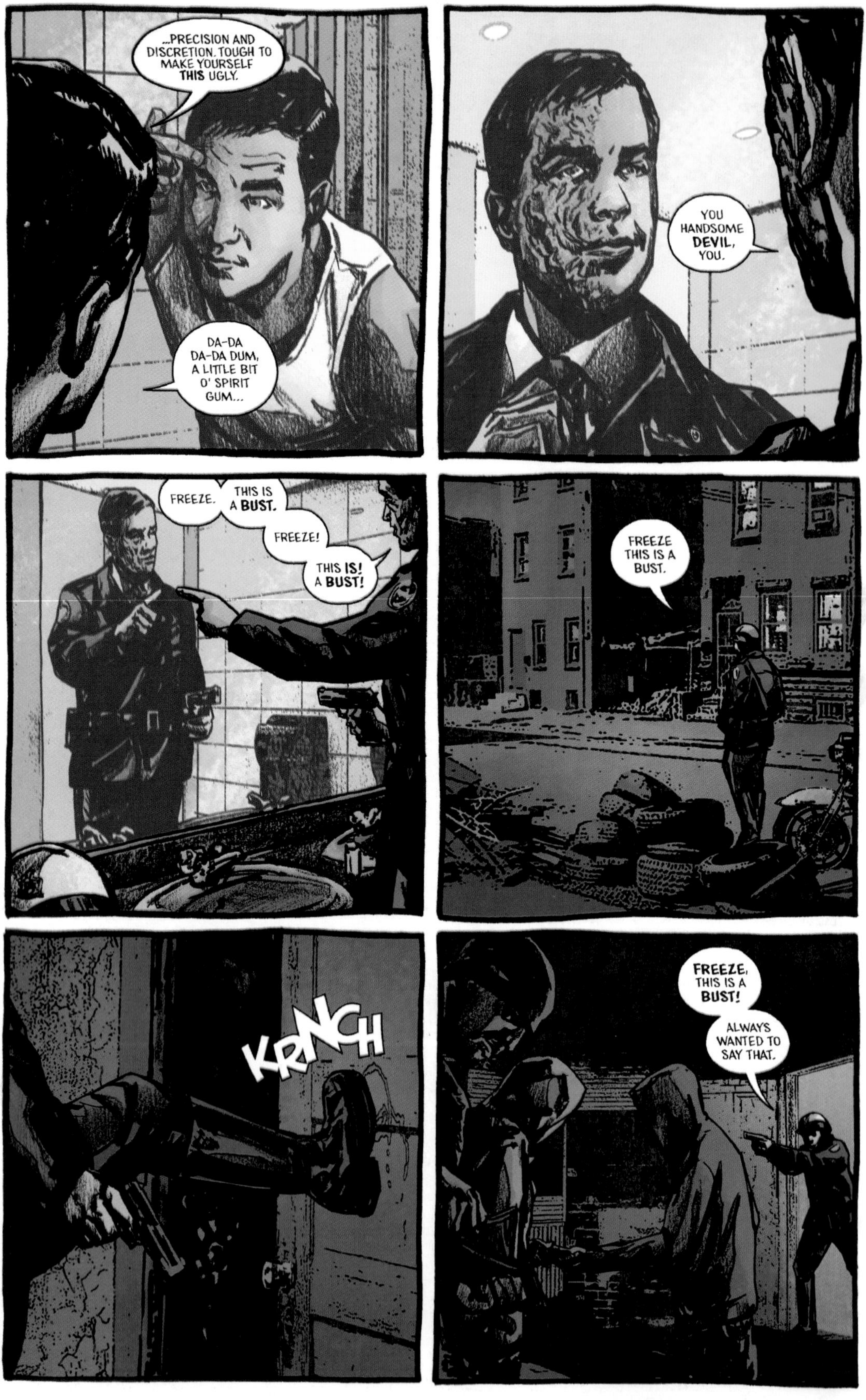
...PRECISION AND DISCRETION. TOUGH TO MAKE YOURSELF **THIS** UGLY.
DA-DA DA-DA DUM, A LITTLE BIT O' SPIRIT GUM...
YOU HANDSOME **DEVIL,** YOU.
FREEZE.
THIS IS A **BUST.**
FREEZE!
THIS **IS!** A **BUST!**
FREEZE THIS IS A BUST.
KRNCH
FREEZE, THIS IS A **BUST!**
ALWAYS WANTED TO SAY THAT.

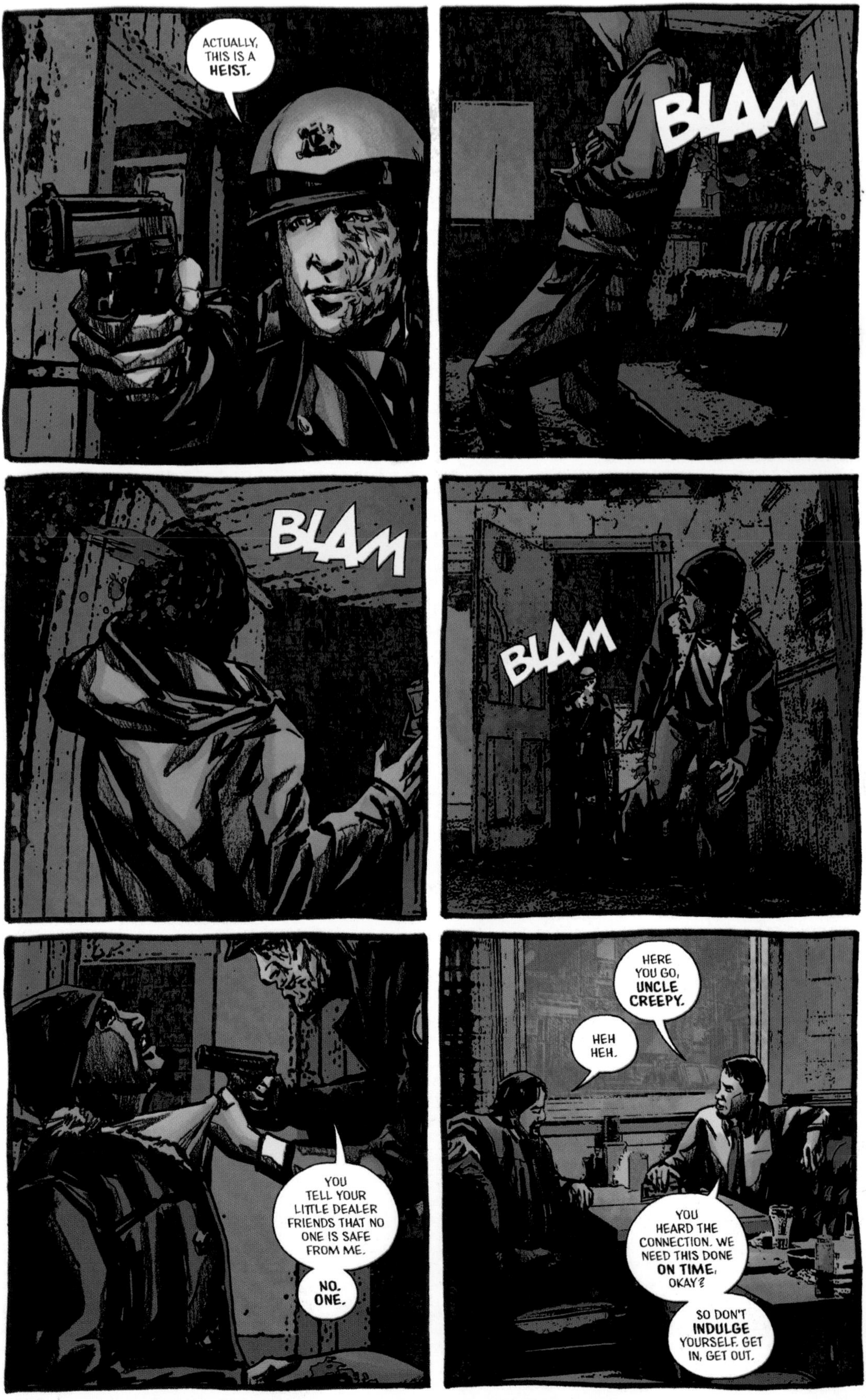
ACTUALLY, THIS IS A HEIST.
BLAM
BLAM
BLAM
YOU TELL YOUR LITTLE DEALER FRIENDS THAT NO ONE IS SAFE FROM ME.
NO. ONE.
HERE YOU GO, UNCLE CREEPY.
HEH HEH.
YOU HEARD THE CONNECTION. WE NEED THIS DONE ON TIME, OKAY?
SO DON'T INDULGE YOURSELF. GET IN, GET OUT.

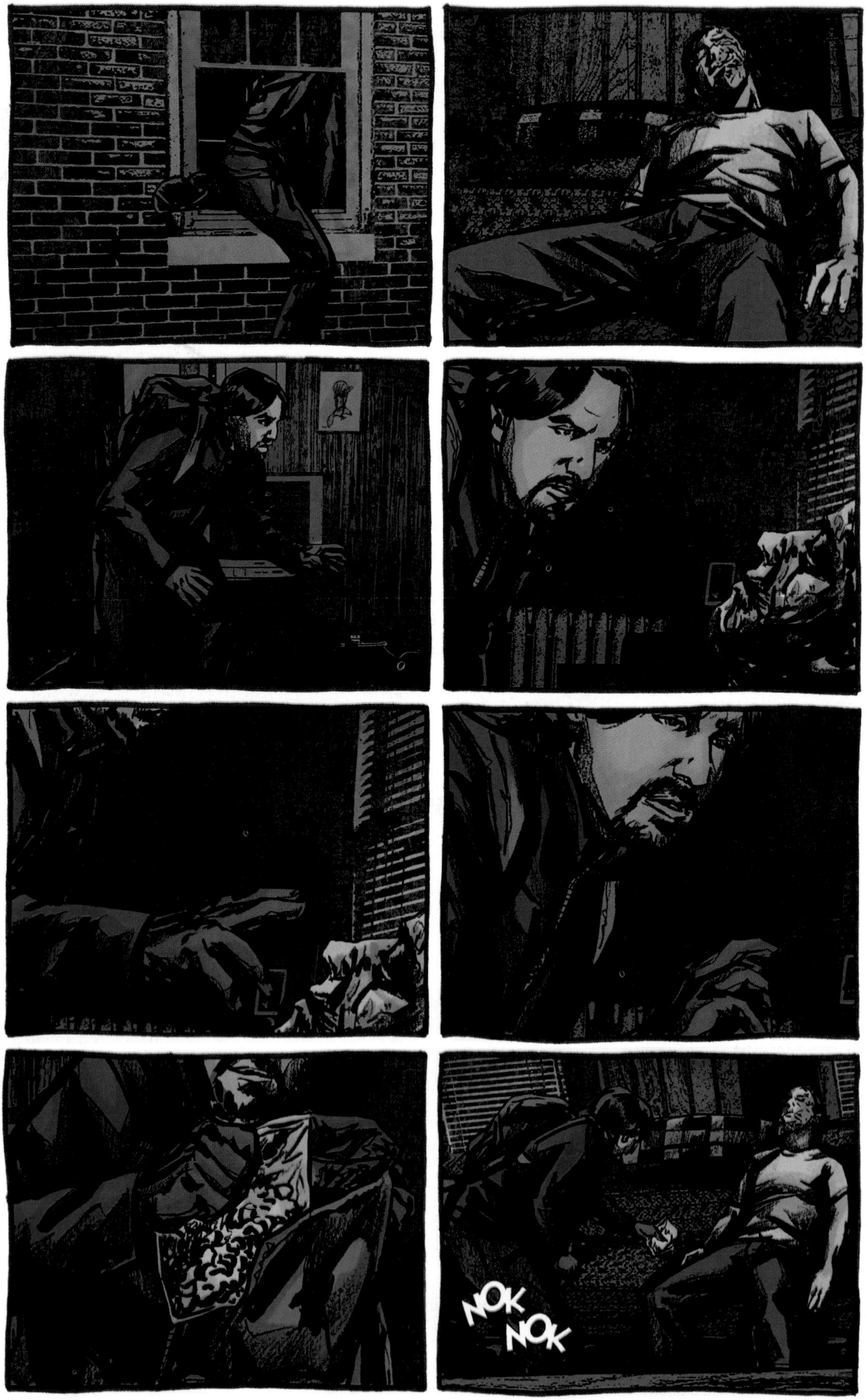
NOK NOK

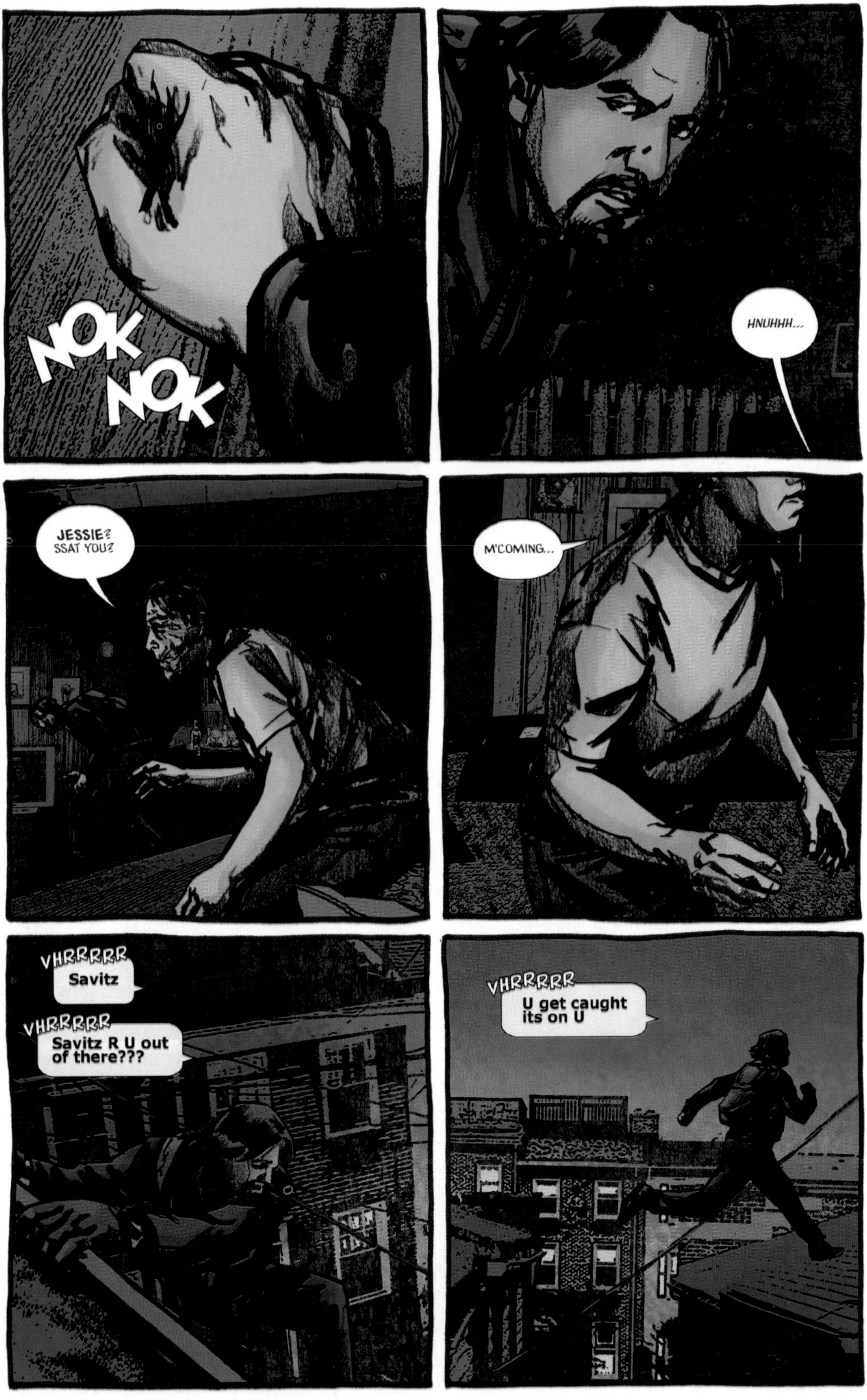
NOK
NOK
HNUHHH...
JESSIE?
SSAT YOU?
M'COMING...
VHRRRRR
Savitz
VHRRRRR
Savitz R U out of there???
VHRRRRR
U get caught its on U

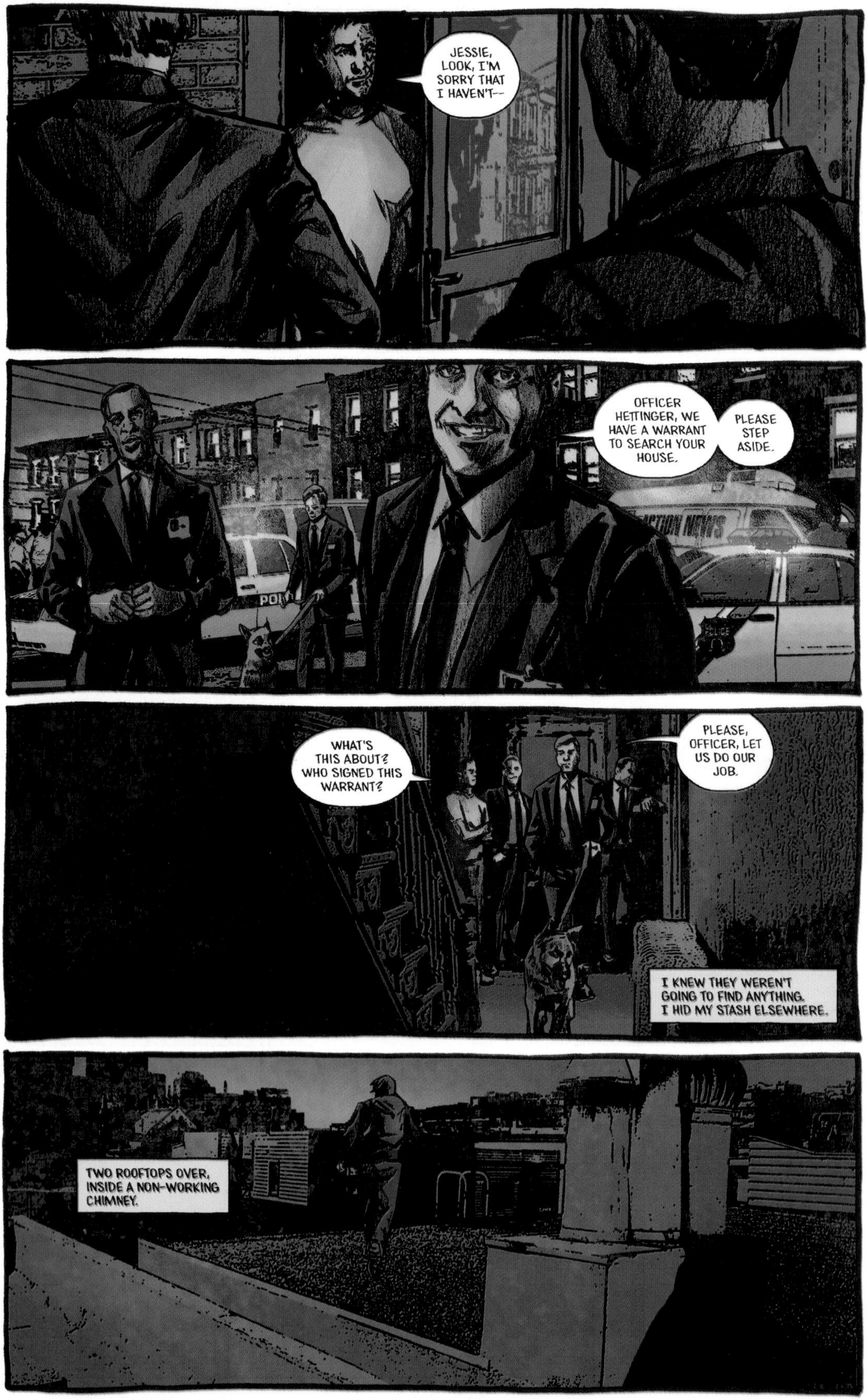
JESSIE, LOOK, I'M SORRY THAT I HAVEN'T--
OFFICER HETTINGER, WE HAVE A WARRANT TO SEARCH YOUR HOUSE.
PLEASE STEP ASIDE.
WHAT'S THIS ABOUT? WHO SIGNED THIS WARRANT?
PLEASE, OFFICER, LET US DO OUR JOB.
I KNEW THEY WEREN'T GOING TO FIND ANYTHING. I HID MY STASH ELSEWHERE.
TWO ROOFTOPS OVER, INSIDE A NON-WORKING CHIMNEY.

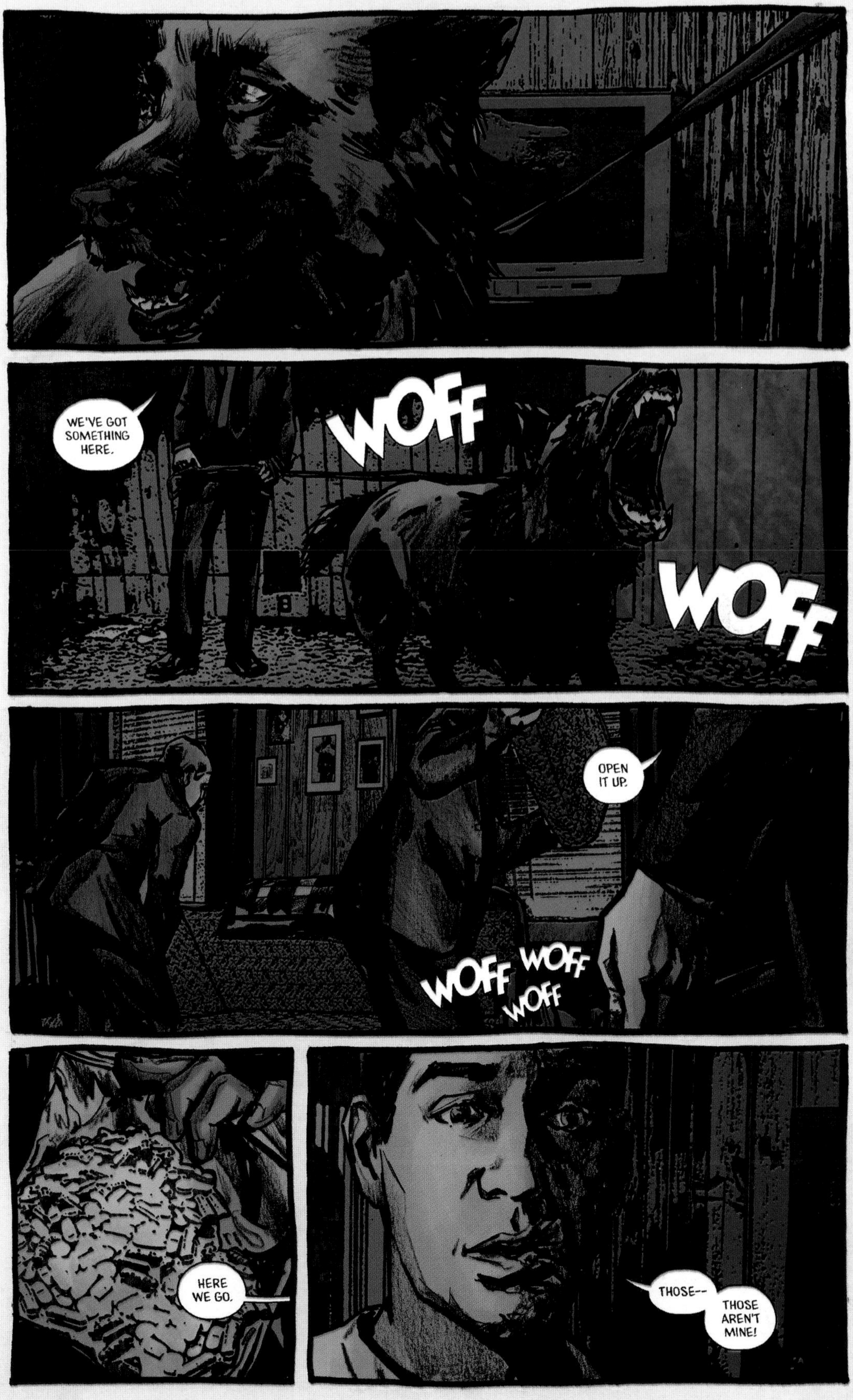
WE'VE GOT SOMETHING HERE.
WOFF
WOFF
OPEN IT UP.
WOFF WOFF
WOFF
HERE WE GO.
THOSE--
THOSE AREN'T MINE!

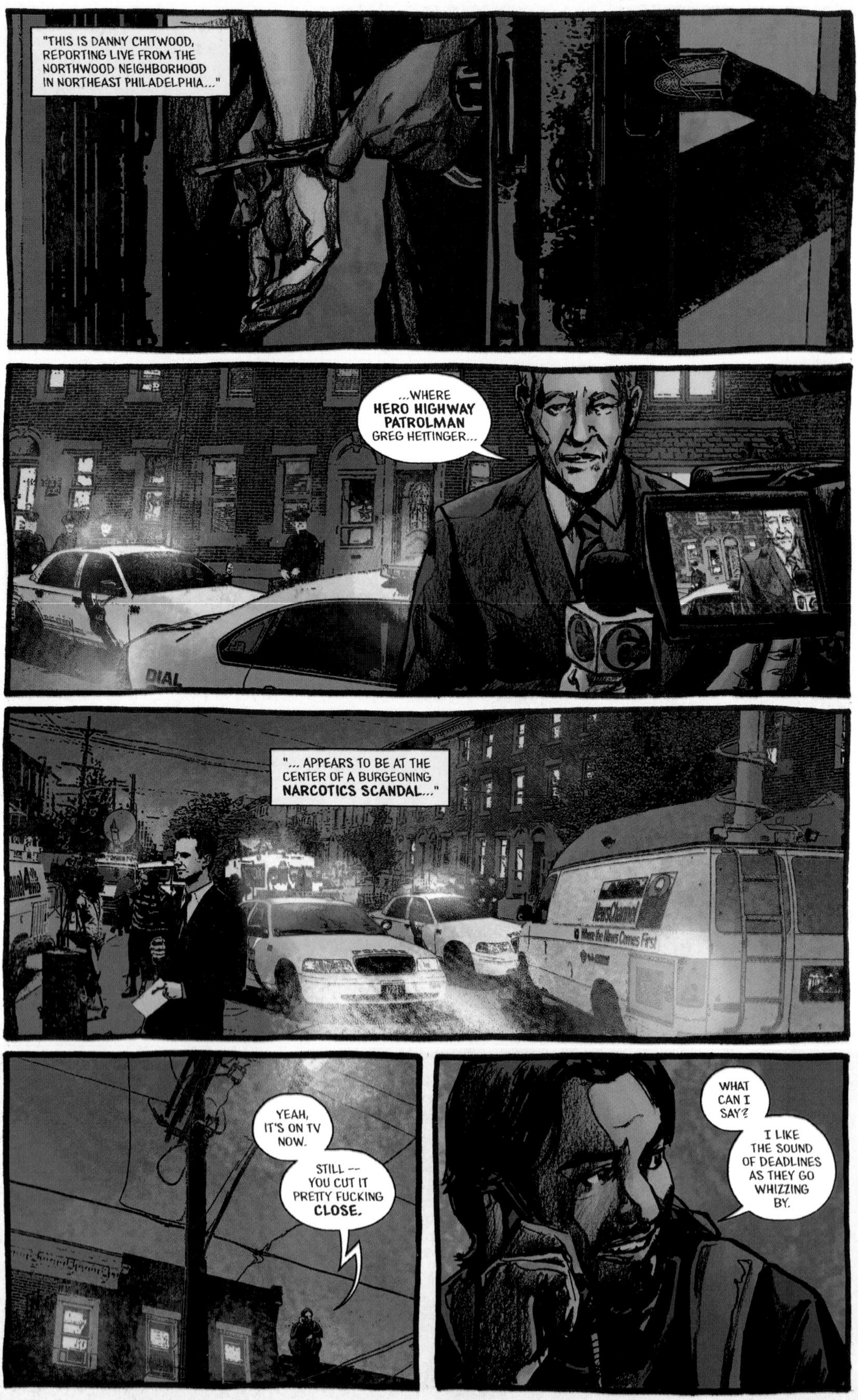
"THIS IS DANNY CHITWOOD, REPORTING LIVE FROM THE NORTHWOOD NEIGHBORHOOD IN NORTHEAST PHILADELPHIA..."
...WHERE HERO HIGHWAY PATROLMAN GREG HETTINGER...
DIAL
"... APPEARS TO BE AT THE CENTER OF A BURGEONING NARCOTICS SCANDAL..."
NewsChannel
Where the News Comes First
YEAH, IT'S ON TV NOW.
STILL -- YOU CUT IT PRETTY FUCKING CLOSE.
WHAT CAN I SAY?
I LIKE THE SOUND OF DEADLINES AS THEY GO WHIZZING BY.

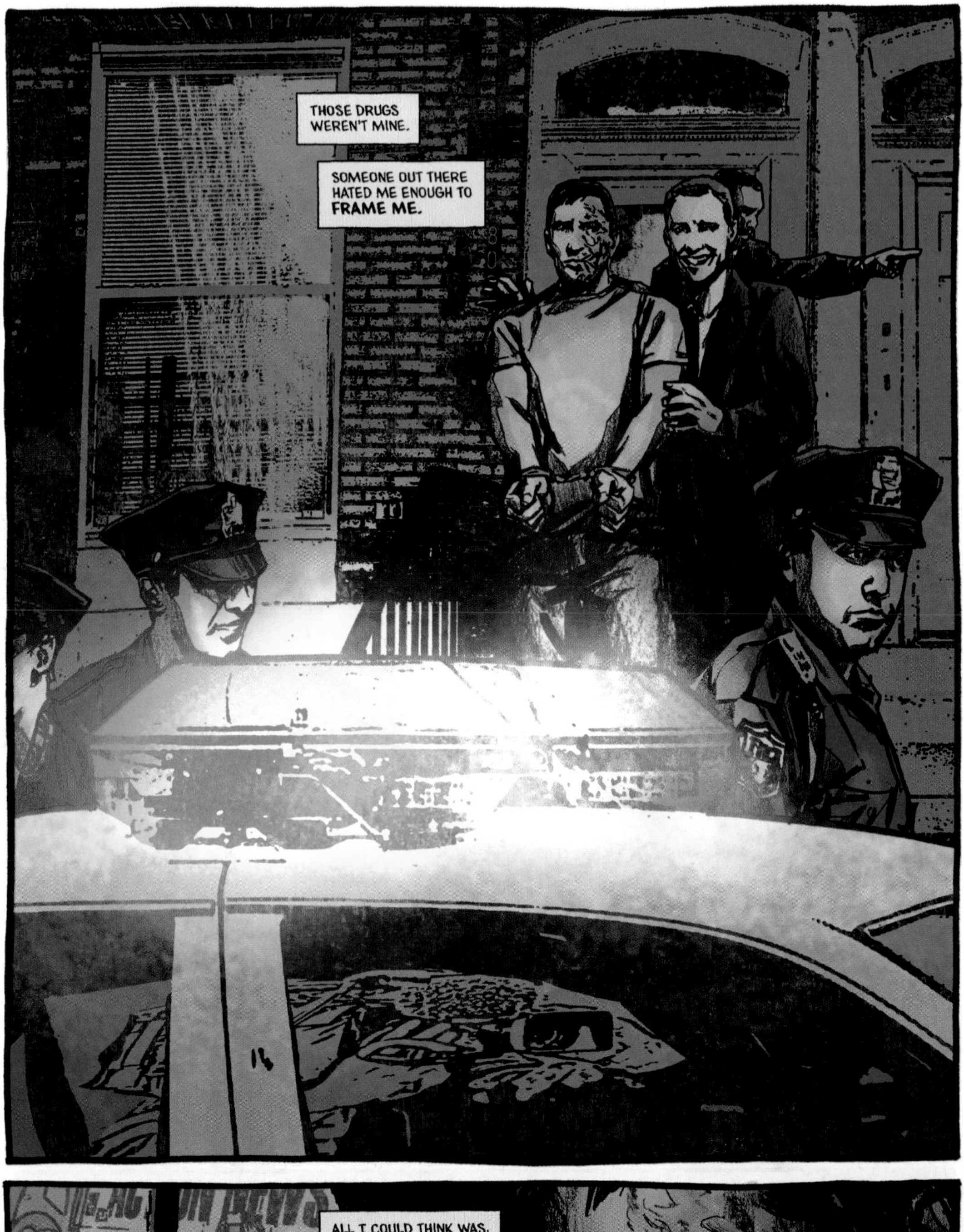
THOSE DRUGS WEREN'T MINE.
SOMEONE OUT THERE HATED ME ENOUGH TO **FRAME ME.**

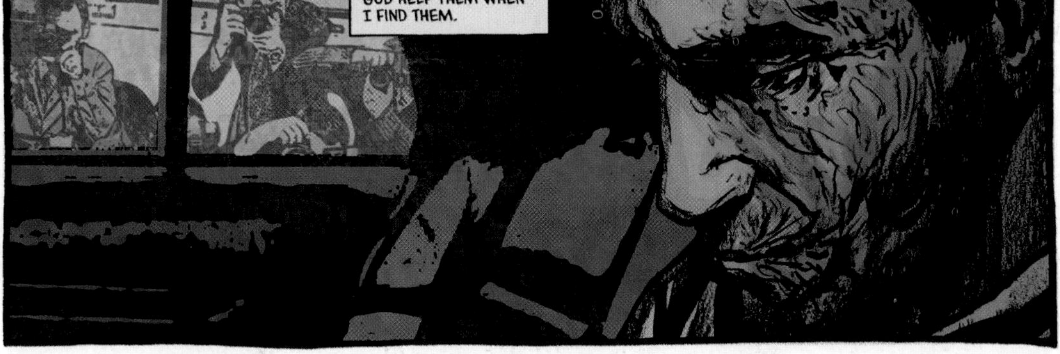
ALL I COULD THINK WAS, GOD HELP THEM WHEN I FIND THEM.

ISSUE THREE

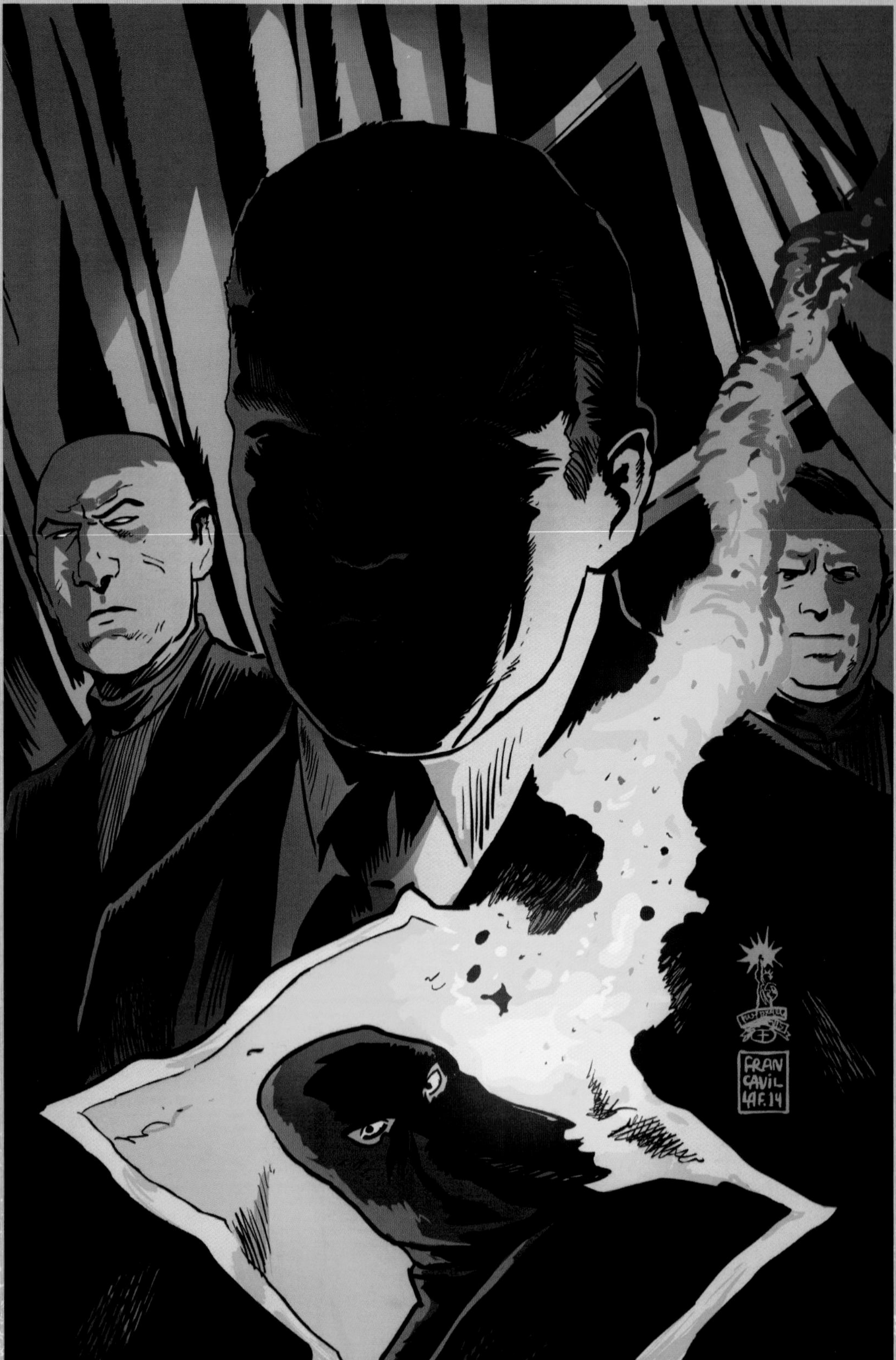
FRAN
CAVIL
4F.14

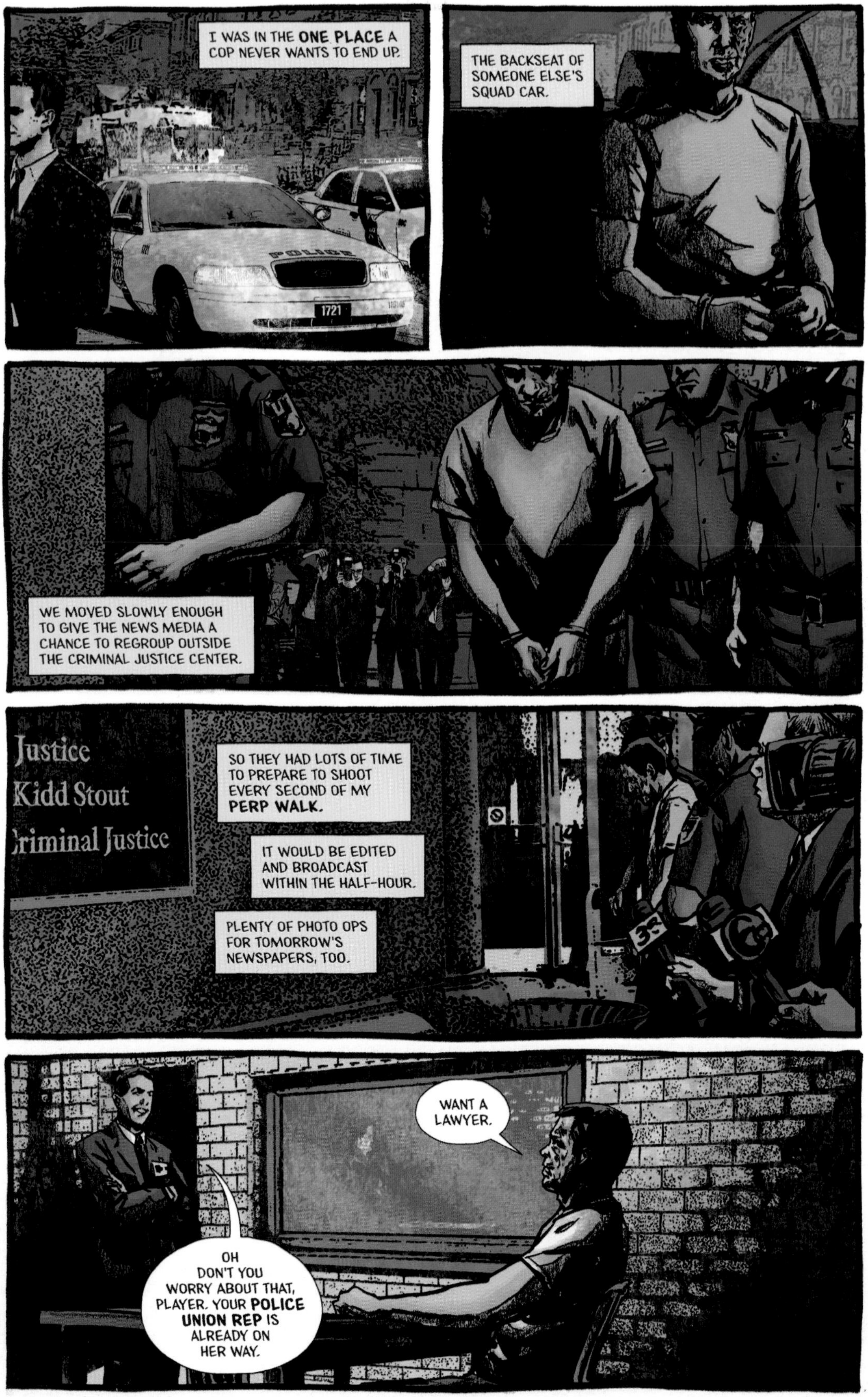
I WAS IN THE ONE PLACE A COP NEVER WANTS TO END UP.
POLICE
1721
THE BACKSEAT OF SOMEONE ELSE'S SQUAD CAR.
WE MOVED SLOWLY ENOUGH TO GIVE THE NEWS MEDIA A CHANCE TO REGROUP OUTSIDE THE CRIMINAL JUSTICE CENTER.
Justice
Kidd Stout
riminal Justice
SO THEY HAD LOTS OF TIME TO PREPARE TO SHOOT EVERY SECOND OF MY PERP WALK.
IT WOULD BE EDITED AND BROADCAST WITHIN THE HALF-HOUR.
PLENTY OF PHOTO OPS FOR TOMORROW'S NEWSPAPERS, TOO.
WANT A LAWYER.
OH DON'T YOU WORRY ABOUT THAT, PLAYER. YOUR POLICE UNION REP IS ALREADY ON HER WAY.

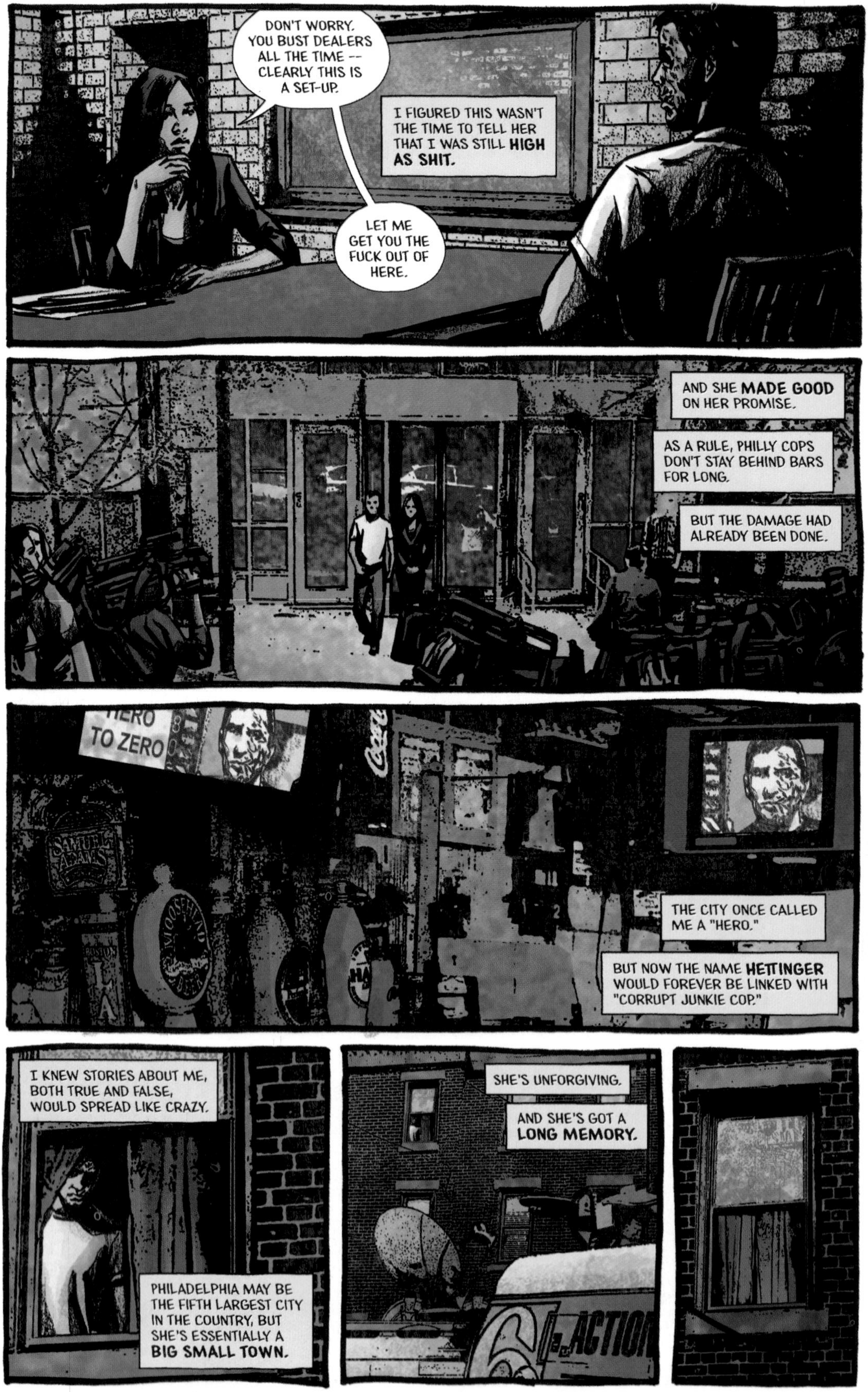
DON'T WORRY. YOU BUST DEALERS ALL THE TIME -- CLEARLY THIS IS A SET-UP.
I FIGURED THIS WASN'T THE TIME TO TELL HER THAT I WAS STILL HIGH AS SHIT.
LET ME GET YOU THE FUCK OUT OF HERE.
AND SHE MADE GOOD ON HER PROMISE.
AS A RULE, PHILLY COPS DON'T STAY BEHIND BARS FOR LONG.
BUT THE DAMAGE HAD ALREADY BEEN DONE.
HERO TO ZERO
THE CITY ONCE CALLED ME A "HERO."
BUT NOW THE NAME HETTINGER WOULD FOREVER BE LINKED WITH "CORRUPT JUNKIE COP."
I KNEW STORIES ABOUT ME, BOTH TRUE AND FALSE, WOULD SPREAD LIKE CRAZY.
PHILADELPHIA MAY BE THE FIFTH LARGEST CITY IN THE COUNTRY, BUT SHE'S ESSENTIALLY A BIG SMALL TOWN.
SHE'S UNFORGIVING.
AND SHE'S GOT A LONG MEMORY.

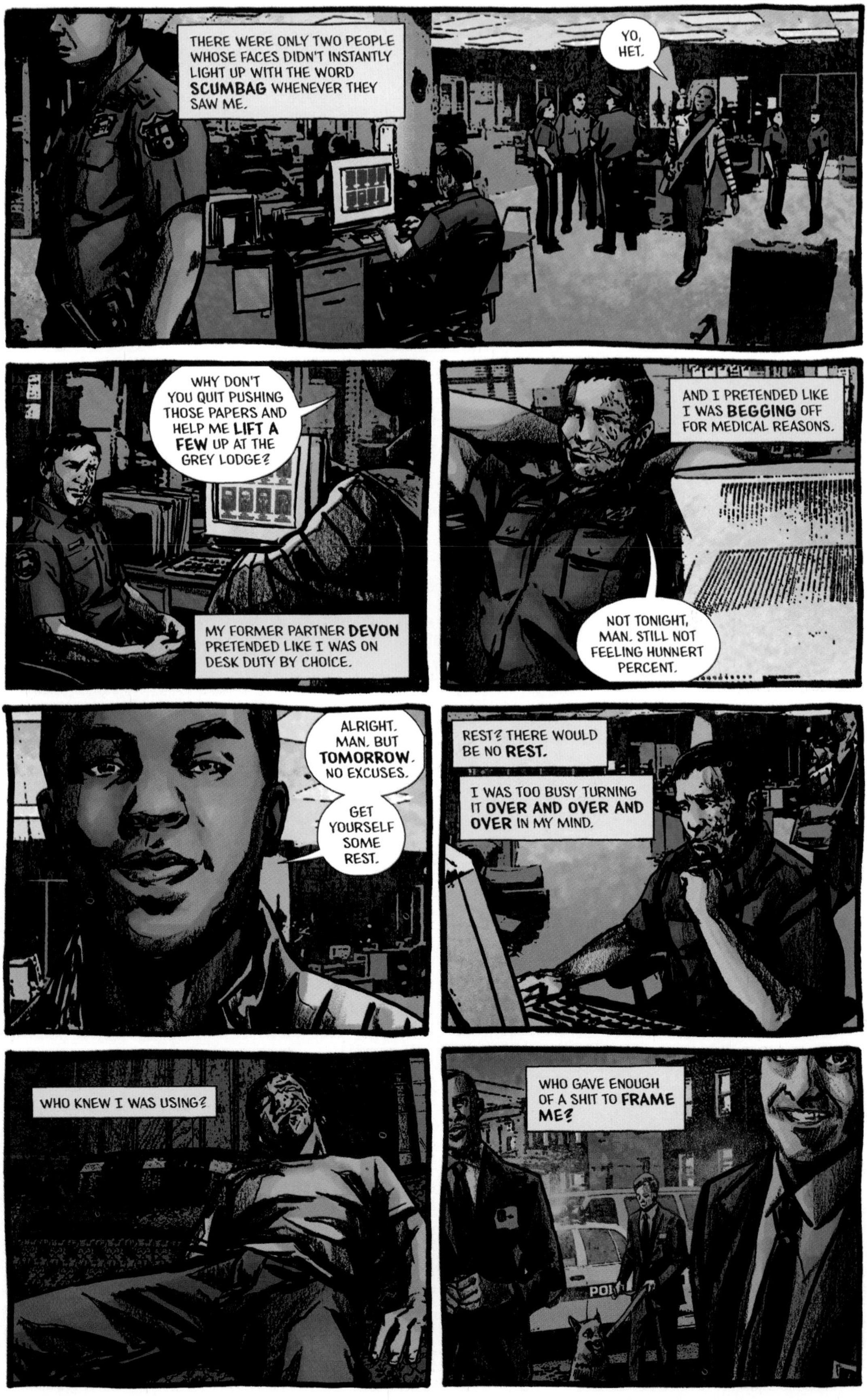
THERE WERE ONLY TWO PEOPLE WHOSE FACES DIDN'T INSTANTLY LIGHT UP WITH THE WORD **SCUMBAG** WHENEVER THEY SAW ME.
YO, HET.
WHY DON'T YOU QUIT PUSHING THOSE PAPERS AND HELP ME **LIFT A FEW** UP AT THE GREY LODGE?
MY FORMER PARTNER **DEVON** PRETENDED LIKE I WAS ON DESK DUTY BY CHOICE.
AND I PRETENDED LIKE I WAS **BEGGING** OFF FOR MEDICAL REASONS.
NOT TONIGHT, MAN. STILL NOT FEELING HUNNERT PERCENT.
ALRIGHT, MAN, BUT **TOMORROW**. NO EXCUSES.
GET YOURSELF SOME REST.
REST? THERE WOULD BE NO **REST**.
I WAS TOO BUSY TURNING IT **OVER AND OVER AND OVER** IN MY MIND.
WHO KNEW I WAS USING?
WHO GAVE ENOUGH OF A SHIT TO **FRAME ME**?

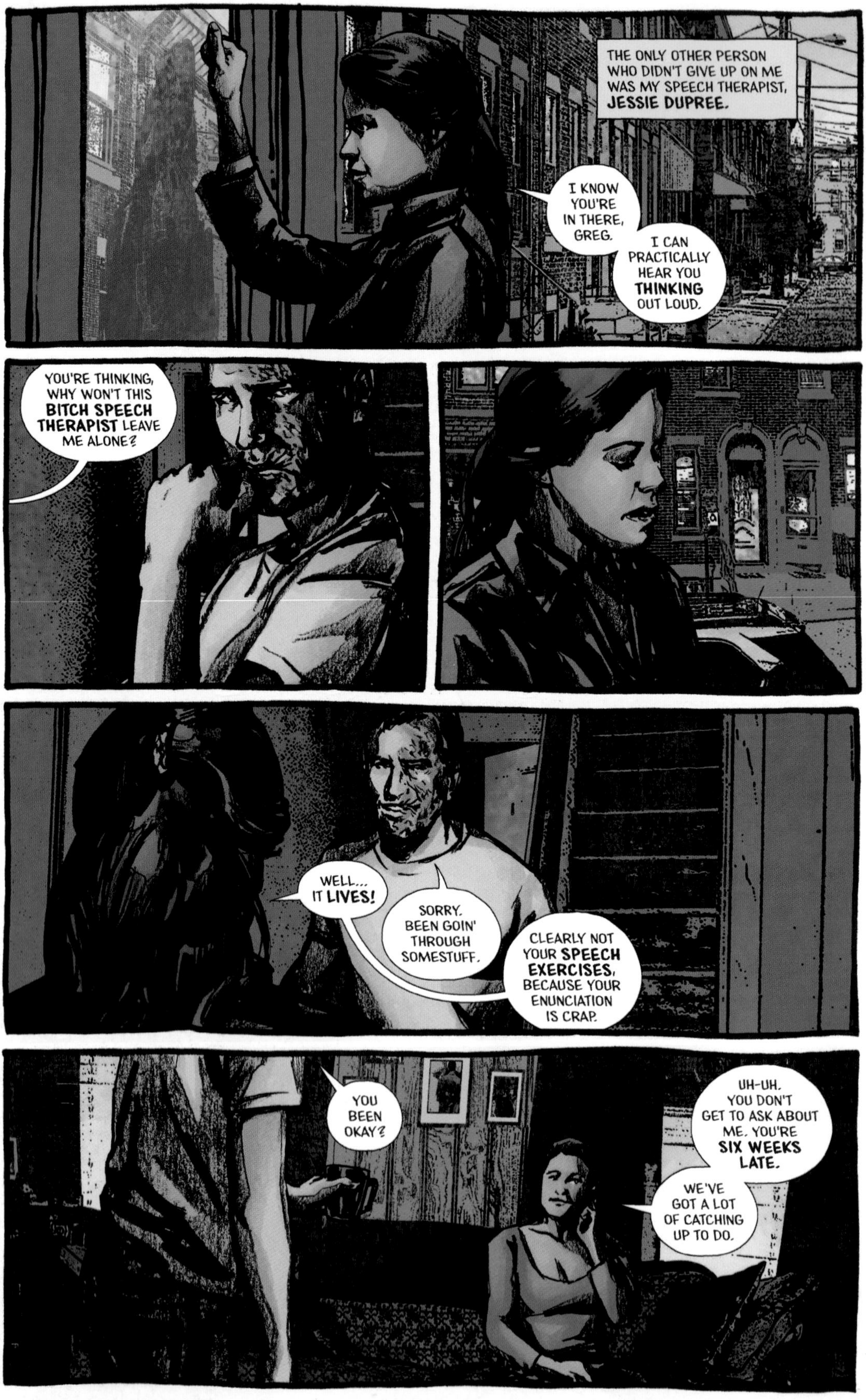
THE ONLY OTHER PERSON WHO DIDN'T GIVE UP ON ME WAS MY SPEECH THERAPIST, JESSIE DUPREE.
I KNOW YOU'RE IN THERE, GREG.
I CAN PRACTICALLY HEAR YOU THINKING OUT LOUD.
YOU'RE THINKING, WHY WON'T THIS BITCH SPEECH THERAPIST LEAVE ME ALONE?
WELL... IT LIVES!
SORRY. BEEN GOIN' THROUGH SOMESTUFF.
CLEARLY NOT YOUR SPEECH EXERCISES, BECAUSE YOUR ENUNCIATION IS CRAP.
YOU BEEN OKAY?
UH-UH. YOU DON'T GET TO ASK ABOUT ME. YOU'RE SIX WEEKS LATE.
WE'VE GOT A LOT OF CATCHING UP TO DO.

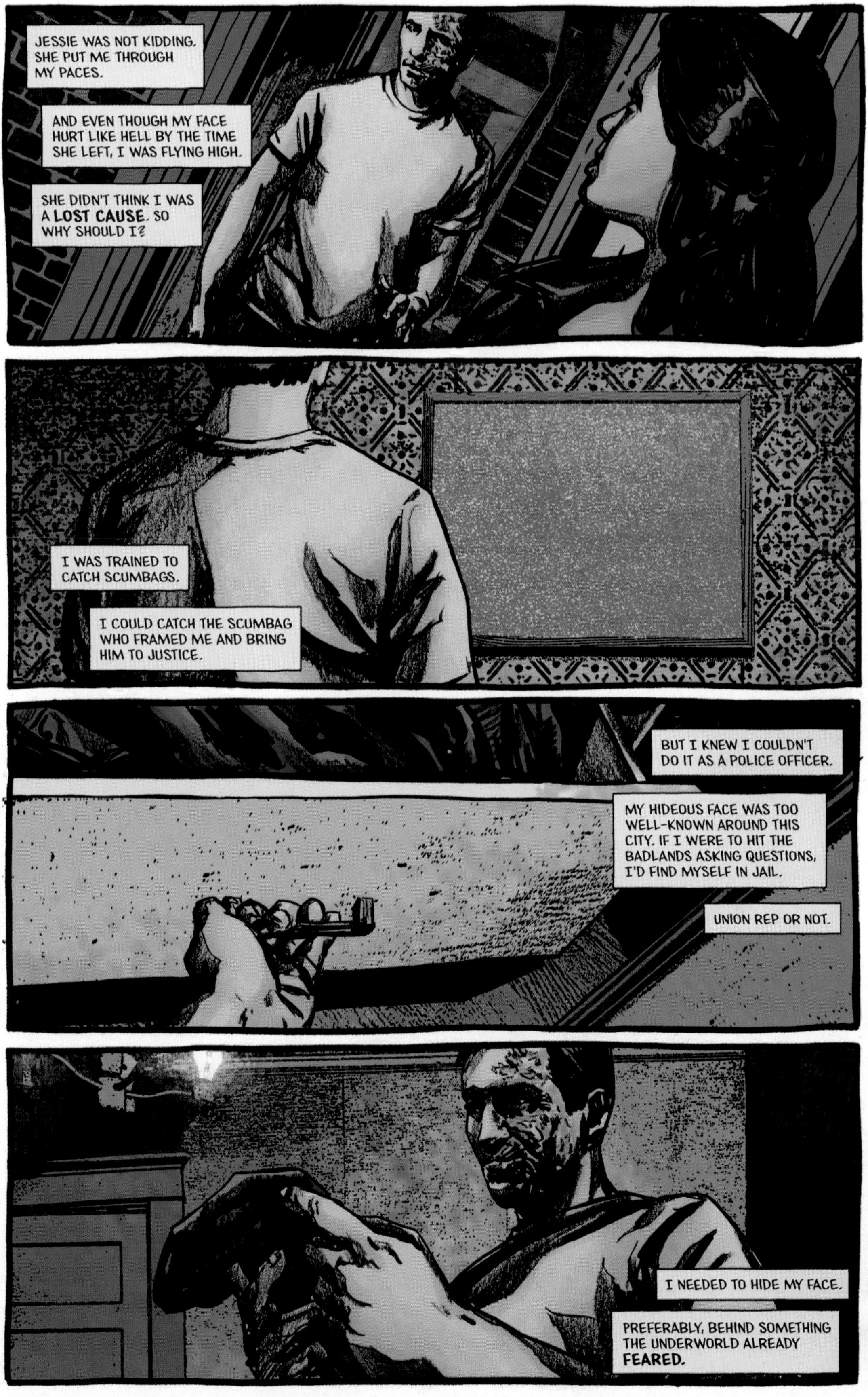
JESSIE WAS NOT KIDDING. SHE PUT ME THROUGH MY PACES.
AND EVEN THOUGH MY FACE HURT LIKE HELL BY THE TIME SHE LEFT, I WAS FLYING HIGH.
SHE DIDN'T THINK I WAS A **LOST CAUSE**. SO WHY SHOULD I?
I WAS TRAINED TO CATCH SCUMBAGS.
I COULD CATCH THE SCUMBAG WHO FRAMED ME AND BRING HIM TO JUSTICE.
BUT I KNEW I COULDN'T DO IT AS A POLICE OFFICER.
MY HIDEOUS FACE WAS TOO WELL-KNOWN AROUND THIS CITY. IF I WERE TO HIT THE BADLANDS ASKING QUESTIONS, I'D FIND MYSELF IN JAIL.
UNION REP OR NOT.
I NEEDED TO HIDE MY FACE.
PREFERABLY, BEHIND SOMETHING THE UNDERWORLD ALREADY **FEARED.**

I THREW MYSELF BACK INTO SPEECH THERAPY LIKE A MAN POSSESSED.

I NEEDED A VOICE TO MATCH THE MASK.

YOU... ME... TELL... ABOVE...

WHY **THESE** WORDS?

S'FOR WORK.

YOU MEAN, **IT. IS. FOR. WORK.**

I ALSO **HIT THE BRAKES** ON THE PILLS, BEST I COULD.

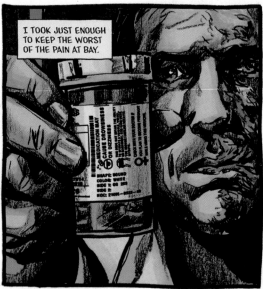

I TOOK JUST ENOUGH TO KEEP THE WORST OF THE PAIN AT BAY.

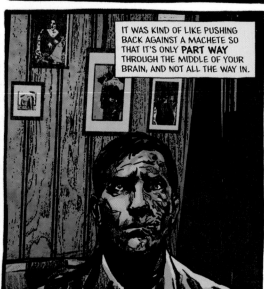

IT WAS KIND OF LIKE PUSHING BACK AGAINST A MACHETE SO THAT IT'S ONLY **PART WAY** THROUGH THE MIDDLE OF YOUR BRAIN, AND NOT ALL THE WAY IN.

I HIT THE WEIGHT ROOM TO GET SOME OF MY STRENGTH AND RANGE OF MOTION BACK.

TOO MUCH TIME WITH MY DVR MACHINE HAD TURNED MY BODY INTO **SORE PUDDING.**

YEAH, IT WAS ALL VERY *ROCKY* OF ME.

FUCK YOU.

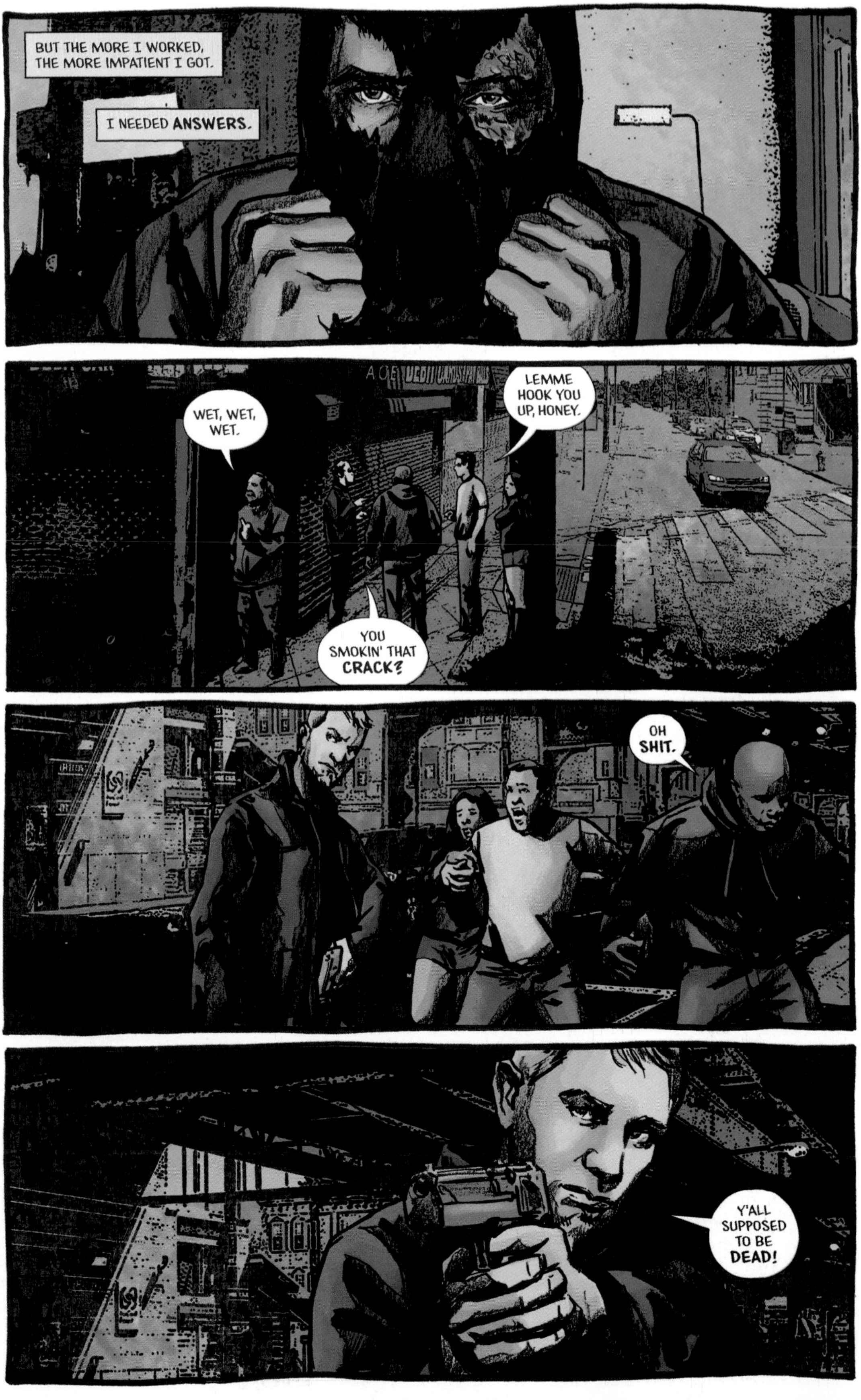
BUT THE MORE I WORKED, THE MORE IMPATIENT I GOT.
I NEEDED **ANSWERS.**
WET, WET, WET.
LEMME HOOK YOU UP, HONEY.
YOU SMOKIN' THAT **CRACK?**
OH **SHIT.**
Y'ALL SUPPOSED TO BE **DEAD!**

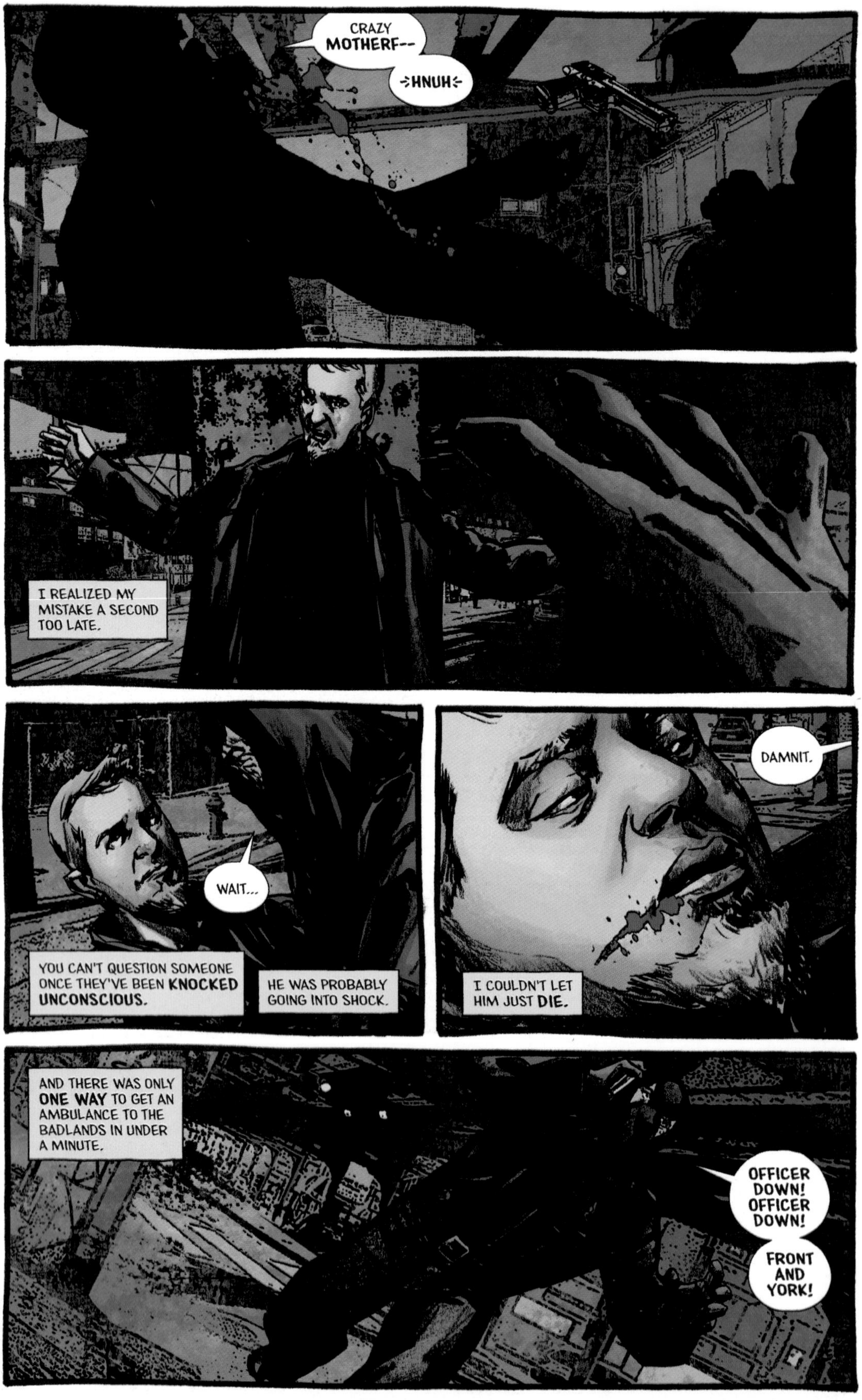
CRAZY MOTHERF--
HNUH
I REALIZED MY MISTAKE A SECOND TOO LATE.
WAIT...
YOU CAN'T QUESTION SOMEONE ONCE THEY'VE BEEN KNOCKED UNCONSCIOUS.
HE WAS PROBABLY GOING INTO SHOCK.
DAMNIT.
I COULDN'T LET HIM JUST DIE.
AND THERE WAS ONLY ONE WAY TO GET AN AMBULANCE TO THE BADLANDS IN UNDER A MINUTE.
OFFICER DOWN! OFFICER DOWN!
FRONT AND YORK!

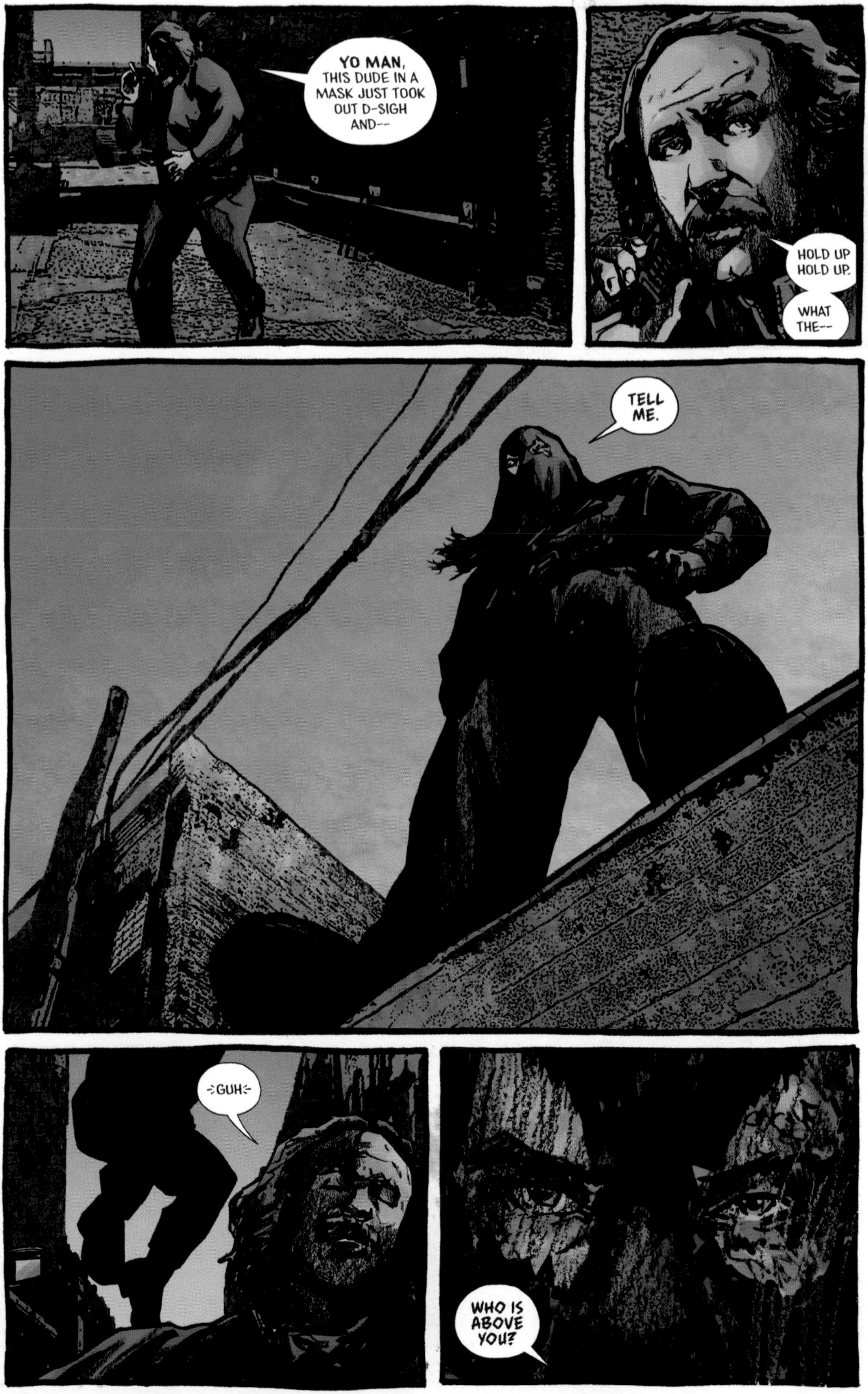
YO MAN, THIS DUDE IN A MASK JUST TOOK OUT D-SIGH AND--
HOLD UP HOLD UP.
WHAT THE--
TELL ME.
GUH
WHO IS ABOVE YOU?

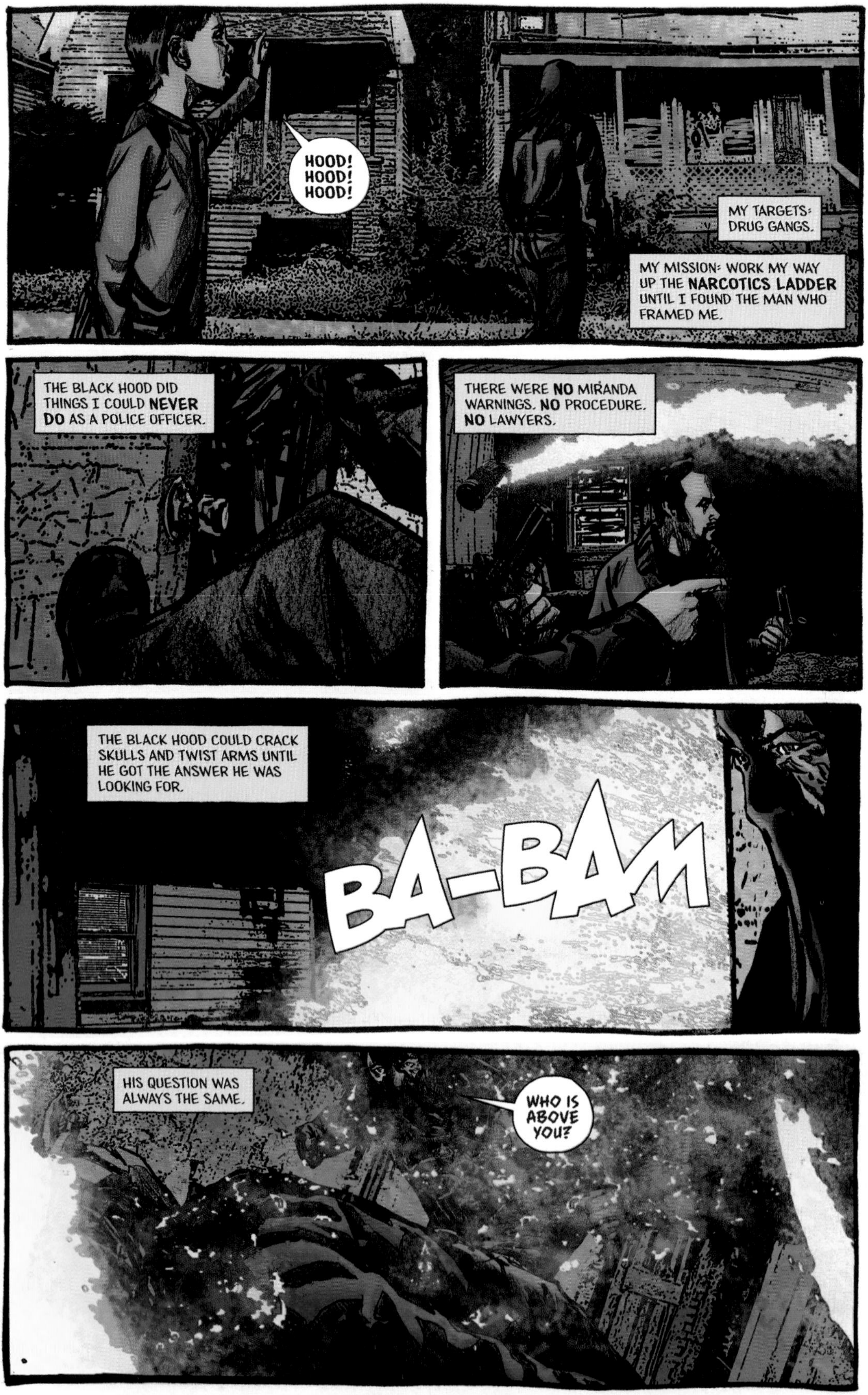
HOOD! HOOD! HOOD!
MY TARGETS: DRUG GANGS.
MY MISSION: WORK MY WAY UP THE **NARCOTICS LADDER** UNTIL I FOUND THE MAN WHO FRAMED ME.
THE BLACK HOOD DID THINGS I COULD **NEVER DO** AS A POLICE OFFICER.
THERE WERE **NO** MIRANDA WARNINGS. **NO** PROCEDURE. **NO** LAWYERS.
THE BLACK HOOD COULD CRACK SKULLS AND TWIST ARMS UNTIL HE GOT THE ANSWER HE WAS LOOKING FOR.
BA-BAM
HIS QUESTION WAS ALWAYS THE SAME.
WHO IS ABOVE YOU?

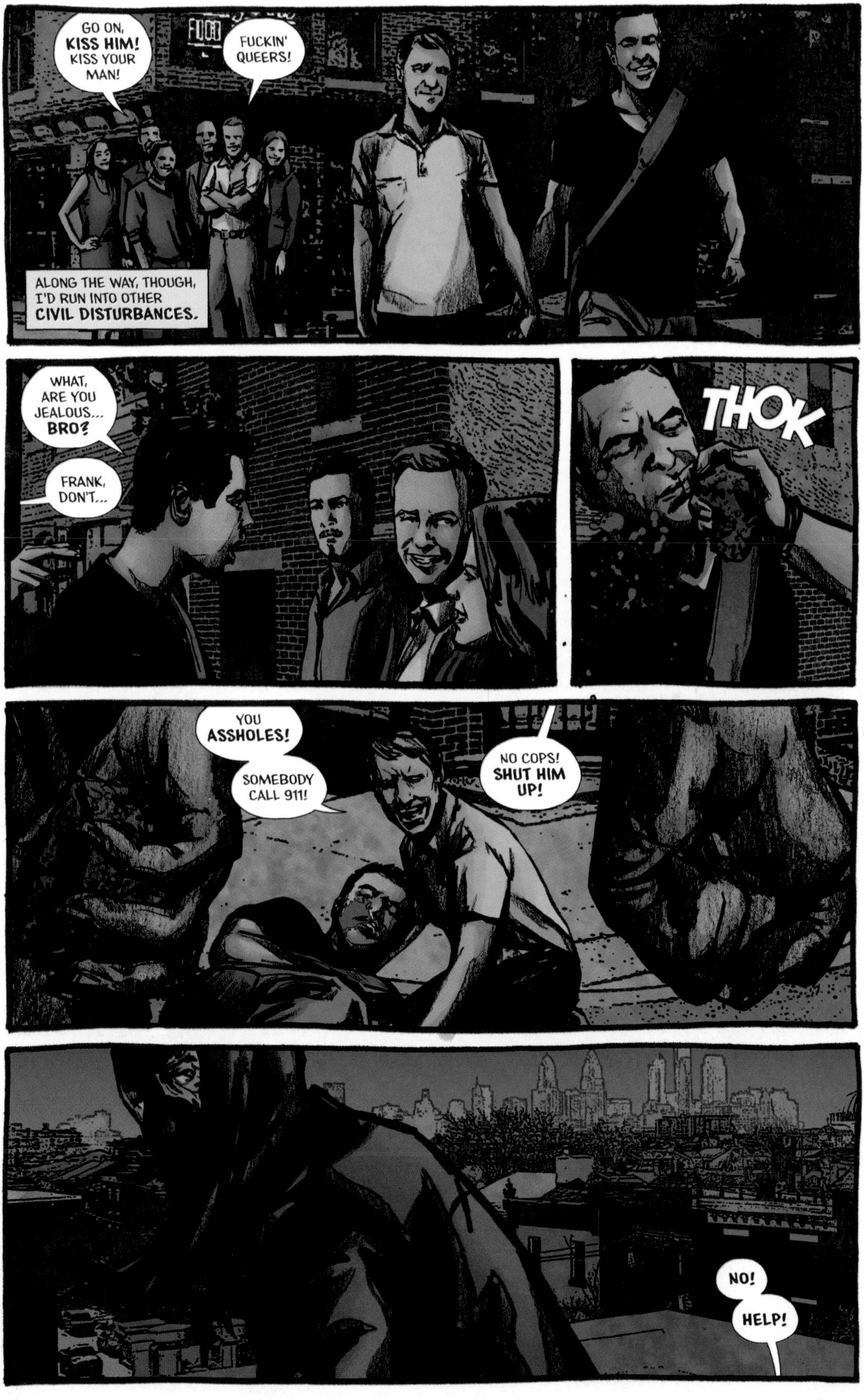
GO ON, KISS HIM! KISS YOUR MAN!
FUCKIN' QUEERS!
ALONG THE WAY, THOUGH, I'D RUN INTO OTHER CIVIL DISTURBANCES.
WHAT, ARE YOU JEALOUS... BRO?
FRANK, DON'T...
THOK
YOU ASSHOLES!
SOMEBODY CALL 911!
NO COPS! SHUT HIM UP!
NO!
HELP!

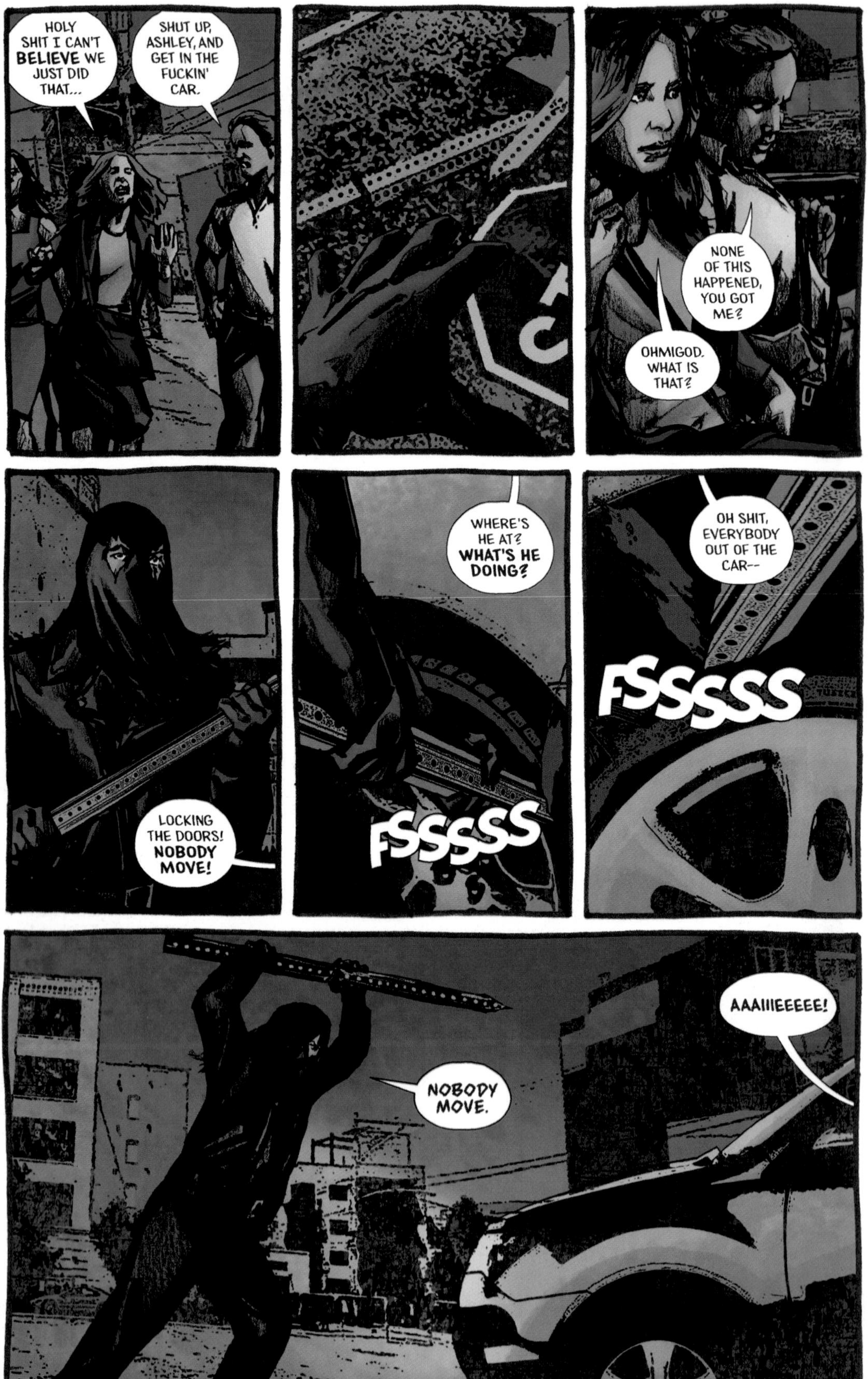
HOLY SHIT I CAN'T BELIEVE WE JUST DID THAT...
SHUT UP, ASHLEY, AND GET IN THE FUCKIN' CAR.
NONE OF THIS HAPPENED, YOU GOT ME?
OHMIGOD. WHAT IS THAT?
LOCKING THE DOORS! NOBODY MOVE!
WHERE'S HE AT? WHAT'S HE DOING?
FSSSSS
OH SHIT, EVERYBODY OUT OF THE CAR--
FSSSSS
NOBODY MOVE.
AAAIIIEEEEE!

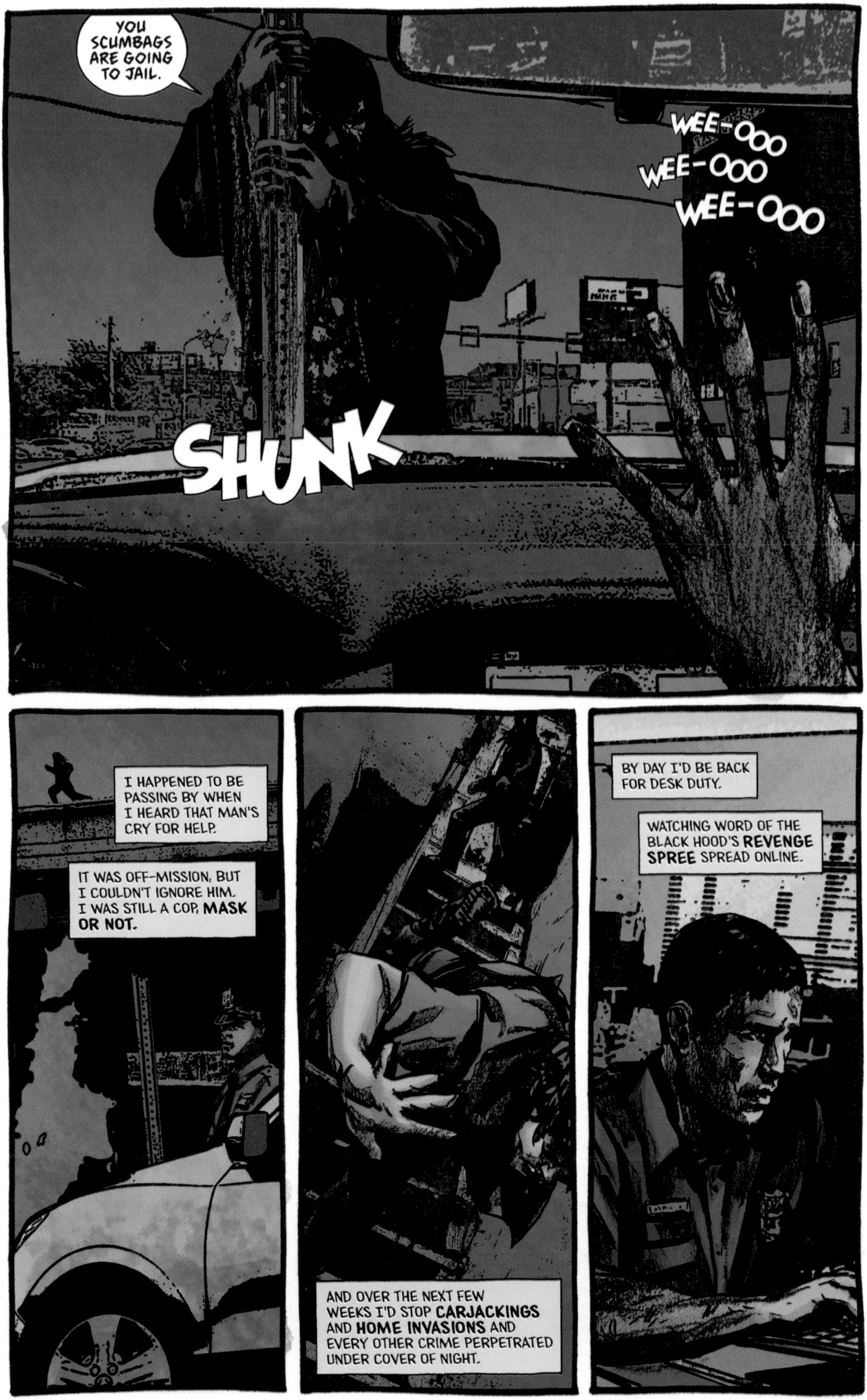
YOU SCUMBAGS ARE GOING TO JAIL.
WEE-OOO
WEE-OOO
WEE-OOO
SHUNK
I HAPPENED TO BE PASSING BY WHEN I HEARD THAT MAN'S CRY FOR HELP.
IT WAS OFF-MISSION, BUT I COULDN'T IGNORE HIM. I WAS STILL A COP, MASK OR NOT.
AND OVER THE NEXT FEW WEEKS I'D STOP CARJACKINGS AND HOME INVASIONS AND EVERY OTHER CRIME PERPETRATED UNDER COVER OF NIGHT.
BY DAY I'D BE BACK FOR DESK DUTY.
WATCHING WORD OF THE BLACK HOOD'S REVENGE SPREE SPREAD ONLINE.

BUT THE BLACK HOOD DIDN'T WANT REVENGE.

HE WANTED NAMES.

WHO'S ABOVE YOU? TELL ME!

I KEPT HITTING THE SAME WALL, THOUGH.

NOBODY WANTED TO **SNITCH** ON THE TOP DOG.

ONLY A FEW WOULD EVEN TELL ME HIS STREET NAME.

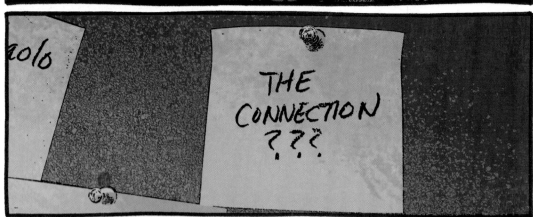

THE CONNECTION ???

THE PAIN WAS STILL ON THE EDGE OF **UNREAL.**

I KEPT TELLING MYSELF, "YOU CAN TAKE THIS, YOU CAN TAKE THIS."

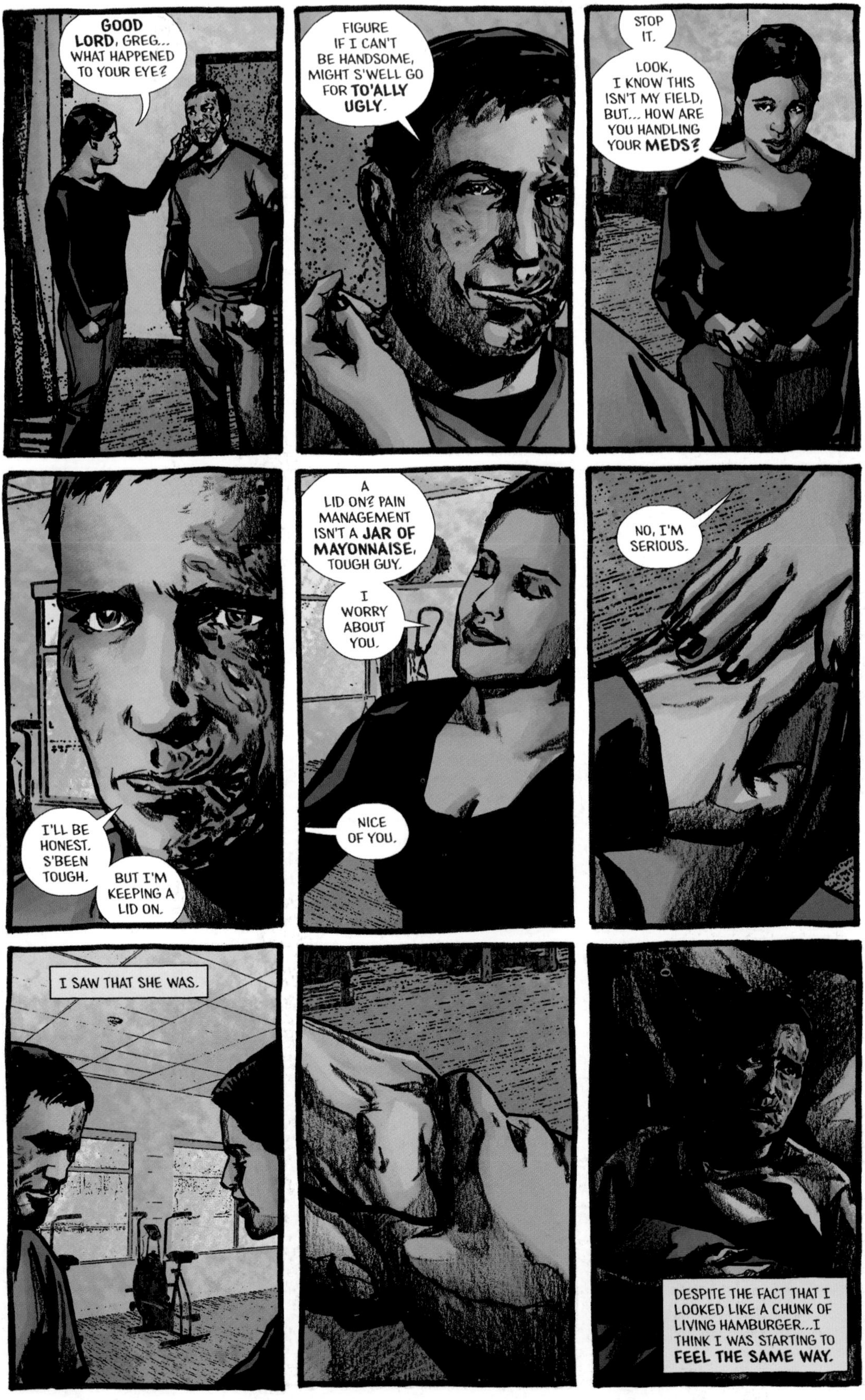
GOOD LORD, GREG... WHAT HAPPENED TO YOUR EYE?
FIGURE IF I CAN'T BE HANDSOME, MIGHT S'WELL GO FOR TO'ALLY UGLY.
STOP IT.
LOOK, I KNOW THIS ISN'T MY FIELD, BUT... HOW ARE YOU HANDLING YOUR MEDS?
I'LL BE HONEST. S'BEEN TOUGH.
BUT I'M KEEPING A LID ON.
A LID ON? PAIN MANAGEMENT ISN'T A JAR OF MAYONNAISE, TOUGH GUY.
I WORRY ABOUT YOU.
NICE OF YOU.
NO, I'M SERIOUS.
I SAW THAT SHE WAS.
DESPITE THE FACT THAT I LOOKED LIKE A CHUNK OF LIVING HAMBURGER... I THINK I WAS STARTING TO FEEL THE SAME WAY.

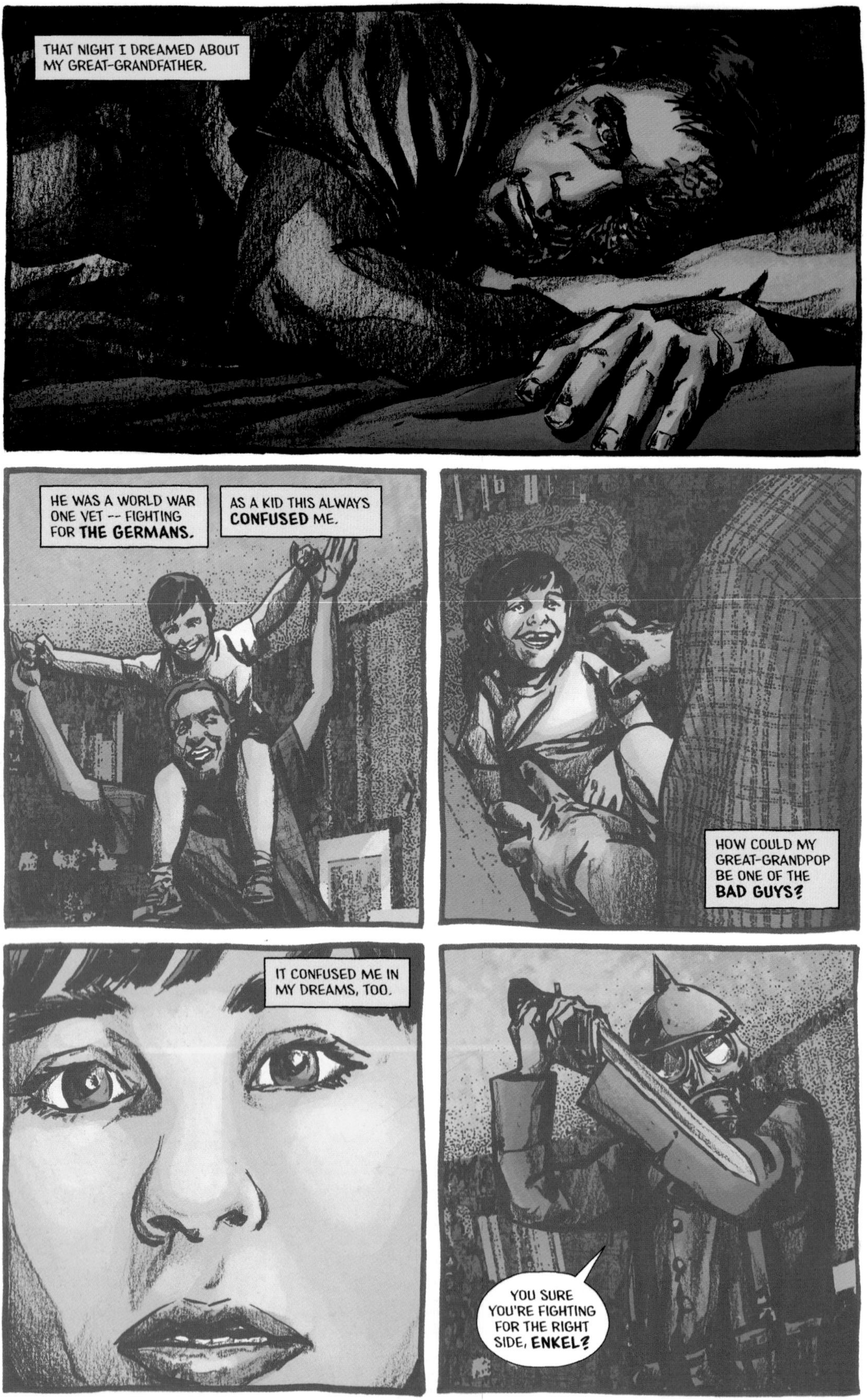
THAT NIGHT I DREAMED ABOUT MY GREAT-GRANDFATHER.
HE WAS A WORLD WAR ONE VET -- FIGHTING FOR **THE GERMANS.**
AS A KID THIS ALWAYS **CONFUSED** ME.
HOW COULD MY GREAT-GRANDPOP BE ONE OF THE **BAD GUYS?**
IT CONFUSED ME IN MY DREAMS, TOO.
YOU SURE YOU'RE FIGHTING FOR THE RIGHT SIDE, **ENKEL?**

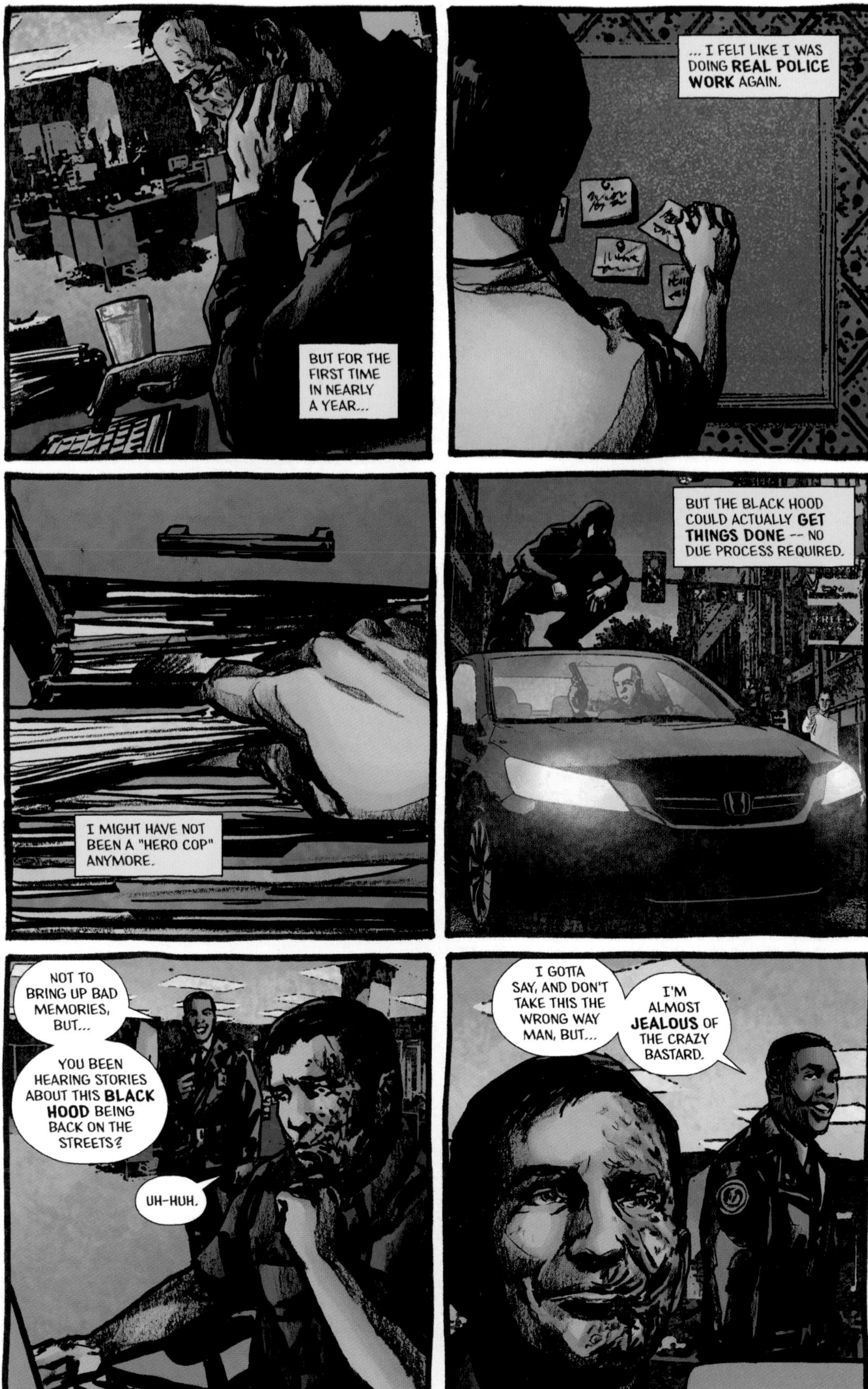
BUT FOR THE FIRST TIME IN NEARLY A YEAR...
... I FELT LIKE I WAS DOING REAL POLICE WORK AGAIN.
I MIGHT HAVE NOT BEEN A "HERO COP" ANYMORE.
BUT THE BLACK HOOD COULD ACTUALLY GET THINGS DONE -- NO DUE PROCESS REQUIRED.
NOT TO BRING UP BAD MEMORIES, BUT...
YOU BEEN HEARING STORIES ABOUT THIS BLACK HOOD BEING BACK ON THE STREETS?
UH-HUH.
I GOTTA SAY, AND DON'T TAKE THIS THE WRONG WAY MAN, BUT...
I'M ALMOST JEALOUS OF THE CRAZY BASTARD.

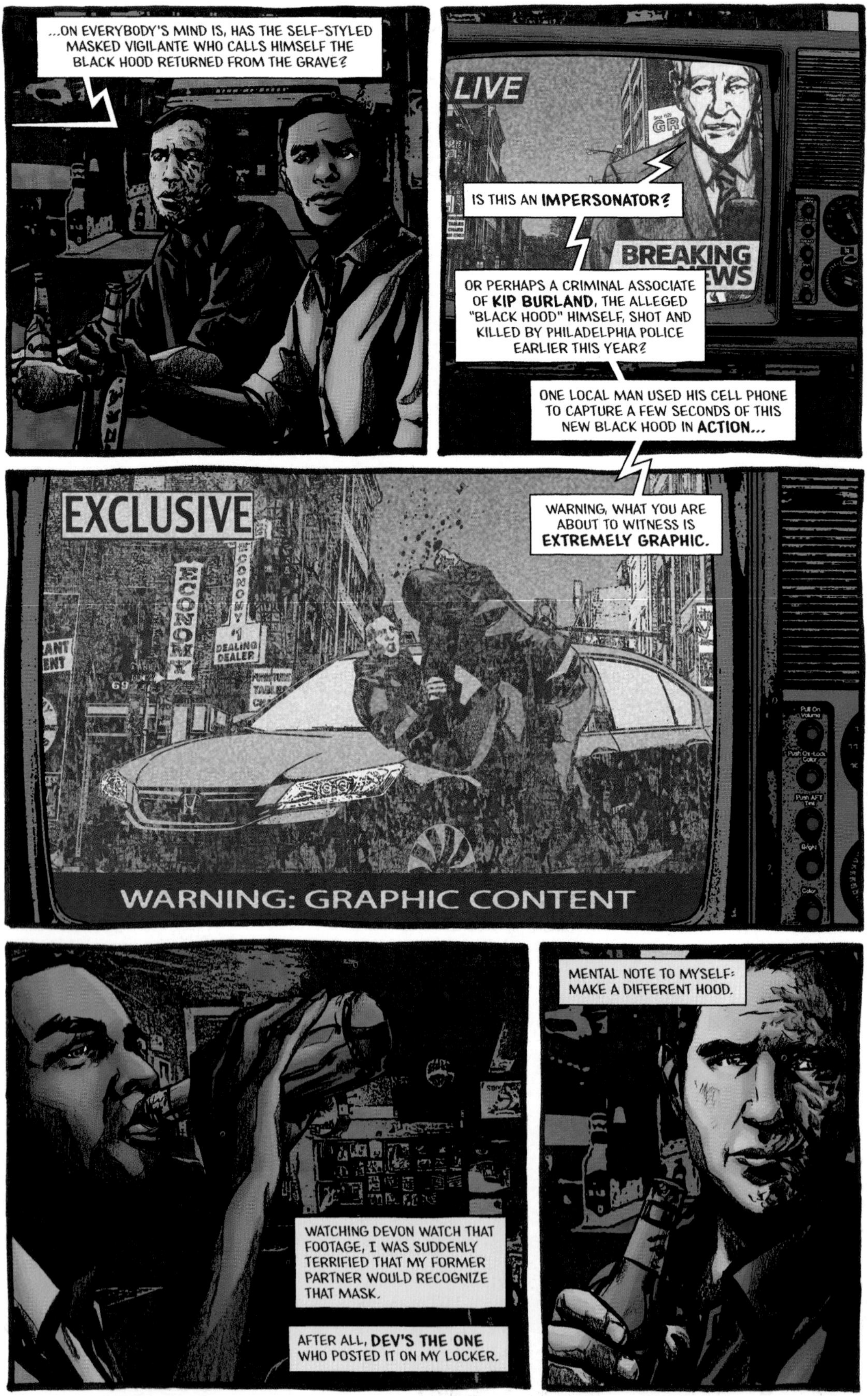
...ON EVERYBODY'S MIND IS, HAS THE SELF-STYLED MASKED VIGILANTE WHO CALLS HIMSELF THE BLACK HOOD RETURNED FROM THE GRAVE?
LIVE
IS THIS AN IMPERSONATOR?
BREAKING NEWS
OR PERHAPS A CRIMINAL ASSOCIATE OF KIP BURLAND, THE ALLEGED "BLACK HOOD" HIMSELF, SHOT AND KILLED BY PHILADELPHIA POLICE EARLIER THIS YEAR?
ONE LOCAL MAN USED HIS CELL PHONE TO CAPTURE A FEW SECONDS OF THIS NEW BLACK HOOD IN ACTION...
EXCLUSIVE
WARNING, WHAT YOU ARE ABOUT TO WITNESS IS EXTREMELY GRAPHIC.
ECONOMY
DEALING DEALER
WARNING: GRAPHIC CONTENT
WATCHING DEVON WATCH THAT FOOTAGE, I WAS SUDDENLY TERRIFIED THAT MY FORMER PARTNER WOULD RECOGNIZE THAT MASK.
AFTER ALL, DEV'S THE ONE WHO POSTED IT ON MY LOCKER.
MENTAL NOTE TO MYSELF: MAKE A DIFFERENT HOOD.

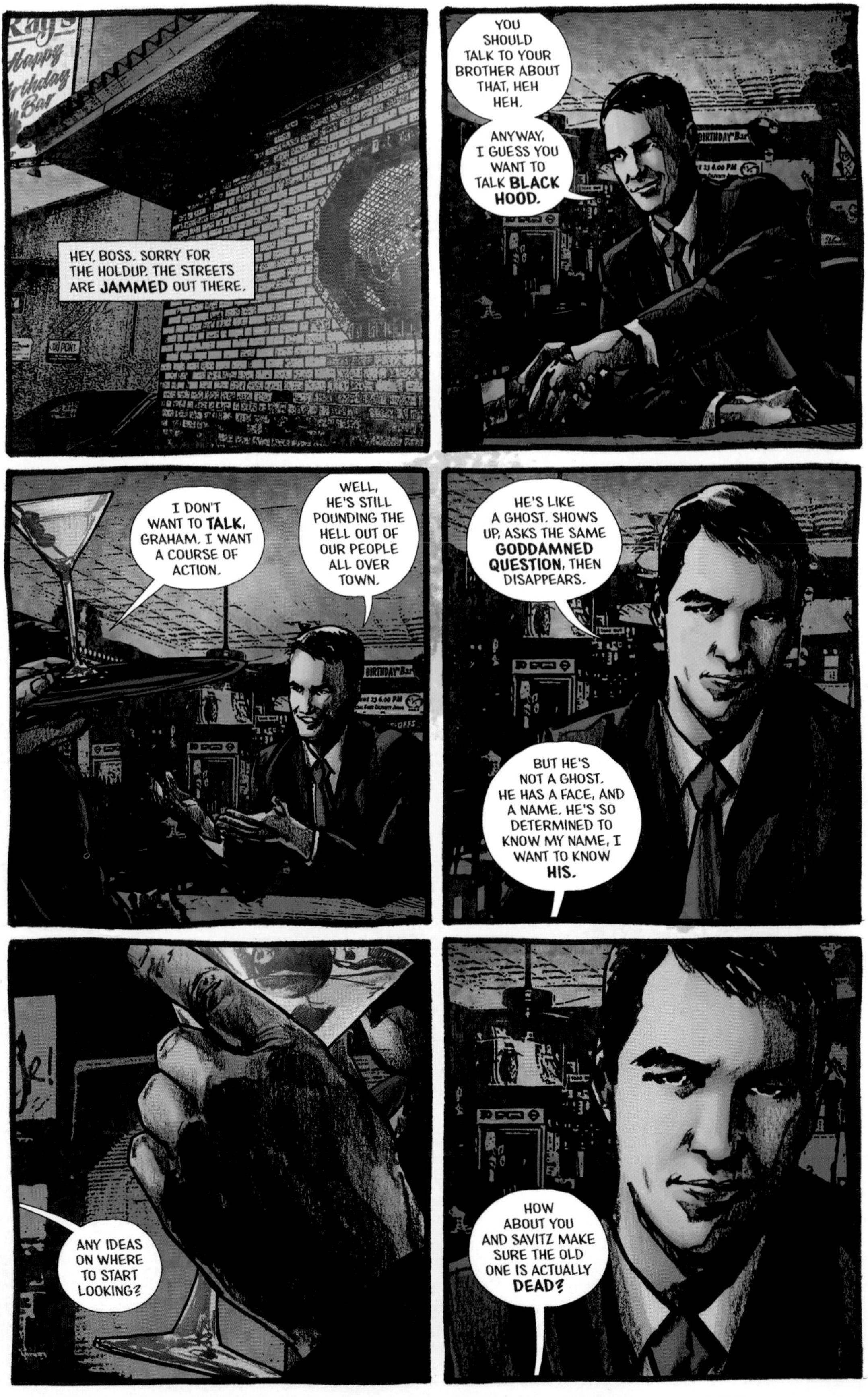
Ray's Happy Birthday Bar
HEY, BOSS. SORRY FOR THE HOLDUP. THE STREETS ARE JAMMED OUT THERE.
YOU SHOULD TALK TO YOUR BROTHER ABOUT THAT, HEH HEH.
ANYWAY, I GUESS YOU WANT TO TALK BLACK HOOD.
I DON'T WANT TO TALK, GRAHAM. I WANT A COURSE OF ACTION.
WELL, HE'S STILL POUNDING THE HELL OUT OF OUR PEOPLE ALL OVER TOWN.
HE'S LIKE A GHOST. SHOWS UP, ASKS THE SAME GODDAMNED QUESTION, THEN DISAPPEARS.
BUT HE'S NOT A GHOST. HE HAS A FACE, AND A NAME. HE'S SO DETERMINED TO KNOW MY NAME, I WANT TO KNOW HIS.
ANY IDEAS ON WHERE TO START LOOKING?
HOW ABOUT YOU AND SAVITZ MAKE SURE THE OLD ONE IS ACTUALLY DEAD?

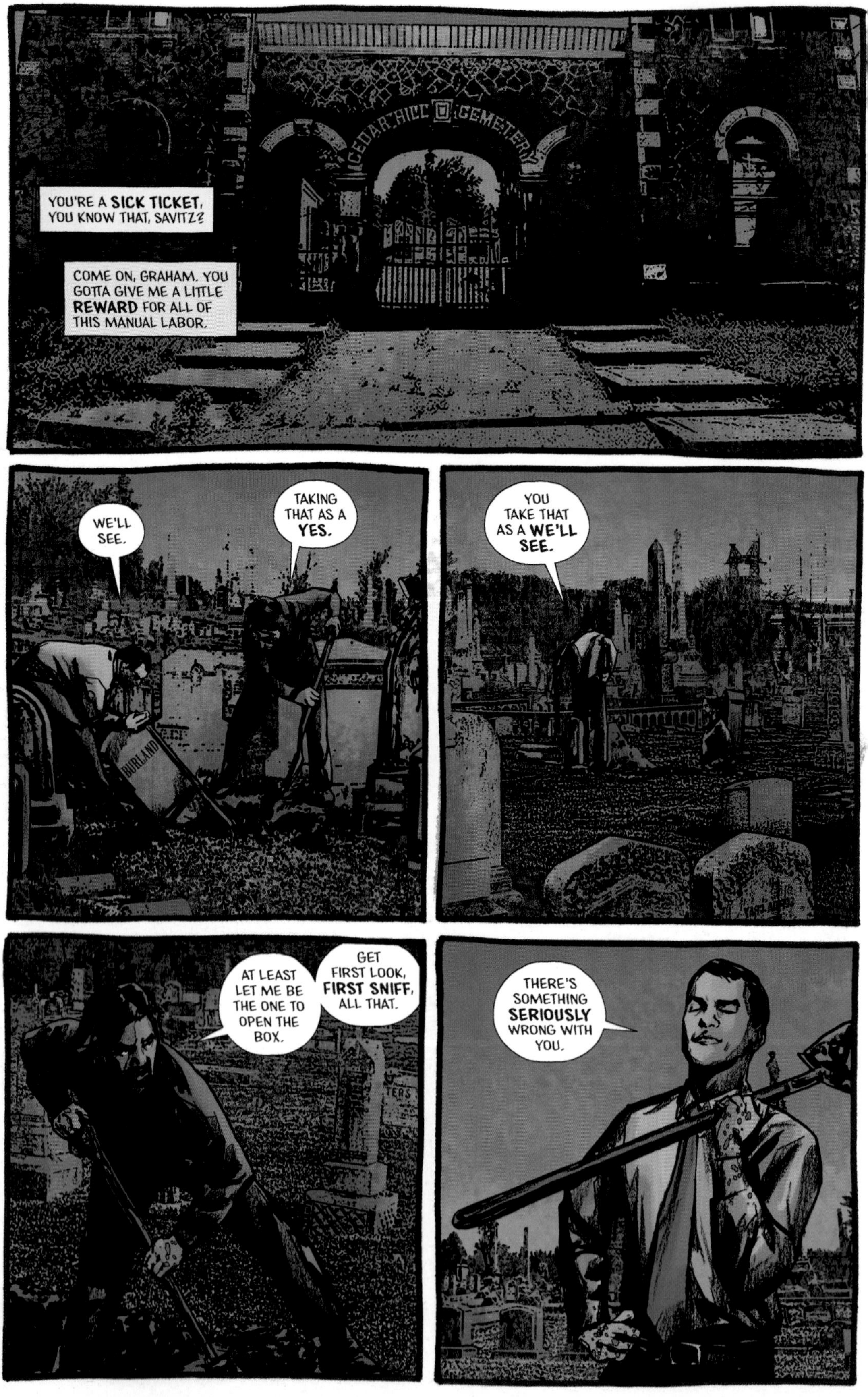
CEDAR HILL CEMETERY
YOU'RE A **SICK TICKET**, YOU KNOW THAT, SAVITZ?
COME ON, GRAHAM. YOU GOTTA GIVE ME A LITTLE **REWARD** FOR ALL OF THIS MANUAL LABOR.
WE'LL SEE.
TAKING THAT AS A **YES.**
BURLAND
YOU TAKE THAT AS A **WE'LL SEE.**
AT LEAST LET ME BE THE ONE TO OPEN THE BOX.
GET FIRST LOOK, **FIRST SNIFF**, ALL THAT.
THERE'S SOMETHING **SERIOUSLY** WRONG WITH YOU.

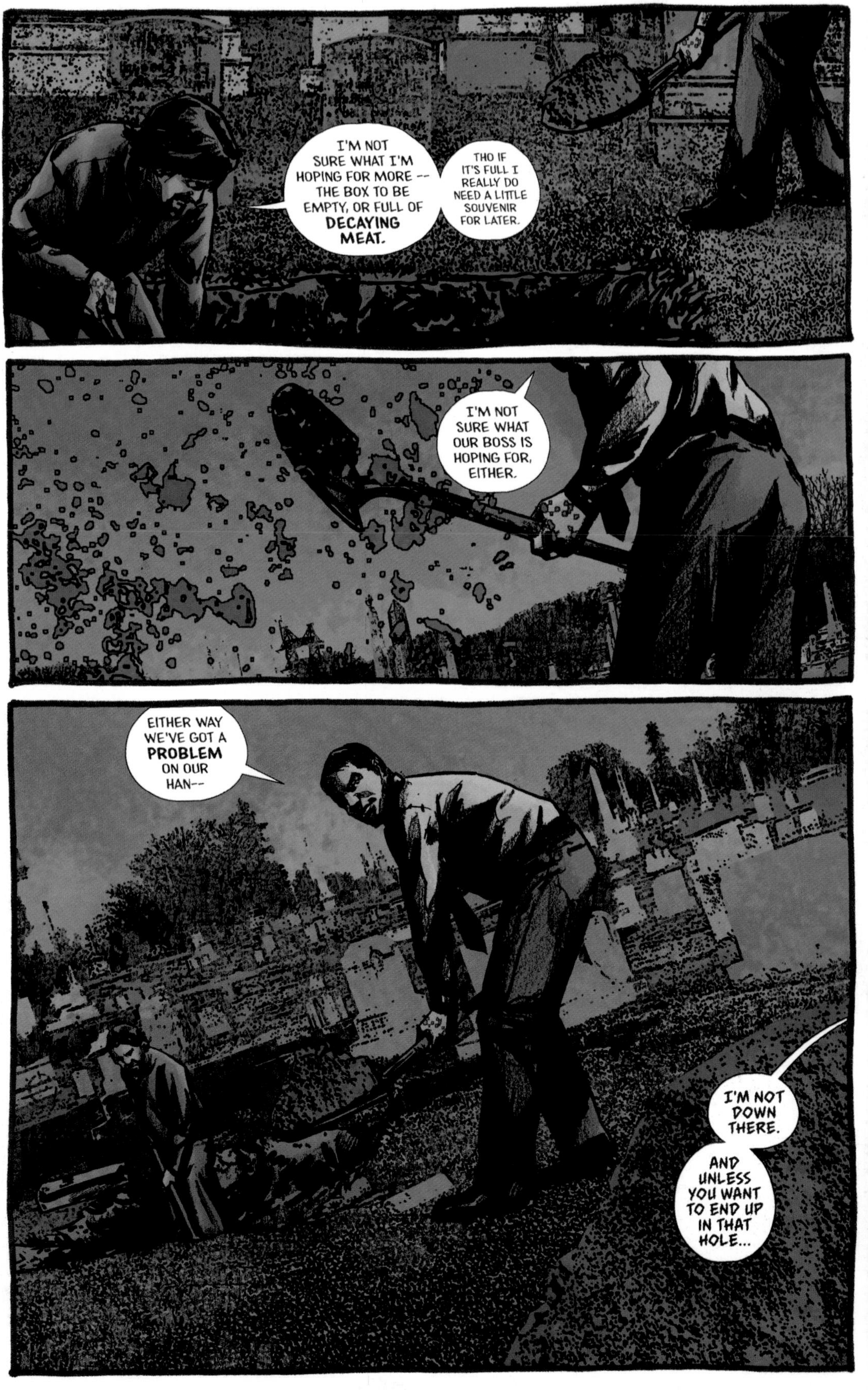
I'M NOT SURE WHAT I'M HOPING FOR MORE -- THE BOX TO BE EMPTY, OR FULL OF DECAYING MEAT.
THO IF IT'S FULL I REALLY DO NEED A LITTLE SOUVENIR FOR LATER.
I'M NOT SURE WHAT OUR BOSS IS HOPING FOR, EITHER.
EITHER WAY WE'VE GOT A PROBLEM ON OUR HAN--
I'M NOT DOWN THERE.
AND UNLESS YOU WANT TO END UP IN THAT HOLE...

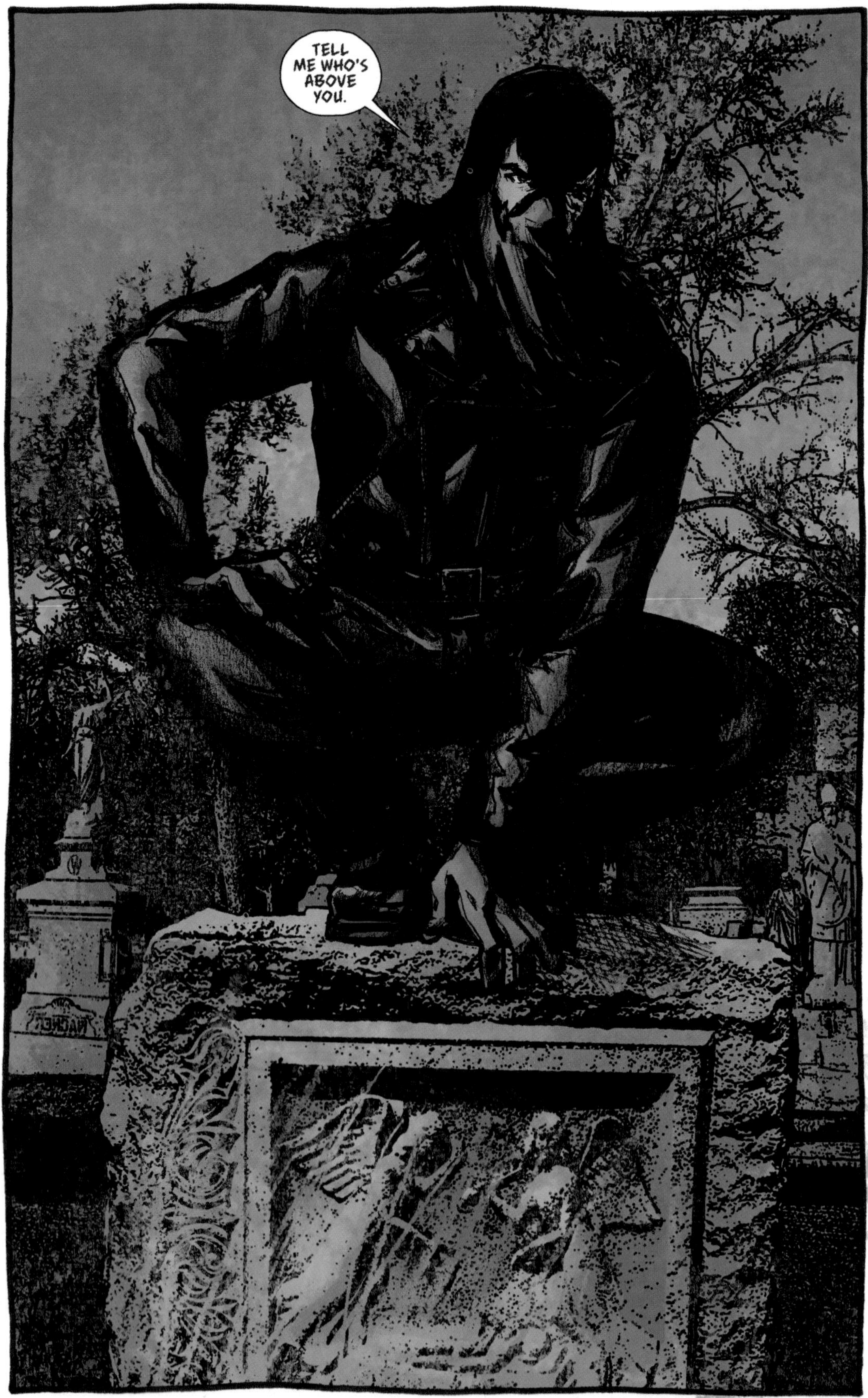
TELL ME WHO'S ABOVE YOU.

ISSUE FOUR

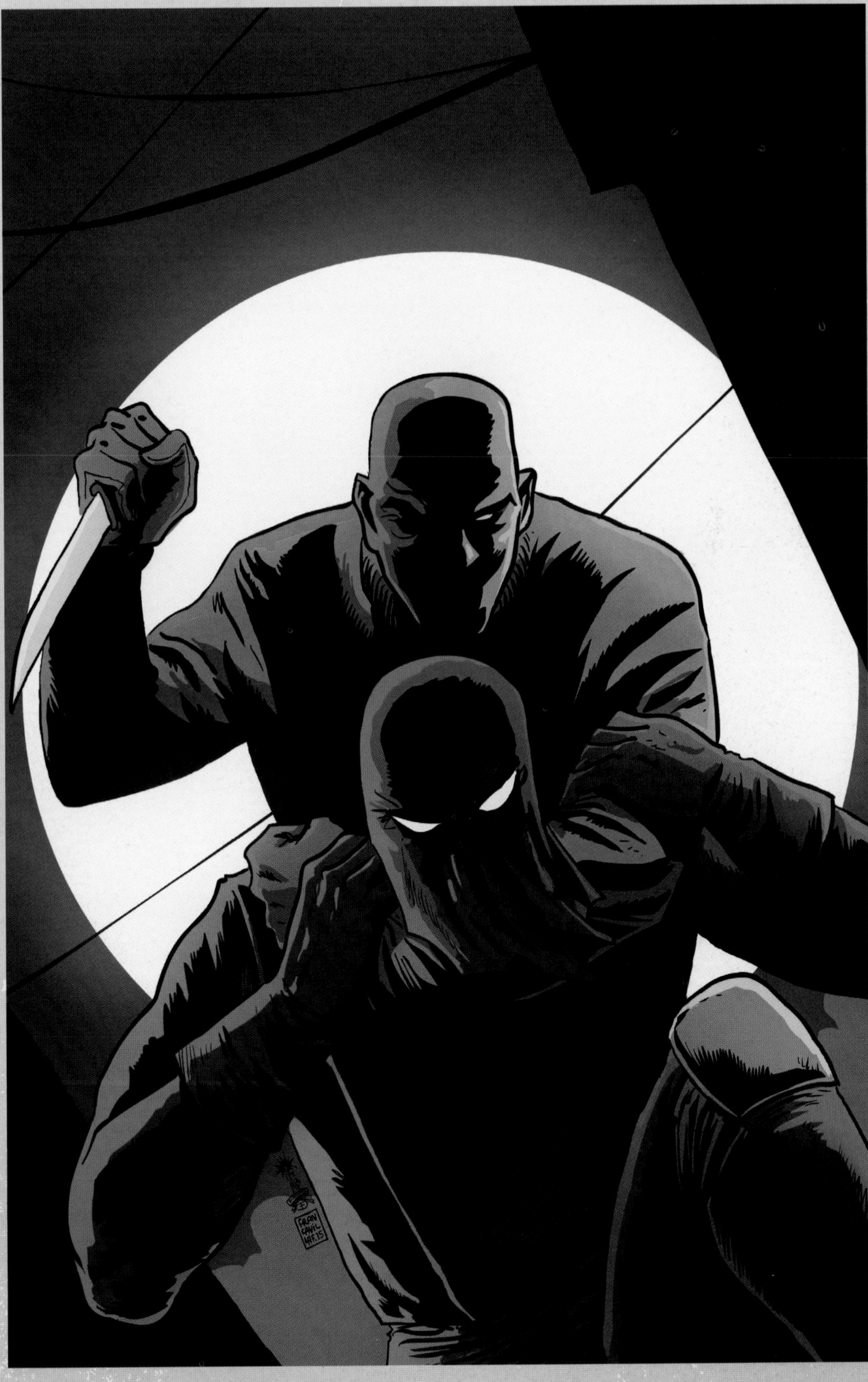

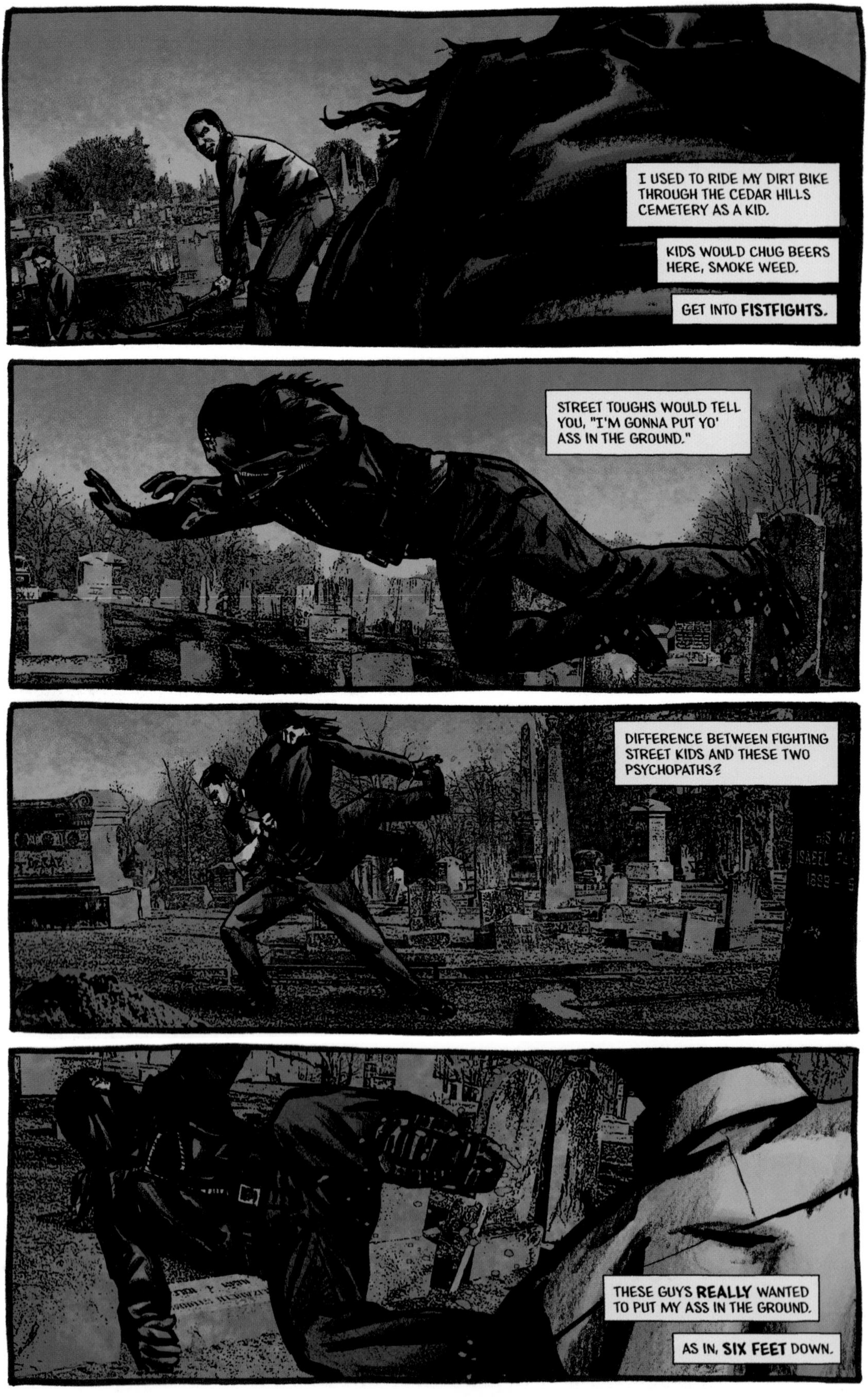
I USED TO RIDE MY DIRT BIKE THROUGH THE CEDAR HILLS CEMETERY AS A KID.
KIDS WOULD CHUG BEERS HERE, SMOKE WEED.
GET INTO **FISTFIGHTS.**
STREET TOUGHS WOULD TELL YOU, "I'M GONNA PUT YO' ASS IN THE GROUND."
DIFFERENCE BETWEEN FIGHTING STREET KIDS AND THESE TWO PSYCHOPATHS?
THESE GUYS **REALLY** WANTED TO PUT MY ASS IN THE GROUND.
AS IN, **SIX FEET** DOWN.

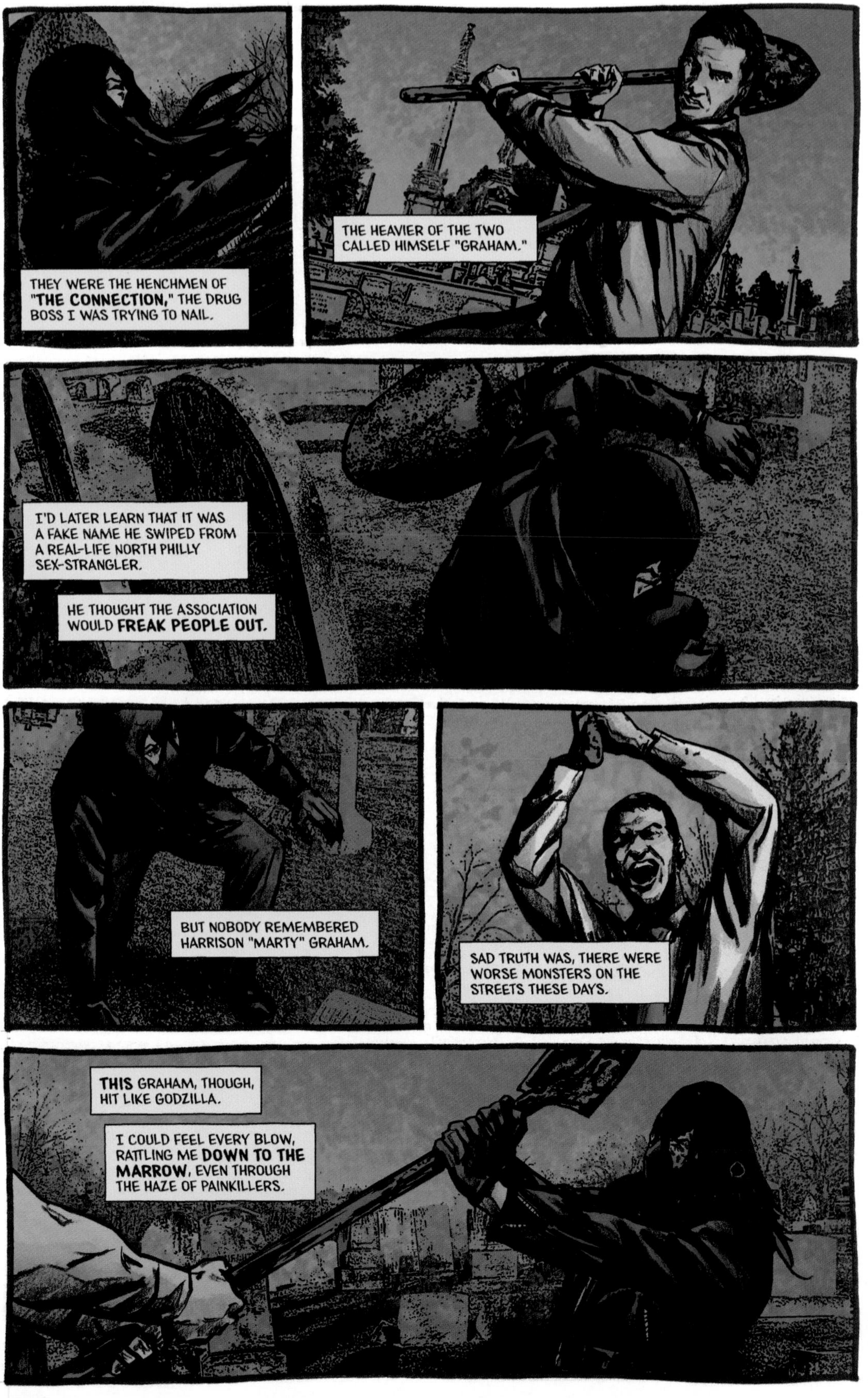
THEY WERE THE HENCHMEN OF "THE CONNECTION," THE DRUG BOSS I WAS TRYING TO NAIL.
THE HEAVIER OF THE TWO CALLED HIMSELF "GRAHAM."
I'D LATER LEARN THAT IT WAS A FAKE NAME HE SWIPED FROM A REAL-LIFE NORTH PHILLY SEX-STRANGLER.
HE THOUGHT THE ASSOCIATION WOULD FREAK PEOPLE OUT.
BUT NOBODY REMEMBERED HARRISON "MARTY" GRAHAM.
SAD TRUTH WAS, THERE WERE WORSE MONSTERS ON THE STREETS THESE DAYS.
THIS GRAHAM, THOUGH, HIT LIKE GODZILLA.
I COULD FEEL EVERY BLOW, RATTLING ME DOWN TO THE MARROW, EVEN THROUGH THE HAZE OF PAINKILLERS.

HIS PARTNER, MEANWHILE... **SAVITZ**...

HE WAS A DIRTY, SNEAKY LITTLE **BASTARD**.

SOMEHOW HE MANAGED TO LIVE IN MY PERIPHERAL VISION.

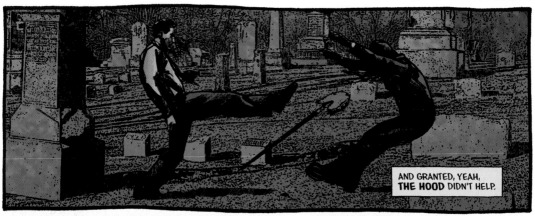

AND GRANTED, YEAH, **THE HOOD** DIDN'T HELP.

THE MOMENT HE SLIPPED OUT OF VIEW, THOUGH...

YOU'D FEEL THIS **COLD NUMBNESS**.

AND YOU'D REALIZE HE'D CUT YOU.

BAD.

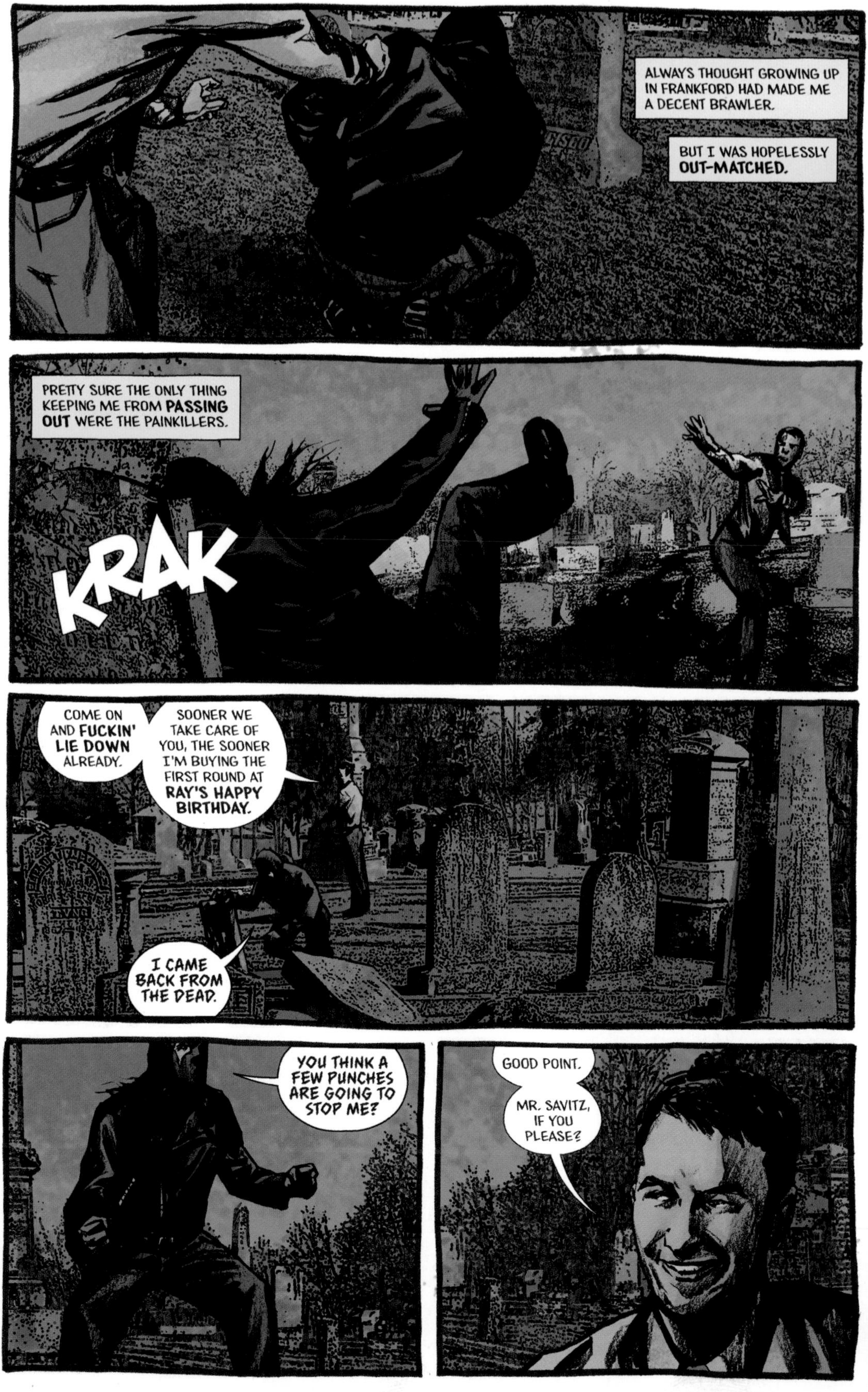

ALWAYS THOUGHT GROWING UP IN FRANKFORD HAD MADE ME A DECENT BRAWLER.
BUT I WAS HOPELESSLY OUT-MATCHED.
PRETTY SURE THE ONLY THING KEEPING ME FROM PASSING OUT WERE THE PAINKILLERS.
KRAK
COME ON AND FUCKIN' LIE DOWN ALREADY.
SOONER WE TAKE CARE OF YOU, THE SOONER I'M BUYING THE FIRST ROUND AT RAY'S HAPPY BIRTHDAY.
I CAME BACK FROM THE DEAD.
YOU THINK A FEW PUNCHES ARE GOING TO STOP ME?
GOOD POINT.
MR. SAVITZ, IF YOU PLEASE?

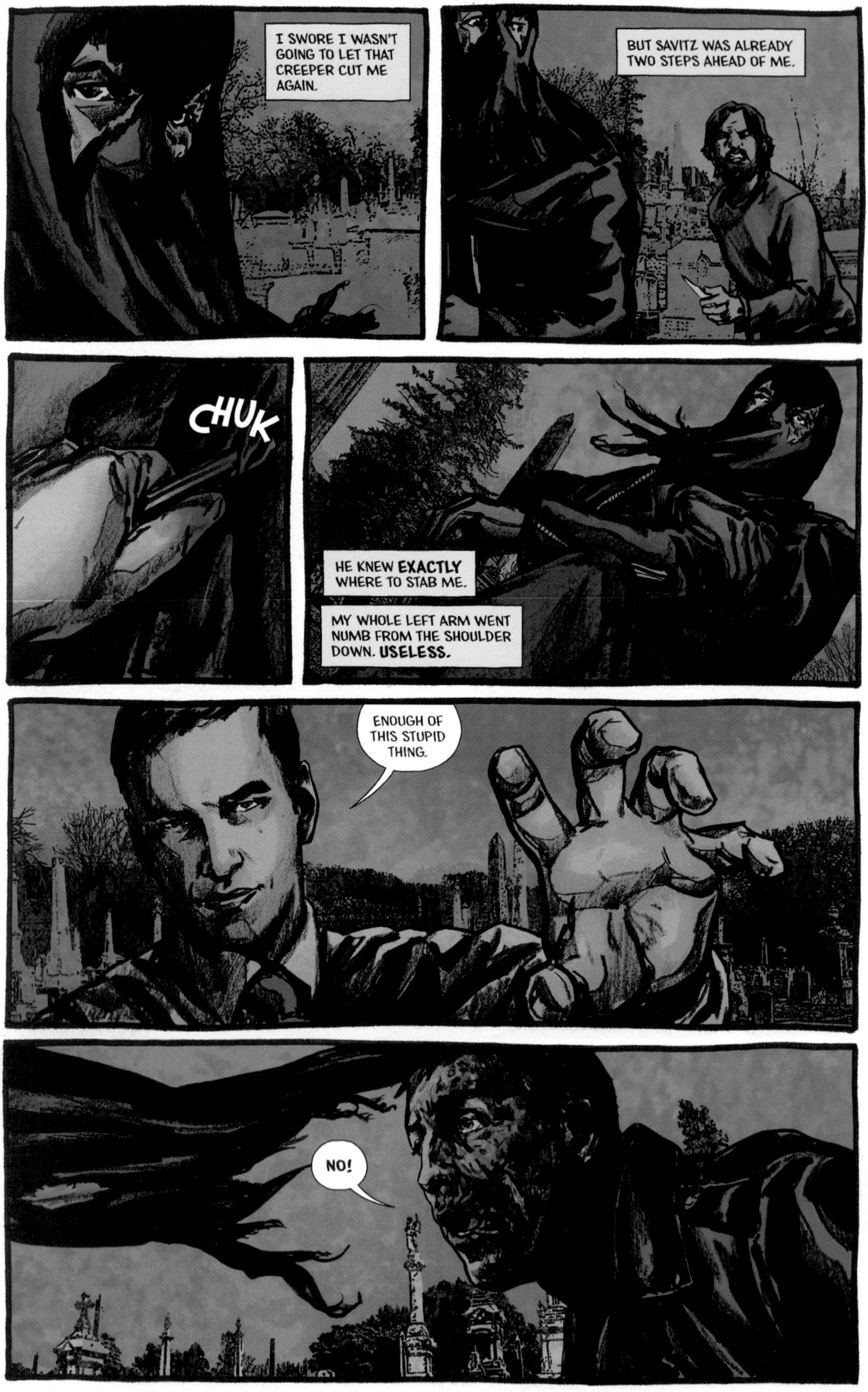
I SWORE I WASN'T GOING TO LET THAT CREEPER CUT ME AGAIN.
BUT SAVITZ WAS ALREADY TWO STEPS AHEAD OF ME.
CHUK
HE KNEW **EXACTLY** WHERE TO STAB ME.
MY WHOLE LEFT ARM WENT NUMB FROM THE SHOULDER DOWN. **USELESS.**
ENOUGH OF THIS STUPID THING.
NO!

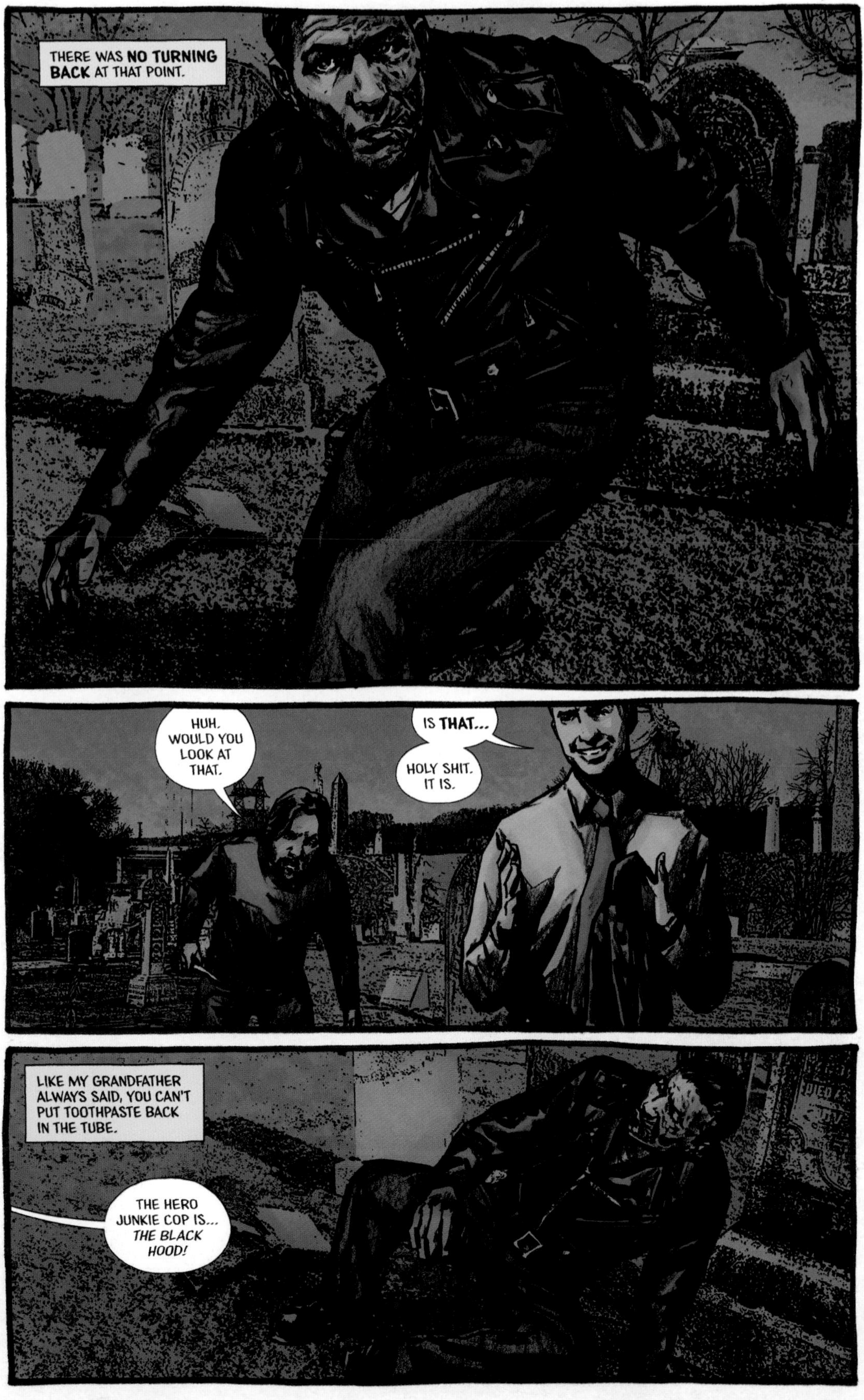
THERE WAS **NO TURNING BACK** AT THAT POINT.
HUH. WOULD YOU LOOK AT THAT.
IS **THAT...**
HOLY SHIT. IT IS.
LIKE MY GRANDFATHER ALWAYS SAID, YOU CAN'T PUT TOOTHPASTE BACK IN THE TUBE.
THE HERO JUNKIE COP IS... *THE BLACK HOOD!*

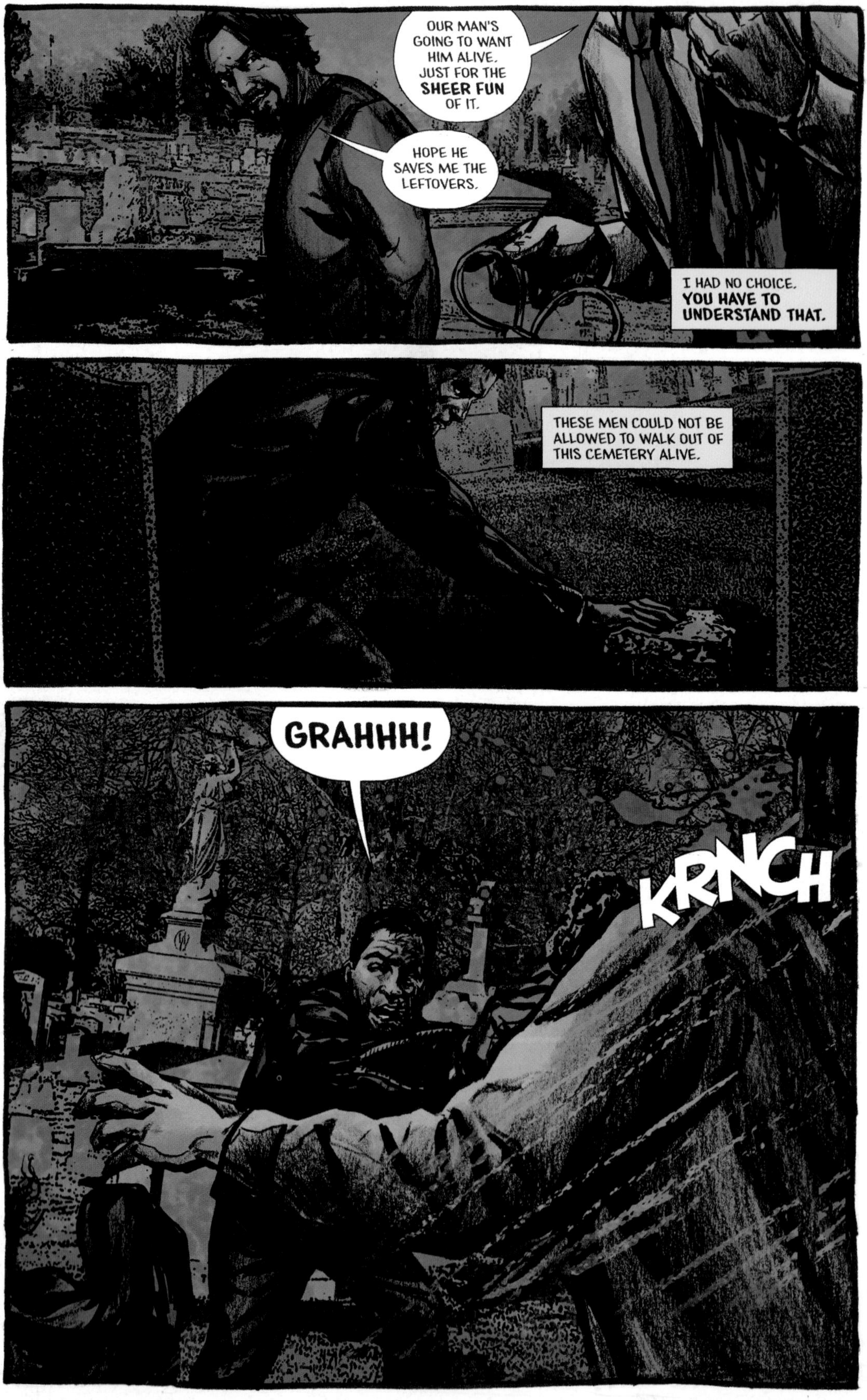
OUR MAN'S GOING TO WANT HIM ALIVE. JUST FOR THE **SHEER FUN** OF IT.
HOPE HE SAVES ME THE LEFTOVERS.
I HAD NO CHOICE. **YOU HAVE TO UNDERSTAND THAT.**
THESE MEN COULD NOT BE ALLOWED TO WALK OUT OF THIS CEMETERY ALIVE.
GRAHHH!
KRNCH

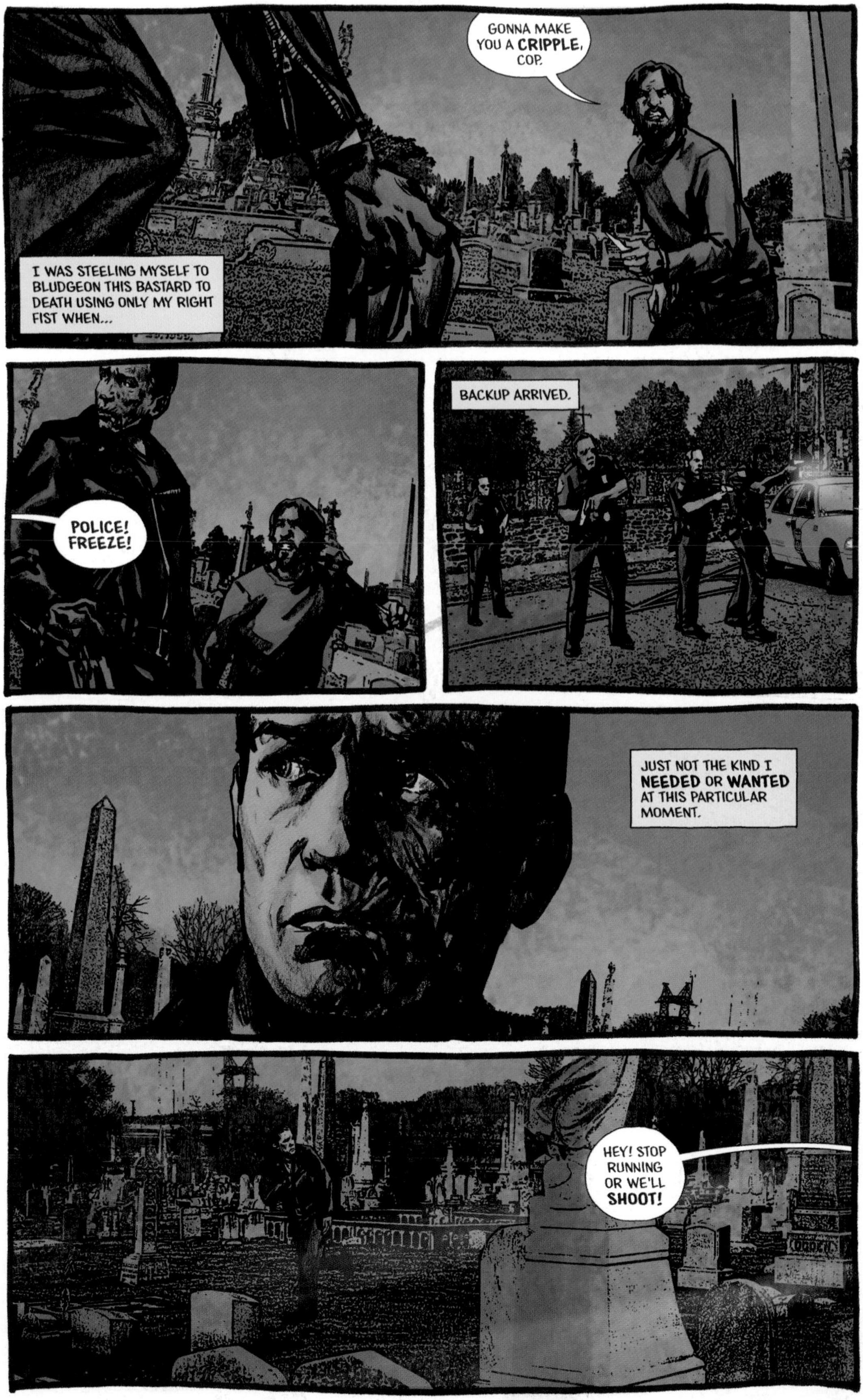
GONNA MAKE YOU A CRIPPLE, COP.
I WAS STEELING MYSELF TO BLUDGEON THIS BASTARD TO DEATH USING ONLY MY RIGHT FIST WHEN...
POLICE! FREEZE!
BACKUP ARRIVED.
JUST NOT THE KIND I NEEDED OR WANTED AT THIS PARTICULAR MOMENT.
HEY! STOP RUNNING OR WE'LL SHOOT!

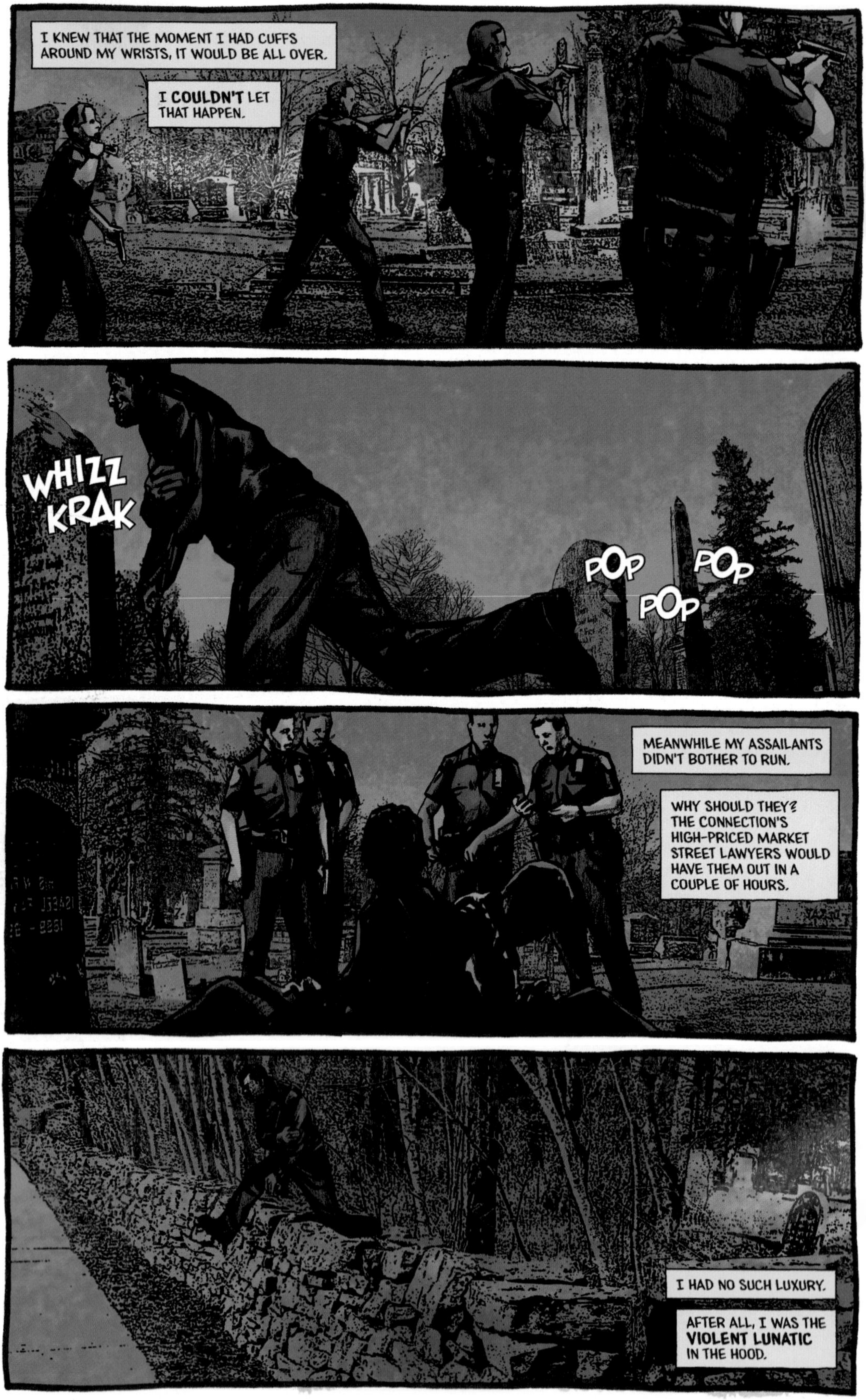
I KNEW THAT THE MOMENT I HAD CUFFS AROUND MY WRISTS, IT WOULD BE ALL OVER.
I **COULDN'T** LET THAT HAPPEN.
WHIZZ
KRAK
POP
POP
POP
MEANWHILE MY ASSAILANTS DIDN'T BOTHER TO RUN.
WHY SHOULD THEY? THE CONNECTION'S HIGH-PRICED MARKET STREET LAWYERS WOULD HAVE THEM OUT IN A COUPLE OF HOURS.
I HAD NO SUCH LUXURY.
AFTER ALL, I WAS THE **VIOLENT LUNATIC** IN THE HOOD.

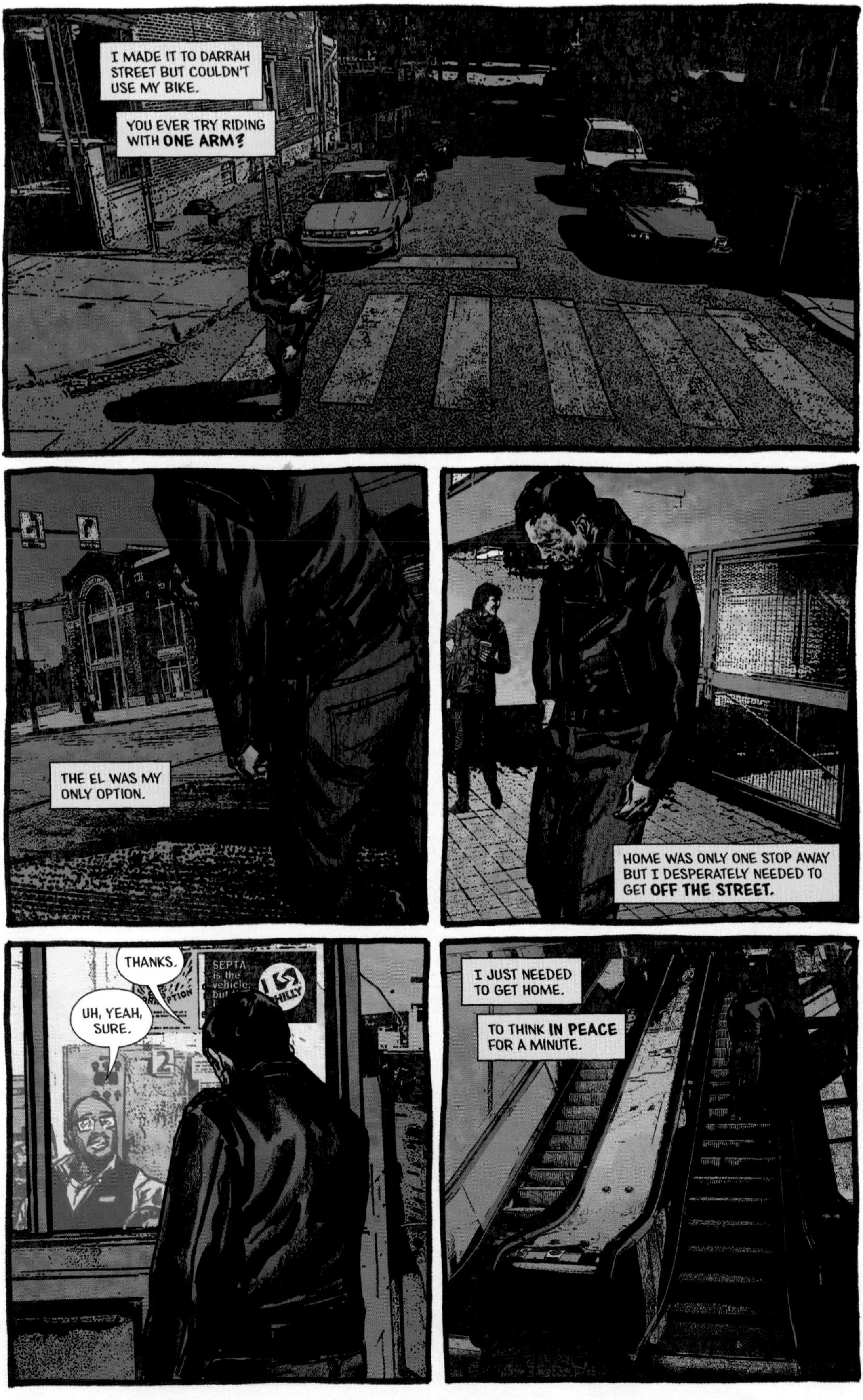
I MADE IT TO DARRAH STREET BUT COULDN'T USE MY BIKE.
YOU EVER TRY RIDING WITH **ONE ARM?**
THE EL WAS MY ONLY OPTION.
HOME WAS ONLY ONE STOP AWAY BUT I DESPERATELY NEEDED TO GET **OFF THE STREET.**
THANKS.
UH, YEAH, SURE.
SEPTA
I JUST NEEDED TO GET HOME.
TO THINK **IN PEACE** FOR A MINUTE.

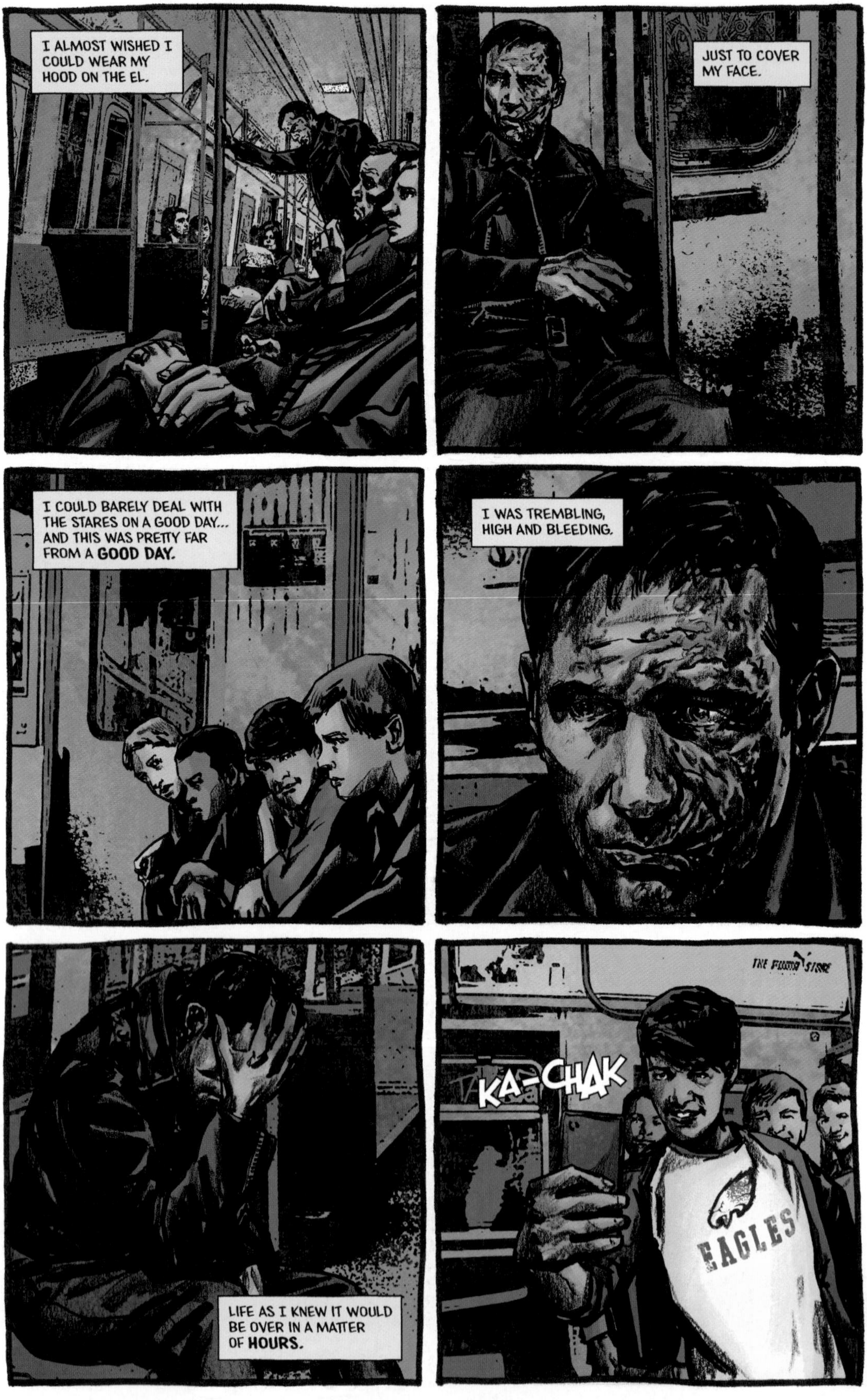
I ALMOST WISHED I COULD WEAR MY HOOD ON THE EL.
JUST TO COVER MY FACE.
I COULD BARELY DEAL WITH THE STARES ON A GOOD DAY... AND THIS WAS PRETTY FAR FROM A GOOD DAY.
I WAS TREMBLING, HIGH AND BLEEDING.
LIFE AS I KNEW IT WOULD BE OVER IN A MATTER OF HOURS.
KA-CHAK
EAGLES

PLEASE.

LEAVE ME ALONE.

HAH HAH HAH HAH HAH HAH HAH

YOUR FACE ALL LIKE HAMBURGER AND SHIT!

EAGLES

GRAHAM AND SAVITZ SAW MY FACE.

THE MINUTE THEY REVEAL MY IDENTITY TO THEIR BOSS-- OR HELL, EVEN THEIR LAWYER-- I WAS A DEAD MAN.

MARKET-FRANKFORD TRAIN MAKING ALL STOPS.

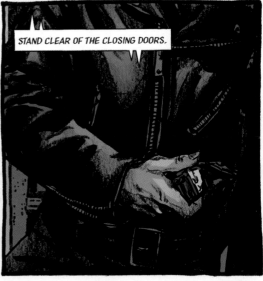

STAND CLEAR OF THE CLOSING DOORS.

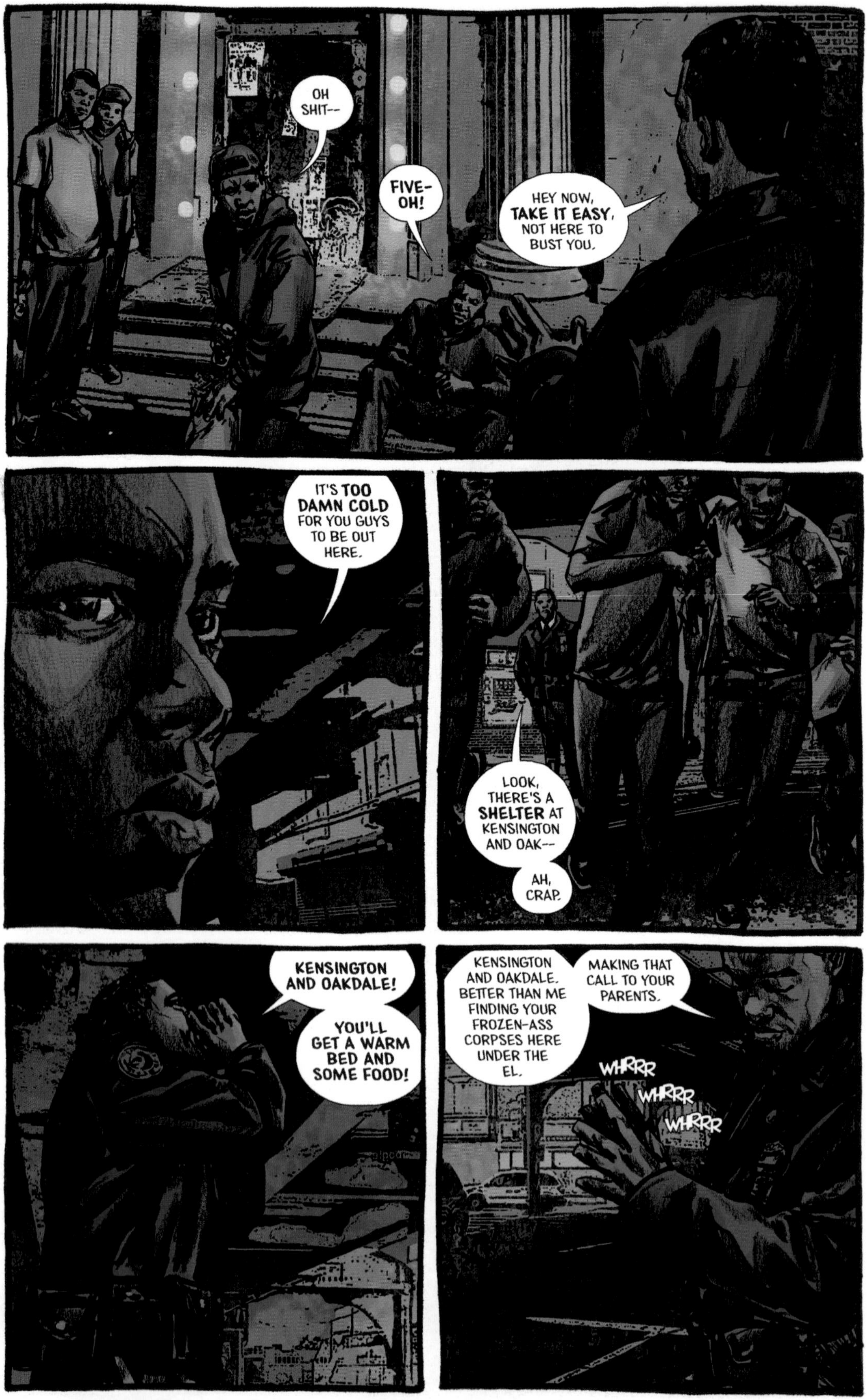
OH SHIT--
FIVE-OH!
HEY NOW, TAKE IT EASY, NOT HERE TO BUST YOU.
IT'S TOO DAMN COLD FOR YOU GUYS TO BE OUT HERE.
LOOK, THERE'S A SHELTER AT KENSINGTON AND OAK--
AH, CRAP.
KENSINGTON AND OAKDALE!
YOU'LL GET A WARM BED AND SOME FOOD!
KENSINGTON AND OAKDALE. BETTER THAN ME FINDING YOUR FROZEN-ASS CORPSES HERE UNDER THE EL.
MAKING THAT CALL TO YOUR PARENTS.
WHRRR
WHRRR
WHRRR

DEV, IT'S ME.

GREG?!

I NEED YOUR HELP, MAN.

"TWO CREEPS NAMED GRAHAM AND SAVITZ ARE ABOUT TO BE BOOKED INTO THE CJC."

The Justice
Juanita Kidd
Center for Crimi

WAIT WAIT...SLOW DOWN.

AREN'T YOU SUPPOSED TO BE RIDING A DESK, MAN?

THOSE TWO PRICKS FRAMED ME. I JUST NEED TIME TO PROVE IT.

...

WHAT ARE YOU ASKING ME, MAN?

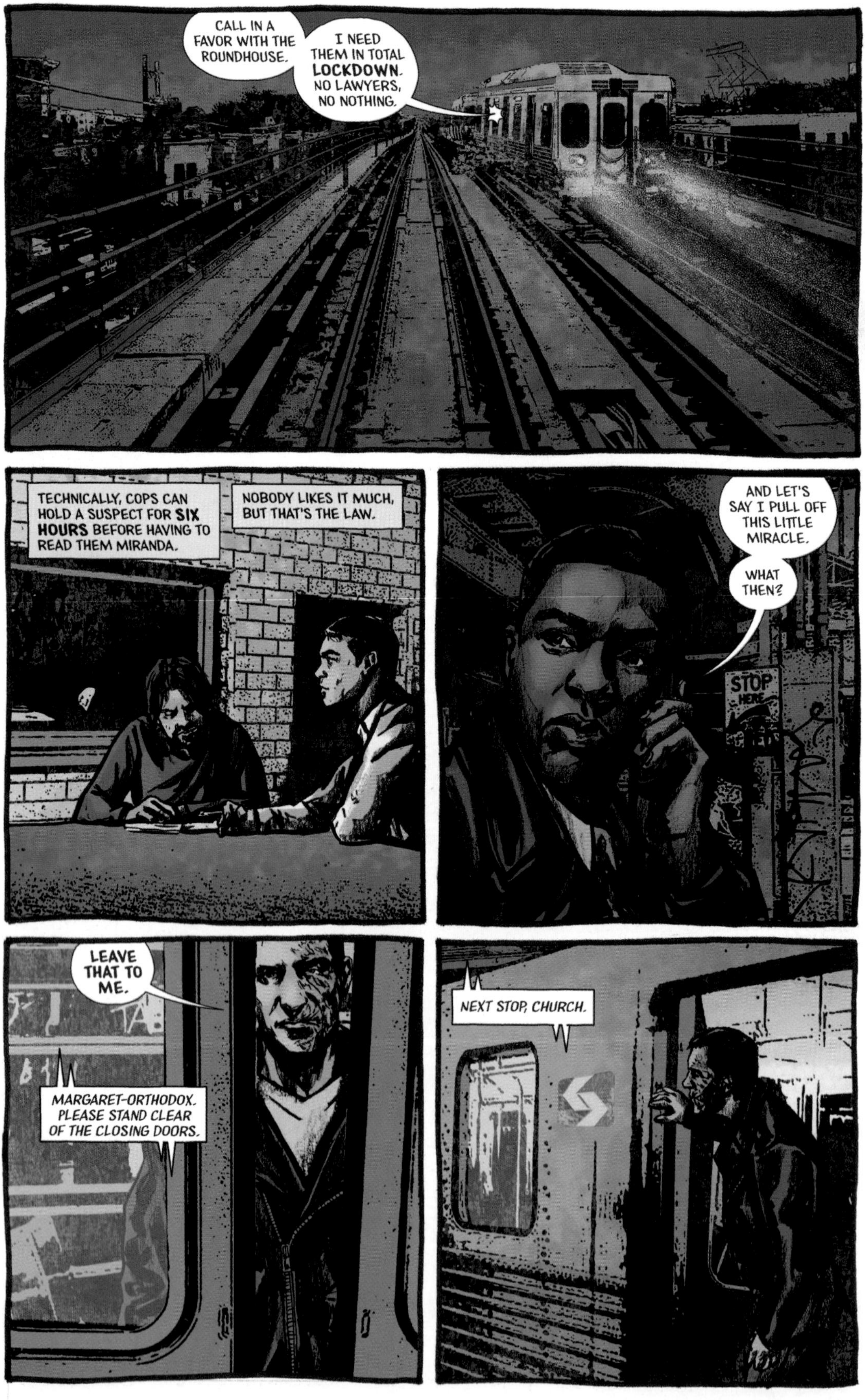

CALL IN A FAVOR WITH THE ROUNDHOUSE.
I NEED THEM IN TOTAL LOCKDOWN. NO LAWYERS, NO NOTHING.
TECHNICALLY, COPS CAN HOLD A SUSPECT FOR SIX HOURS BEFORE HAVING TO READ THEM MIRANDA.
NOBODY LIKES IT MUCH, BUT THAT'S THE LAW.
AND LET'S SAY I PULL OFF THIS LITTLE MIRACLE.
WHAT THEN?
STOP HERE
LEAVE THAT TO ME.
MARGARET-ORTHODOX. PLEASE STAND CLEAR OF THE CLOSING DOORS.
NEXT STOP, CHURCH.

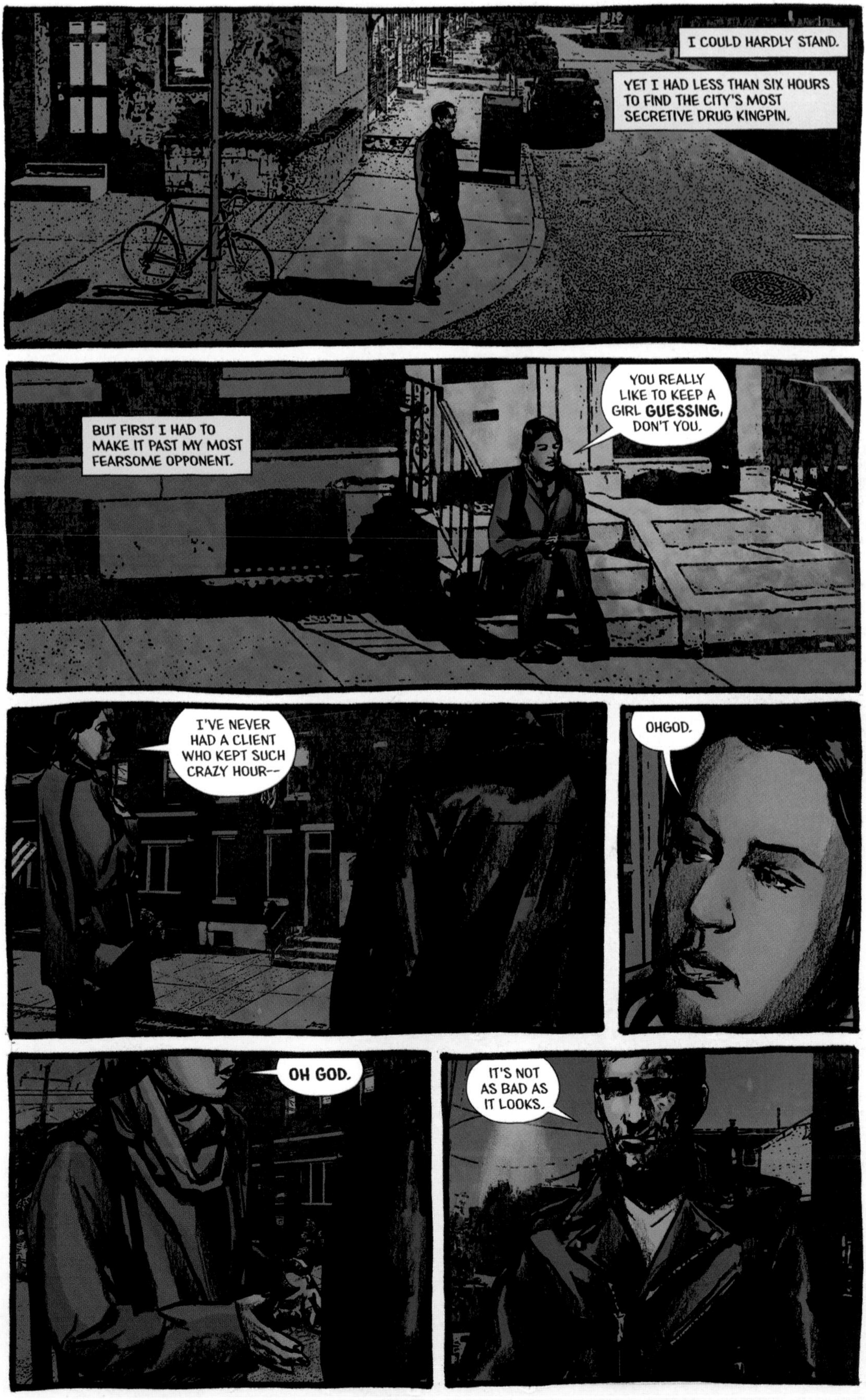
I COULD HARDLY STAND.
YET I HAD LESS THAN SIX HOURS TO FIND THE CITY'S MOST SECRETIVE DRUG KINGPIN.
BUT FIRST I HAD TO MAKE IT PAST MY MOST FEARSOME OPPONENT.
YOU REALLY LIKE TO KEEP A GIRL GUESSING, DON'T YOU.
I'VE NEVER HAD A CLIENT WHO KEPT SUCH CRAZY HOUR--
OHGOD.
OH GOD.
IT'S NOT AS BAD AS IT LOOKS.

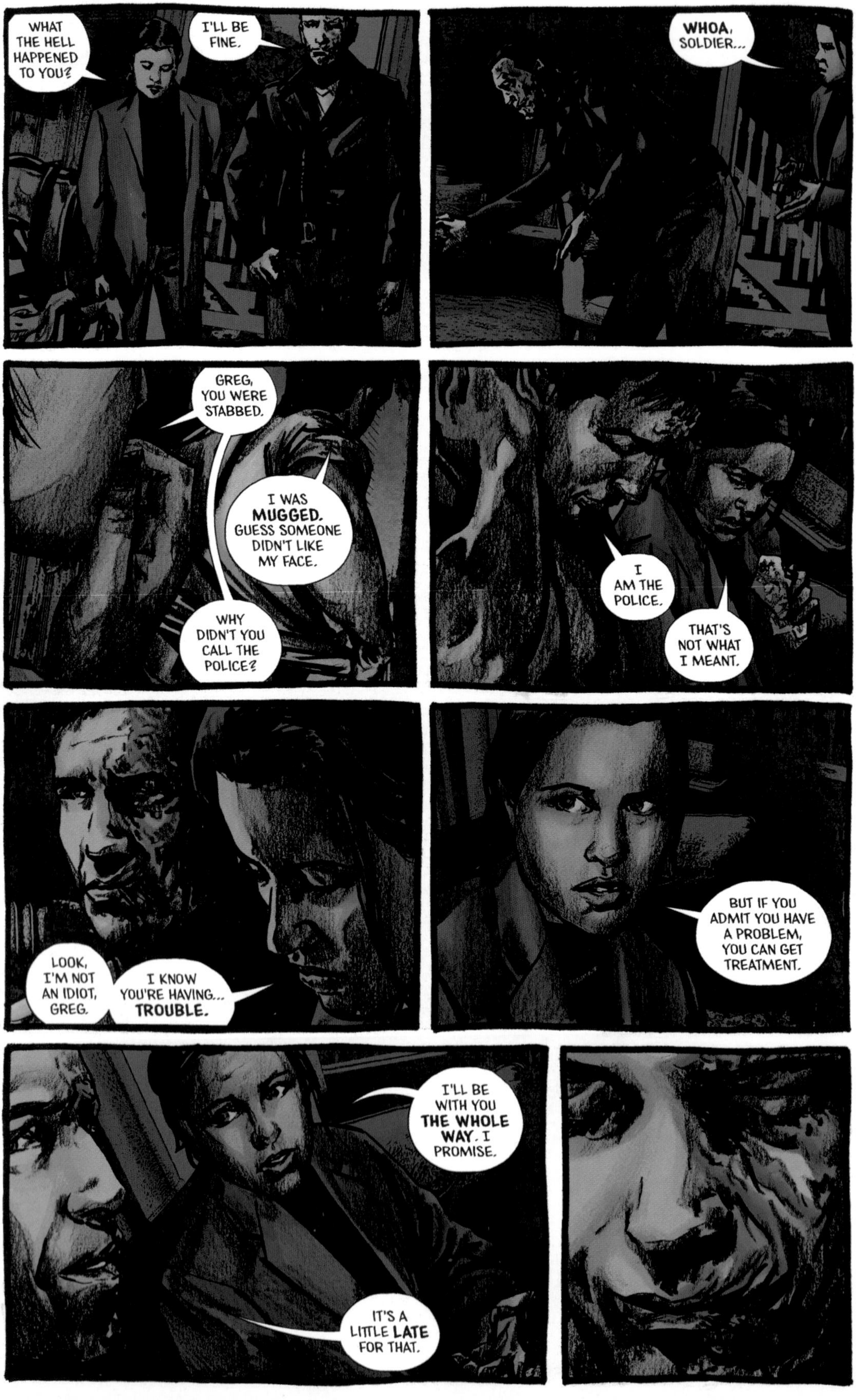
WHAT THE HELL HAPPENED TO YOU?
I'LL BE FINE.
WHOA, SOLDIER...
GREG, YOU WERE STABBED.
I WAS MUGGED. GUESS SOMEONE DIDN'T LIKE MY FACE.
WHY DIDN'T YOU CALL THE POLICE?
I AM THE POLICE.
THAT'S NOT WHAT I MEANT.
LOOK, I'M NOT AN IDIOT, GREG.
I KNOW YOU'RE HAVING... TROUBLE.
BUT IF YOU ADMIT YOU HAVE A PROBLEM, YOU CAN GET TREATMENT.
I'LL BE WITH YOU THE WHOLE WAY. I PROMISE.
IT'S A LITTLE LATE FOR THAT.

NO. I'M **NOT** GOING TO LET YOU DO THIS TO YOURSELF.

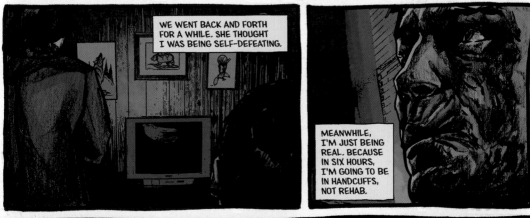

WE WENT BACK AND FORTH FOR A WHILE. SHE THOUGHT I WAS BEING SELF-DEFEATING.

MEANWHILE, I'M JUST BEING REAL. BECAUSE IN SIX HOURS, I'M GOING TO BE IN HANDCUFFS, NOT REHAB.

FINE. YOU DON'T WANT MY HELP, I CAN TAKE A HINT.

JESSIE, I HAVE SOMETHING TO TELL YOU.

TELL **SOMEONE** ELSE.

I'M THE BLACK HOOD.

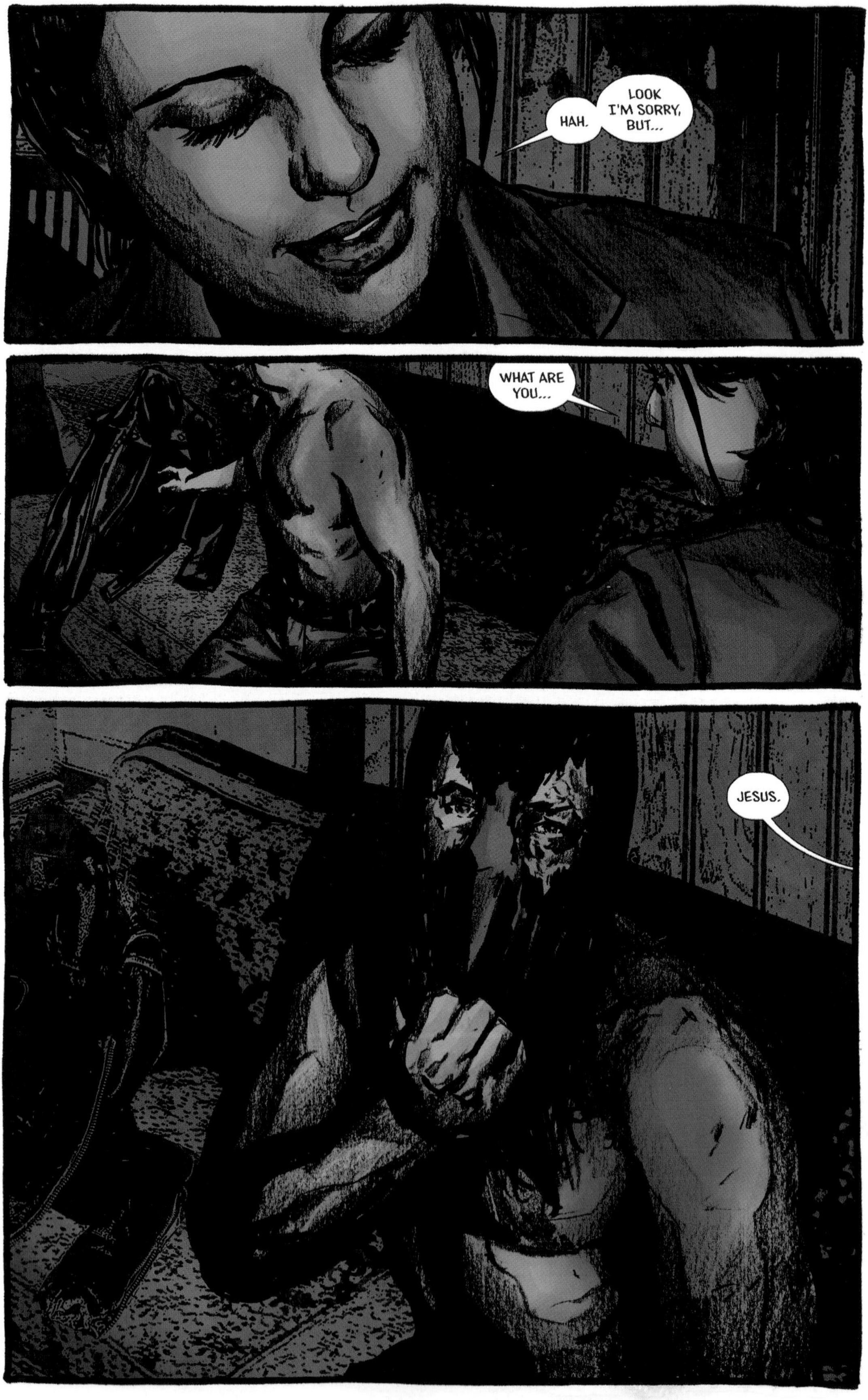
HAH.
LOOK I'M SORRY, BUT...
WHAT ARE YOU...
JESUS.

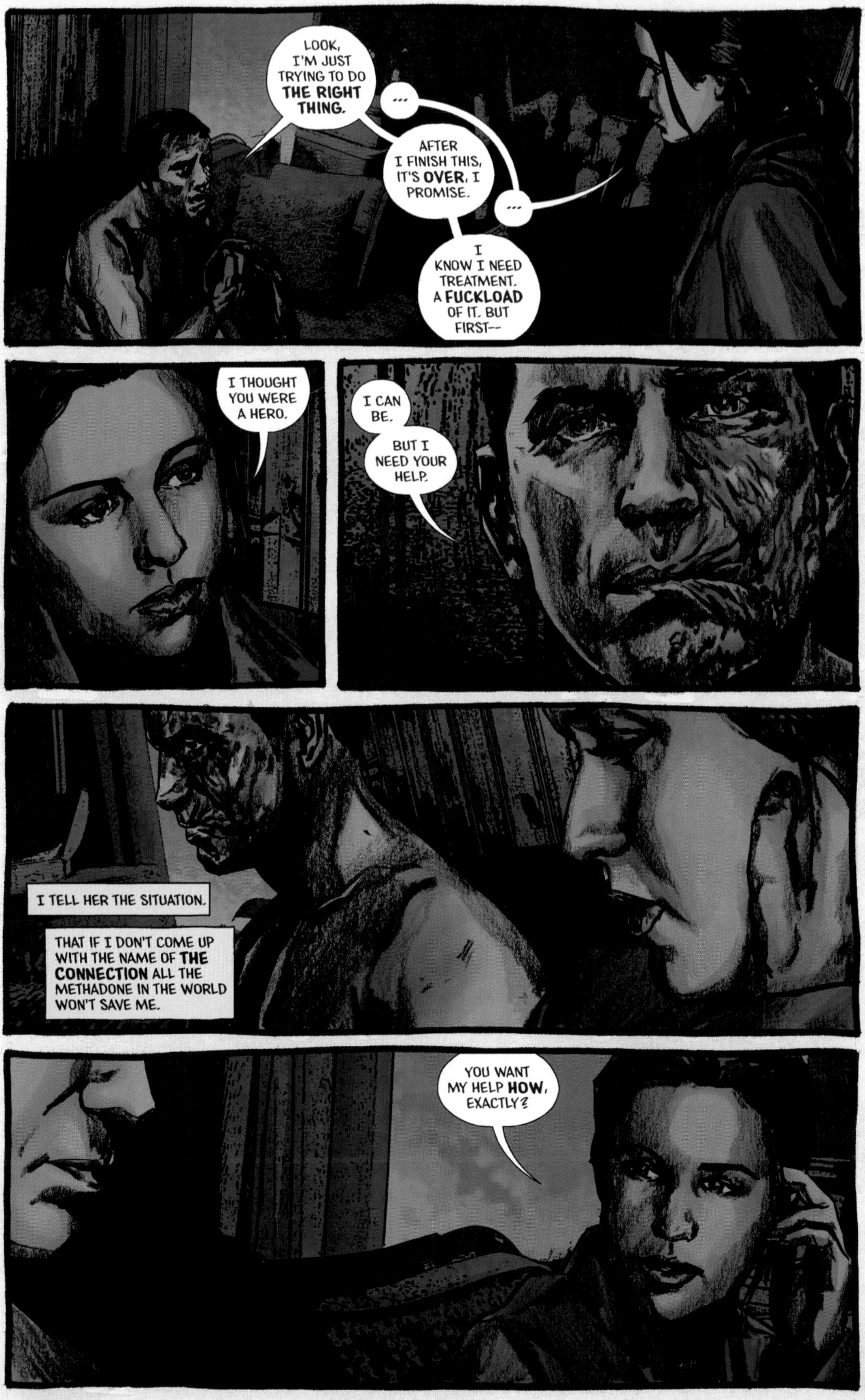
LOOK, I'M JUST TRYING TO DO THE RIGHT THING.
...
AFTER I FINISH THIS, IT'S OVER, I PROMISE.
...
I KNOW I NEED TREATMENT. A FUCKLOAD OF IT. BUT FIRST--
I THOUGHT YOU WERE A HERO.
I CAN BE.
BUT I NEED YOUR HELP.
I TELL HER THE SITUATION.
THAT IF I DON'T COME UP WITH THE NAME OF THE CONNECTION ALL THE METHADONE IN THE WORLD WON'T SAVE ME.
YOU WANT MY HELP HOW, EXACTLY?

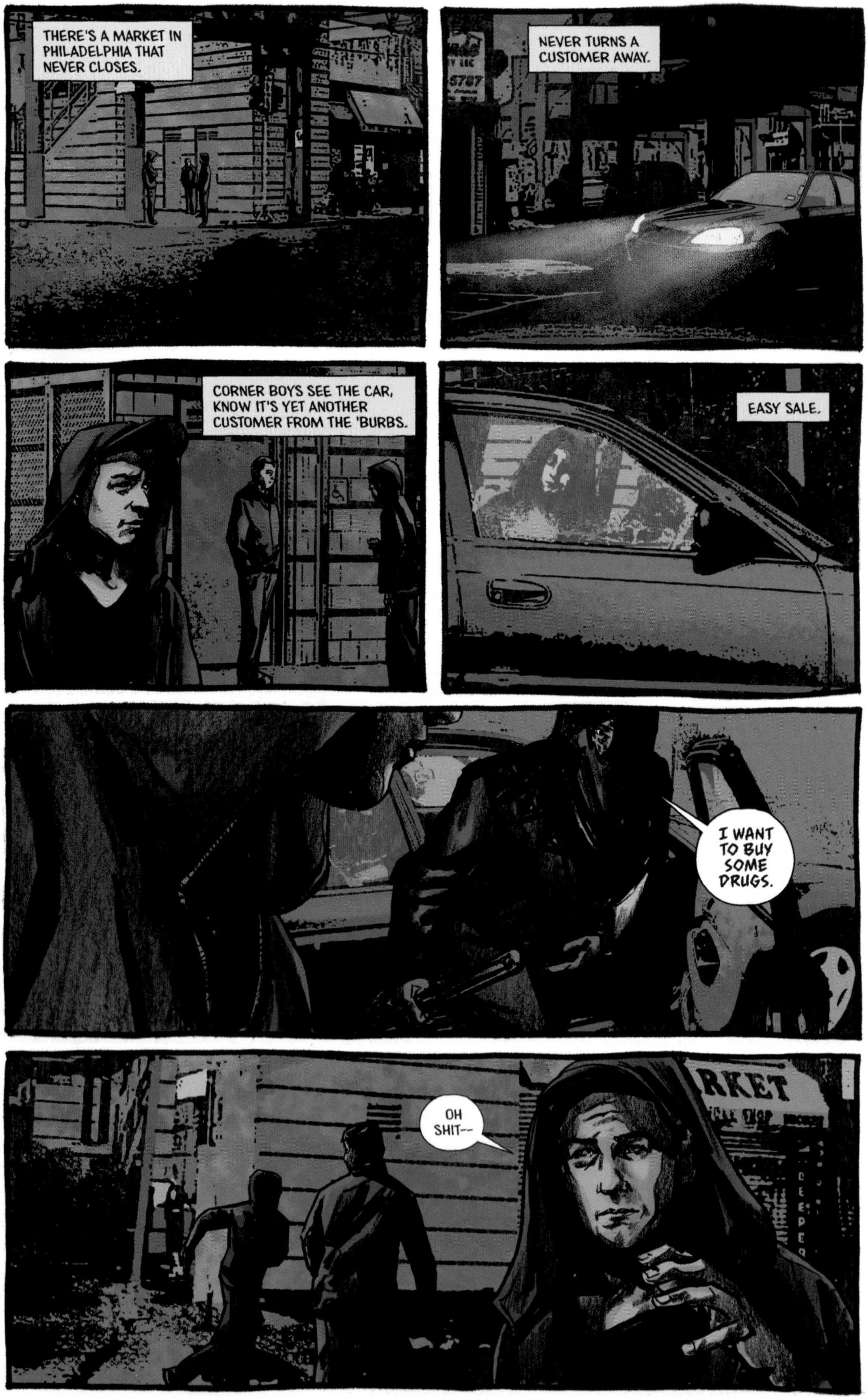
THERE'S A MARKET IN PHILADELPHIA THAT NEVER CLOSES.
NEVER TURNS A CUSTOMER AWAY.
CORNER BOYS SEE THE CAR, KNOW IT'S YET ANOTHER CUSTOMER FROM THE 'BURBS.
EASY SALE.
I WANT TO BUY SOME DRUGS.
OH SHIT--
RKET

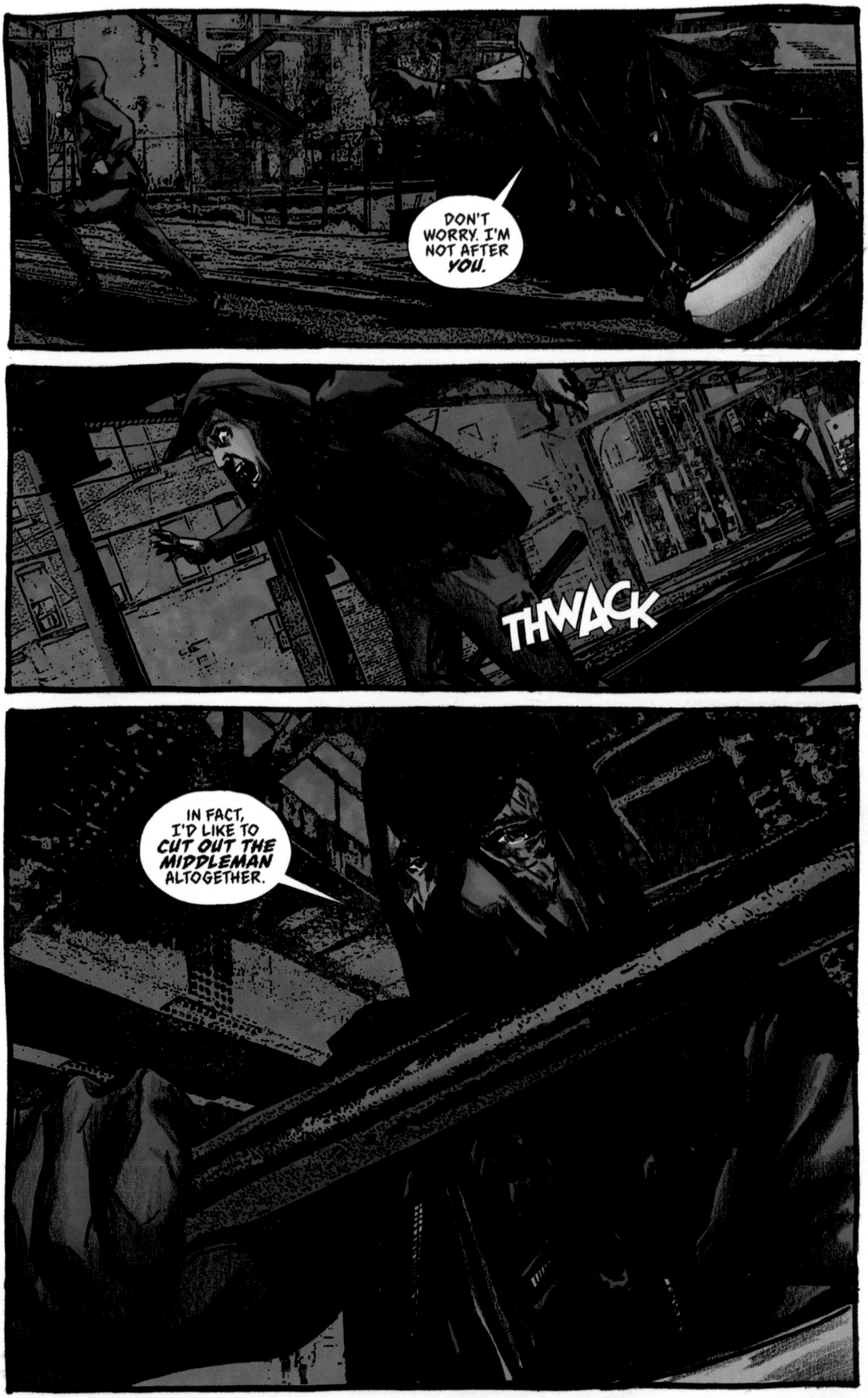
DON'T WORRY. I'M NOT AFTER YOU.
THWACK
IN FACT, I'D LIKE TO CUT OUT THE MIDDLEMAN ALTOGETHER.

ISSUE FIVE

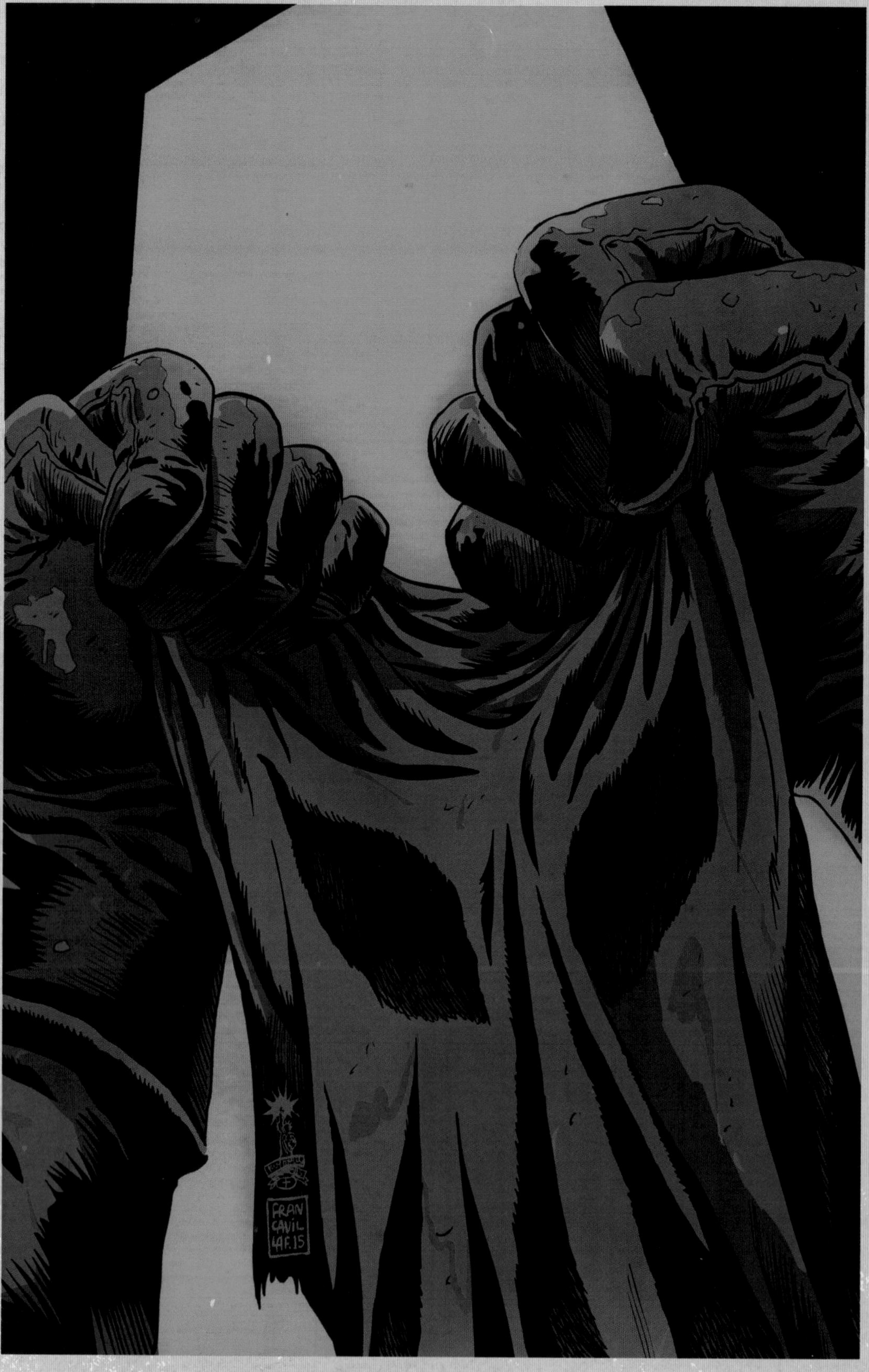
FRAN
CAVIL
LAF.15

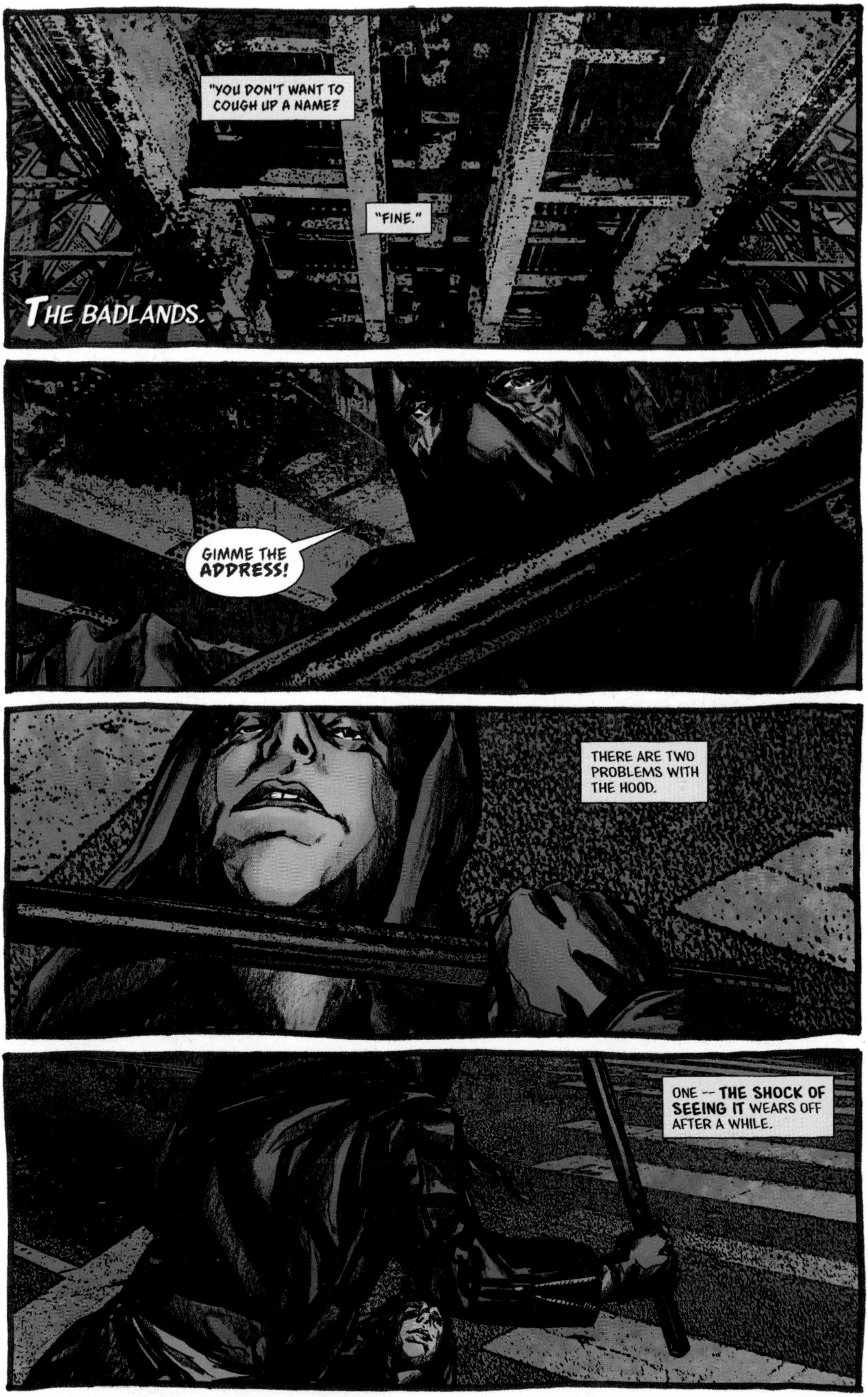
"YOU DON'T WANT TO COUGH UP A NAME?
"FINE."
THE BADLANDS.
GIMME THE ADDRESS!
THERE ARE TWO PROBLEMS WITH THE HOOD.
ONE -- THE SHOCK OF SEEING IT WEARS OFF AFTER A WHILE.

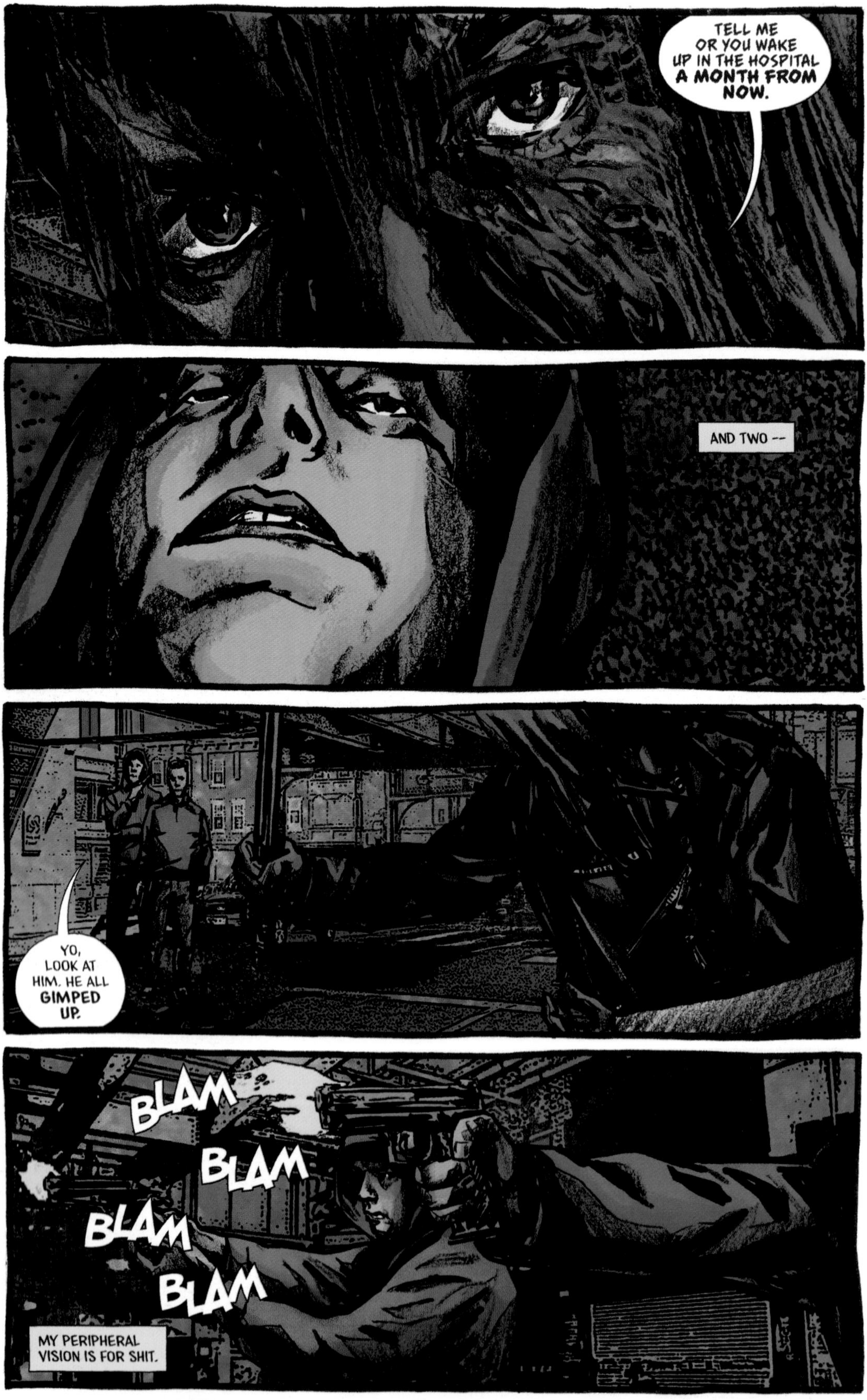
TELL ME OR YOU WAKE UP IN THE HOSPITAL **A MONTH FROM NOW.**
AND TWO --
YO, LOOK AT HIM. HE ALL **GIMPED** UP.
BLAM
BLAM
BLAM
BLAM
MY PERIPHERAL VISION IS FOR SHIT.

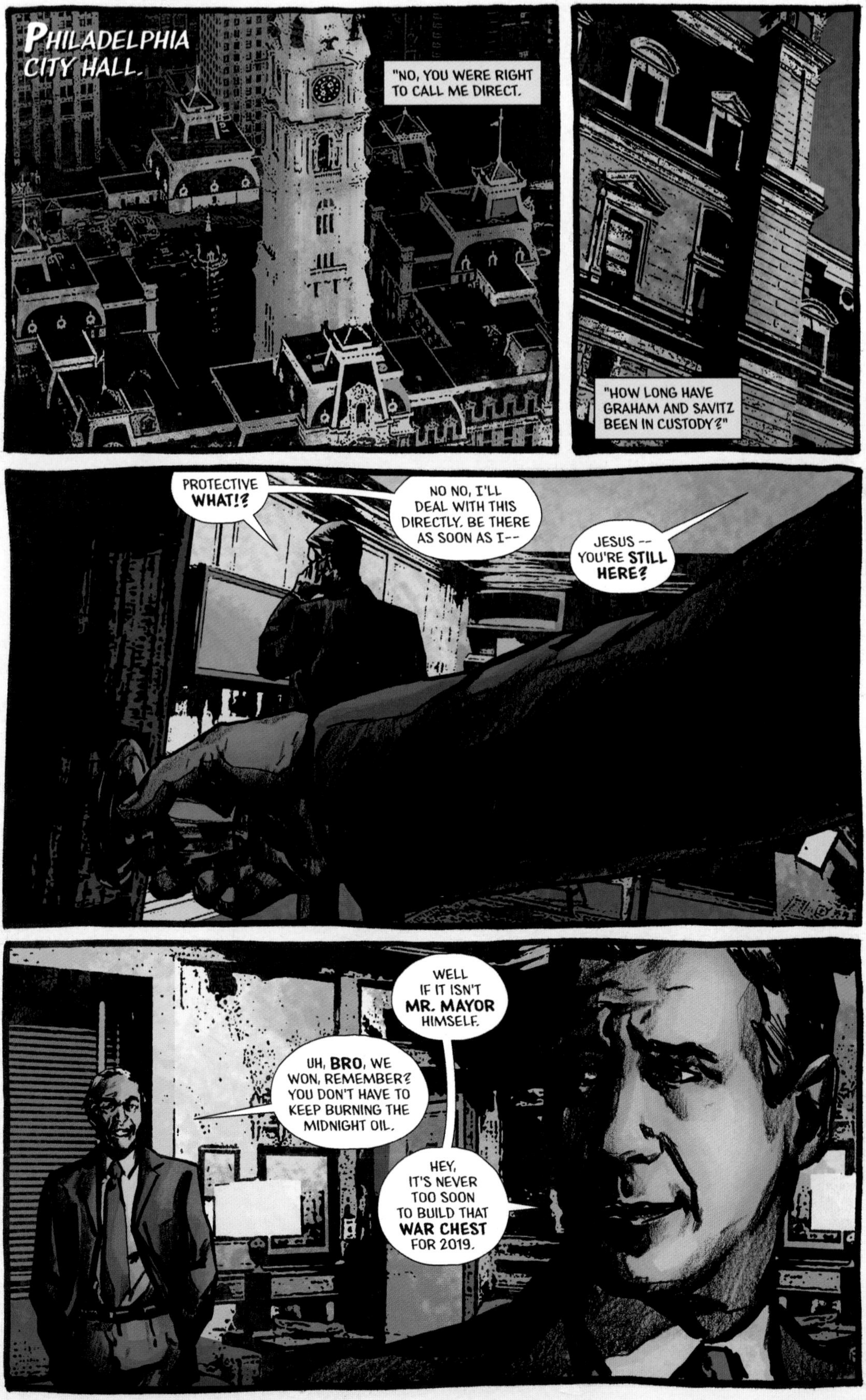
PHILADELPHIA CITY HALL.
"NO, YOU WERE RIGHT TO CALL ME DIRECT.
"HOW LONG HAVE GRAHAM AND SAVITZ BEEN IN CUSTODY?"
PROTECTIVE WHAT!?
NO NO, I'LL DEAL WITH THIS DIRECTLY. BE THERE AS SOON AS I--
JESUS -- YOU'RE STILL HERE?
WELL IF IT ISN'T MR. MAYOR HIMSELF.
UH, BRO, WE WON, REMEMBER? YOU DON'T HAVE TO KEEP BURNING THE MIDNIGHT OIL.
HEY, IT'S NEVER TOO SOON TO BUILD THAT WAR CHEST FOR 2019.

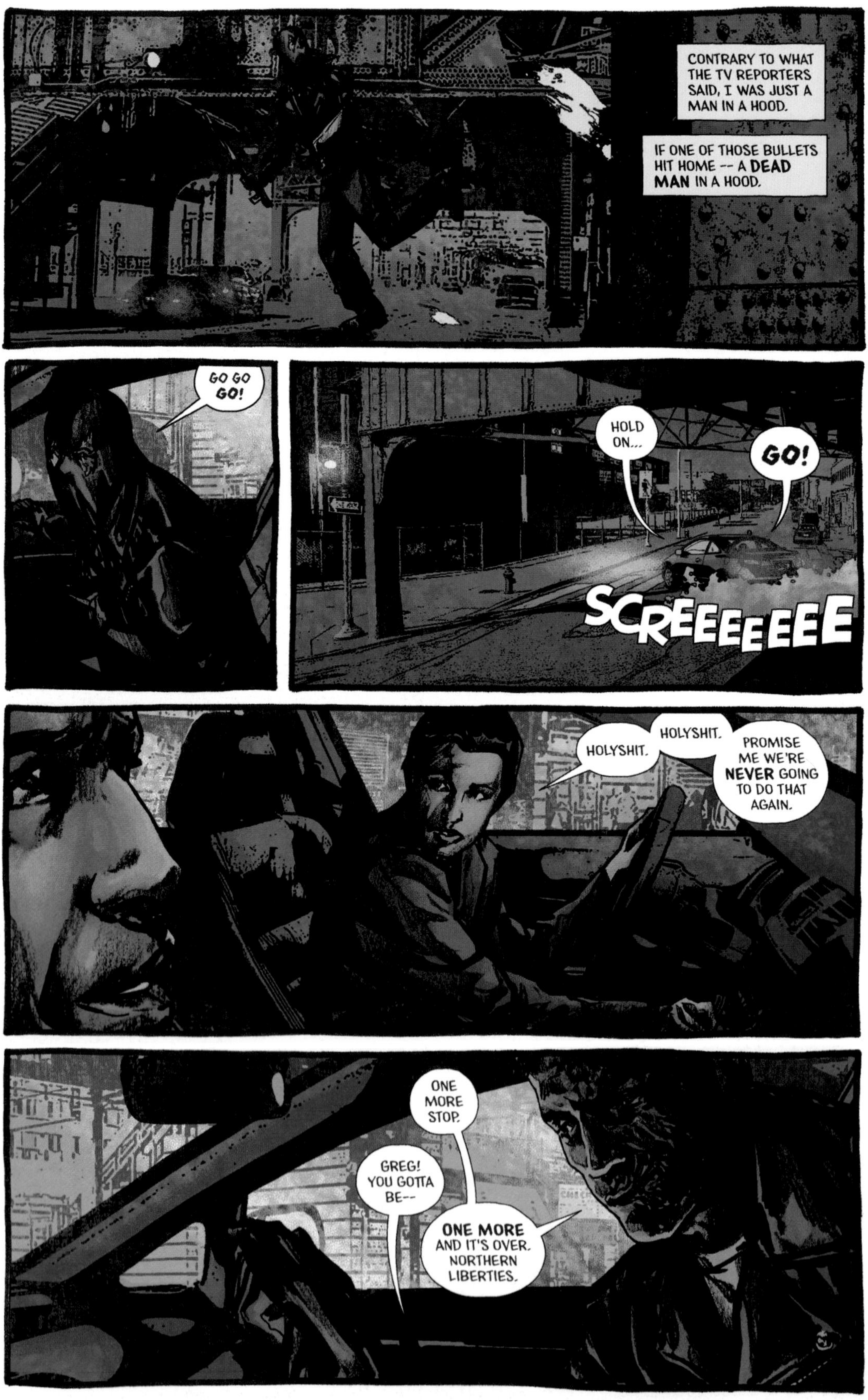
CONTRARY TO WHAT THE TV REPORTERS SAID, I WAS JUST A MAN IN A HOOD.
IF ONE OF THOSE BULLETS HIT HOME -- A DEAD MAN IN A HOOD.
GO GO GO!
HOLD ON...
GO!
SCREEEEEEEE
HOLYSHIT.
HOLYSHIT.
PROMISE ME WE'RE NEVER GOING TO DO THAT AGAIN.
ONE MORE STOP.
GREG! YOU GOTTA BE--
ONE MORE AND IT'S OVER. NORTHERN LIBERTIES.

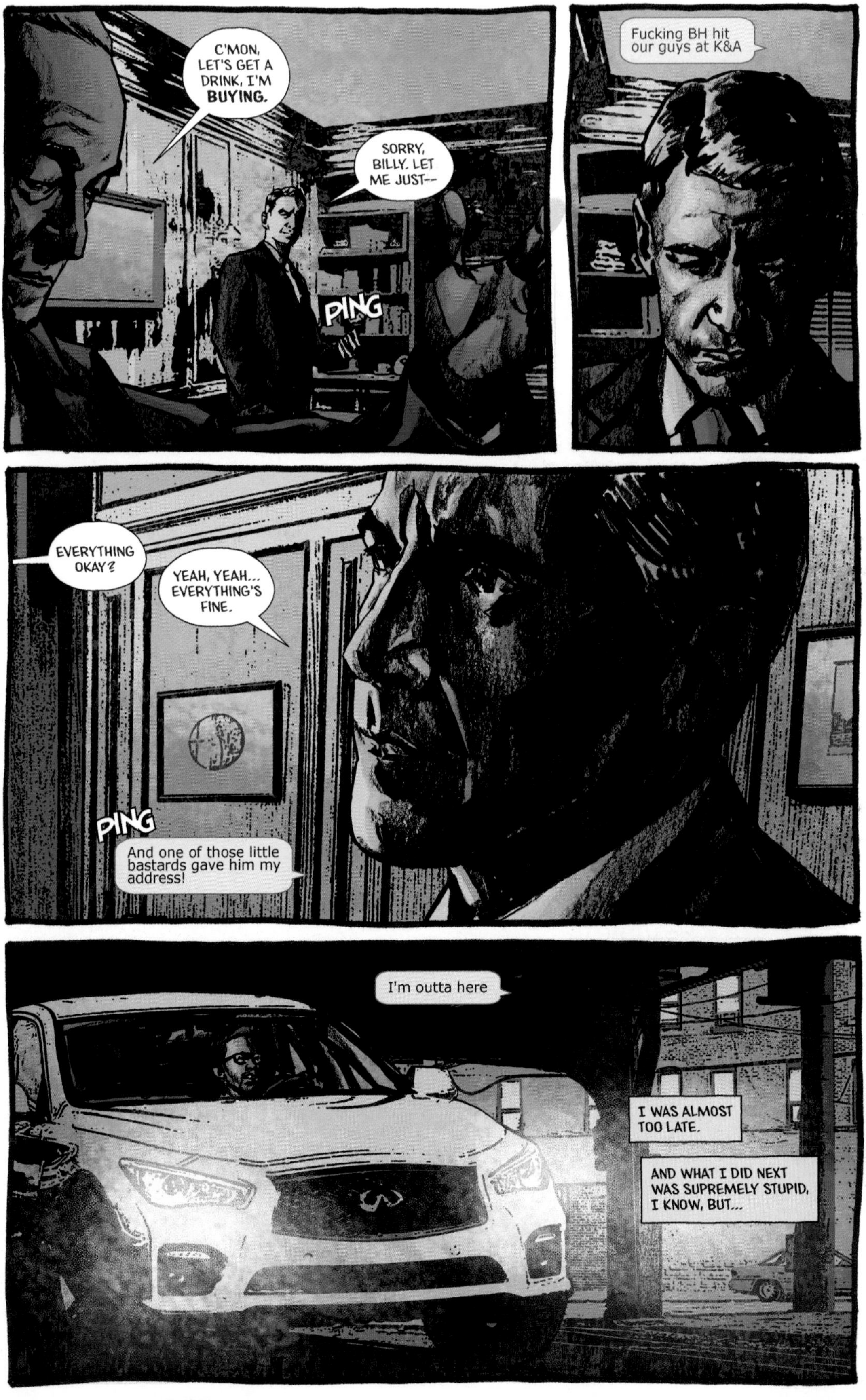

C'MON, LET'S GET A DRINK, I'M **BUYING.**
SORRY, BILLY. LET ME JUST--
PING
Fucking BH hit our guys at K&A
EVERYTHING OKAY?
YEAH, YEAH... EVERYTHING'S FINE.
PING
And one of those little bastards gave him my address!
I'm outta here
I WAS ALMOST TOO LATE.
AND WHAT I DID NEXT WAS SUPREMELY STUPID, I KNOW, BUT...

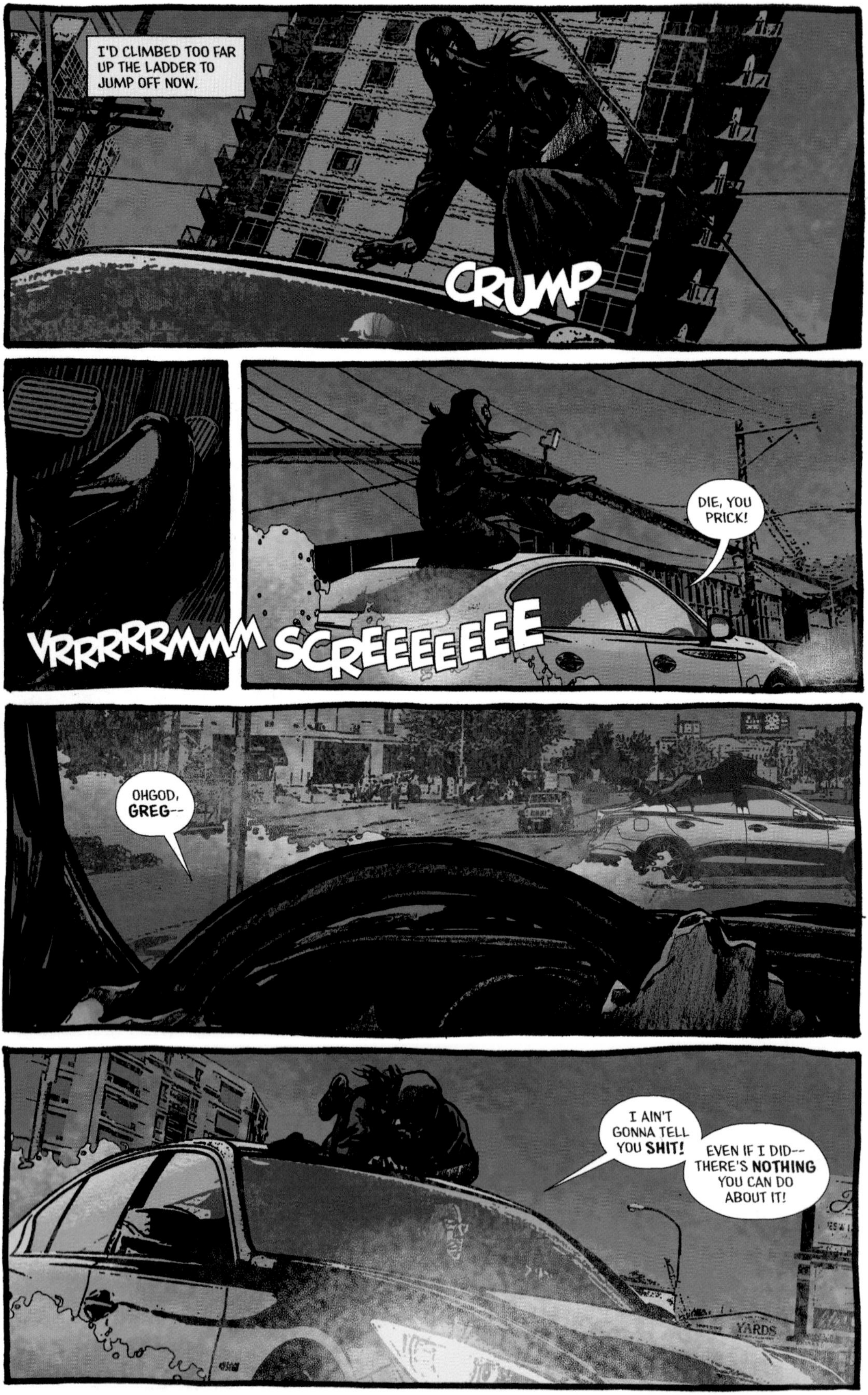
I'D CLIMBED TOO FAR UP THE LADDER TO JUMP OFF NOW.
CRUMP
VRRRRRMMM
SCREEEEEEE
DIE, YOU PRICK!
OHGOD, GREG--
I AIN'T GONNA TELL YOU SHIT!
EVEN IF I DID-- THERE'S NOTHING YOU CAN DO ABOUT IT!
YARDS

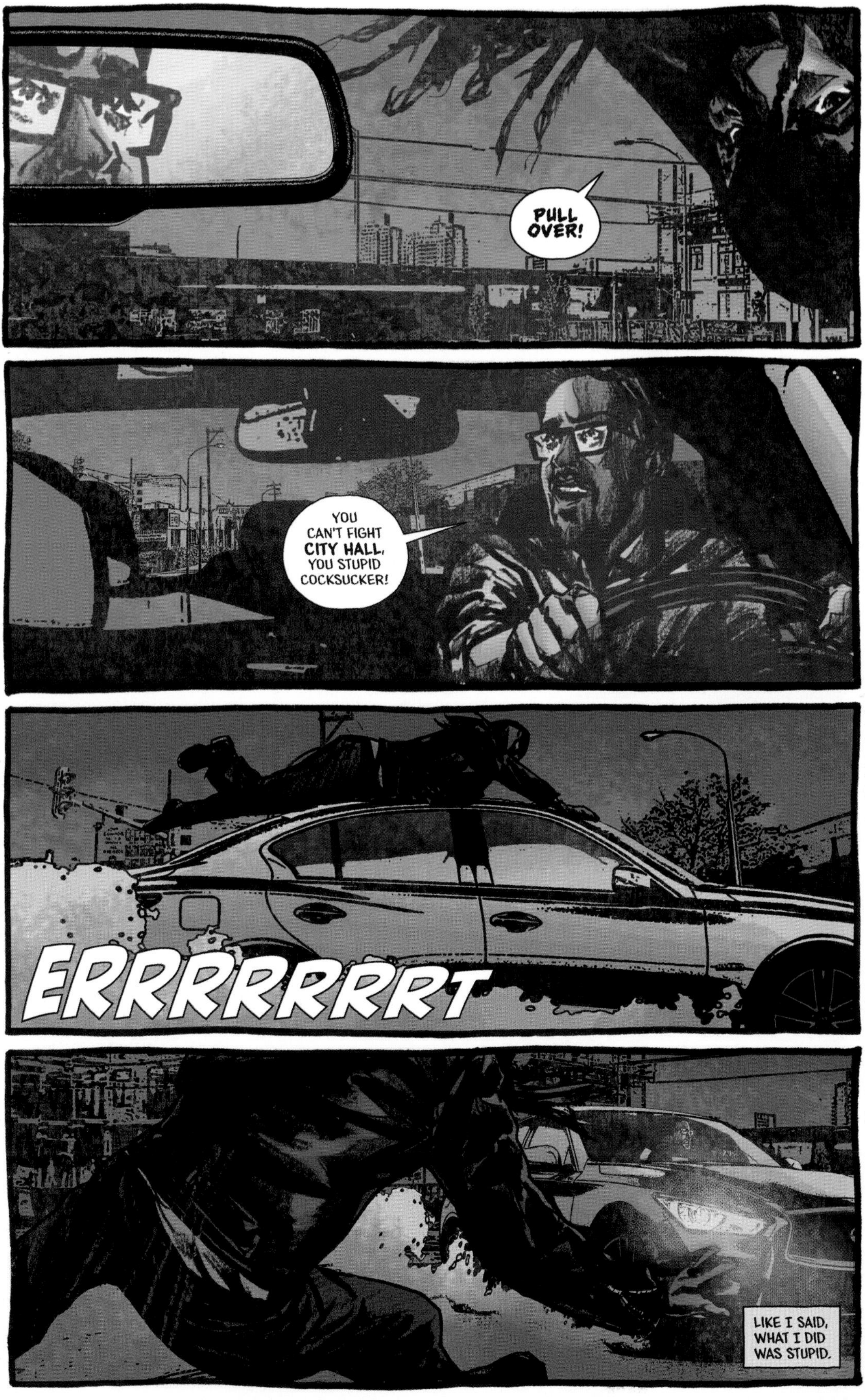
PULL OVER!
YOU CAN'T FIGHT CITY HALL, YOU STUPID COCKSUCKER!
ERRRRRRRT
LIKE I SAID, WHAT I DID WAS STUPID.

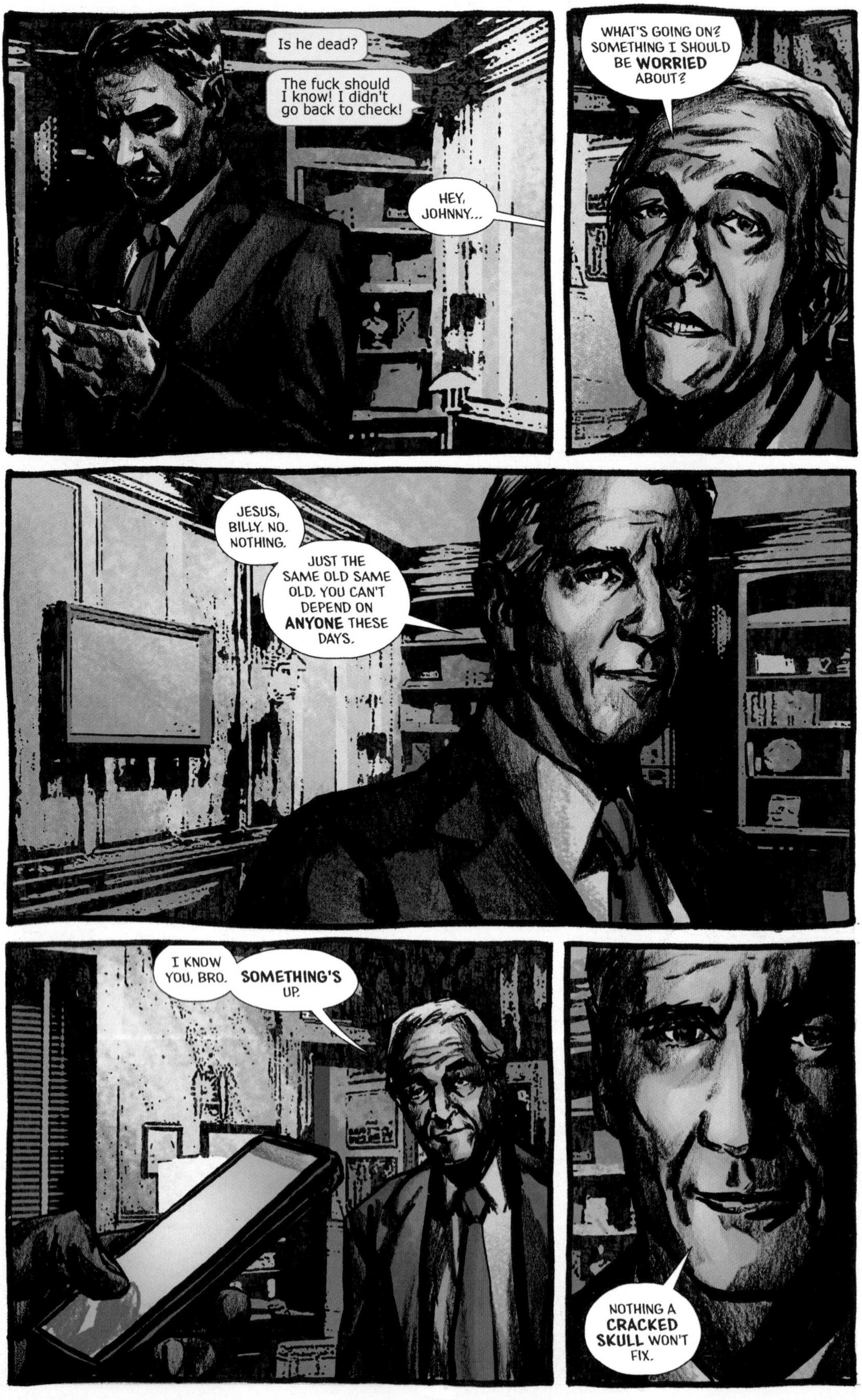
Is he dead?
The fuck should I know! I didn't go back to check!
HEY, JOHNNY...
WHAT'S GOING ON? SOMETHING I SHOULD BE WORRIED ABOUT?
JESUS, BILLY. NO. NOTHING.
JUST THE SAME OLD SAME OLD. YOU CAN'T DEPEND ON ANYONE THESE DAYS.
I KNOW YOU, BRO.
SOMETHING'S UP.
NOTHING A CRACKED SKULL WON'T FIX.

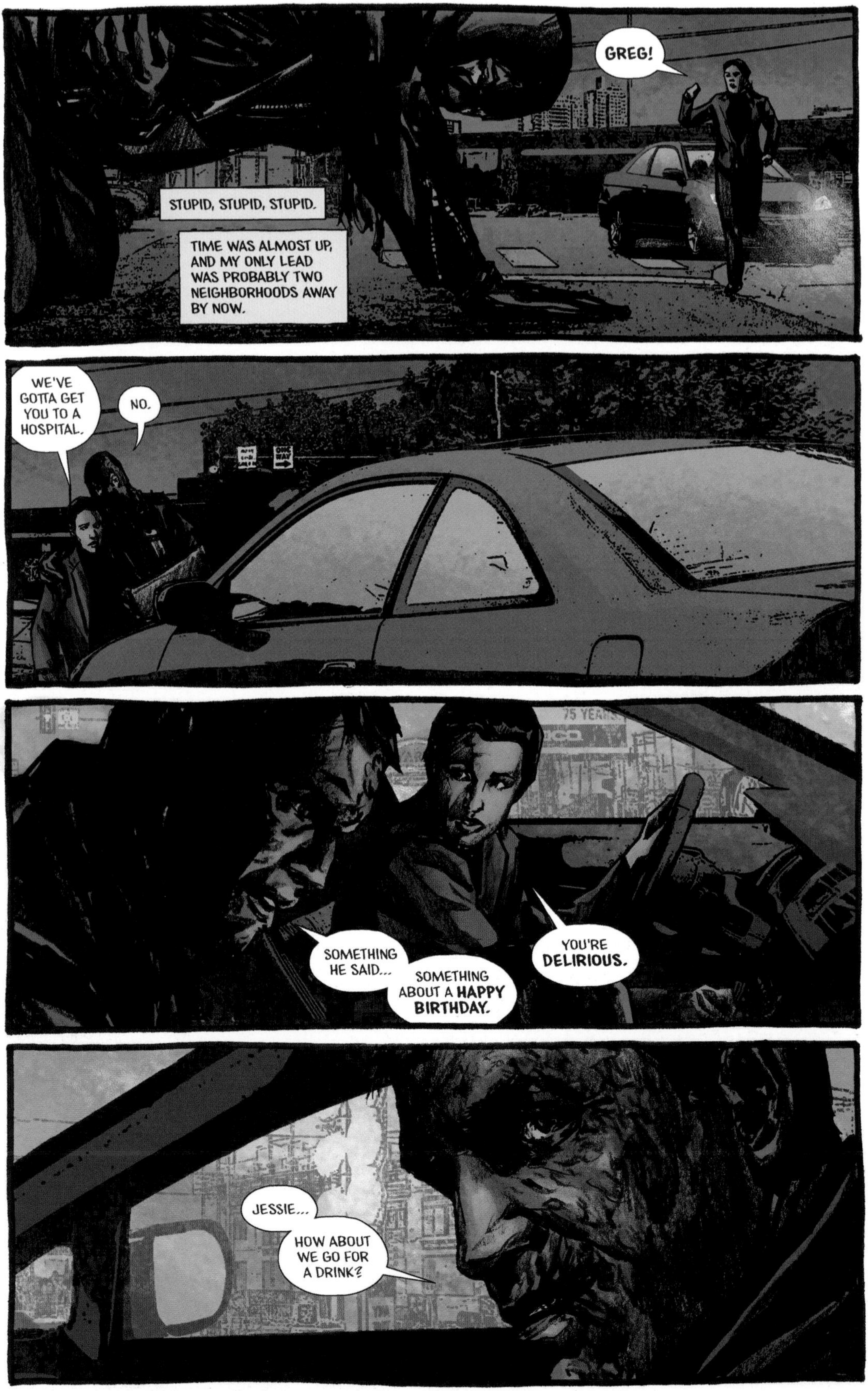
GREG!
STUPID, STUPID, STUPID.
TIME WAS ALMOST UP, AND MY ONLY LEAD WAS PROBABLY TWO NEIGHBORHOODS AWAY BY NOW.
WE'VE GOTTA GET YOU TO A HOSPITAL.
NO.
SOMETHING HE SAID...
SOMETHING ABOUT A HAPPY BIRTHDAY.
YOU'RE DELIRIOUS.
JESSIE...
HOW ABOUT WE GO FOR A DRINK?

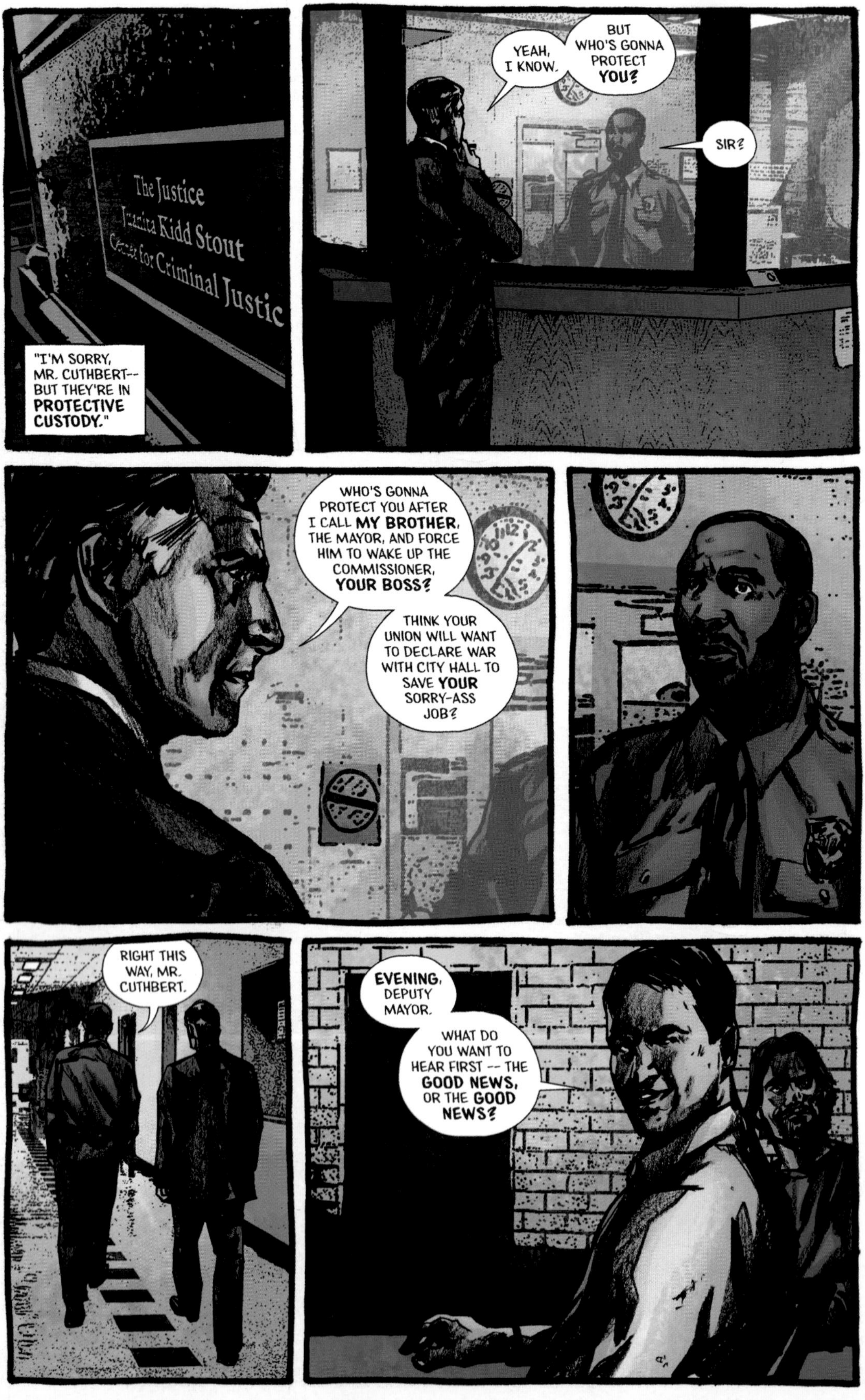
The Justice
Juanita Kidd Stout
Center for Criminal Justic
"I'M SORRY, MR. CUTHBERT-- BUT THEY'RE IN PROTECTIVE CUSTODY."
YEAH, I KNOW.
BUT WHO'S GONNA PROTECT YOU?
SIR?
WHO'S GONNA PROTECT YOU AFTER I CALL MY BROTHER, THE MAYOR, AND FORCE HIM TO WAKE UP THE COMMISSIONER, YOUR BOSS?
THINK YOUR UNION WILL WANT TO DECLARE WAR WITH CITY HALL TO SAVE YOUR SORRY-ASS JOB?
RIGHT THIS WAY, MR. CUTHBERT.
EVENING, DEPUTY MAYOR.
WHAT DO YOU WANT TO HEAR FIRST -- THE GOOD NEWS, OR THE GOOD NEWS?

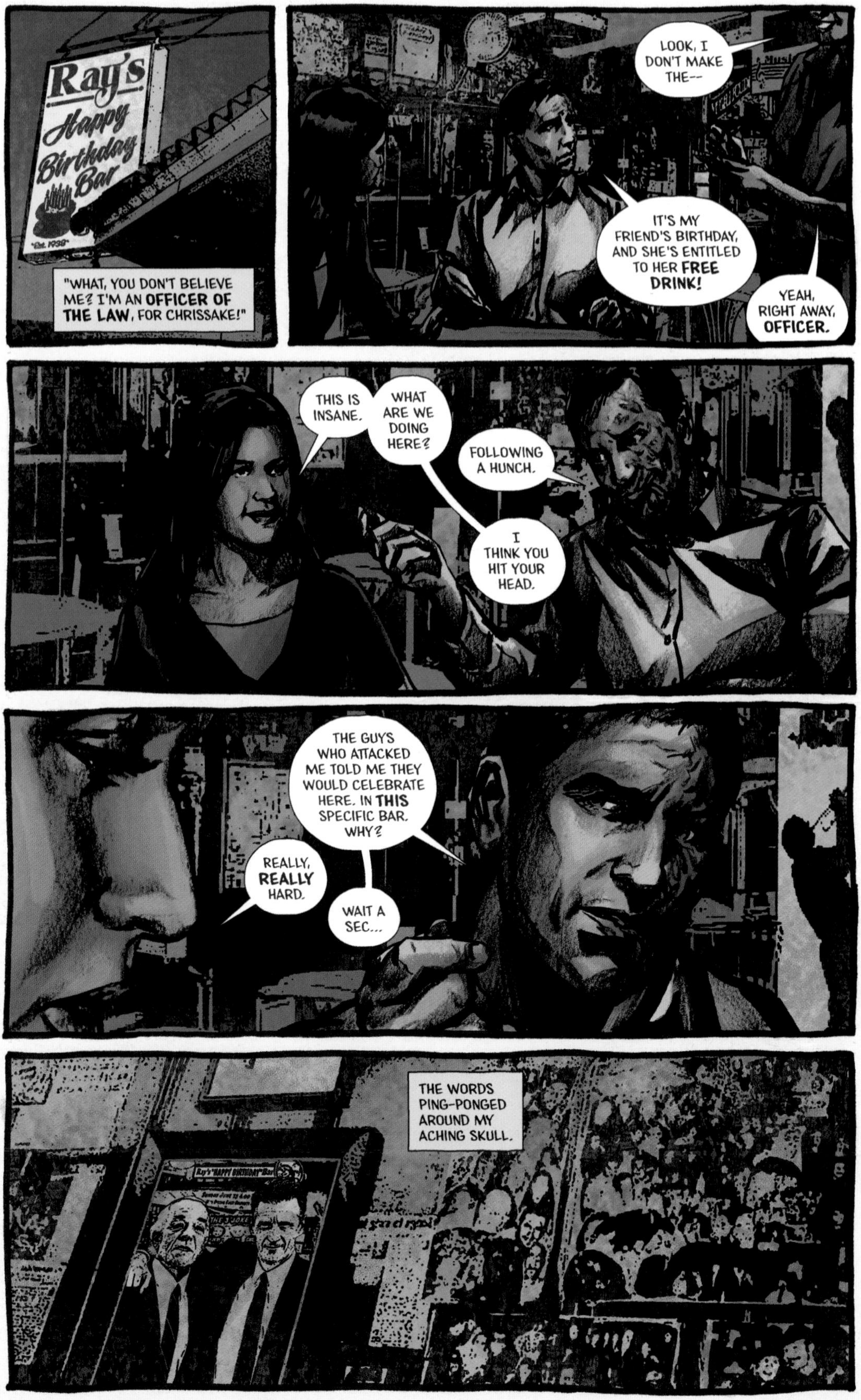

Ray's Happy Birthday Bar
"WHAT, YOU DON'T BELIEVE ME? I'M AN **OFFICER OF THE LAW**, FOR CHRISSAKE!"
LOOK, I DON'T MAKE THE--
IT'S MY FRIEND'S BIRTHDAY, AND SHE'S ENTITLED TO HER **FREE DRINK!**
YEAH, RIGHT AWAY, **OFFICER.**
THIS IS INSANE.
WHAT ARE WE DOING HERE?
FOLLOWING A HUNCH.
I THINK YOU HIT YOUR HEAD.
THE GUYS WHO ATTACKED ME TOLD ME THEY WOULD CELEBRATE HERE. IN **THIS** SPECIFIC BAR. WHY?
REALLY, **REALLY** HARD.
WAIT A SEC...
THE WORDS PING-PONGED AROUND MY ACHING SKULL.

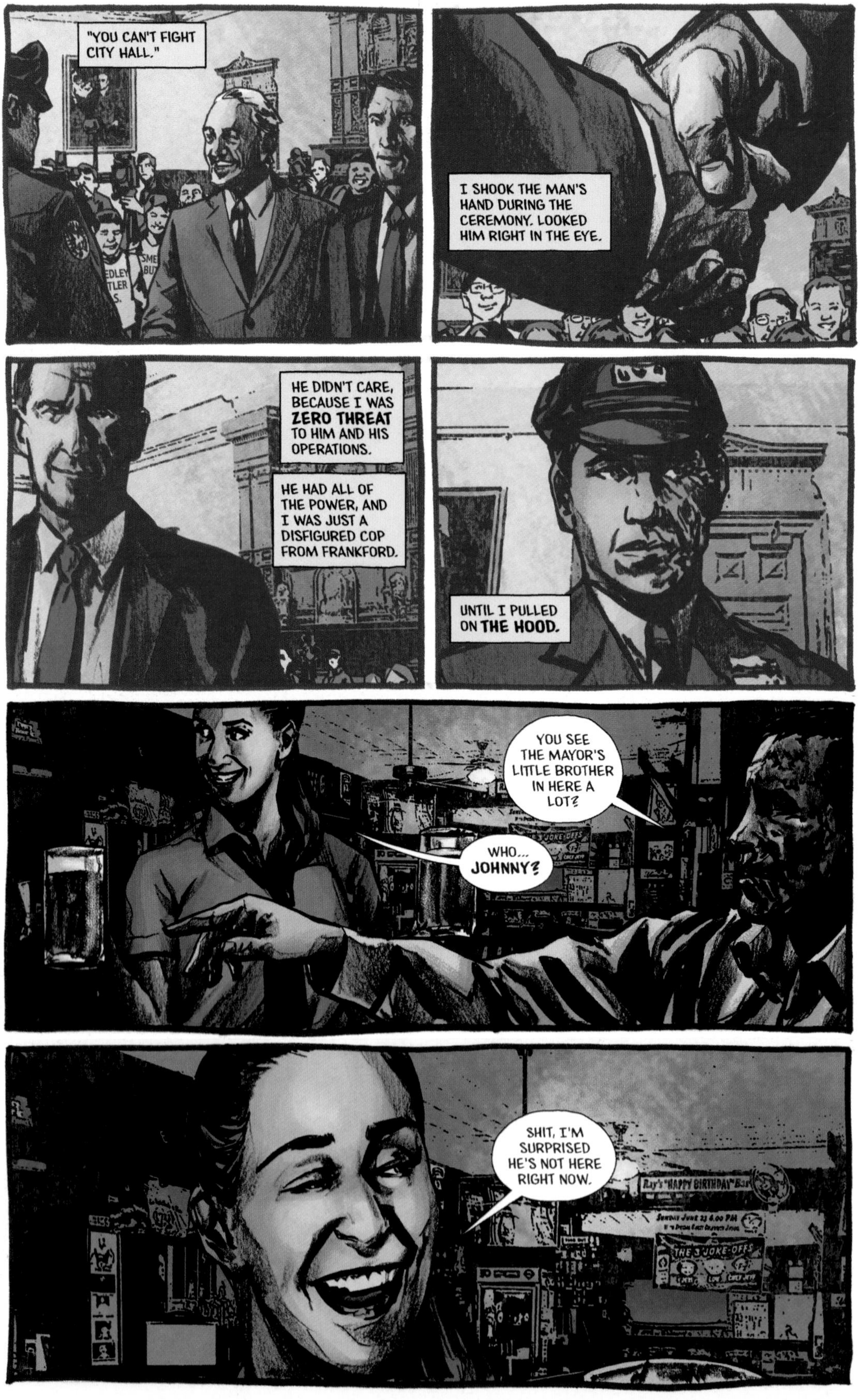
"YOU CAN'T FIGHT CITY HALL."
I SHOOK THE MAN'S HAND DURING THE CEREMONY. LOOKED HIM RIGHT IN THE EYE.
HE DIDN'T CARE, BECAUSE I WAS ZERO THREAT TO HIM AND HIS OPERATIONS.
HE HAD ALL OF THE POWER, AND I WAS JUST A DISFIGURED COP FROM FRANKFORD.
UNTIL I PULLED ON THE HOOD.
YOU SEE THE MAYOR'S LITTLE BROTHER IN HERE A LOT?
WHO... JOHNNY?
SHIT, I'M SURPRISED HE'S NOT HERE RIGHT NOW.
Ray's "HAPPY BIRTHDAY" Bar
THE 3 JOKE-OFFS

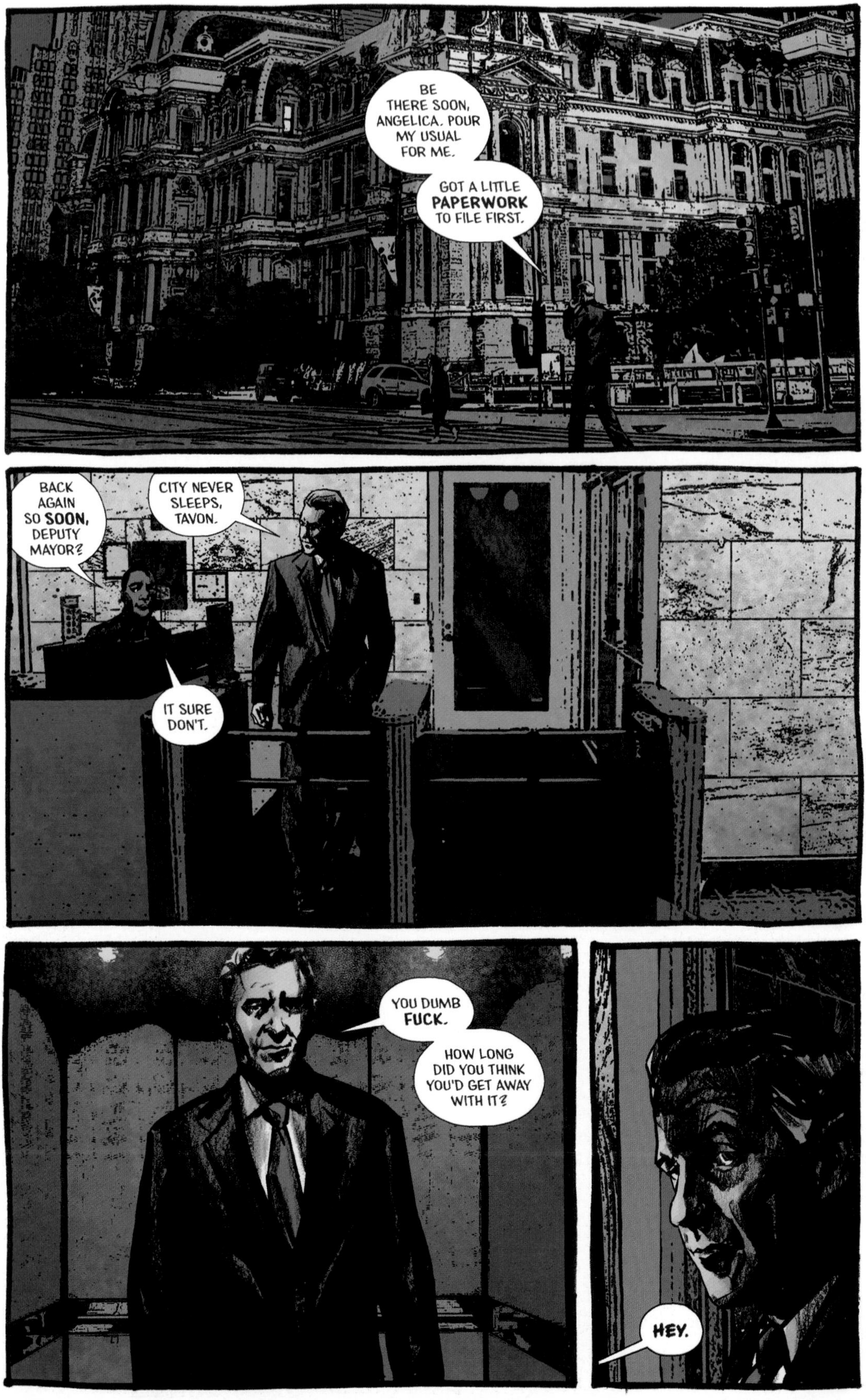
BE THERE SOON, ANGELICA. POUR MY USUAL FOR ME.
GOT A LITTLE **PAPERWORK** TO FILE FIRST.
BACK AGAIN SO **SOON,** DEPUTY MAYOR?
CITY NEVER SLEEPS, TAVON.
IT SURE DON'T.
YOU DUMB **FUCK.**
HOW LONG DID YOU THINK YOU'D GET AWAY WITH IT?
HEY.

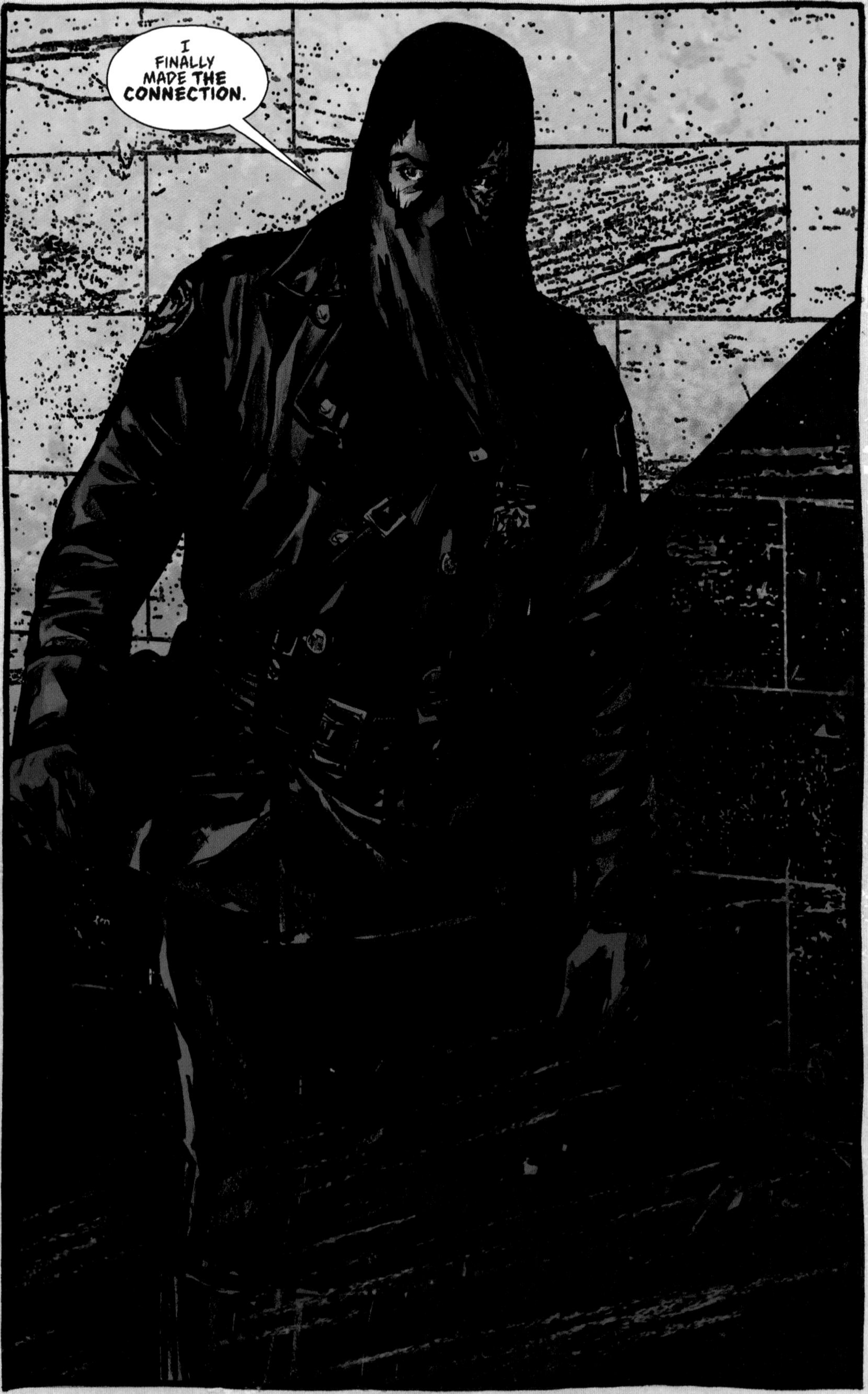
I FINALLY MADE THE CONNECTION.

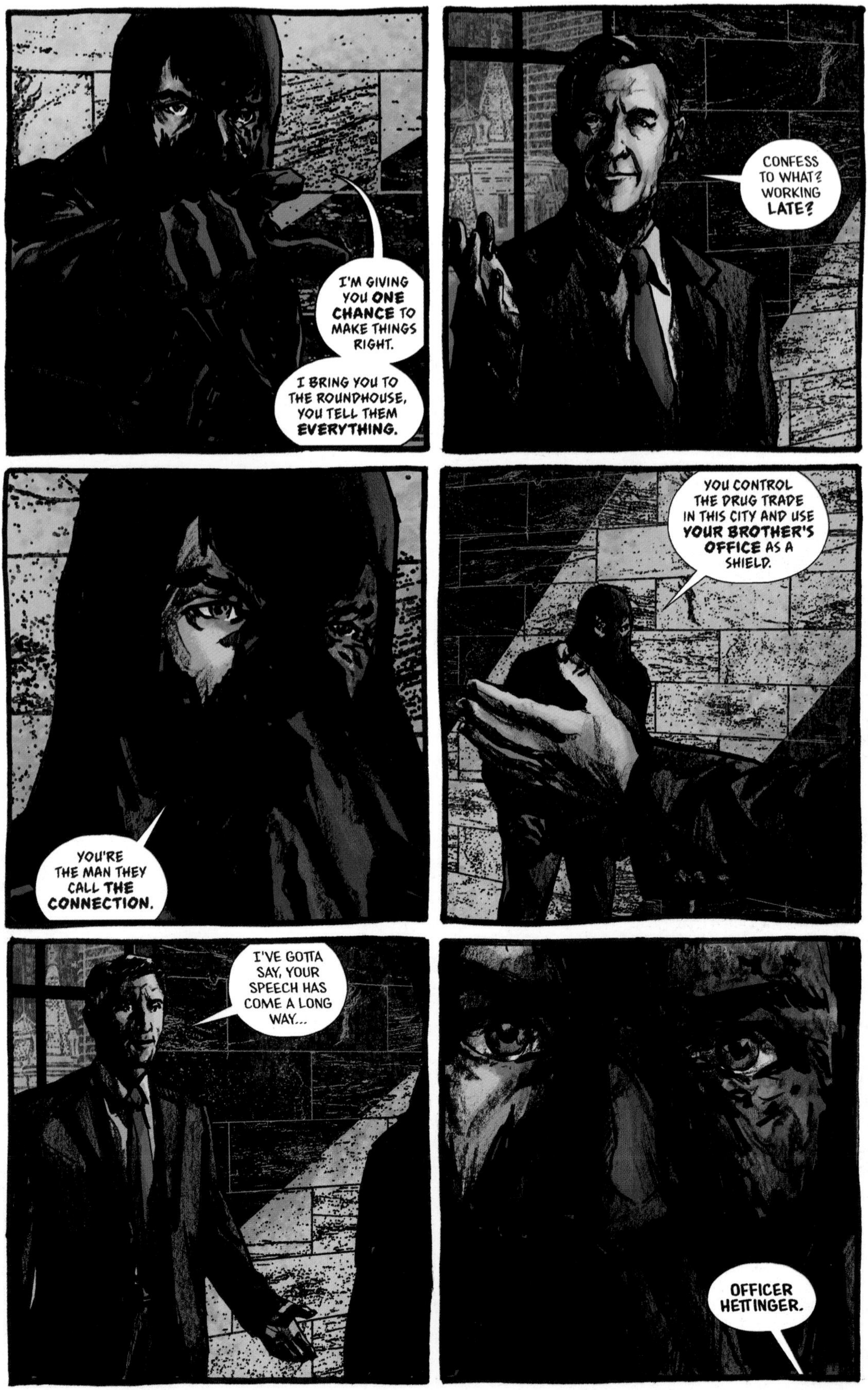
I'M GIVING YOU ONE CHANCE TO MAKE THINGS RIGHT.
I BRING YOU TO THE ROUNDHOUSE, YOU TELL THEM EVERYTHING.
CONFESS TO WHAT? WORKING LATE?
YOU'RE THE MAN THEY CALL THE CONNECTION.
YOU CONTROL THE DRUG TRADE IN THIS CITY AND USE YOUR BROTHER'S OFFICE AS A SHIELD.
I'VE GOTTA SAY, YOUR SPEECH HAS COME A LONG WAY...
OFFICER HETTINGER.

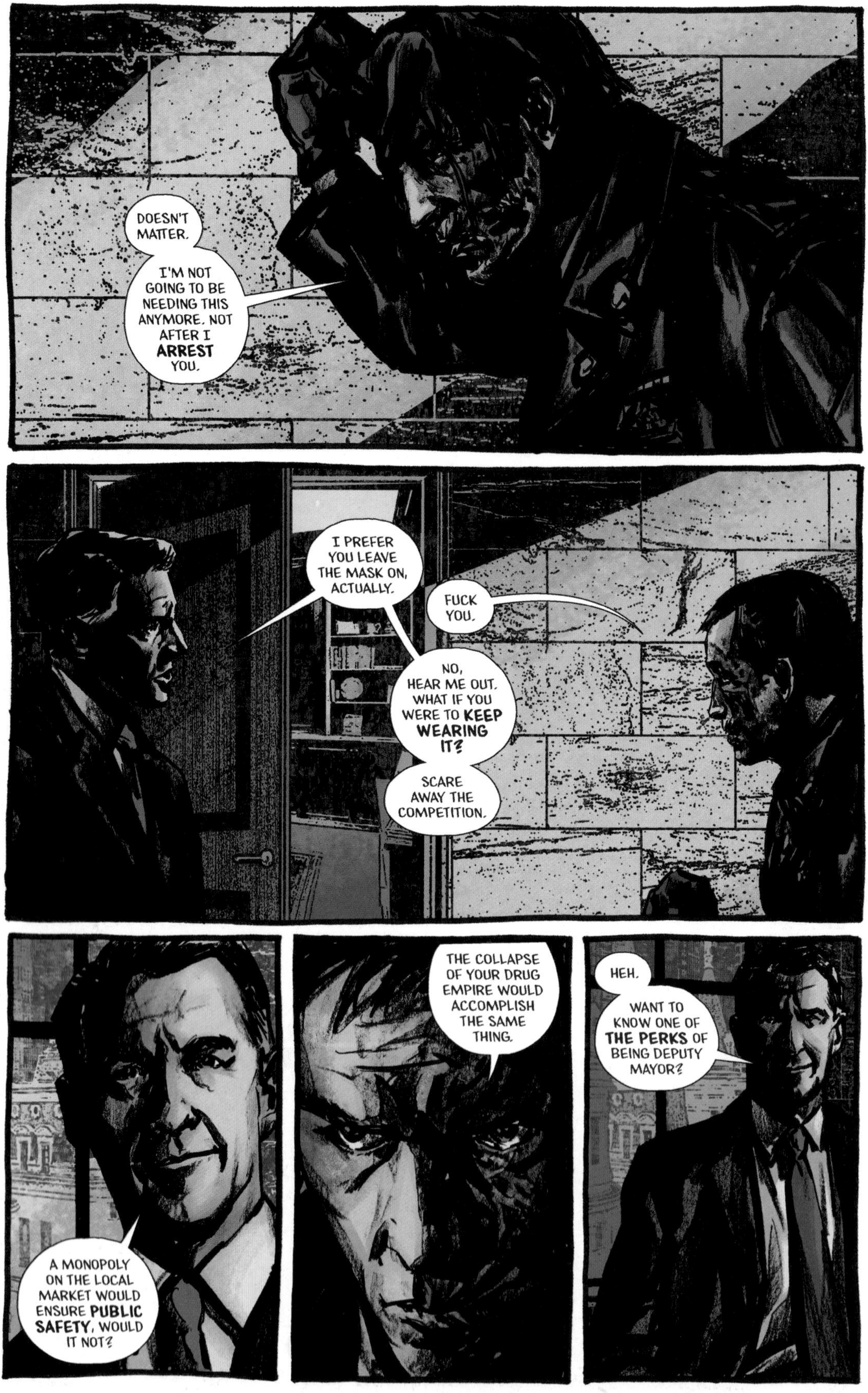
DOESN'T MATTER.
I'M NOT GOING TO BE NEEDING THIS ANYMORE. NOT AFTER I **ARREST** YOU.
I PREFER YOU LEAVE THE MASK ON, ACTUALLY.
FUCK YOU.
NO, HEAR ME OUT. WHAT IF YOU WERE TO **KEEP WEARING IT?**
SCARE AWAY THE COMPETITION.
A MONOPOLY ON THE LOCAL MARKET WOULD ENSURE **PUBLIC SAFETY**, WOULD IT NOT?
THE COLLAPSE OF YOUR DRUG EMPIRE WOULD ACCOMPLISH THE SAME THING.
HEH.
WANT TO KNOW ONE OF **THE PERKS** OF BEING DEPUTY MAYOR?

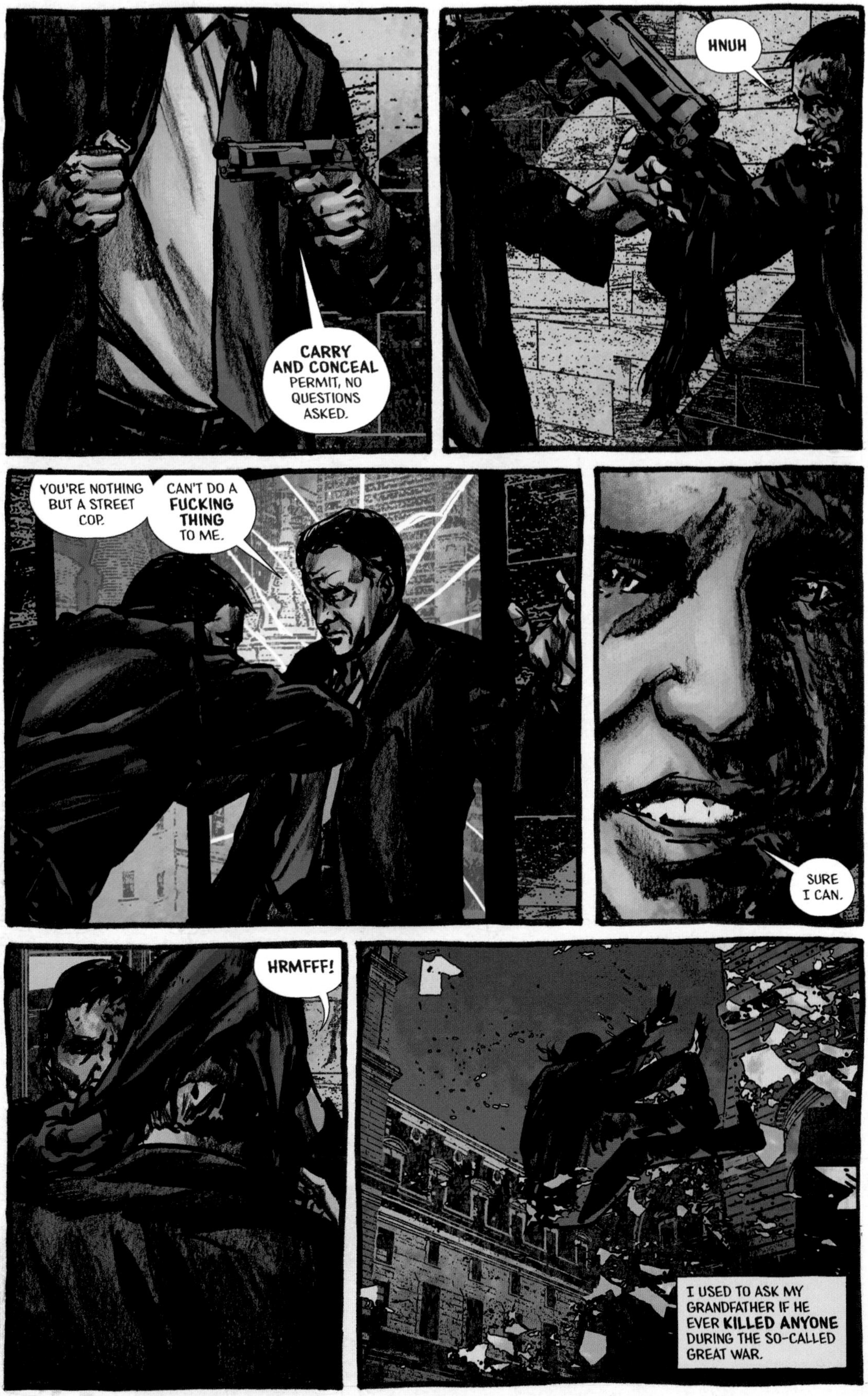
CARRY AND CONCEAL PERMIT, NO QUESTIONS ASKED.
HNUH
YOU'RE NOTHING BUT A STREET COP.
CAN'T DO A FUCKING THING TO ME.
SURE I CAN.
HRMFFF!
I USED TO ASK MY GRANDFATHER IF HE EVER KILLED ANYONE DURING THE SO-CALLED GREAT WAR.

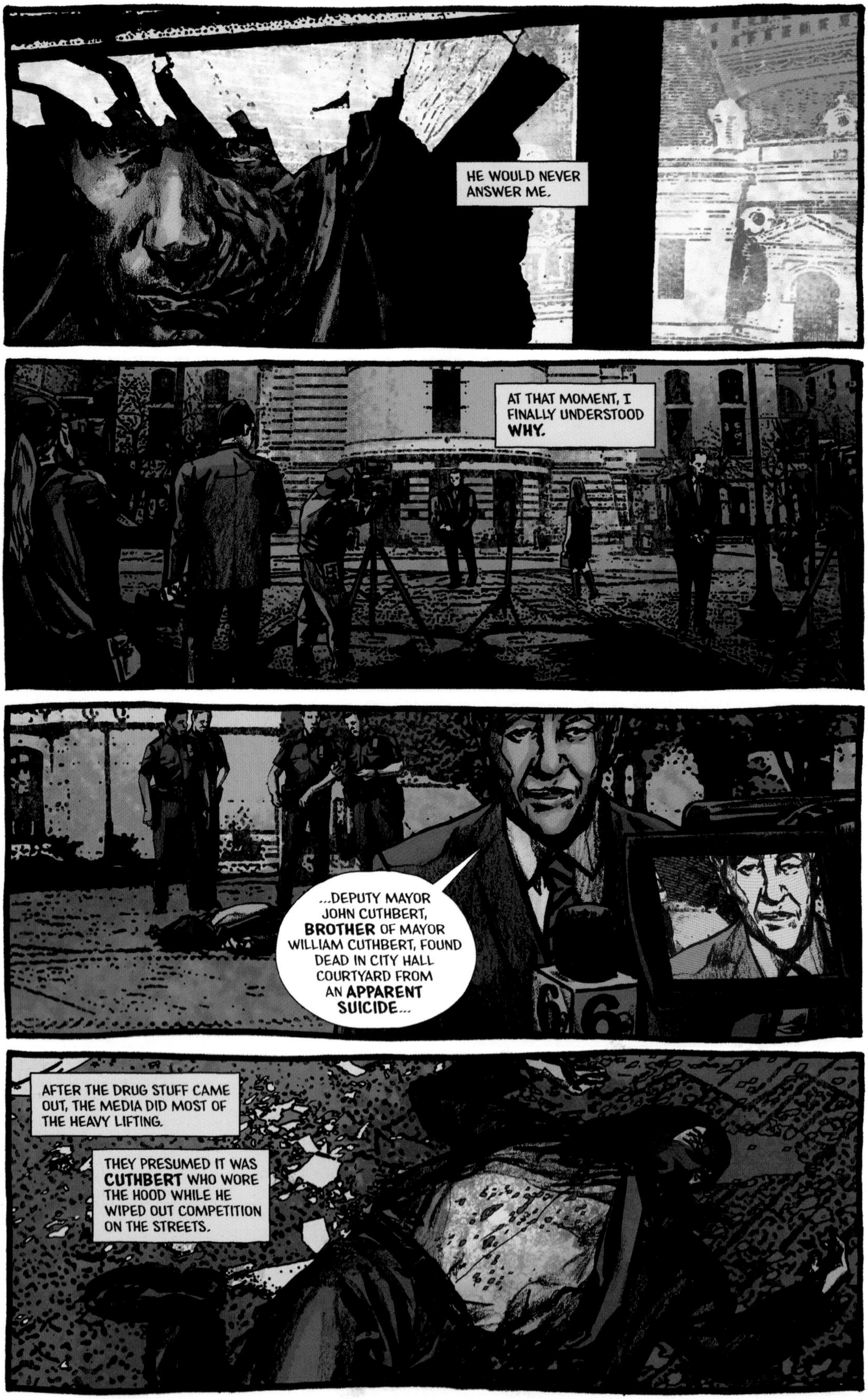
HE WOULD NEVER ANSWER ME.
AT THAT MOMENT, I FINALLY UNDERSTOOD **WHY.**
...DEPUTY MAYOR JOHN CUTHBERT, **BROTHER** OF MAYOR WILLIAM CUTHBERT, FOUND DEAD IN CITY HALL COURTYARD FROM AN **APPARENT SUICIDE**...
AFTER THE DRUG STUFF CAME OUT, THE MEDIA DID MOST OF THE HEAVY LIFTING.
THEY PRESUMED IT WAS **CUTHBERT** WHO WORE THE HOOD WHILE HE WIPED OUT COMPETITION ON THE STREETS.

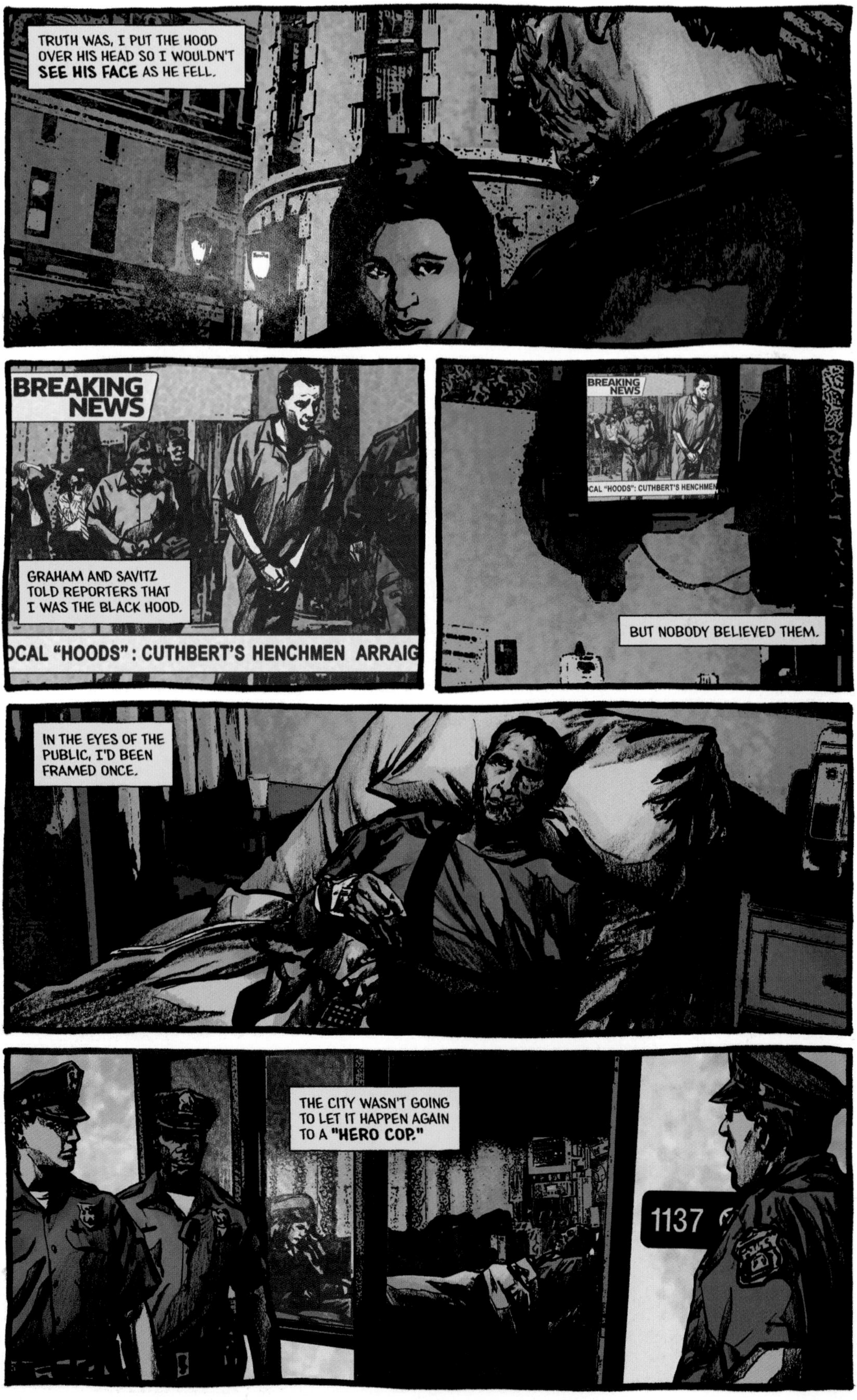
TRUTH WAS, I PUT THE HOOD OVER HIS HEAD SO I WOULDN'T **SEE HIS FACE** AS HE FELL.
BREAKING NEWS
GRAHAM AND SAVITZ TOLD REPORTERS THAT I WAS THE BLACK HOOD.
OCAL "HOODS": CUTHBERT'S HENCHMEN ARRAIG
BREAKING NEWS
OCAL "HOODS": CUTHBERT'S HENCHMEN
BUT NOBODY BELIEVED THEM.
IN THE EYES OF THE PUBLIC, I'D BEEN FRAMED ONCE.
THE CITY WASN'T GOING TO LET IT HAPPEN AGAIN TO A **"HERO COP."**
1137

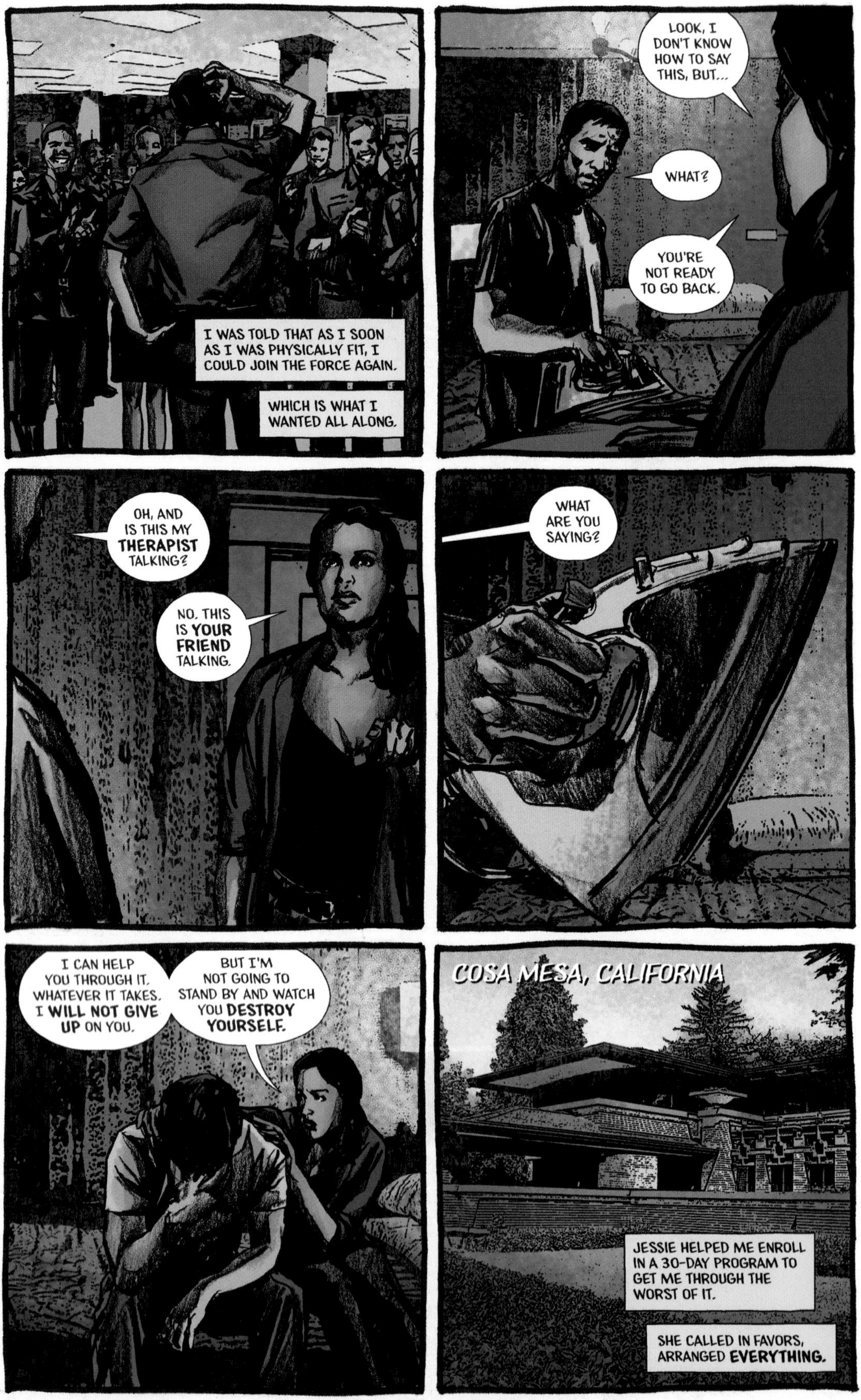
I WAS TOLD THAT AS I SOON AS I WAS PHYSICALLY FIT, I COULD JOIN THE FORCE AGAIN.
WHICH IS WHAT I WANTED ALL ALONG.
LOOK, I DON'T KNOW HOW TO SAY THIS, BUT...
WHAT?
YOU'RE NOT READY TO GO BACK.
OH, AND IS THIS MY **THERAPIST** TALKING?
NO. THIS IS **YOUR FRIEND** TALKING.
WHAT ARE YOU SAYING?
I CAN HELP YOU THROUGH IT. WHATEVER IT TAKES. I **WILL NOT GIVE UP** ON YOU.
BUT I'M NOT GOING TO STAND BY AND WATCH YOU **DESTROY YOURSELF.**
COSA MESA, CALIFORNIA
JESSIE HELPED ME ENROLL IN A 30-DAY PROGRAM TO GET ME THROUGH THE WORST OF IT.
SHE CALLED IN FAVORS, ARRANGED **EVERYTHING.**

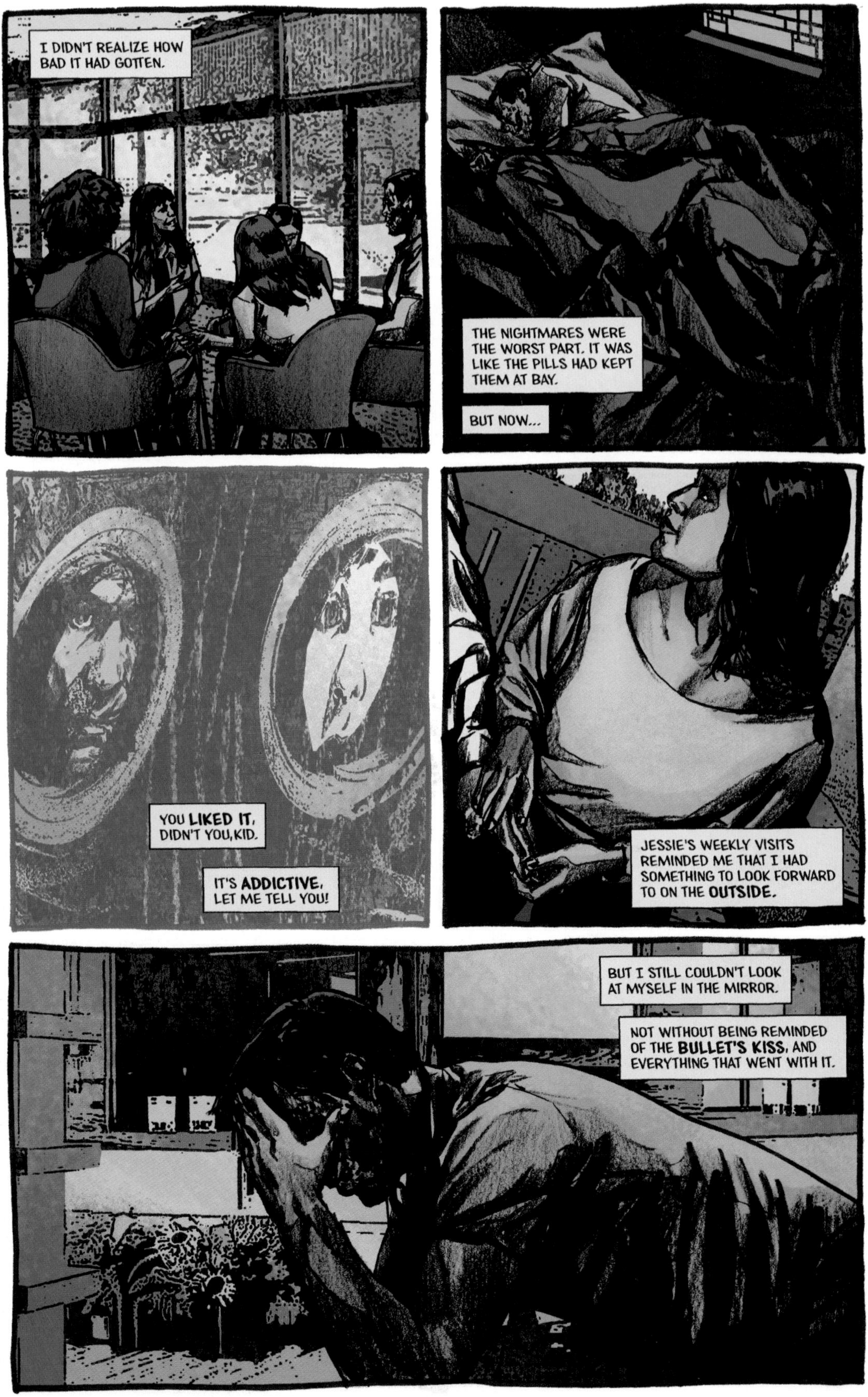
I DIDN'T REALIZE HOW BAD IT HAD GOTTEN.
THE NIGHTMARES WERE THE WORST PART. IT WAS LIKE THE PILLS HAD KEPT THEM AT BAY.
BUT NOW...
YOU LIKED IT, DIDN'T YOU, KID.
IT'S ADDICTIVE, LET ME TELL YOU!
JESSIE'S WEEKLY VISITS REMINDED ME THAT I HAD SOMETHING TO LOOK FORWARD TO ON THE OUTSIDE.
BUT I STILL COULDN'T LOOK AT MYSELF IN THE MIRROR.
NOT WITHOUT BEING REMINDED OF THE BULLET'S KISS, AND EVERYTHING THAT WENT WITH IT.

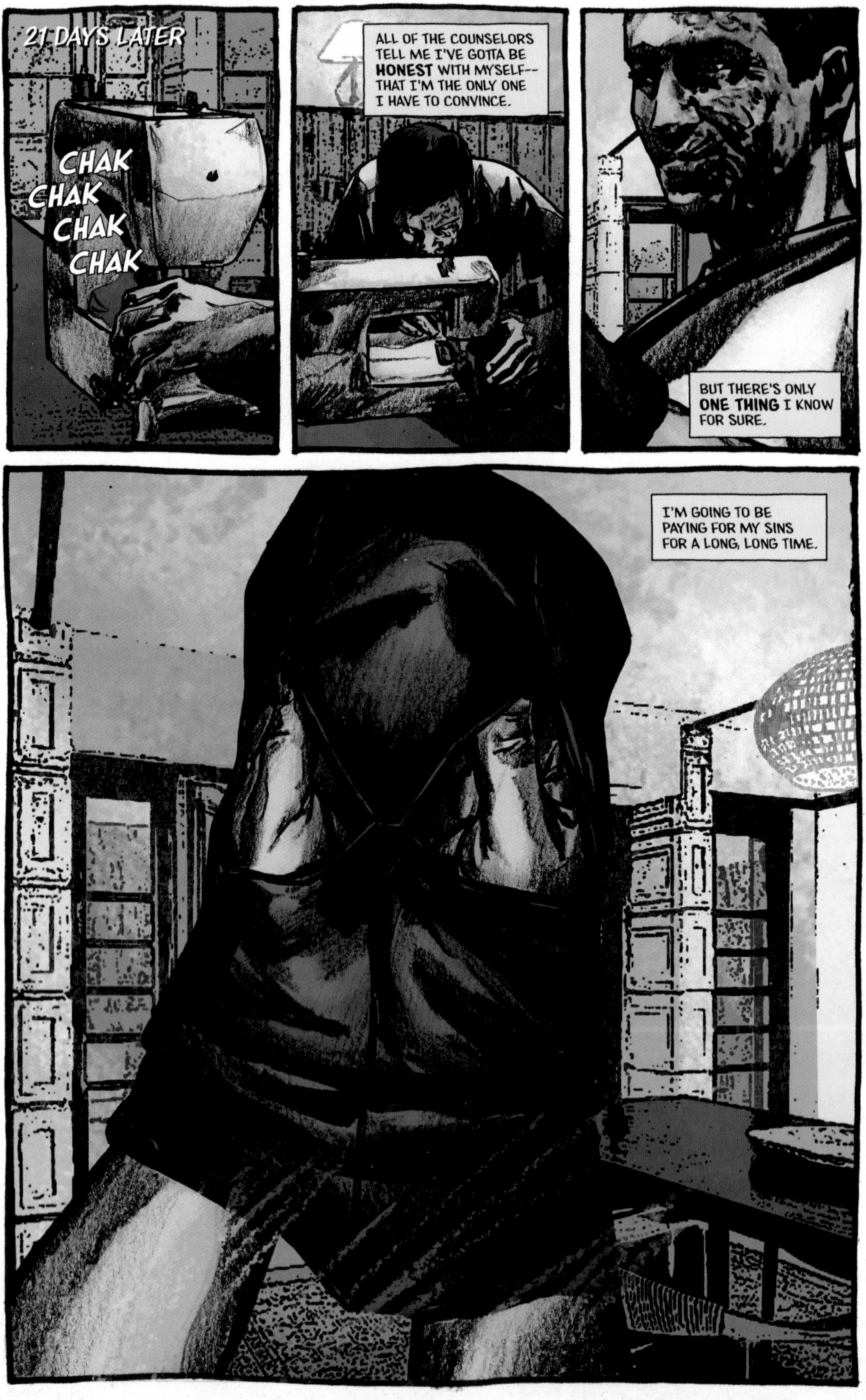
21 DAYS LATER
CHAK
CHAK
CHAK
CHAK
ALL OF THE COUNSELORS TELL ME I'VE GOTTA BE **HONEST** WITH MYSELF-- THAT I'M THE ONLY ONE I HAVE TO CONVINCE.
BUT THERE'S ONLY **ONE THING** I KNOW FOR SURE.
I'M GOING TO BE PAYING FOR MY SINS FOR A LONG, LONG TIME.

ISSUE SIX

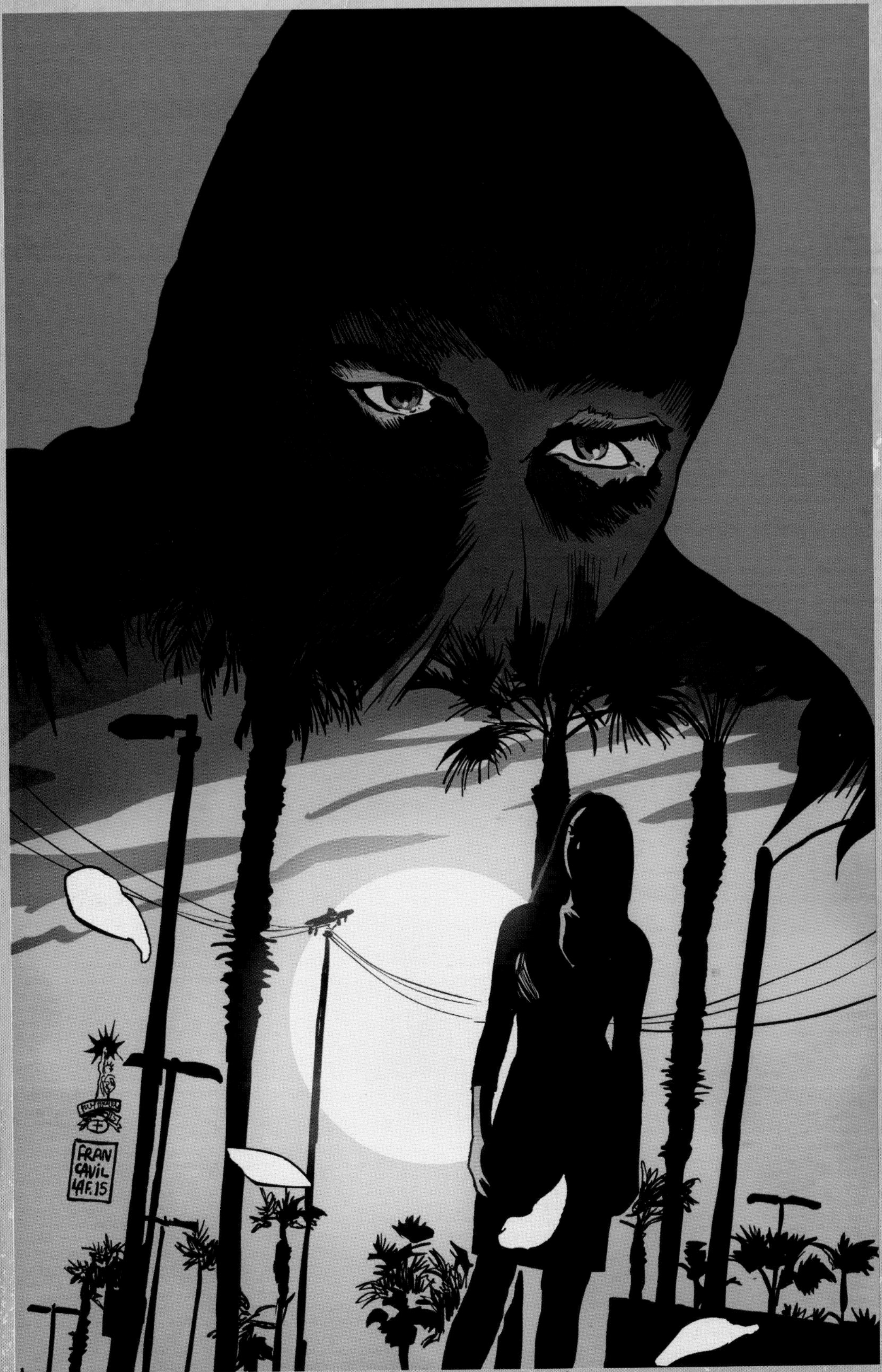
FRAN CAVIL 14F.15

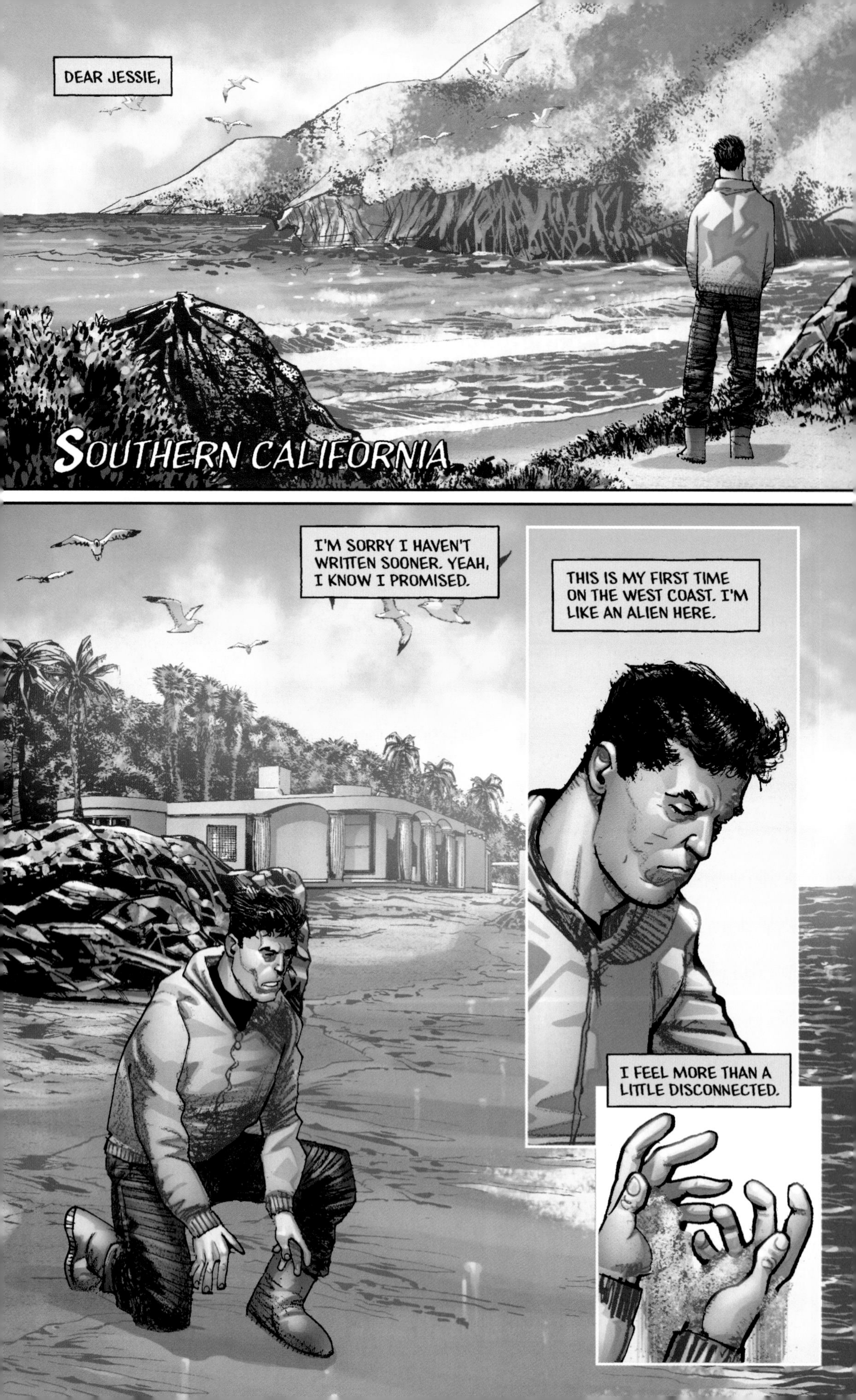
DEAR JESSIE,
SOUTHERN CALIFORNIA
I'M SORRY I HAVEN'T WRITTEN SOONER. YEAH, I KNOW I PROMISED.
THIS IS MY FIRST TIME ON THE WEST COAST. I'M LIKE AN ALIEN HERE.
I FEEL MORE THAN A LITTLE DISCONNECTED.

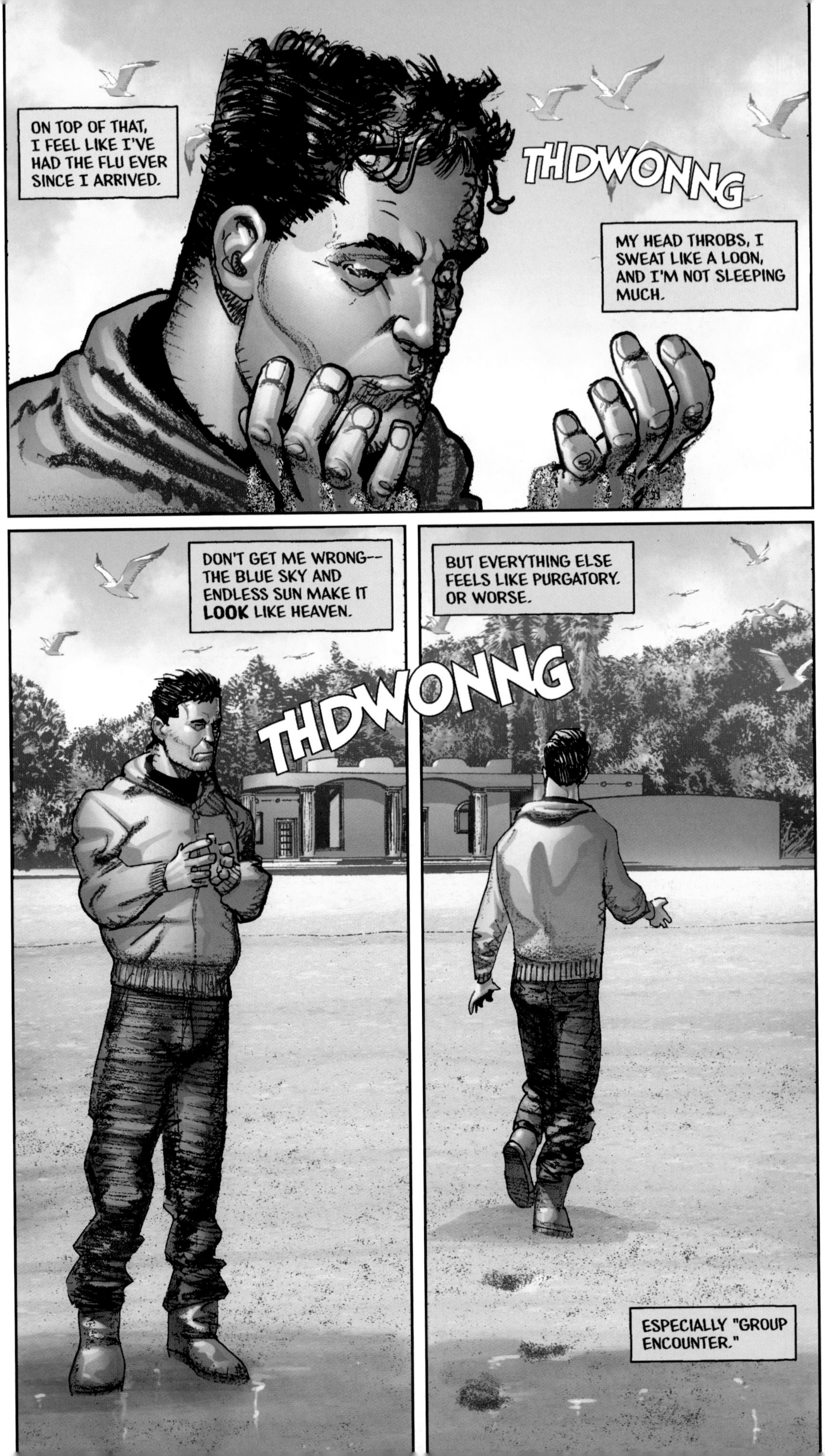
ON TOP OF THAT, I FEEL LIKE I'VE HAD THE FLU EVER SINCE I ARRIVED.
THDWONNG
MY HEAD THROBS, I SWEAT LIKE A LOON, AND I'M NOT SLEEPING MUCH.
DON'T GET ME WRONG-- THE BLUE SKY AND ENDLESS SUN MAKE IT LOOK LIKE HEAVEN.
BUT EVERYTHING ELSE FEELS LIKE PURGATORY. OR WORSE.
THDWONNG
ESPECIALLY "GROUP ENCOUNTER."

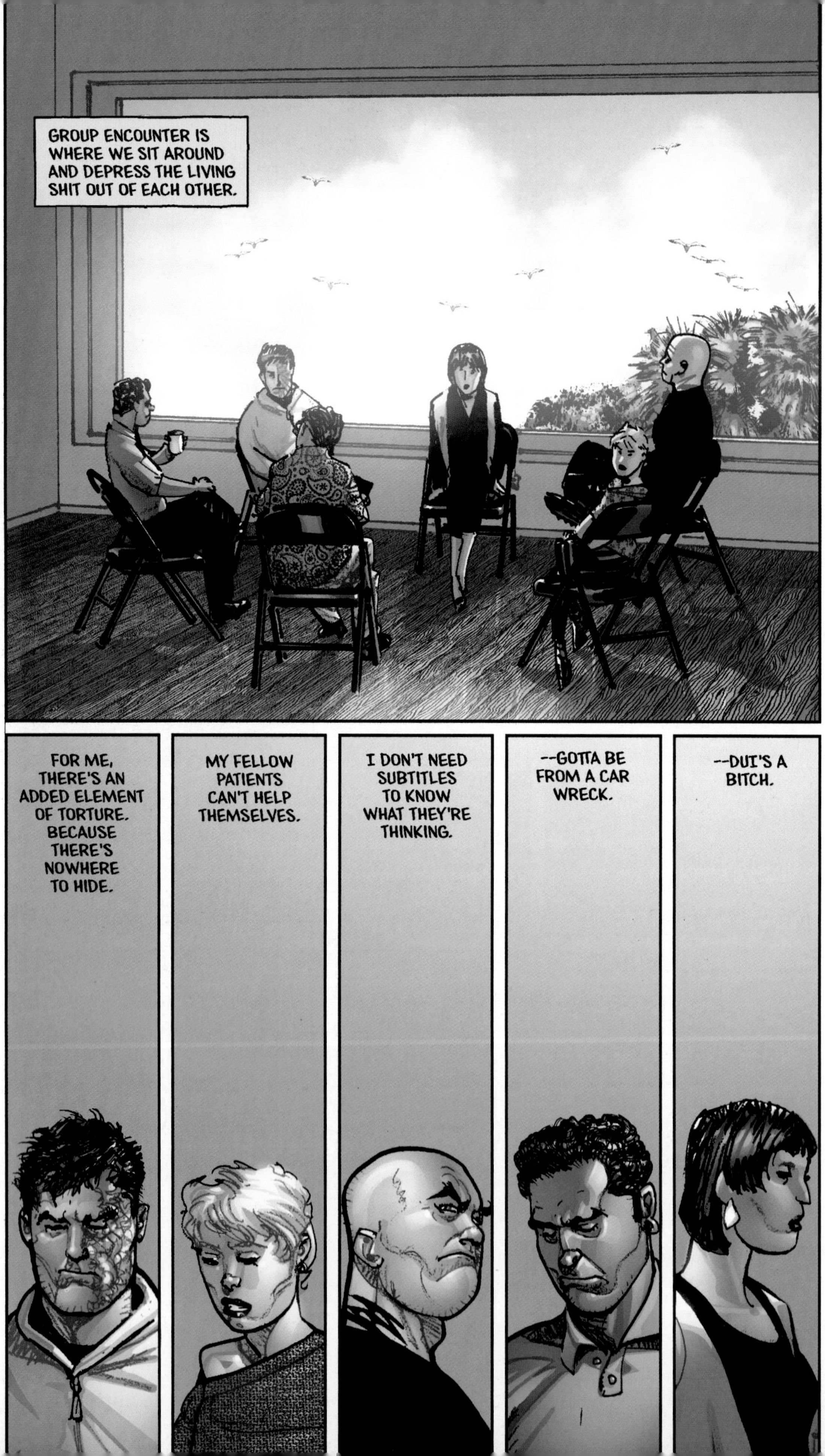
GROUP ENCOUNTER IS WHERE WE SIT AROUND AND DEPRESS THE LIVING SHIT OUT OF EACH OTHER.
FOR ME, THERE'S AN ADDED ELEMENT OF TORTURE. BECAUSE THERE'S NOWHERE TO HIDE.
MY FELLOW PATIENTS CAN'T HELP THEMSELVES.
I DON'T NEED SUBTITLES TO KNOW WHAT THEY'RE THINKING.
--GOTTA BE FROM A CAR WRECK.
--DUI'S A BITCH.

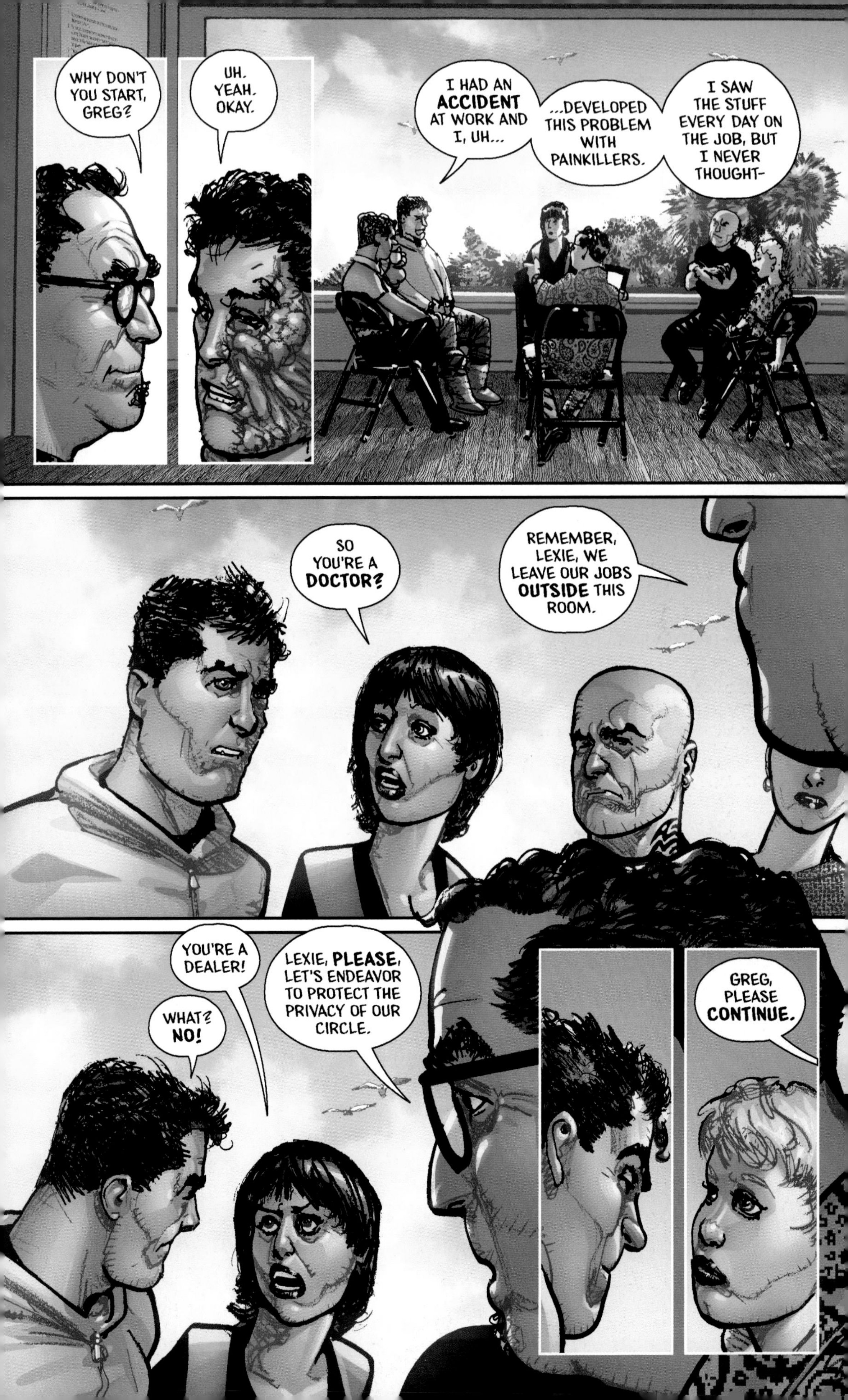
WHY DON'T YOU START, GREG?
UH. YEAH. OKAY.
I HAD AN ACCIDENT AT WORK AND I, UH...
...DEVELOPED THIS PROBLEM WITH PAINKILLERS.
I SAW THE STUFF EVERY DAY ON THE JOB, BUT I NEVER THOUGHT-
SO YOU'RE A DOCTOR?
REMEMBER, LEXIE, WE LEAVE OUR JOBS OUTSIDE THIS ROOM.
YOU'RE A DEALER!
WHAT? NO!
LEXIE, PLEASE, LET'S ENDEAVOR TO PROTECT THE PRIVACY OF OUR CIRCLE.
GREG, PLEASE CONTINUE.

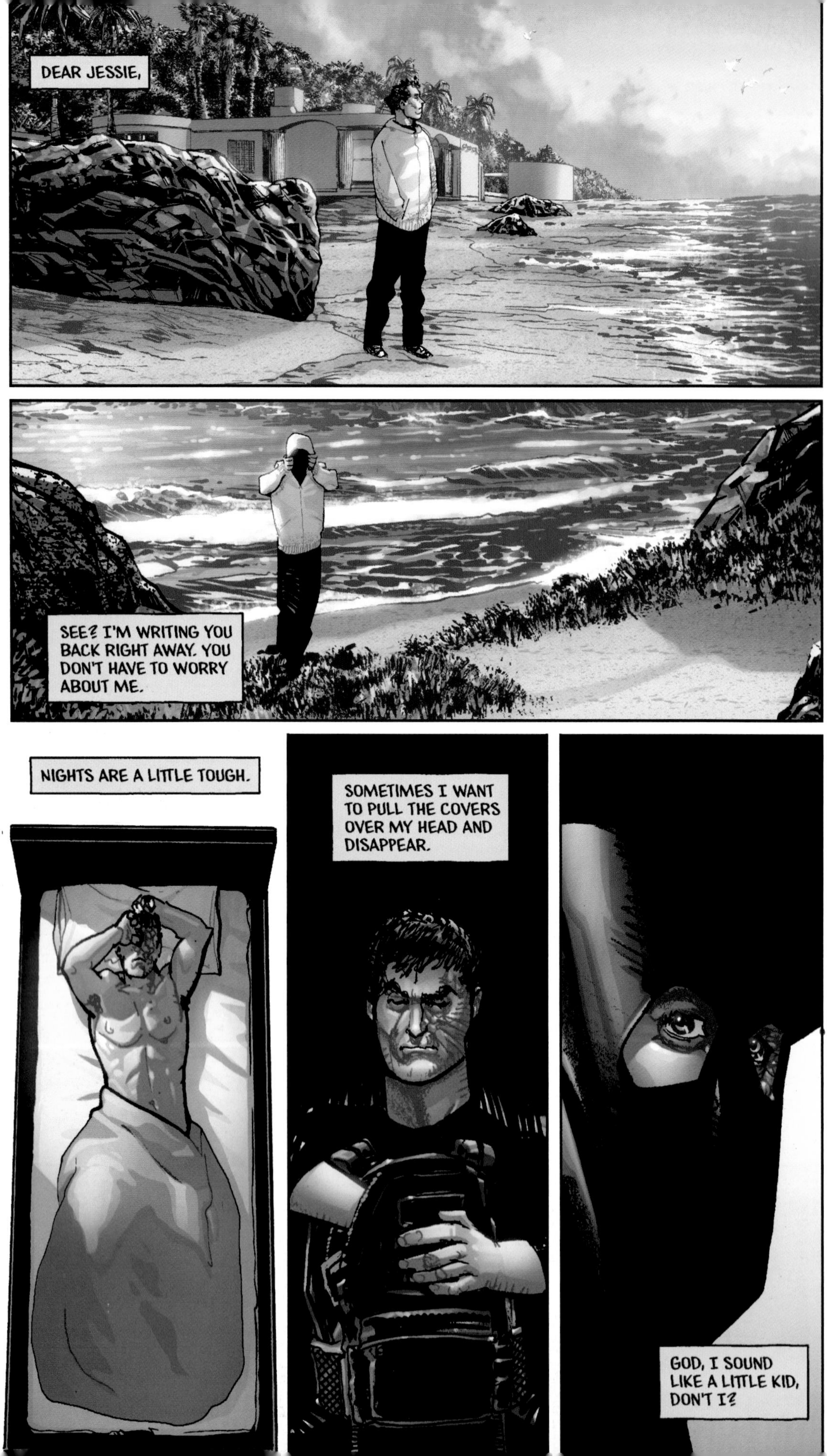
DEAR JESSIE,
SEE? I'M WRITING YOU BACK RIGHT AWAY. YOU DON'T HAVE TO WORRY ABOUT ME.
NIGHTS ARE A LITTLE TOUGH.
SOMETIMES I WANT TO PULL THE COVERS OVER MY HEAD AND DISAPPEAR.
GOD, I SOUND LIKE A LITTLE KID, DON'T I?

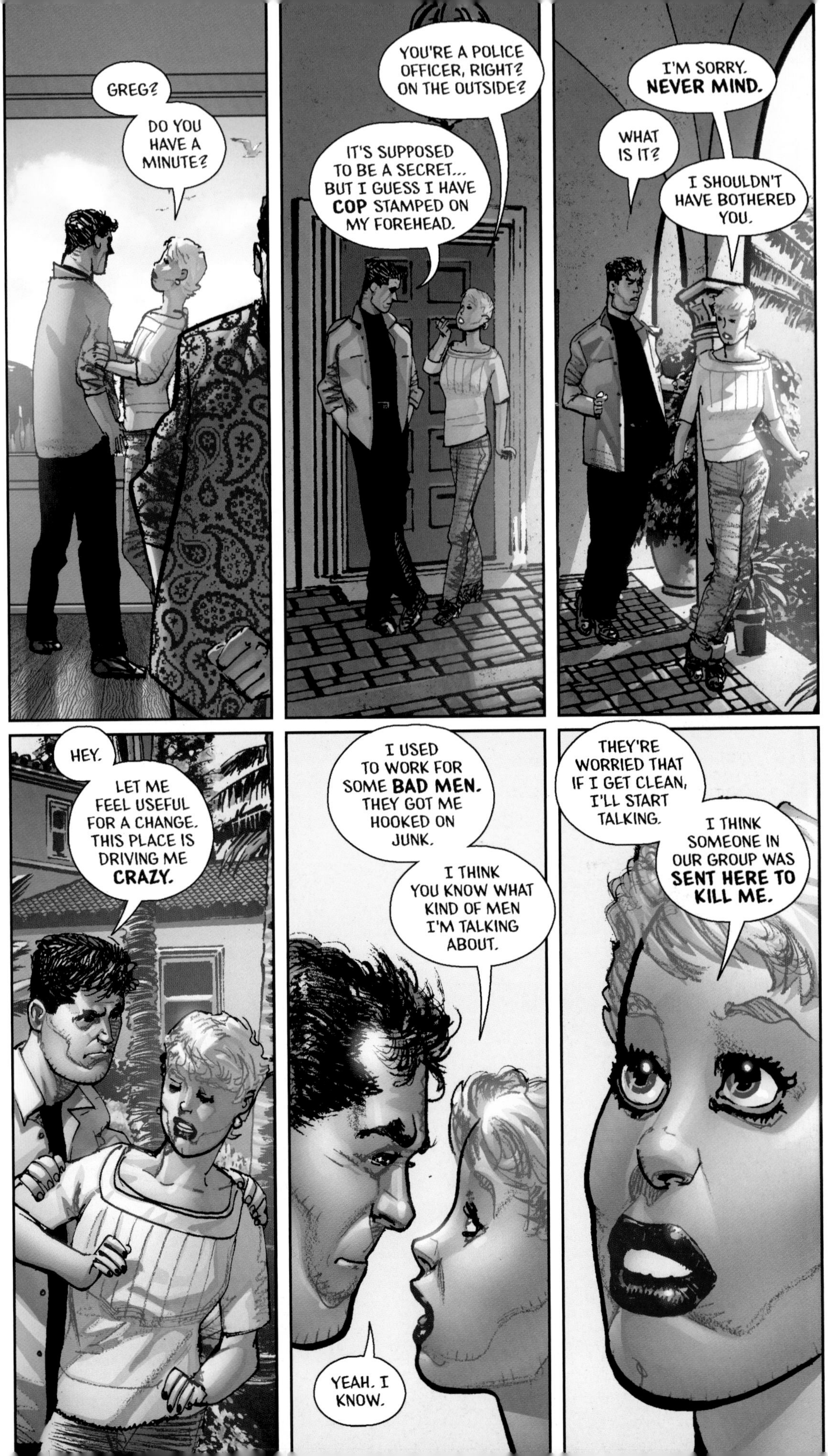
GREG?
DO YOU HAVE A MINUTE?
YOU'RE A POLICE OFFICER, RIGHT? ON THE OUTSIDE?
IT'S SUPPOSED TO BE A SECRET... BUT I GUESS I HAVE **COP** STAMPED ON MY FOREHEAD.
WHAT IS IT?
I'M SORRY. **NEVER MIND.**
I SHOULDN'T HAVE BOTHERED YOU.
HEY.
LET ME FEEL USEFUL FOR A CHANGE. THIS PLACE IS DRIVING ME **CRAZY.**
I USED TO WORK FOR SOME **BAD MEN.** THEY GOT ME HOOKED ON JUNK.
I THINK YOU KNOW WHAT KIND OF MEN I'M TALKING ABOUT.
YEAH. I KNOW.
THEY'RE WORRIED THAT IF I GET CLEAN, I'LL START TALKING.
I THINK SOMEONE IN OUR GROUP WAS **SENT HERE TO KILL ME.**

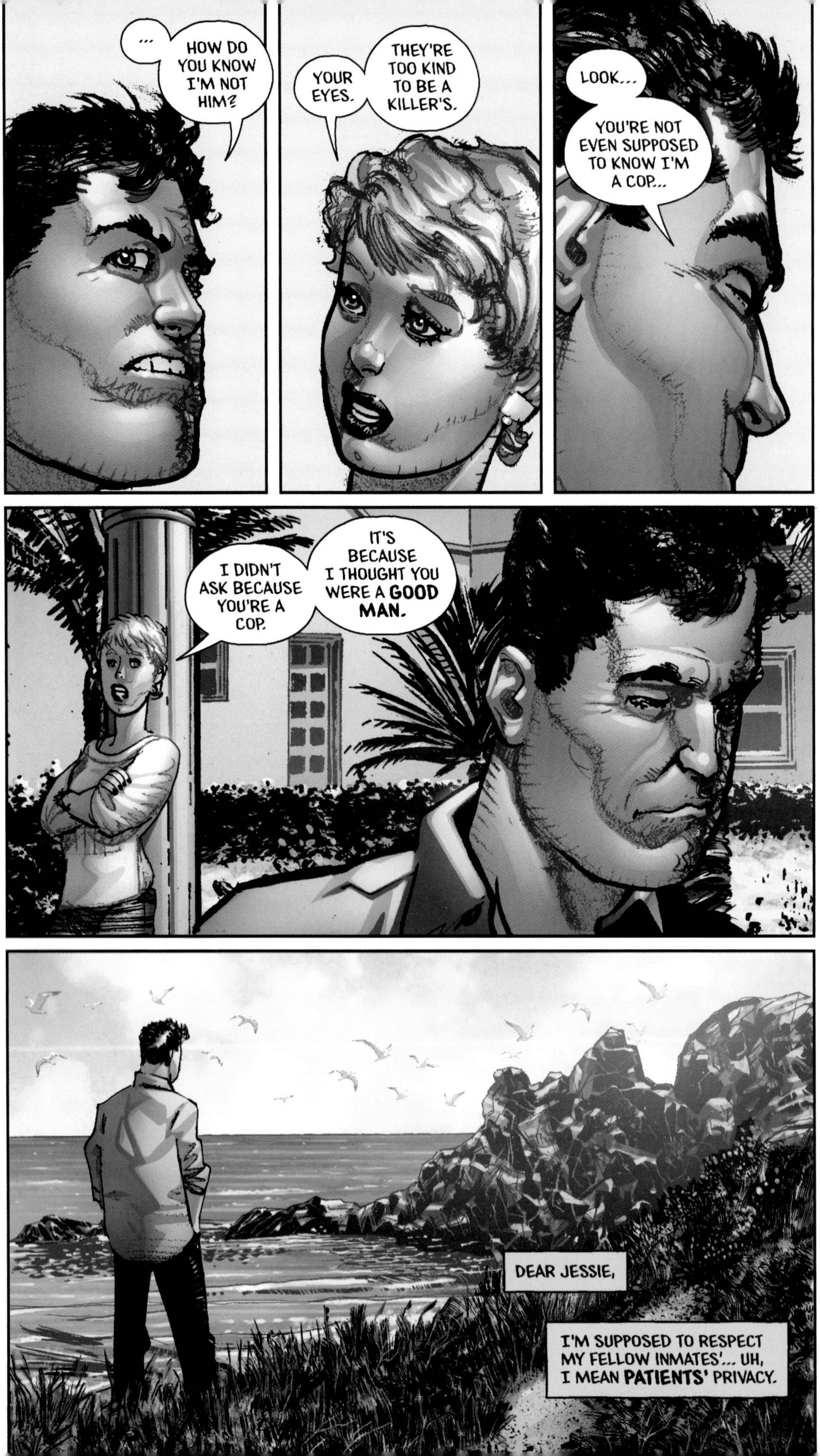
...
HOW DO YOU KNOW I'M NOT HIM?
YOUR EYES.
THEY'RE TOO KIND TO BE A KILLER'S.
LOOK...
YOU'RE NOT EVEN SUPPOSED TO KNOW I'M A COP...
I DIDN'T ASK BECAUSE YOU'RE A COP.
IT'S BECAUSE I THOUGHT YOU WERE A **GOOD MAN.**
DEAR JESSIE,
I'M SUPPOSED TO RESPECT MY FELLOW INMATES'... UH, I MEAN **PATIENTS'** PRIVACY.

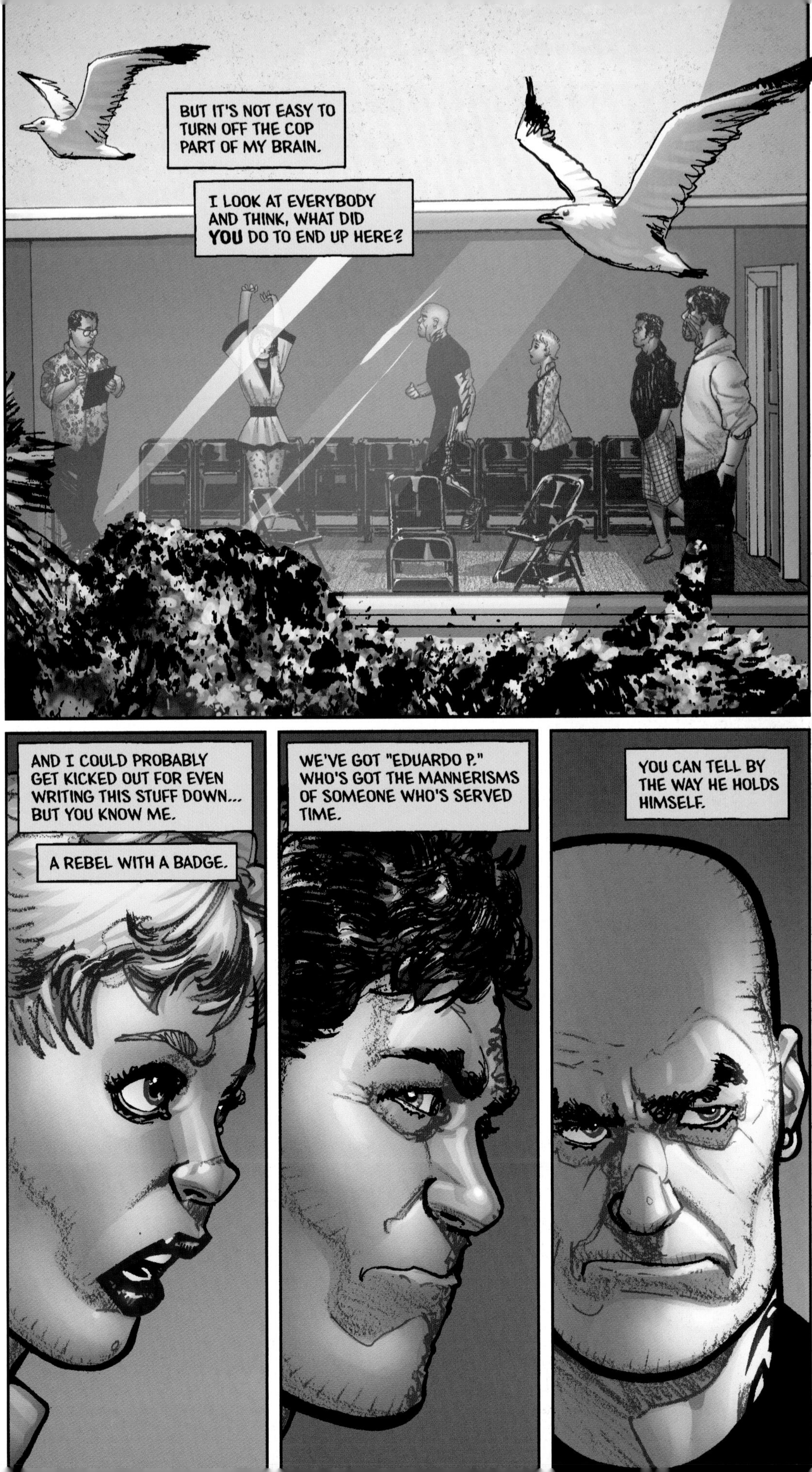
BUT IT'S NOT EASY TO TURN OFF THE COP PART OF MY BRAIN.
I LOOK AT EVERYBODY AND THINK, WHAT DID YOU DO TO END UP HERE?
AND I COULD PROBABLY GET KICKED OUT FOR EVEN WRITING THIS STUFF DOWN... BUT YOU KNOW ME.
A REBEL WITH A BADGE.
WE'VE GOT "EDUARDO P." WHO'S GOT THE MANNERISMS OF SOMEONE WHO'S SERVED TIME.
YOU CAN TELL BY THE WAY HE HOLDS HIMSELF.

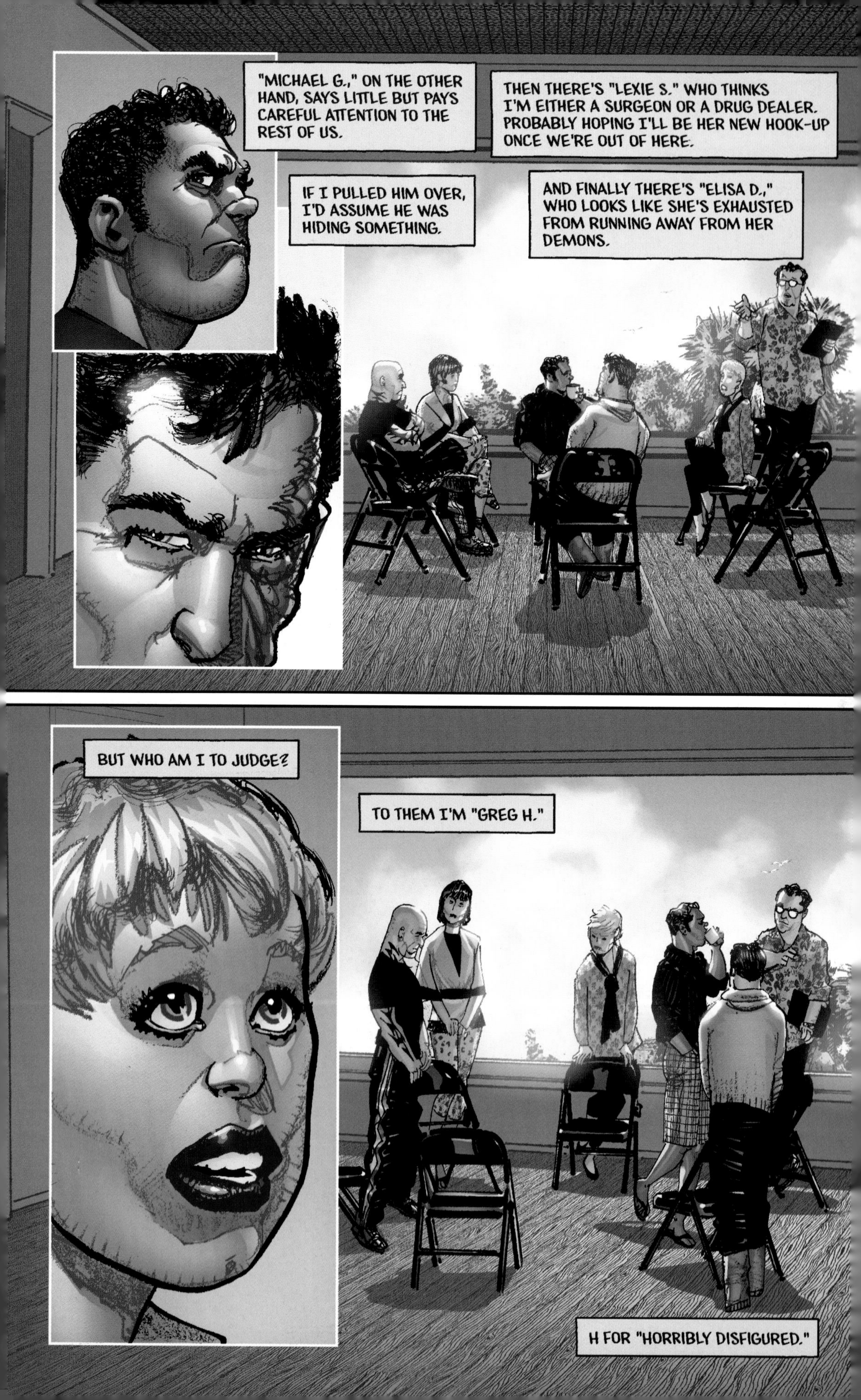
"MICHAEL G.," ON THE OTHER HAND, SAYS LITTLE BUT PAYS CAREFUL ATTENTION TO THE REST OF US.
IF I PULLED HIM OVER, I'D ASSUME HE WAS HIDING SOMETHING.
THEN THERE'S "LEXIE S." WHO THINKS I'M EITHER A SURGEON OR A DRUG DEALER. PROBABLY HOPING I'LL BE HER NEW HOOK-UP ONCE WE'RE OUT OF HERE.
AND FINALLY THERE'S "ELISA D.," WHO LOOKS LIKE SHE'S EXHAUSTED FROM RUNNING AWAY FROM HER DEMONS.
BUT WHO AM I TO JUDGE?
TO THEM I'M "GREG H."
H FOR "HORRIBLY DISFIGURED."

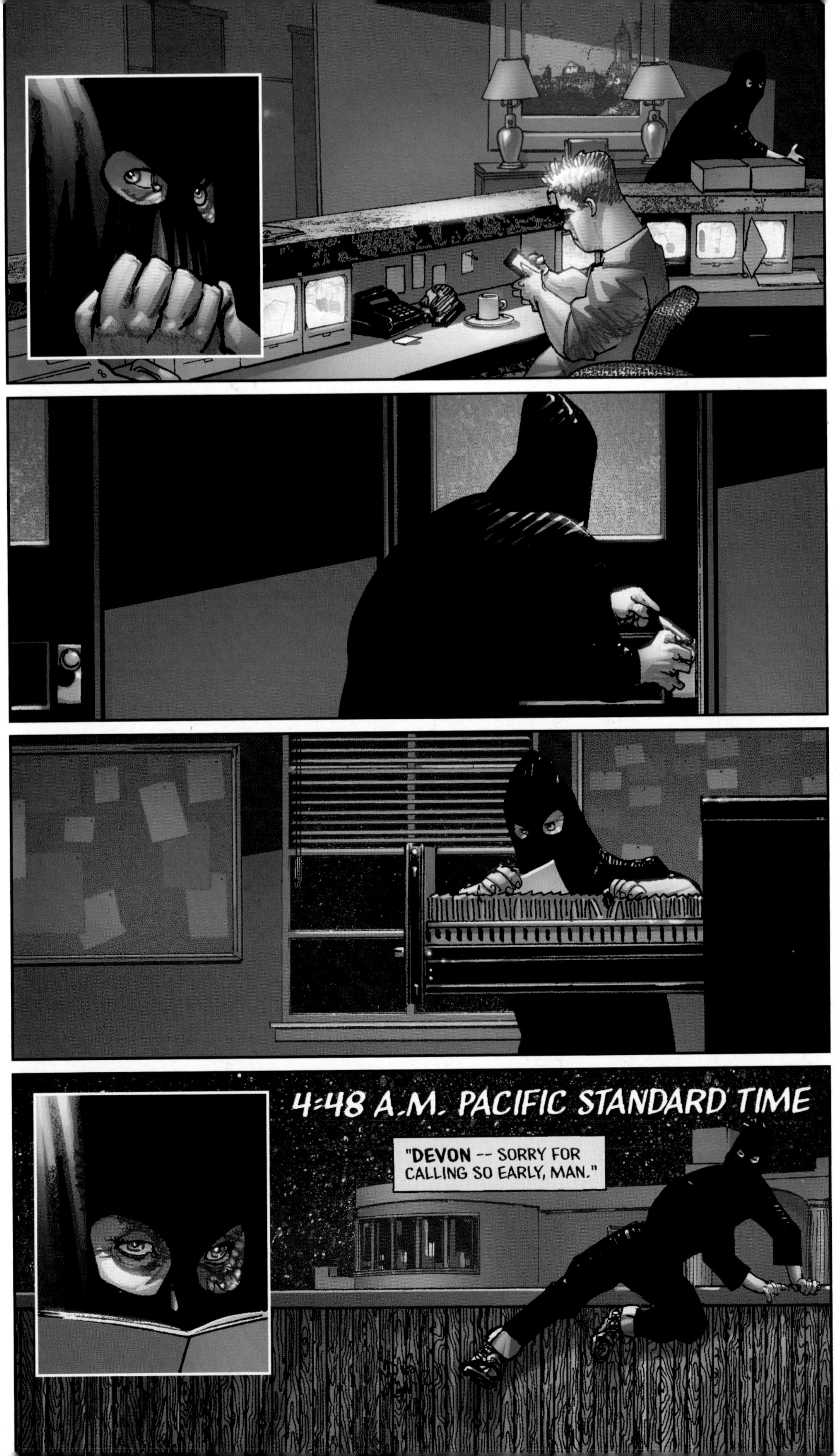
4:48 A.M. PACIFIC STANDARD TIME
"DEVON -- SORRY FOR CALLING SO EARLY, MAN."

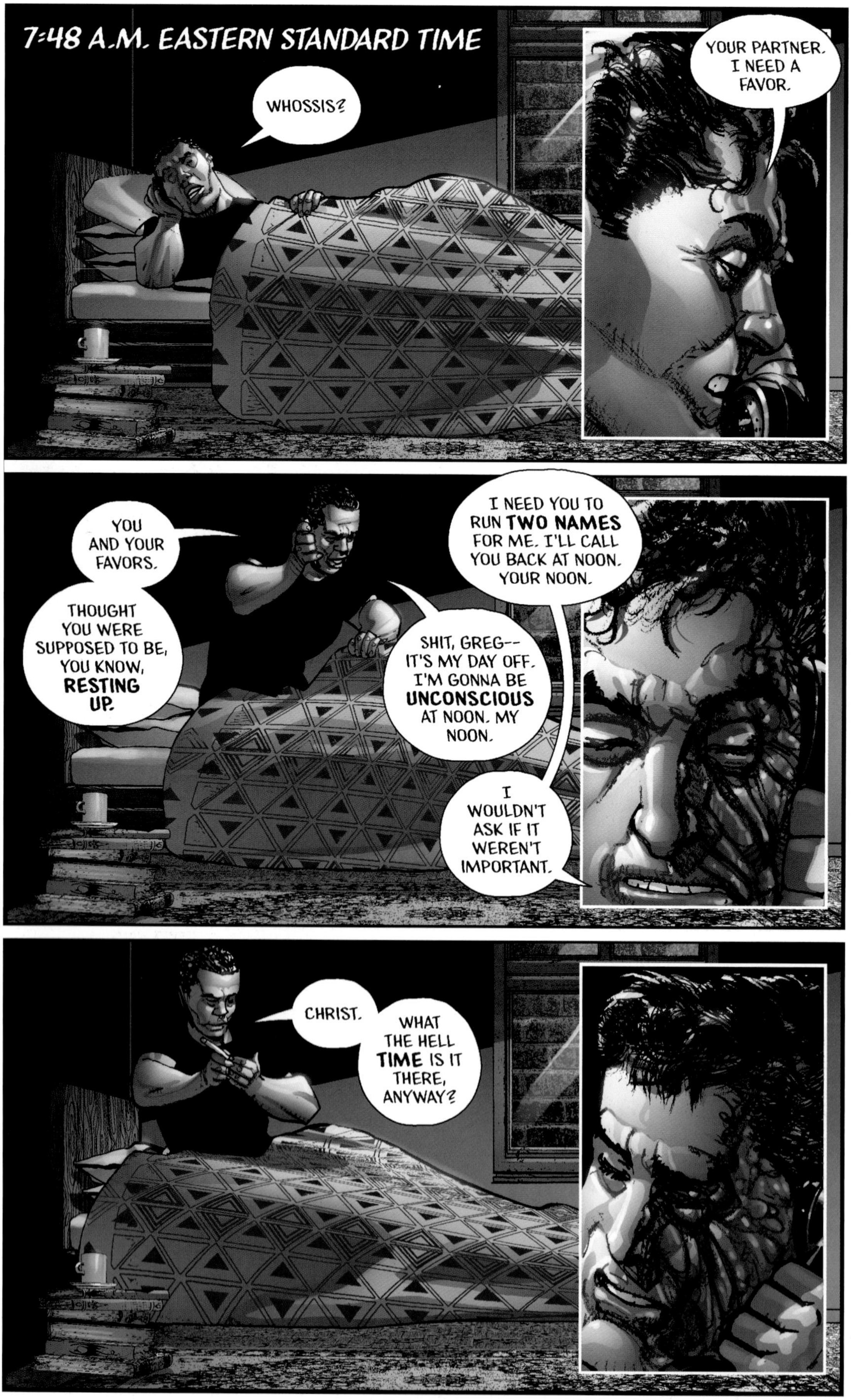
7:48 A.M. EASTERN STANDARD TIME
WHOSSIS?
YOUR PARTNER. I NEED A FAVOR.
YOU AND YOUR FAVORS.
THOUGHT YOU WERE SUPPOSED TO BE, YOU KNOW, **RESTING UP.**
I NEED YOU TO RUN **TWO NAMES** FOR ME. I'LL CALL YOU BACK AT NOON. YOUR NOON.
SHIT, GREG-- IT'S MY DAY OFF. I'M GONNA BE **UNCONSCIOUS** AT NOON. MY NOON.
I WOULDN'T ASK IF IT WEREN'T IMPORTANT.
CHRIST.
WHAT THE HELL **TIME** IS IT THERE, ANYWAY?

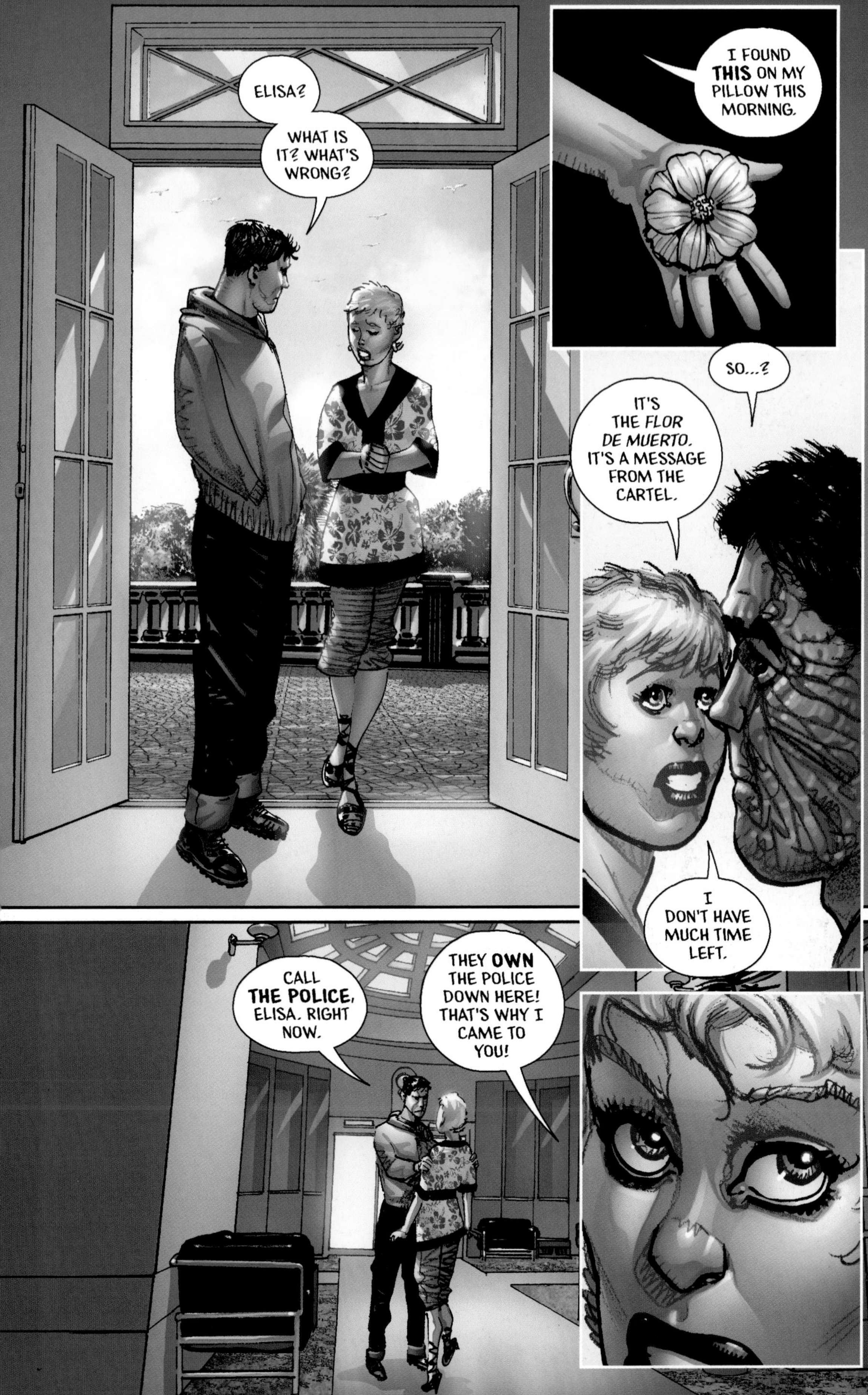
ELISA?
WHAT IS IT? WHAT'S WRONG?
I FOUND THIS ON MY PILLOW THIS MORNING.
SO...?
IT'S THE FLOR DE MUERTO. IT'S A MESSAGE FROM THE CARTEL.
I DON'T HAVE MUCH TIME LEFT.
CALL THE POLICE, ELISA. RIGHT NOW.
THEY OWN THE POLICE DOWN HERE! THAT'S WHY I CAME TO YOU!

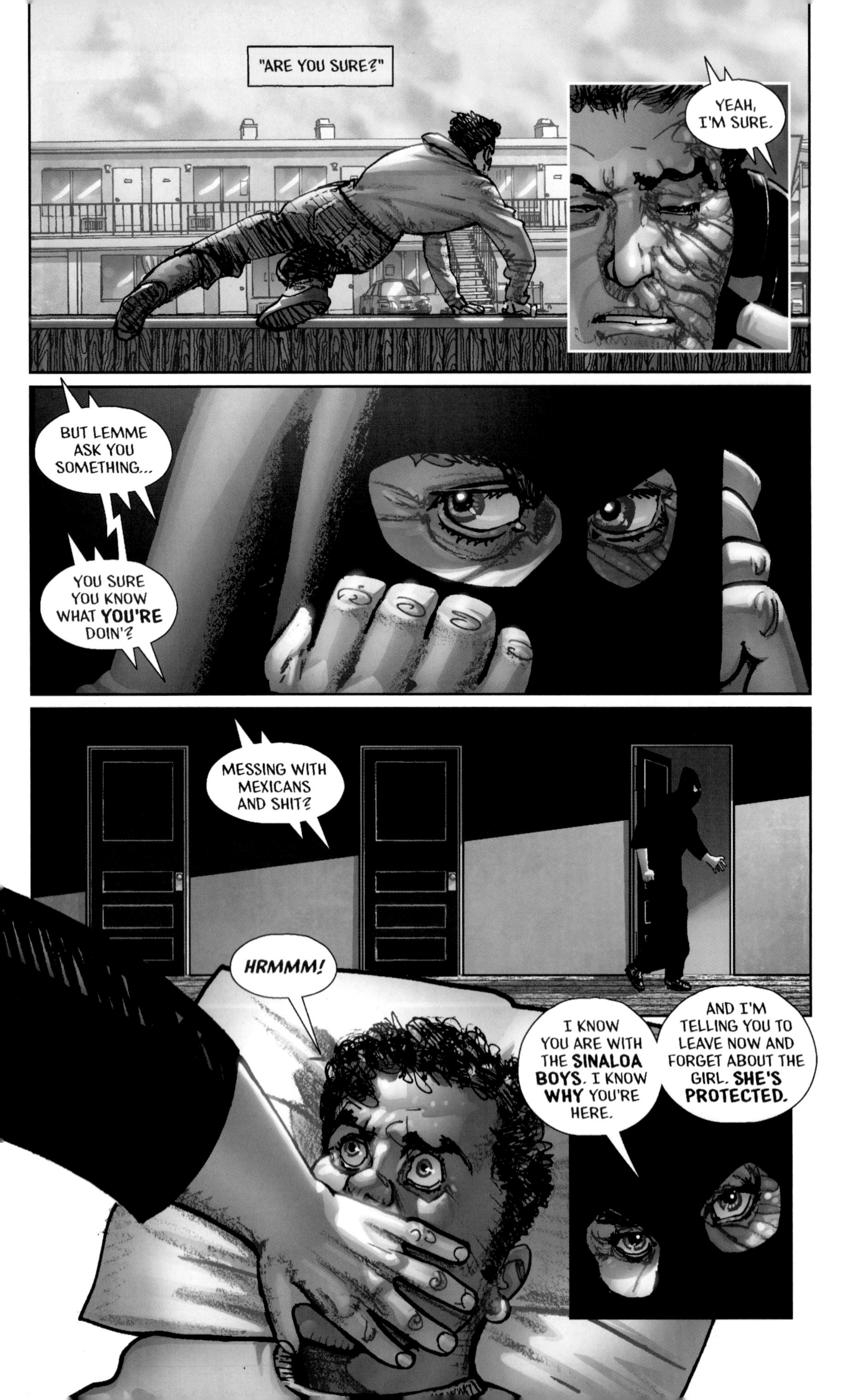
"ARE YOU SURE?"
YEAH, I'M SURE.
BUT LEMME ASK YOU SOMETHING...
YOU SURE YOU KNOW WHAT YOU'RE DOIN'?
MESSING WITH MEXICANS AND SHIT?
HRMMM!
I KNOW YOU ARE WITH THE SINALOA BOYS. I KNOW WHY YOU'RE HERE.
AND I'M TELLING YOU TO LEAVE NOW AND FORGET ABOUT THE GIRL. SHE'S PROTECTED.

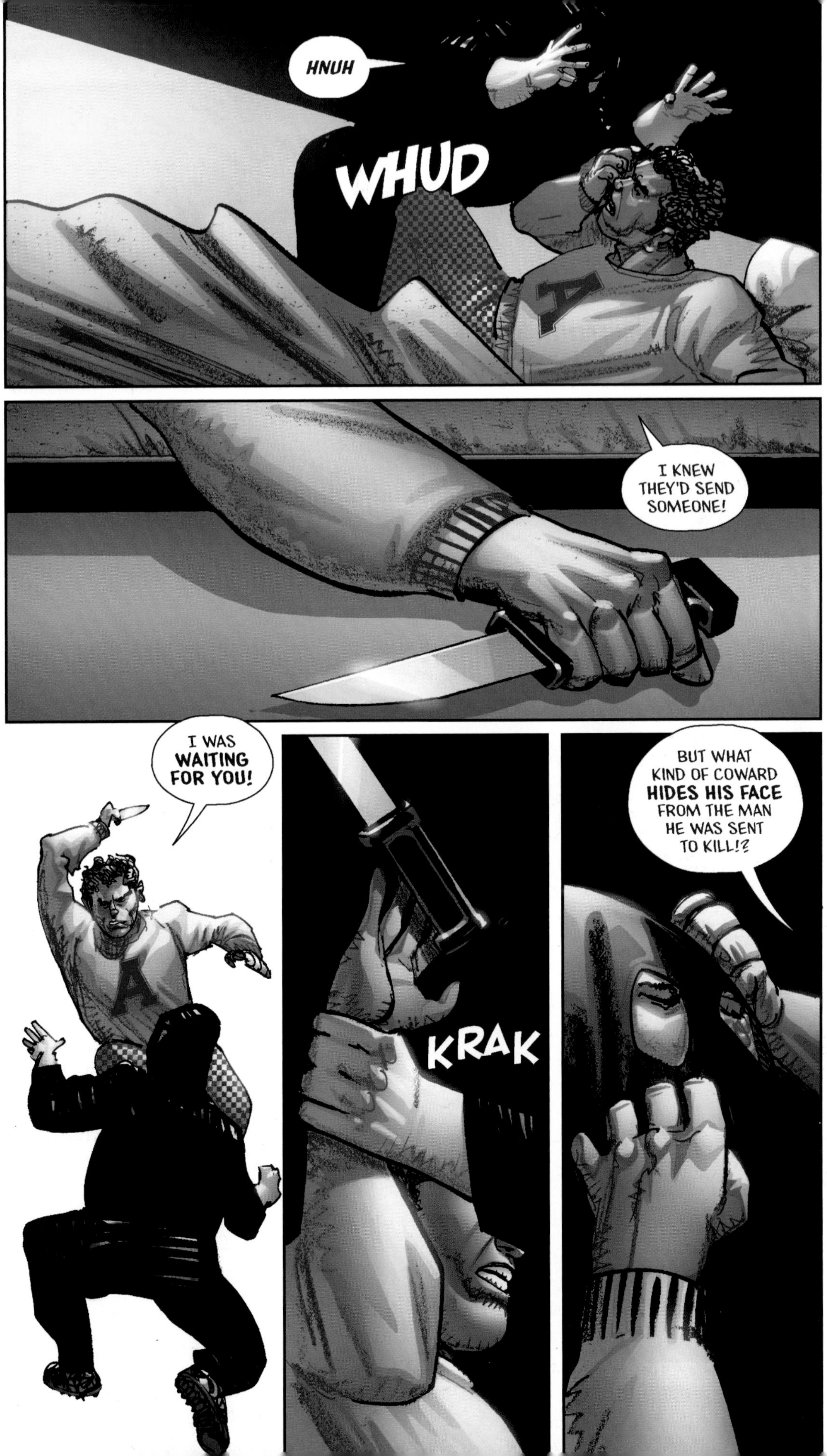
HNUH
WHUD
I KNEW THEY'D SEND SOMEONE!
I WAS WAITING FOR YOU!
KRAK
BUT WHAT KIND OF COWARD HIDES HIS FACE FROM THE MAN HE WAS SENT TO KILL!?

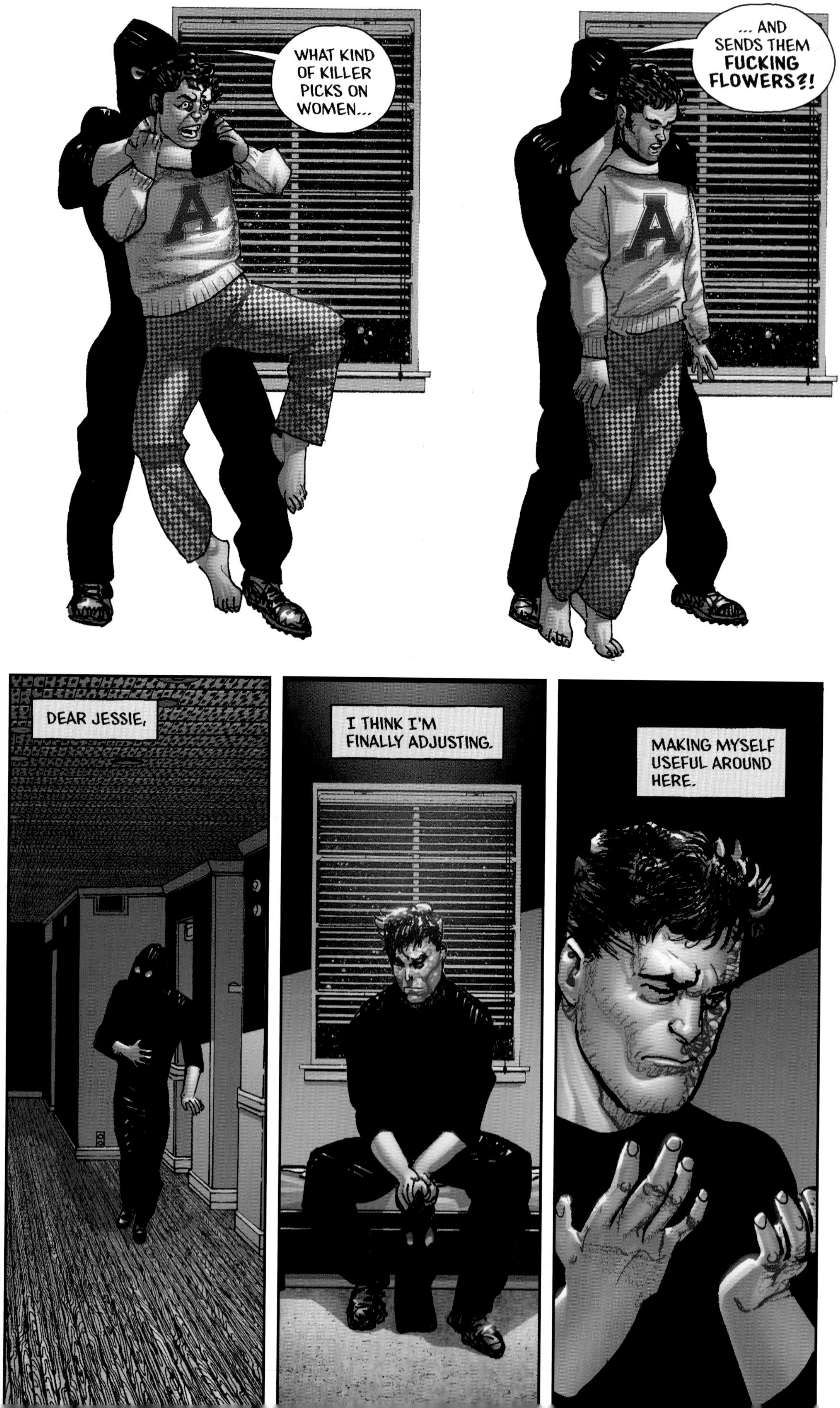
WHAT KIND OF KILLER PICKS ON WOMEN...
... AND SENDS THEM FUCKING FLOWERS?!
DEAR JESSIE,
I THINK I'M FINALLY ADJUSTING.
MAKING MYSELF USEFUL AROUND HERE.

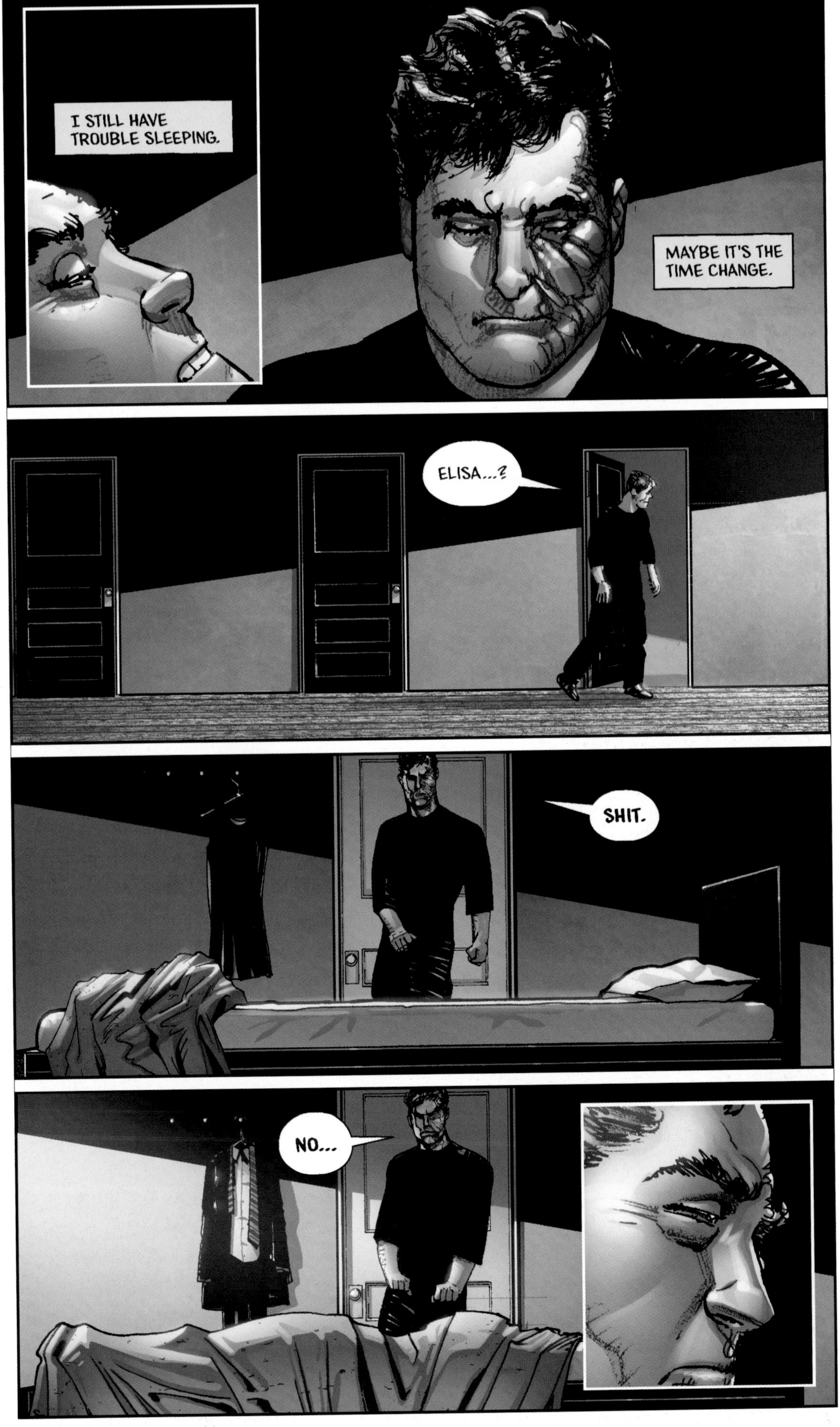
I STILL HAVE TROUBLE SLEEPING.
MAYBE IT'S THE TIME CHANGE.
ELISA...?
SHIT.
NO...

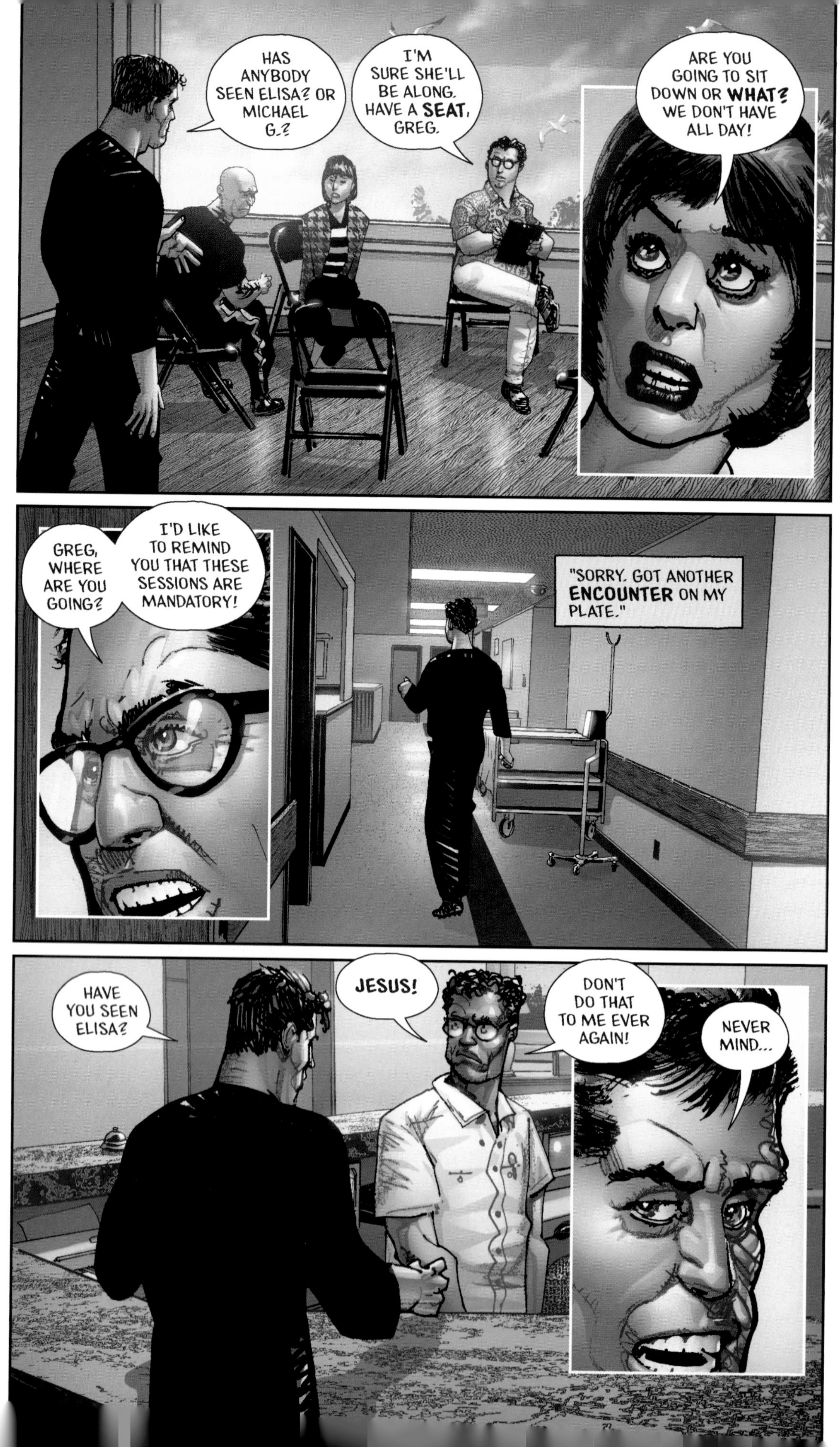
HAS ANYBODY SEEN ELISA? OR MICHAEL G.?
I'M SURE SHE'LL BE ALONG. HAVE A SEAT, GREG.
ARE YOU GOING TO SIT DOWN OR WHAT? WE DON'T HAVE ALL DAY!
GREG, WHERE ARE YOU GOING?
I'D LIKE TO REMIND YOU THAT THESE SESSIONS ARE MANDATORY!
"SORRY. GOT ANOTHER ENCOUNTER ON MY PLATE."
HAVE YOU SEEN ELISA?
JESUS!
DON'T DO THAT TO ME EVER AGAIN!
NEVER MIND...

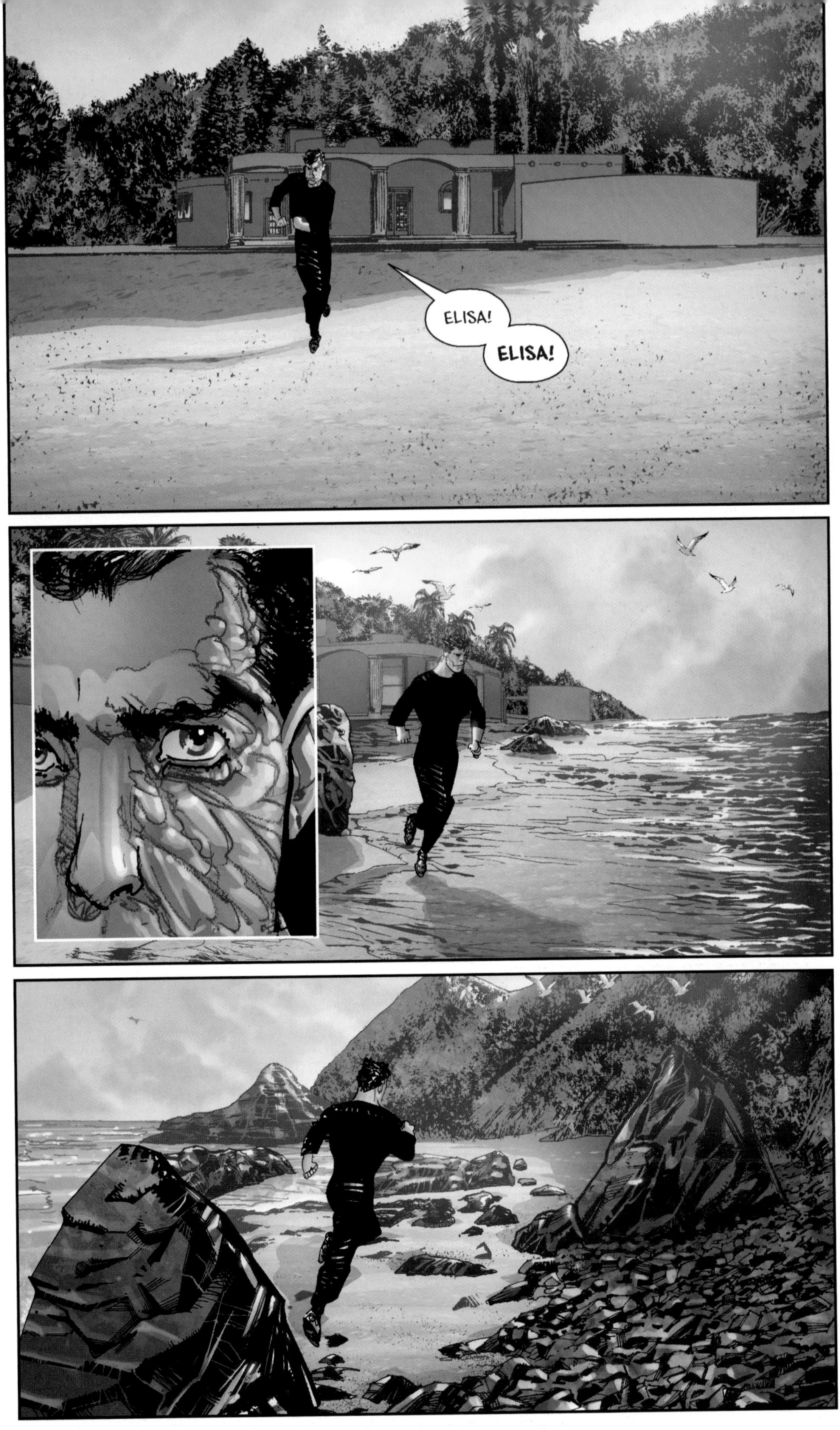
ELISA!
ELISA!

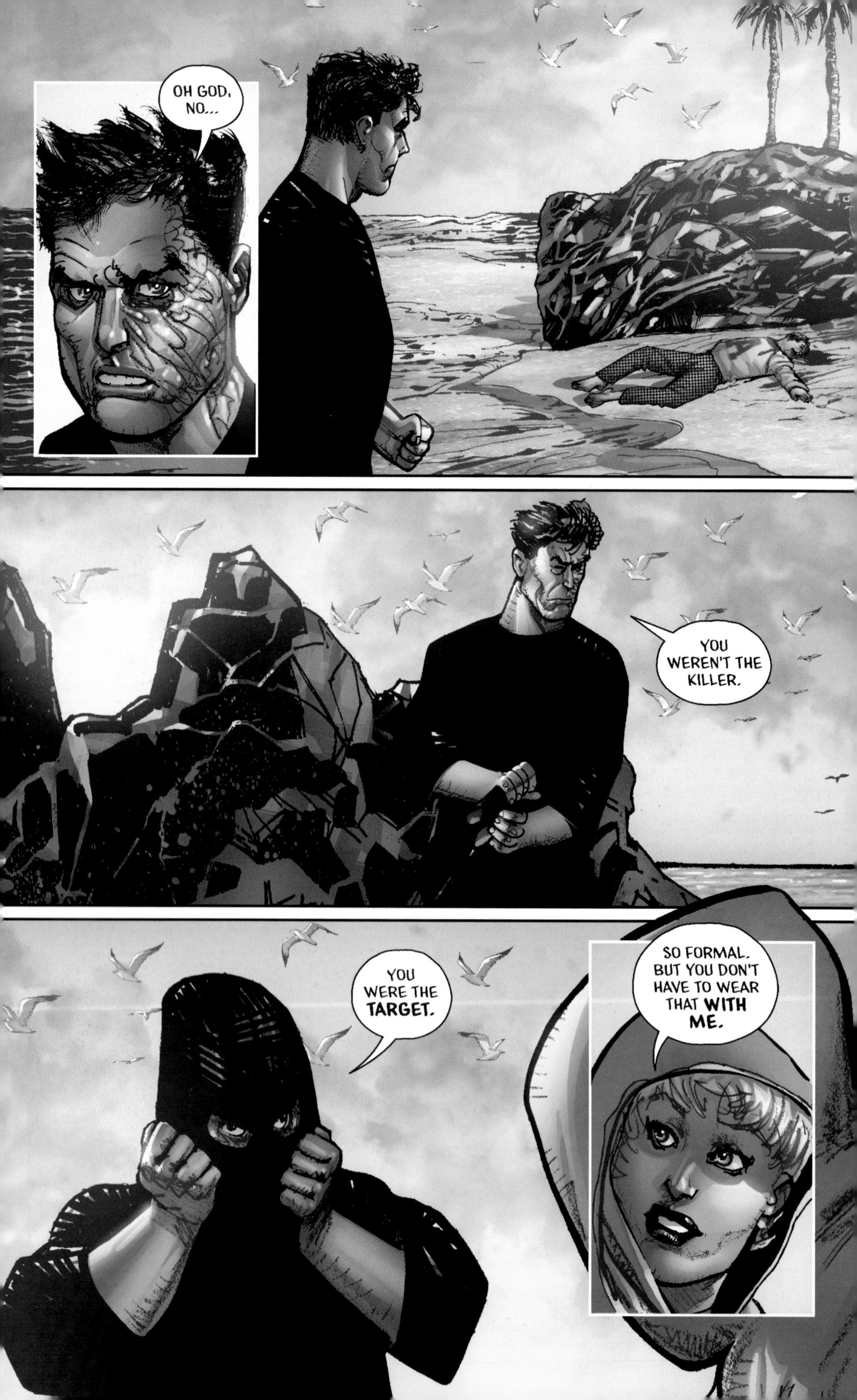
OH GOD, NO...
YOU WEREN'T THE KILLER.
YOU WERE THE **TARGET.**
SO FORMAL. BUT YOU DON'T HAVE TO WEAR THAT **WITH ME.**

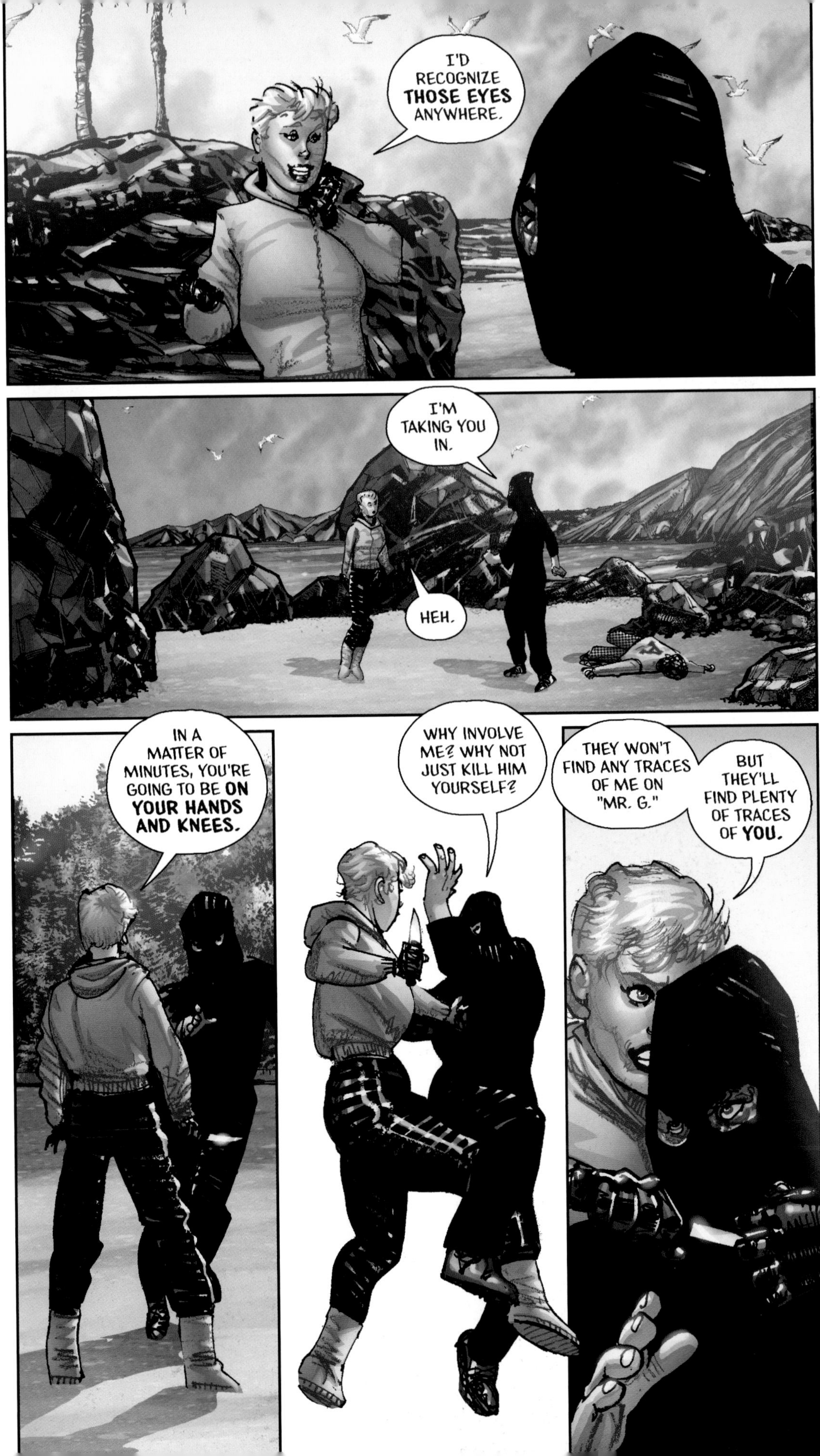
I'D RECOGNIZE THOSE EYES ANYWHERE.
I'M TAKING YOU IN.
HEH.
IN A MATTER OF MINUTES, YOU'RE GOING TO BE ON YOUR HANDS AND KNEES.
WHY INVOLVE ME? WHY NOT JUST KILL HIM YOURSELF?
THEY WON'T FIND ANY TRACES OF ME ON "MR. G."
BUT THEY'LL FIND PLENTY OF TRACES OF YOU.

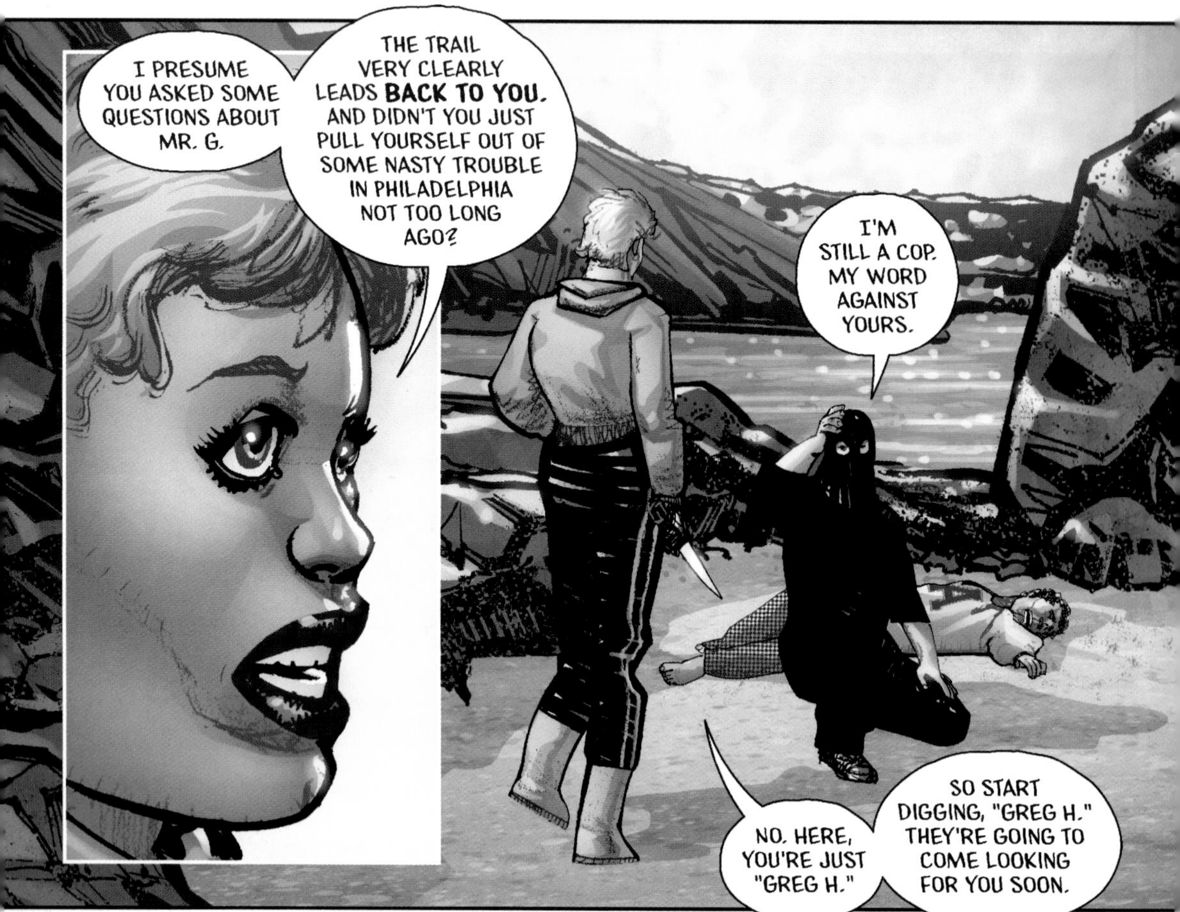
I PRESUME YOU ASKED SOME QUESTIONS ABOUT MR. G.
THE TRAIL VERY CLEARLY LEADS **BACK TO YOU.** AND DIDN'T YOU JUST PULL YOURSELF OUT OF SOME NASTY TROUBLE IN PHILADELPHIA NOT TOO LONG AGO?
I'M STILL A COP. MY WORD AGAINST YOURS.
NO. HERE, YOU'RE JUST "GREG H."
SO START DIGGING, "GREG H." THEY'RE GOING TO COME LOOKING FOR YOU SOON.

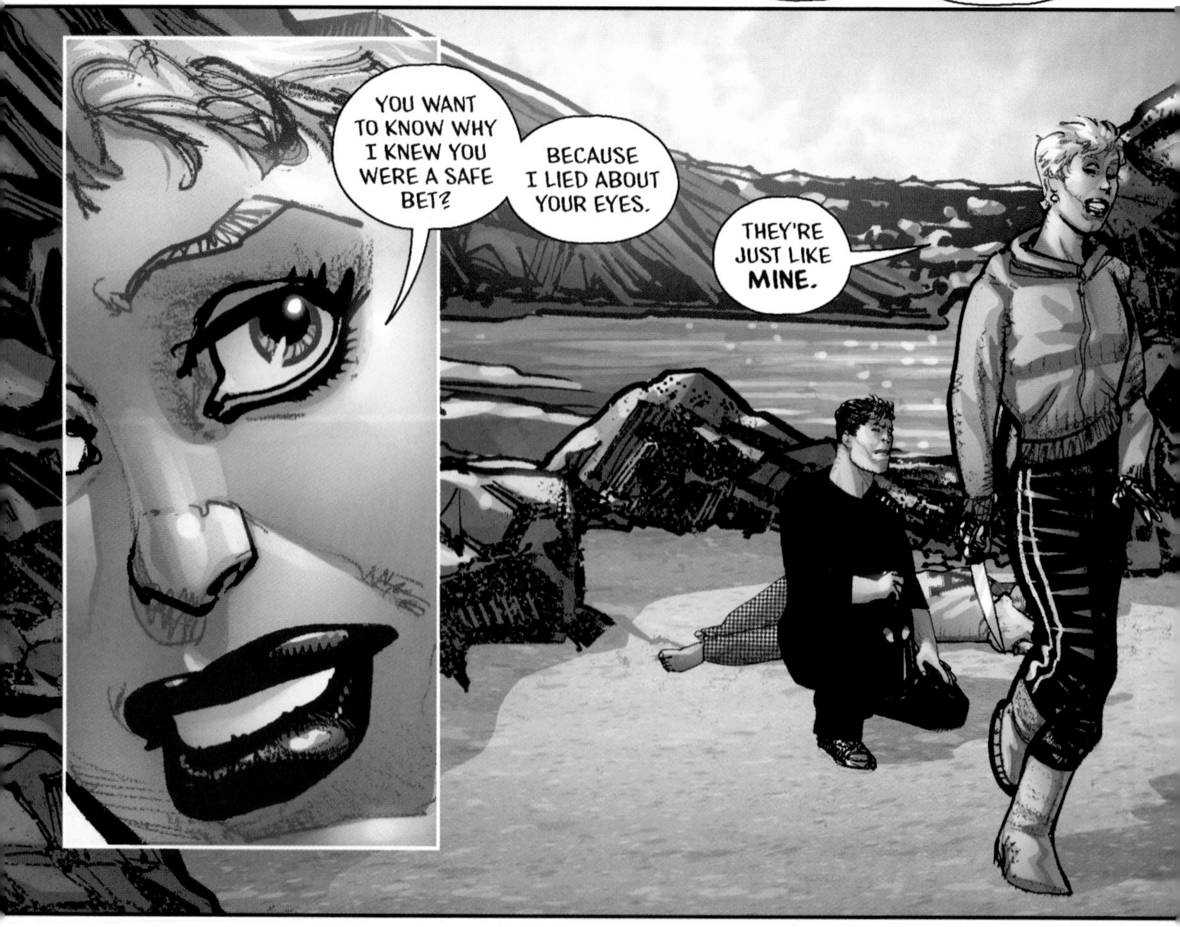
YOU WANT TO KNOW WHY I KNEW YOU WERE A SAFE BET?
BECAUSE I LIED ABOUT YOUR EYES.
THEY'RE JUST LIKE **MINE.**

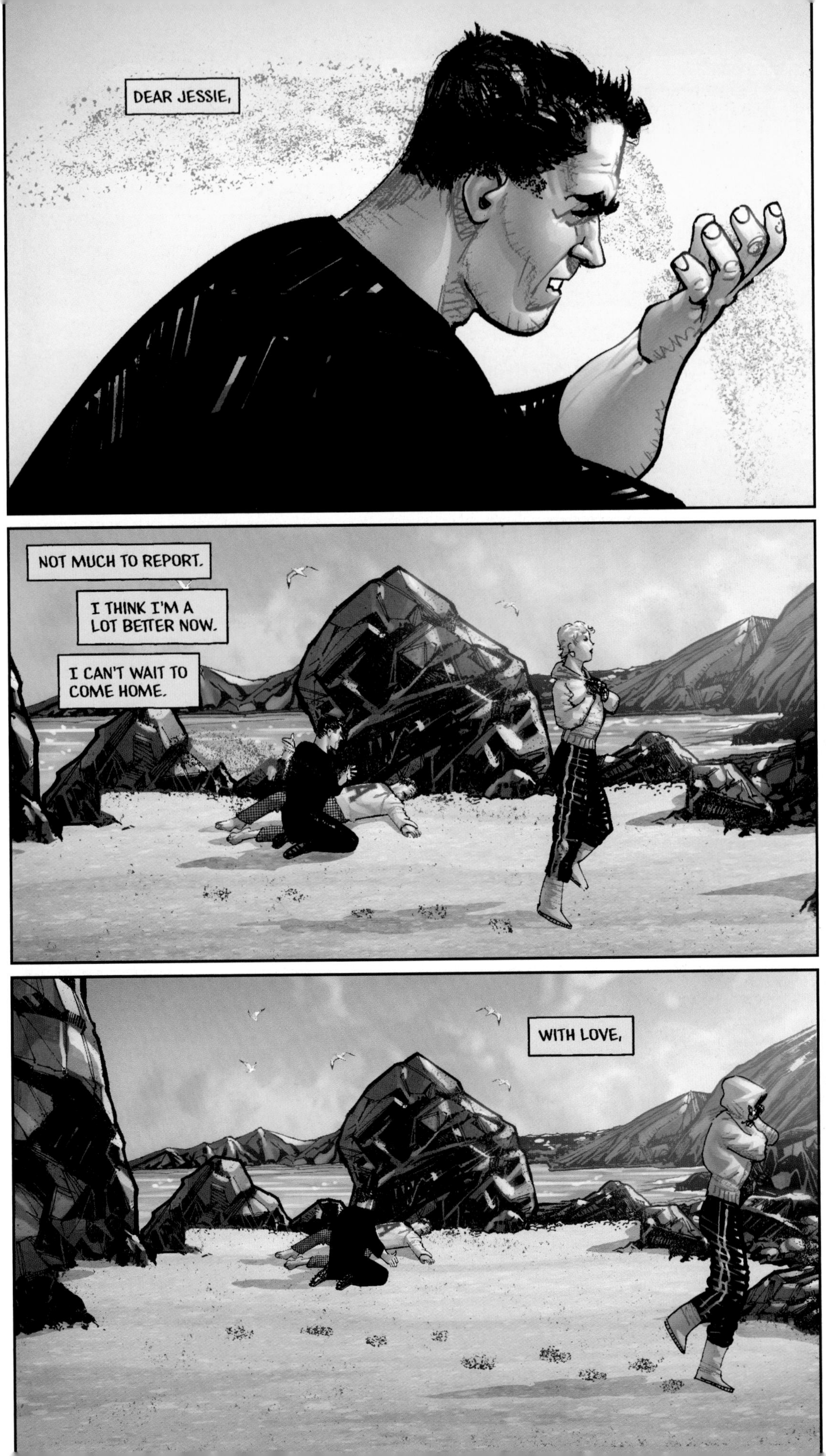
DEAR JESSIE,
NOT MUCH TO REPORT.
I THINK I'M A LOT BETTER NOW.
I CAN'T WAIT TO COME HOME.
WITH LOVE,

AFTERWORD BY SERIES EDITOR ALEX SEGURA

The Black Hood was one of those rare projects where the idealized version and final product are virtually identical. When I was asked to spearhead a relaunch of Archie's dark vigilante, I knew I wanted a take that wasn't beholden to superhero tropes, or too saddled by continuity.

"It'd be great if someone like Duane Swierczynski would write it..." I thought on the train to work. I've known Duane a long time, and you'd be hard-pressed to find a more professional and talented writer. As we considered artists, the company knew the book needed a look that screamed "real" and veered as far from the four-color trappings of mainstream superhero fare as possible. "So, someone like Michael Gaydos?" Expecting a polite dismissal from both, we asked. To my surprise, Duane and Michael said yes. I knew we were onto something special when Duane turned in his first pass at the script. It was dark, in-your-face and fearless. In the same vein, Michael is a no-frills pro, turning in impeccable, gritty and unique linework regularly. I always say the best guys make it look easy. Duane and Michael made it look very easy.

This book is the first chapter in an epic crime saga in comic form as told by two masters, ably assisted by the likes of Kelly Fitzpatrick, Rachel Deering, Jamie Rotante, Vincent Lovallo and special guest star Howard Chaykin. It's one of the things I'm most proud of, and I couldn't have asked for a more engaging and memorable take on the Black Hood, courtesy of the best team in comics. Thanks to Jon Goldwater and Mike Pellerito for their faith in this book

I hope you enjoyed your trip down the seedy streets of Philadelphia — just watch your back.

VARIANT COVER GALLERY

ISSUE ONE

HOWARD CHAYKIN
WITH JESUS ABURTO

FRANCESCO FRANCAVILLA

DAVID MACK

DAVID WILLIAMS

COMICSPRO EXCLUSIVE COVER

MICHAEL GAYDOS

ISSUE TWO

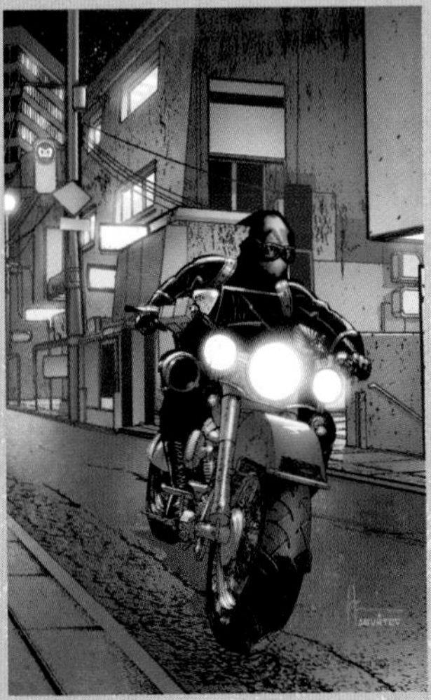

HOWARD CHAYKIN
WITH JESUS ABURTO

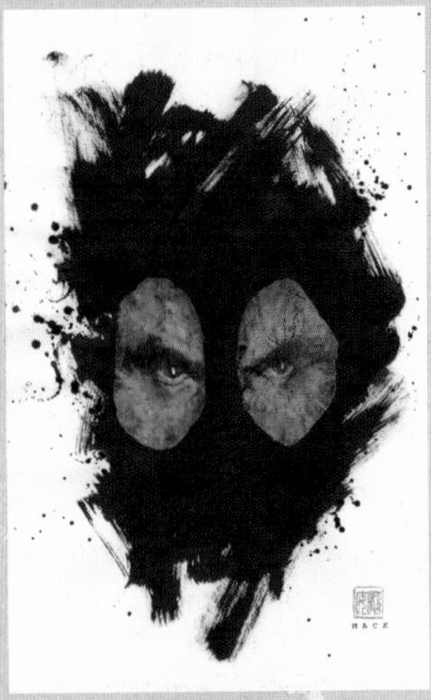

DAVID MACK

ISSUE THREE

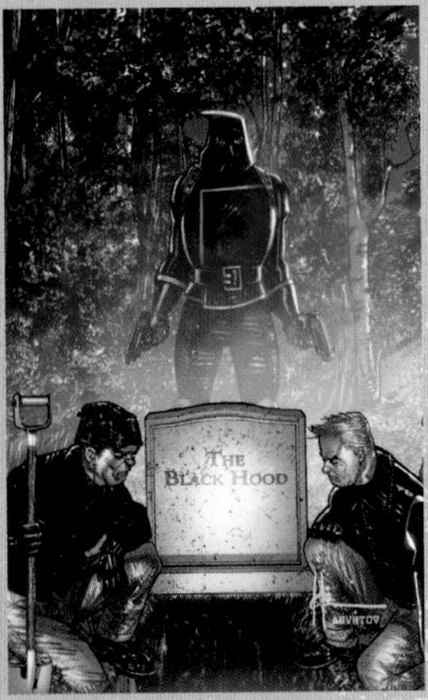
THE BLACK HOOD

HOWARD CHAYKIN
WITH JESUS ABURTO

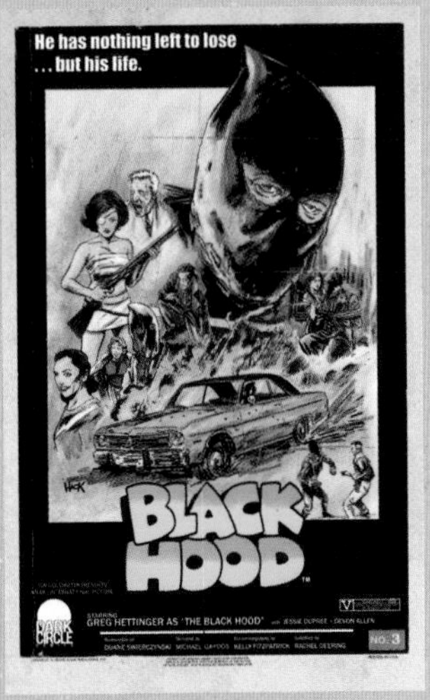
He has nothing left to lose
. . . but his life.
BLACK HOOD
NO. 3

ROBERT HACK

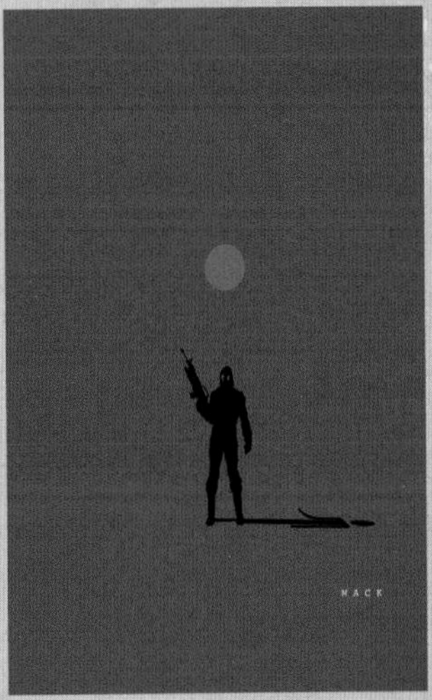

DAVID MACK

ISSUE FOUR

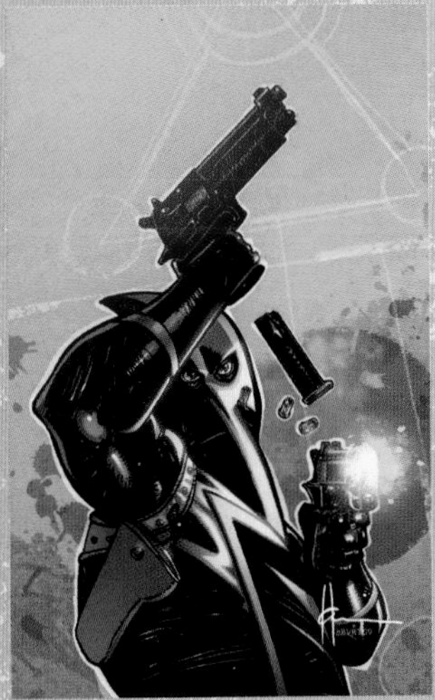

HOWARD CHAYKIN
WITH JESUS ABURTO

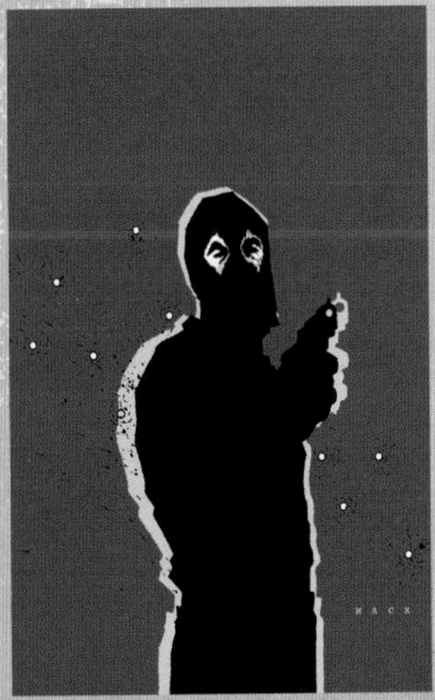

DAVID MACK

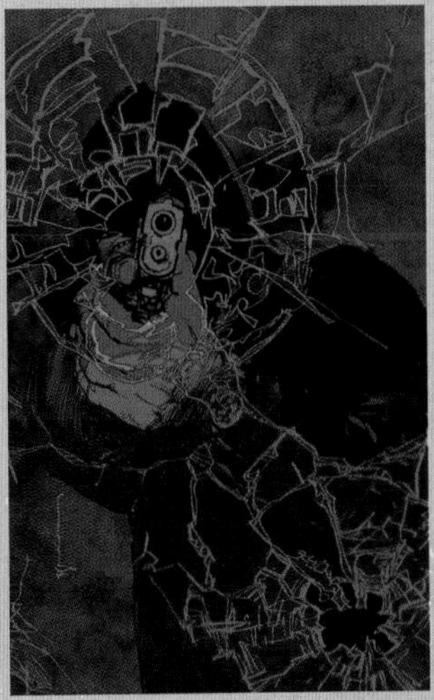

BILL SIENKIEWICZ

ISSUE FIVE

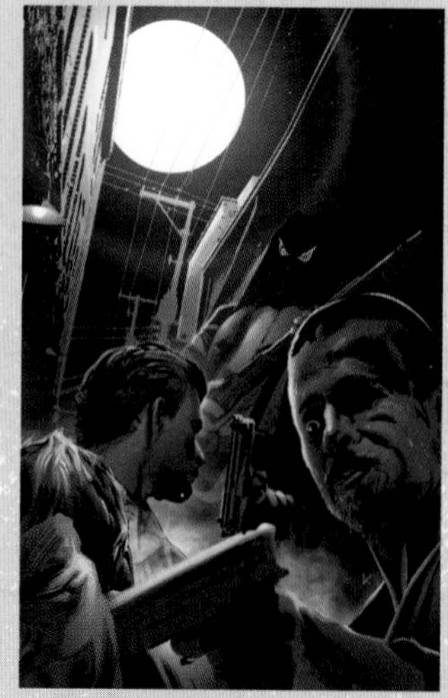

DENNIS CALERO

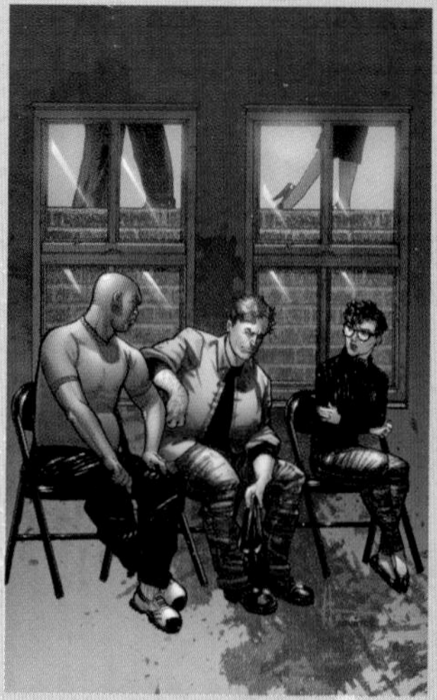

HOWARD CHAYKIN
WITH JESUS ABURTO

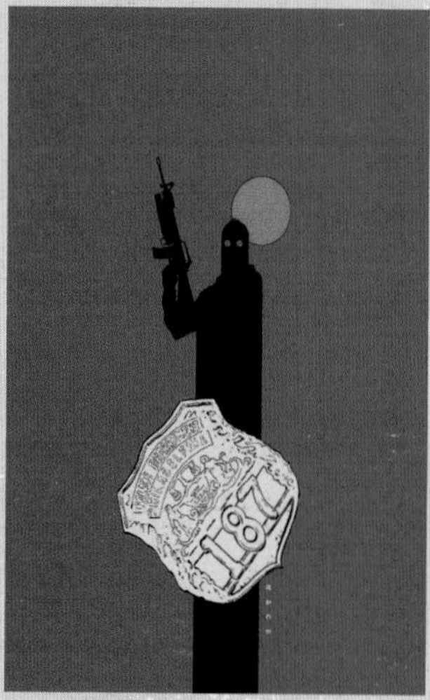
187

DAVID MACK

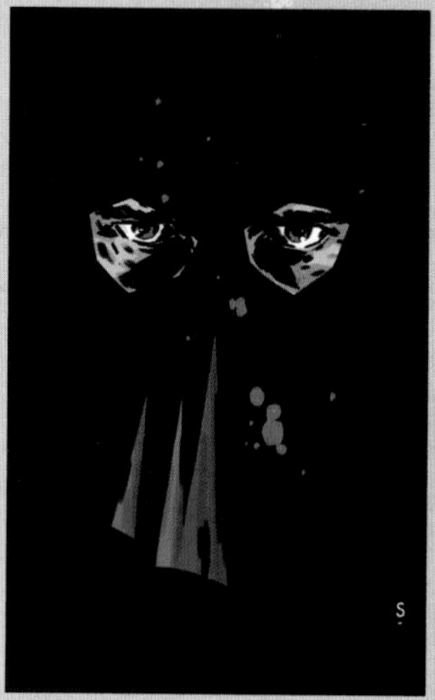

MATTHEW DOW SMITH

ISSUE SIX

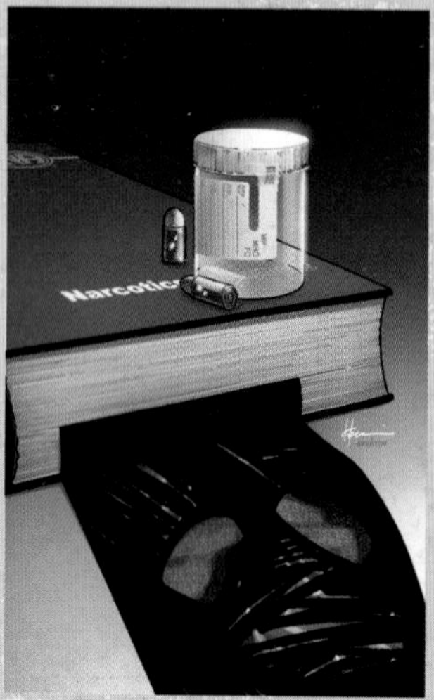
Narcotics

HOWARD CHAYKIN
WITH JESUS ABURTO

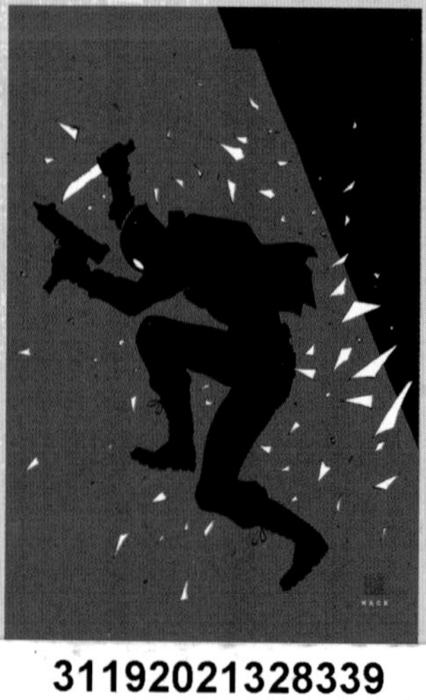

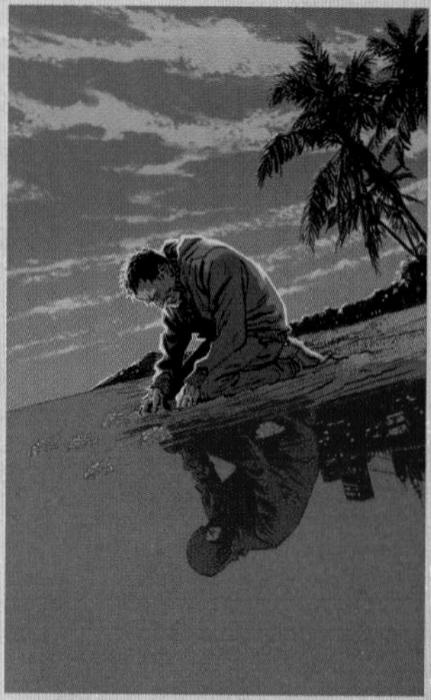

GREG SMALLWOOD